STONEBEARER'S REDEMPTION

SHADOW BARRIER TRILOGY, BOOK THREE

JODI L. MILNER

To Mike
For showing us all the power of change and acceptance

PROLOGUE

A coastal breeze swept through the open window, knocking a letter with a thick wax seal off the stack perched on the corner of Darius's desk and into his lap. After a cursory glance, he tossed it into the heap to be burned with the others. If the King of Fortzala really wanted something important, he'd have sent one of his pimpled squires to deliver the message, or worse, come himself.

Hannah, a Seeker who had served as his personal secretary for the past decade, made a pained sound in her throat. "You should at least see what it is." She wiped the nib of her pen and set it next to her ledger alongside the small cake she'd been enjoying, before plucking the letter from the pile. "Maybe something new has come up?"

"Nonsense. You know him as well as I do. This—" He snatched the letter back. "—is a complaint, no doubt about the new Stonebearer Counselor we sent him."

"Master Tomas is one of our best diplomatic minds. What complaint could he have about the man?"

Darius cracked the letter open, more to prove he was right than to see the contents. "See, right there." He pointed to the tidy script. "Too ugly. Says here he scares the ladies of the court." He let the letter fall back into the pile. "Now that's just unfair. It's not like Tomas wanted that scar."

"Would you like me to send him a reprimand?" A frightfully gleeful expression spread on Hannah's face, making Darius recoil slightly. "It's been ages since I've delivered a good tongue-lashing."

"You already know the answer to that. The man's got a tendency to send armies against people who irritate him. As much as our Guardians could use the excitement, I'd prefer to avoid bloodshed." Darius eyed the remaining stack of papers, trying to ignore the sinking suspicion that more of them had spawned while he wasn't looking. "Check the roster and see if there's anyone left willing to take Tomas's place."

Hannah gave a curt nod before turning her attention to the shelves behind her desk and thumbed her way through the older ledgers perched there. Darius leaned back in his chair and rested an arm over his eyes as he tried to ignore the deep thrum of power that resonated through the thick stone walls of the stronghold. Most days he didn't mind. Living in the very beating heart of the Stonebearer stronghold meant someone was always testing or creating something at any given time. It was the price of progress, nothing more.

This time, it was different. Rose, his companion, was up to something as big and ambitious as her reputation. The invisible bond between them made her intentions, her emotions, and above all, her flows of power known to him.

The last time she'd been this intent, it had resulted in the creation of the traveling posts, a linked system of motherstone that allowed Stonebearers the world over to travel vast distances in moments. The Stonebearer Society hailed it as a crowning achievement that nothing could top in terms of scale and sheer usefulness. Not that Darius was keeping count, but in the twenty-some-odd years since its creation, it had halted no fewer than four separate wars. That alone made the risks of its use worth it.

This new idea of hers remained a mystery, but he suspected it had much to do with correcting the traveling post's shortcomings. They'd learned from sad experience that many Stonebearers weren't strong enough to use the posts safely. It drained their life away like water through a hole in a bucket. Even strong Stonebearers found themselves exhausted. The only exceptions were those from the Traveler's sept whose talent provided them a safeguard against the strain. This drawback had never sat well with Rose. Even so many years later, he still caught her sketching diagrams on ways she could fix it.

Hannah studied the cover of one of her ledgers before giving it a perfunctory wipe with her sleeve and setting it back on the shelf to fetch another. She spread it on her desk and ran a finger down one of the pages.

"Has he really gone through twelve different Seekers?"

The question brought Darius's thoughts back to the task at hand. "And four healers, I believe, during that nasty business when the plague ransacked the capitol. Even then he was picky."

Just then, a much stronger power surge coursed through the building. The walls vibrated with it like a massive drum. A sharp pull drew Darius's attention inward. Whatever Rose was doing, it wasn't just chasing the natural veins of motherstone that ran through the earth; it had also danced in uncomfortable circles where the power dwelt inside him and had taken hold of the focusing pendant that hung at his throat. Hannah stood with both hands braced on the desk and shot him a worried glance, clearly feeling the pull as well.

"That's not a good sign." He hurried from his office and out into the colonnaded great hall. Hannah followed close behind.

"You're right, this is different." Her hand grasped at the stone hanging from the fine chain around her neck. "Shall I summon a Healer, just in case? Or a Guardian?"

The implication struck Darius hard. Rose had been skirting the line of what was allowed and what was forbidden for years. If she'd finally crossed it, she'd have to face justice just like anyone else.

He didn't answer Hannah, didn't want to. Involving a Stonebearer Guardian always complicated things, and the last thing he wanted to do was make the situation, whatever it was, worse.

At the center of the Great Hall, he was met with a disconcerting silence. The Stonebearers and dignitaries going about their business there all stood stock still. Visible threads of Rose's power wove through the space, piercing the heart of each soul present.

Hannah drew closer to a bearded older man, a Bender named Ezrom, who carried a basket full of supplies. When she poked his shoulder, he didn't respond. "She's doing something to them, something she wouldn't dare do to either of us."

"We best get to the bottom of this, and quickly." Darius let the searing heat of the power fill him and hurried to the testing chamber. He yanked on the door only to find it sealed. Rose had never done that in the past, but then again, she'd never targeted her brothers and sisters in the craft either.

Opening a power-sealed door in Khanrosh was a matter of finding two people who could insert the proper sequence, a safeguard he'd insisted on when they first built the place. He counted himself lucky that Hannah had an uncanny knack of knowing all sorts of things that she technically shouldn't know. She matched his actions, smoothly feeding in the correct series of glyphs. The seals holding the doors secure became visible and rotated around themselves until they released with a satisfying thud.

Darius rushed inside, utterly unprepared for the sight that greeted him. Rose stood in the center of the room where hundreds, no, thousands, of separate threads clung to her before stretching out in all directions. Sequences and patterns fell from her fingers in a dance, one after the next, as they rode down the different threads and out of sight. Circling her feet, the ring of protective glyphs set into the floor pulsed in time with her work. In the center of that circle, a ribbon of her power pierced the earth into the thick vein of motherstone that ran beneath the stronghold.

Drawing from that well was dangerous at best, as its raw unfiltered power could overwhelm even the strongest wielder. More than a few had lost their minds by trying.

"What is the meaning of this?" Darius fought to keep the anger from his voice, but it shoved itself against his throat.

She faltered at the sound of his voice. The rhythm of her casting paused for a brief moment, long enough to allow him to spot the Bender glyphs woven in tight rings around the last pattern as it disappeared out into the world. Defiance shone in her gaze. She'd always pushed the boundaries, but this time she'd broken them, and she knew it. Bender glyphs caused things to change by rearranging their structure. Causing people to change by erasing memories, altering their mood, or compelling them to act was a practice that had been forbidden for centuries.

She resumed her work. "Turn around. Leave. I don't need your help."

Stubborn woman. Darius let his power flare beneath his skin, a subtle threat of what he could do if necessary. Yes, he loved Rose more than life itself, but he had a responsibility to the people of their world. He wouldn't let her use bending glyphs on them, even in the name of progress.

"This is wrong. Release them."

"I can't. Not without causing harm." To her credit, her voice remained calm, passive even.

"We'll find another way, a safer way." He drew himself closer, needing more than anything to understand what would push her this far.

"This is for everyone's good. You'll see." With a flick of her hand, several snakelike ribbons of power leapt up to keep him back. She'd never done that before, not to him.

Hannah pulled the doors closed behind her and planted herself firmly in front of them. "I could have sworn I saw a compulsion sequence in there. Cut her off. Sever the flows before it's too late."

Darius's heart sank. For years, Rose had entertained this whim of setting anchors into those nearest her as a safeguard, always for the good of Stonebearer Society, always to help people get the aid they needed as quickly as possible. With news of more of their people trying, and failing, to safely use her traveling posts, her fixation had become more absurd. Hers was the kind of curiosity that demanded attention. When she talked to him about it, he'd entertained her whims with the hope that once her curiosity was satiated, she'd move on as she had before. Now, he could see that she'd used him.

"Rose, we've discussed this." He kept his arms open, showing that he had no intention of hurting her. "This isn't the answer. You can't do this to people, it isn't right."

"Forty-three people died last month, some only children, because our council couldn't gather resources fast enough to go to their aid. Don't talk to me about what's right. What's the use in having all of this power when we can't step in and put an end to horrors like that?" She sent another cascade of green-tinged glyphs down the threads and swayed slightly. What she was doing was costing her. "I can't let it happen again. Won't let it happen."

The clatter of armored Guardians echoed through the hall and toward them. A flash of power shone from the door as Hannah resealed it against entry. A wicked smile crossed Rose's face before she schooled herself to calm and sent more sequences down her threads. "You must let me finish what I've started. It's the only way."

"You're controlling them?" His mouth went dry. "You'd turn the Guardians against me? For this?"

"Let me finish and I won't have to."

"Each of those things she's releasing turns someone else into one of her puppets." Hannah worked furiously, creating elaborate sequences that she sent skittering down Rose's threads, dozens at a time. "I'll sever anyone who hasn't been compromised. Force her to release the others. She's right, if we cut those, their minds will tear. She must withdraw."

There was no good answer. No safe bet. No guarantee that anything Darius did would alter what had already been set in motion. He'd known Rose for the better part of two centuries. He knew how stubborn she was when she dug in. The harder he pushed her to stop, the harder she'd fight. If he was going to free those souls she'd sunk her anchors into, he'd have to counteract the glyphs she'd spun.

The power flowed differently in his veins than it did others, often acting on intuition and instinct rather than following orderly patterns and studied sequences. When he needed it most, when times were dire and options were few, it drew from the deep intelligence of the world itself to do what was necessary. If he ever needed help with anything, it was in this moment. A gauntleted fist pounded on the door.

"I'll do what I can," he told Hannah. "Keep the Guardians out."

He cleared his mind and allowed the potency of his need fill him. Glyphs formed over his outstretched palms and a presence urged him to move closer. Rose shrieked and lashed out at him with snake-like ribbons in a vain attempt to keep him back. They clashed against his flows and fell away.

"They're forcing the seals," Hannah shouted over the noise. "Whatever you're going to do, do it quickly."

As he drew closer to Rose, the deep intelligence guided him and through him created layers within layers of patterns that laced around her in an elaborate sphere. He had to trust that this was the right thing, that it would be enough to remove Rose's influence from those she'd already corrupted.

"Stay away," Rose begged. "I can do so much good. Let me have this." The resolve in her voice shrunk down into something small and scared as his sphere grew larger. A new series of glyphs formed between her hands, something ugly, born of desperation and fear. If she released it within the confined space, there was no telling what it might do.

He passed through the layers, sparking each one to life as he went, and wrapped her tightly in his arms. This close, she couldn't strike him without harming herself or her precious threads. Each layer burst into different colors of shining stars, thousands of them. They sought out the threads and began their work, some flying outward along their lengths, some working their way inward.

She trembled in his grasp, then arched her back with a hiss of pain. "It's too much. Make it stop."

Back and forth the stars raced, undoing what she'd done not unlike unthreading a loom. With each pass, she clung to him a little tighter and her cries grew weaker. Still, none of the threads fell away. Her stubborn strength began to fade, and yet she held on.

The noise behind the door quieted, her grip on the Guardian's minds too weak to compel them.

"I beg you. Let them go. I won't lose you over this." He pressed a kiss into her hair and prayed she'd see sense. Even so, he prepared a flow to sustain her. If all that was needed was more time, he could keep her alive.

When she met his gaze, there was a fresh determination in her eyes. "No."

Her connection to the vein of motherstone pulsed as she pulled strength from it. His stars slowed, then stopped, leaving the two of them suspended in the middle of their own night sky. He poured his need to cut her free back into the intelligence. A new pattern emerged, something much bigger than before, big enough that it made Darius hesitate. While the power itself held a wisdom he couldn't dream of matching, it had no awareness of how much he could safely give. The Guardians began their assault on the doors once more.

"Hannah, I need you."

She pressed her hands against the door and sent a fresh webbing of glyphs streaking across its surface. "Will it end this?"

Darius didn't get a chance to answer. Rose gripped him by the throat, her face wild and pleading as tendrils of her power pierced his mind and wrapped around his heart. She pulled power from him in grasping hungry gulps while pushing her will against his.

Hannah wasted no time. The moment his sphere faltered a fraction she darted in, gripped him by the shoulder, and pressed in her own ribbon of power. The moment he felt her presence, he sparked the new pattern to life. The stars, which Rose had halted in their journey, burst back into motion and moved along the threads like lightning.

Rose dug deeper into him, ripping at the center of his power with what felt like sharp claws. The effort to keep his own flows intact made his head spin. Dark shapes crossed his vision. His awareness shrank down to her, Hannah, and the chaos surrounding them.

Hannah shook him, but her words sounded far away. "We must see it through. Don't give in, not when we're this close."

Another voice came to him, this one smooth like fine silk. "It's for the best. You need to let go now."

He trusted that voice. He loved that voice. He began to withdraw his flows from the complex web of light spinning circles around them.

"What are you doing?" The fear in Hannah's voice shifted to dismay. "You have to maintain the sequence or we'll lose it, lose everything."

That wasn't right. Rose needed his help, he was sure of it, and his sequences needed to be pulled away. The light, the chaos, the noise, none of it made sense. He drew back the supporting threads, one at a time, watching with relief as the chaos calmed.

Hannah released her grip on him. "You've left me no choice. I'm sorry."

A brilliant light formed at the corner of Darius's vision as she released a swarm of cutting glyphs. They buzzed into the space, severing the thousands of threads as if they were no more than stalks of wheat. Rose stiffened in his arms and arched her back as her face contorted into a silent scream. Her hold on his mind broke away, and reality slammed back into place.

"No, Hannah, stop!" he managed to cry out, but not before her cutting glyphs collided with what remained of his flow.

Instead of severing it, their two forces merged into something new. It blossomed into the space, sweeping up the ends of the cut lines and twisting them in on themselves. Darius dug deep, needing something, anything, to put all to right, but the intelligence didn't stir. His mind was still fractured and struggling from Rose's intrusion. From the chaos grew new patterns and sequences, broken dark things that merged and expanded, fueled by the raw wild power Rose continued to pull from the motherstone beneath them.

This was how people died using the power. They lost control. With the last of his flagging strength, he wrapped layers of protection around the three of them and hoped it would be enough. The chaos grew more violent, more frantic. Its deafening roar fought against the room's protective warding.

Rose's eyes shone with madness. He held her tighter. If they were to die, they'd die together.

"I have to save them." She struggled in his arms. With a wrenching twist, she pulled on the tendril she'd wrapped around the core of his power, and something gave way.

The roar intensified, shaking the very stones of the building around them. Darius fought to remain conscious.

He pulled her closer as darkness spotted his vision. "I love you."

When the world tore, all turned to silence.

CHAPTER 1

At the Tower of Amul Dun, a most welcome calm had settled over its glyph-laced walls, and Katira was grateful for the stillness. Enough turmoil had filled her first months at the Tower to last a lifetime.

Regardless of this calm, her time as an apprentice was still filled with lessons and other duties from the moment she woke up to the moment she went to bed. The days passed by in an unremarkable smooth succession, one after another after another.

Afternoon sun beat down across Katira's back as she bent over her mother's old garden plot and studied the sanaresina blossoms, which had started to open only a few days before. Her light linen tunic stuck to her back, and she craved even the smallest of breezes in the rare summer heat. The garden itself was situated on a narrow terrace built into the side of the mountain just outside the stronghold's outer walls, close enough to the massive Keep to be protected, but far enough away that being there felt like an escape.

Next to her, Isben sat on the ground as he dug at a patch of bindweed that had crept beneath the taller herbs and threatened to choke them. He uttered a steady stream of grumbles under his breath as he tugged at the invasive creeper. Had it not been for her insisting on him needing a break from his studies in the library, he wouldn't be here at all.

Katira plucked one of the red sanaresina flowers and held it up to him. "Do you see how the seedpod is starting to form? It's too late to harvest this blossom."

Isben glanced up and pushed at the hair where it had stuck to his face, leaving a dark streak. "I thought these just bloomed. Is it too late for all of them?"

On the nearby steps, Cassim, the Tower's second most renowned healer after Master Firen, sat and fanned himself with his hand. "If it's too late, do you mind explaining why we are out here in this blasted heat?" he asked, wiping his face with the sleeve of his cream-colored shirt.

He'd ditched his healer's robes the moment they'd left the cool of the Tower and stepped onto the sunbaked terrace, piling them in a heap on the step beside him. Onyx, his pet raven, poked her beak through the folds, hoping to find the sunflower seeds he kept in his pocket just for her.

"Because many of them are still good." She plucked a ripe blossom from the same plant and set it into her basket. "Anyway, a good herbalist tends to their garden every day. Weeds must be pulled, the soil checked, fruits and flowers harvested at the proper time, seeds collected—"

"Is this one I'm supposed to dig out, or leave where it is?" Isben pointed his trowel toward a plant with velvety soft leaves, one of the seedlings they'd planted that spring.

"Leave it. It's lamb's ear. Good for cuts and ground cover." Katira moved closer and stroked one of the soft leaves. That close to Isben, the dusty vanilla scent of old books and stories clinging to his clothes from the endless hours he spent in the massive Tower library rose off him.

"I understand all that." Cassim cut her off with a huff. "Couldn't we have come out later tonight when it's cooler?"

"You're whining. It's not a good look for you." She pinched back several of the lamb's ears longer stalks and set them in the basket.

"Besides, sanaresina is most potent if harvested in the heat of the day. That's worth a little discomfort, don't you think?"

Cassim scooted Onyx back when she got too curious about his shirt pocket. "You really do sound like your mother. She taught you well."

Katira paused between pickings, the sharp ache of grief catching her off guard. Isben stopped digging and regarded her carefully. He'd experienced the loss of his own master not long after Mamar had died and understood. Months had passed, but the reminders still hurt.

Decades before she was born, if not longer, Mamar had tended to these same beds. Katira imagined her kneeling and caring for this garden the same way she'd worked in the cottage garden back in Namragan, with tenderness and a wealth of experience.

"I wish I could have had more time with her. Worked this garden with her. It would have been so beautiful." Katira plucked several sanaresina blossoms in quick succession, no longer stopping to explain. They stained her fingertips pink and released the smell of pepper and camphor into the air. She breathed in and closed her eyes, letting her mother's memory come and go.

"I did it again, didn't I?" Cassim levered himself to his feet and brushed the dust from his hands. "You know I would never say anything to hurt you on purpose. Right? I miss her too."

"It's okay. I always think about her here. Her, and home, and how things used to be." She picked up her basket and the small trowel.

Cassim lifted the basket from her hand. "Tell you what, why don't the two of you take the afternoon off? I can take care of today's pickings easily enough." His gaze jumped from Katira to Isben and for a moment, Katira caught a twinkle there. He was up to something. "Besides, it will give me an excuse to put off cleaning my disaster of an office for another day."

Isben stammered before answering, his cheeks going pink. "But we're supposed to spend another two hours with you, and after that, study in the library until the evening bell." It wasn't exactly a protest. A change in schedule was as rare as it was welcome.

"It's okay." Cassim waved them off with the basket hanging securely from his elbow and Onyx perched on his shoulder. "Run along. Healer's orders. The rest will do both of you good." He gathered up his discarded robe and made his way back into the sheltered cool of the Tower.

Katira, unsure of what had just happened, exchanged a look with Isben. As Cassim disappeared through the heavy door, Isben snatched up his shovel and returned it to the small shed at the garden's edge.

"I know exactly where we can go." He glanced at the sun's position and nodded to himself. "It's perfect for an afternoon like this. Come on."

Katira crossed her arms, skeptical. She'd gone on a handful of his adventures before, which usually ended up with them exploring dusty storerooms or wandering the dark corridors that stretched deep into the mountain. "I'd rather not go to the rooftop. It's far too hot today."

"No. It's a surprise. You haven't been there."

She raised an eyebrow.

"I promise you'll like it. If we leave now, we'll have enough time to enjoy it."

Somewhere new. After months of not venturing further from Amul Dun than the garden, Katira thought she'd seen everything. Her curiosity got the best of her.

Katira chased after Isben as he hurried through dusty abandoned hallways and up twisted staircases. The last time she'd been in this part of the keep, the threat of shadow hounds lurked in every shadow. For now, that threat was extinguished, but being there still made her stomach turn.

Halfway down one of the corridors, he flashed her a wicked grin before ducking through a slanted doorway. She bent to follow him, finding herself in a cramped dusty room where the back wall had fallen away. Isben stood at the broken edge of the floor, looking down.

"Is this what you wanted to show me? I've seen ruined parts of the keep before." Katira approached the edge but couldn't bring herself to go as close as he had.

"You have to trust me. Come on." He beckoned her to the farthest corner of the room.

When Katira came closer, a short ledge came into view, and beyond that, a rustic trail leading up the mountainside. "You can't be serious. Do you know how much trouble we could get in?"

"It's not far." He reached out, urging her to take his hand. "We'll make sure to be back before anyone even knows we left."

No matter how much Katira refused to admit it, Isben had a knack for talking her into things. She let him pull her across the ledge and onto the hidden trail. The trail was too narrow to walk side-by-side, so Katira followed behind as Isben led the way.

"I'm guessing you won't give me any clues?"

"That would ruin the surprise. You're far too good at figuring things out. All I can say is this is a place I used to go when I needed to clear my head."

They worked their way along the trail past looming granite slabs and low scrubby brush. Here and there, several of the rocks appeared as if they had been molded and reformed to allow a person to pass. Bender work.

Curiosity struck again. "How long has this trail been here?"

"Hard to say. A few decades at least." He tapped one of the altered rocks with the toe of his boot. "I'm guessing that more than a few in the Tower know about it."

The trail twisted and turned down a steep slope before depositing them on a much larger path rutted by wagon wheels. Pine trees mingled with gnarled chokecherry and the shade beneath the trees felt delicious on Katira's skin.

Isben paused next to a granite slab that blocked the view of the trail ahead. "Close your eyes."

"Why?"

"Just do it. I want to make this as dramatic as possible."

Katira let out her breath in a huff. "Fine, but you better not toss me into a pond." She closed her eyes and held out her hands.

"It was only the one time. Admit it, you had fun."

With his hands in hers, the connection between them opened a fraction. Papan, her father, had explained that because of how the power of the Khandashii worked, even as an unbonded companionship they could sense each other when they touched. In that moment, Isben's excitement coursed through him in fresh sparkling waves. As he led her forward, the whispers of pine faded into a hard echoing silence. The air itself changed, transforming from the warm heat of wooded earth to that of stone after rain. The ground beneath her feet grew hard and flat.

He released her hands. "Here we are. Open your eyes."

The sight that greeted Katira confused her at first. It was as if someone had taken a giant knife and cut the mountain into a vast square chamber. Large blocks dotted the ground in different states of being cut into smooth sided cubes and rectangles. It was both beautiful and barren.

"What is this place?" she asked.

He rested his hip against the block closest to him and watched her as she took in the sight. "Amul Dun's granite quarry."

"It's so quiet." She returned to his side and sat on the block, tugging at him to join her. "I can see why you like it here."

Together, they soaked in the silence. Their work as apprentices meant long days of practice and study. Katira rolled the stiffness from her neck and breathed deep, letting the tension fall away. Cassim was right, she needed a rest.

One of the things she loved most about Isben was how he knew when she needed to talk or when she'd prefer to sit and think. He traced the series of small crescent shaped scars that dotted her bare arm while he waited until she was ready to break the silence. Working outside in Mamar's garden had darkened her skin, making the scars stand out. His touch awoke memories of the shadow hound attacks they both had survived. They'd been lucky.

"What are you thinking about?" she asked, needing to turn her thoughts somewhere else.

"You."

"Really?" His all-too-honest answer made her laugh. "That's none too interesting. I would have sworn you were thinking about how to combine those new glyphs Master Aro taught you."

"Maybe later." He scratched at his chin. "But for now, I'm enjoying this moment. Watching you is like seeing this place for the first time all over again."

Katira rolled her eyes. "We really do need to get out more, especially if you keep talking like that." She leaned back to better see the sky framed in the square of the quarry. The two necklaces she wore beneath her tunic shifted against her skin. She pulled them out and held them loosely in her fist. From one hung her apprentice stone, which represented her future. From the other a simple locket, a bittersweet reminder of the life she once knew.

Isben touched the side of the locket. "Have you been wearing that all this time?"

"Not always. Working in Mamar's garden brings back a lot of memories. It helps me remember." She ran a thumb over its polished surface. Often just holding the locket was enough to help push away the homesickness.

"May I?" Isben touched its edge. "I've always wanted to take a better look at it."

Katira hadn't looked inside the locket in weeks, hadn't felt the need to. When she'd first arrived at the Tower and said goodbye to Elan, her childhood sweetheart, she had two lockets woven with Bender glyphs that would show pictures of the other that changed over time. While it seemed like a good idea then, now it only served to remind her of the life she'd left behind.

Isben noticed her hesitation. "You don't have to."

She set the locket into his waiting palm. "It's okay." And it was. She had nothing to hide from him.

He brought it closer to his face, carefully examining its surface the same way he studied an item he intended to bend with the power. When he finally clicked it open, Katira made a point not to look.

"When did you open this last?" His tone grew serious.

She took the locket from his hand, afraid of what she might see. "Weeks ago, why?"

"Take a look."

Elan's picture made her breath catch in her throat. Dirt and ash streaked the sides of his face, and a fresh gash marred his forehead over his left eyebrow. He looked hunted, scared. She snapped the locket closed, unwilling to believe that what she'd seen was true, and pressed it between her palms.

Isben leaned closer and wrapped an arm around her. "I'm so sorry. I had no idea."

She swallowed down the shock of it. *To do nothing is death,* Papan would say. There had to be an explanation. Letting her emotions get the best of her wouldn't help her find it.

"What do you think happened?"

"It could be something innocent. A fire, perhaps." Isben offered. "I didn't know him well, but he seems like the type to run into danger if someone needed help. He did it for you."

"Maybe." Katira wanted that to be the answer, but her gut said otherwise. Isben's concerned gaze said otherwise. She'd have to look again, closer this time. She took a breath to steady her nerves and flicked the locket open once more. Elan's dirty face, the anger in his brow, the fear in his eyes, all spoke of a different kind of threat — one that he wasn't prepared to deal with.

"What in the ..." Isben pulled her hand closer to him. "Are those—"

Katira spotted it as soon as he said it. Dark shining eyes peered at her from behind Elan's shoulder. Shadow hounds.

"It's not possible, is it? Maybe it's some sort of trick of the light. We're turning this into something it isn't." As much as she didn't like it, Katira knew what she saw. No amount of trying to convince herself otherwise was going to change it.

Isben shook his head. "The locket doesn't work that way. If it's in the picture, it's real."

"They can't be in the world at all." Katira argued, still in denial. Elan wasn't in danger, he just wasn't. "Wrothe can't open the barrier without someone on this side to help her. Shadow hounds can't enter."

"That's not technically true." Isben scooted off the block and started to pace. "Amul Dun is reinforced with protective glyphs and wards, and Wrothe wasn't strong enough to open the barrier here by herself. The rest of the world doesn't have those protections, so shadow hounds can slip through where the barrier is thinnest. We still don't know exactly how. Part of Master Regulus's research was to learn how it all worked so we could put an end to it. We both know how that turned out."

"We must tell my father and the High Lady. If Wrothe is hatching a new plan, she must be stopped." Katira slipped her locket back safely around her neck. "Do you think that Wrothe is behind this?"

"I don't think we can rule her out. She's devious and mean. She lost her anchor here, but who knows what she's still capable of?"

Katira hopped down from the granite block and made her way to the narrow cut leading out of the quarry. "Hurry! If that monster is hatching a new plan, she has to be stopped."

When she didn't hear Isben's steps behind her, she turned back. Something on the far side of the quarry had caught his attention. A low growl broke the silence. The sound twisted Katira's stomach into a knot.

Impossible.

In the months following Wrothe's attack on Amul Dun and Master Ternan's trial, Katira hadn't heard of a single hound spotted anywhere near the Tower. She had let herself believe, like many did, that the threat was over, that the hounds and Wrothe were trapped in the mirror realm forever.

Clearly, she was wrong. It was as if their talk of shadow hounds had forced one to appear. It didn't make any sense.

Isben moved toward Katira one cautious step at a time, not

turning his back on the hound. He didn't speak until he was close enough to whisper.

"Do you think it knows we're here?"

"Of course it knows we're here." Katira pulled her apprentice stone free and bound it to her palm with its chain. "We weren't being quiet."

"I suppose running is out of the question, then?" He did the same with his stone and readied himself for a fight.

During their first encounters with shadow hounds, they'd been ill prepared. This time would be different. Issa, the captain of Lady Alystra's personal guard, had taken it upon herself to train them so they'd be prepared should they need to protect themselves.

Katira took up a defensive position several steps from Isben. Her fingers curled around the practical working knife she kept at her belt. She couldn't help thinking about the first time she faced a shadow hound with only the tiny knife Elan had given her for her birthday. And just like Elan, it didn't suit her needs. The knife she wore now had been crafted by her father specifically for her. *Quality would serve you better than sentimentality,* he told her. Now that she was facing down a real enemy, she couldn't agree more.

"Issa keeps saying we're not ready. I pray we can prove her wrong," Isben murmured under his breath as he drew his own knife.

They'd only started practicing with daggers and hunting knives that past month, and only with dummies and targets. Using those techniques on something alive felt wrong. Katira's purpose was centered around healing, not killing.

"I can't tell you how much I hate this." She hoped he couldn't hear how her voice trembled.

They stalked forward with silent steps, listening for the skitter of claws on stone. The fading daylight filled the quarry with pockets of deep shadow, providing plenty of cover. In a flash of shining eyes and scrambling limbs, a single hound bolted out of one shadow to that of the nearest corner, its instincts to find freedom stronger than that of wanting to attack. Katira opened herself to her power, welcoming the wave of searing heat, the clarity of thought, and the emotionless space where she and the power worked as one. She spared a glance toward Isben, signaling her intentions, before releasing a bolt of energy toward where the hound cowered.

It moved like a shot, streaking across the yard in a blur. Isben stood ready to intercept, the lines on his arms glowing and his long-bladed knife alive with glyphs. With a quick stride, he flowed into the hound's escape path and swung his blade in a smooth arc.

The hound dodged away, changing direction at the last second. Katira charged forward, summoning glyphs that chased up the steel of her own blade.

"Come get me!" she taunted as she bent lower to the ground and waved her bare arm to entice the hound to strike.

Issa believed that a hound without its pack fell into the same reliable patterns. This one should be no different. Katira shook her arm again. The hound turned and charged, jaws open wide to reveal razor-sharp teeth.

Katira held her position and waited for the perfect time to strike. Patience was much easier in the training yard when her target didn't want to rip out her throat. The hound bounded forward, readying itself to leap and in doing so, exposing its vulnerable underbelly. A quick end to a needless battle was always best. Or as Issa said, *Don't dawdle. Don't give second chances. Strike true, strike cleanly, strike once.*

As soon as the hound's feet left the ground, Katira shifted her weight and stabbed her knife upward, aiming for the heart. At the last moment, the hound twisted again, causing her strike to miss by a fraction. Instead of running for the shelter of the shadows, the hound rebounded directly toward her, vicious jaws open.

Isben fired a bolt of energy, knocking the beast away before it could make contact.

Katira swore under her breath. Her strike was meant to end the fight, and it hadn't. One of them would have to try again. When she glanced at Isben to coordinate their next move, she found him grinning at her, clearly pleased at himself for keeping the hound off her.

He signaled for her to stay back and ready as he closed in on where the hound had retreated.

Katira maintained her position. Either the hound would lunge at Isben when he got too close, or it would flee and she could intercept it. As soon as Isben stepped into the shadow where it waited, it burst straight toward her.

She dove forward with her blade, grimacing at how it caught on the beast's fur before slicing its throat. It staggered away several steps before stopping and panting for breath. With a whine, its long limbs buckled and it collapsed to the quarry floor.

There was no joy in the victory. Issa had taught them over and over that all death was to be respected, even for one of these beasts.

Isben replaced his long dagger back into its sheath and came up beside her. "I know that wasn't easy for you. Are you okay?"

Katira wiped her blade clean before tucking it away. "I don't understand. They were supposed to be trapped in their world. Why was that one even here?"

"It could have slipped in through one of those thin spots I was talking about." He crouched down next to the hound to get a better look. "I know it doesn't make it any better, but we got rid of something that wasn't supposed to be here in the first place."

"I can still hate it."

Lines of soft peach and violet streaked across the sky. Cooler air swirled down into the quarry from the canyon above, heralding the night's approach.

Isben sighed and straightened. "As hard as it is, this is our duty as Stonebearers. We keep the world safe from monsters. To do nothing is—"

She cut him off. "Don't say it. I know."

"By rock and ruin, what is the meaning of this?" The startled curse echoed from the narrow entrance to the quarry.

A tall woman with dark cropped hair rushed toward them. Her distinct yellow tunic trimmed in purple identified her as a member of Lady Alystra's personal guard. Katira knew her only through what she'd overheard from Issa. Her name was Leandra, and she was definitely not one to be crossed. In many ways she was a lot like Issa, except half as kind and twice as strict. Having her show up spelled trouble for the both of them.

"What are you two doing here?" Leandra demanded as she

scanned the quarry, loosening her sword from its scabbard. "I declared this area off-limits."

When her gaze fell on the dead shadow hound, she slammed the sword back into its scabbard. "Well, that's just perfect. How do they expect me to study these things now?"

Isben opened his mouth to say something, but she stopped him with a glare that could have melted iron.

"I don't want to hear your attempt at an excuse. Save it for the High Lady. You're both coming with me."

CHAPTER 2

The rich red tapestries and carpets outside the High Lady's office held onto the summer's heat, making Katira's grey apprentice robe feel twice as heavy. It was one thing to get caught; it was quite another to face an interrogation that would determine their punishment. She twisted the wide sleeve into a rope and wound it tight around her fingers. If she pulled hard enough, the resulting pinch distracted her from the discomfort of waiting. Namragan was in trouble, and the sooner she could tell the High Lady, the better.

Next to her, Isben shifted back and forth on the balls of his feet. His hands twitched at his sides and his lanky golden hair stood out at all angles. A streak of dirt ran across his cheek.

Katira wanted to be mad at him. Going to the quarry was his idea. She should have never agreed to venture beyond Amul Dun's walls, or at least she should have taken more than a second to think it through. Had she not been so thrilled at the idea of spending an afternoon with him, she wouldn't be slowly cooking in her own guilt.

On the other side of the heavy door, Leandra, Papan, and Issa were locked in a heated discussion. Katira couldn't make out a single word, regardless of how hard she listened. She could imagine it well enough. Leandra would demand justice and recompense for her ruined experiment. Issa would ask for details and clarifications. And Papan, well, Katira could never be sure what he would do.

She had put him in a difficult situation once again. Ever since they'd assigned him to be her master, he'd been at odds with himself. As her father, he wanted to shield her from any discomfort or suffering. As her master, he was required to cause it to help her learn. No matter what he did, it pricked at his conscience. To complicate things further, his obligation as a General forced him to put the Tower's needs first. He couldn't defend her and serve the Tower's needs when they were at odds with each other like this. He would have to choose between them.

When Katira had first arrived in the hallway, she'd tried to sense him through the connection that linked his master and her apprentice stones. Even the smallest clue about how he felt regarding the situation would give her an idea of how things might turn out. She should have known that it was pointless to try. The second he'd heard about what happened, he'd closed himself off from her.

"Hey," Isben started, "for what it's worth, I'm sorry."

Katira released the edge of her tortured sleeve and pressed it flat against her thigh. "Don't be. I'm just as much to blame."

"I'm trying to ask for forgiveness here, would you stop that?"

"If I end up doing laundry because of you, you'll need to do far more than ask for forgiveness." She nudged him with her elbow. "You'll need to work for it."

He bit his lip as he tried to hide a smile. "You said you were also to blame. Doesn't that mean we're even?"

"We'll see."

The discussion inside the High Lady's office quieted. Leandra opened the door and ushered Katira and Isben inside with a jerk of her head. As expected, Leandra's stern face revealed nothing. Inside the well-appointed room, a stack of books propped open the large window and let in a welcome evening breeze. Papan and Issa appeared relaxed and at ease, but Katira knew better. Issa often adopted a similar pose during training to put an attacker off guard. From there, she could strike, viper-quick and deadly, if the situation required it.

As Katira entered the room, she tried to catch Papan's gaze, hoping for him to give her a sign that things would be okay. But as much as she willed it, he didn't turn. The door behind the stately desk swung open and Lady Alystra strode in. She took her place behind the desk and looked at each of them in turn with her piercing, knowledgeable gaze.

On an unspoken cue, Papan and Issa moved to stand on either side of Katira and Isben, acting more like jailers than mentors. Leandra remained fixed at her position next to the door. In unison, they gave the ceremonial bow, bending at the waist with a fist pressed to their chests.

Lady Alystra had always been practical. Given the heat, instead of ceremonial robes, she opted to wear a simple belted linen dress the color of golden wheat. Intricate lines of flowery embroidery chased up the loose sleeves and around the neck. She'd knotted her fine white hair high on the back of her head to keep it off her neck, something Katira was itching to do with her own hair the second they were excused.

The chair next to her remained empty. Katira would have preferred its usual occupant to be there. Bremin, Lady Alystra's master advisor and companion, was Papan's close friend. He would have been one more person to speak in her and Isben's favor.

"Let's get this over with," Lady Alystra said as she arranged herself in the chair behind the desk.

Katira clutched the locket in her fist. The news concerning Namragan couldn't wait another minute. "My Lady, there's something important I have to tell you."

"Silence!" Leandra ordered. "You'll speak only when asked."

The High Lady pushed back her sleeves and leaned forward, all business. "Thank you. Leandra told me what she witnessed, but I want to hear your side of the story. What were you two doing in the quarry?"

Even with Papan a step out of view, Katira felt his attention drilling into the back of her head. It pushed her to speak.

"There's something going on you need to know about. Something I saw in…"

Lady Alystra cut her off with an upheld hand. "I'm not interested in excuses. If you can't contain your outbursts to the subject at hand, I'll have to ask you to leave."

Katira bit her tongue, the sooner they got this out of the way, the sooner she could tell Lady Alystra about what they saw in the locket. "Cassim gave us the afternoon off. Master Regulus used to take Isben up to the quarry to get away from things, and I'd never been—"

"It's my fault, my Lady," Isben jumped in to explain. "Katira wouldn't have gone had I not suggested it. As for the hound, once it had spotted us, we had no choice but to kill it. Neither of us knew about it being held there for a reason."

Katira clenched her teeth to stop herself from arguing with Isben in front of the High Lady, but she couldn't allow him to take the entirety of the blame either. "Isben wouldn't have gone if it weren't for me. We both killed that hound. I submit that we both shoulder whatever punishment you see fit to give us."

The High Lady arched an eyebrow. "I'll make that decision, if you don't mind. I've found that if anything requires sneaking, it's generally a bad idea." Her gaze flicked back to Papan and she looked almost amused. "Wouldn't you agree, Master Jarand?"

He gave a nod. Amusement creased the corner of his eye. "Yes, my lady."

Issa also smirked for the briefest of seconds. Clearly there was something in his past where he'd gotten himself in trouble for the same thing. Katira made a mental note to ask him about it later.

"I won't drag this out," Lady Alystra continued, "You both knew better than to leave the Tower without permission, and now a valuable test subject needs to be replaced. Seeing as Bremin is currently out on my errand and it's Leandra you've inconvenienced, I'll leave it to her to decide what your punishment will be. That will be all." Without another word, she stood to leave.

Katira hadn't released the locket. She couldn't leave without making her voice heard. "There are shadow hounds in Namragan," she blurted out.

Lady Alystra stopped, her hand rested on the doorway leading into her private quarters. "What did you say?"

Katira placed the locket in her palm and held it forward. "Shadow hounds. In Namragan. I've been trying to tell you since I got here."

The High Lady returned to her desk. "How do you know this?"

At the same time, Papan took the locket from her hand. He knew what it was and what it did. "What did you see?"

"Look for yourself. There must have been an attack in the village."

Papan flipped it open and showed the picture inside to both Lady Alystra and Issa. "You would tell me if there was trouble there." A troubled look crossed his face. "Wouldn't you?"

"Not until things were confirmed, no."

"So, there is something then." Papan gripped the edge of the desk. "How long have you known?"

The wall he'd built to prevent Katira from reading his emotions cracked under the weight of this new discovery. She sensed bits and pieces of his utter astonishment mingled with outrage. Namragan was the closest thing he had to living a normal peaceful life. Lady Alystra knew what lengths he'd go to in order to protect it.

"My network caught wind of a possible problem and reported it to me a few days ago. Bremin is investigating it as we speak. He'll send word if any other action is necessary."

"That's not enough. You should have told me. Let me do something." The muscles of Papan's jaw tensed. He hovered on the edge of lashing out.

Issa stepped closer. While she was Papan's friend, she was still the captain of Lady Alystra's personal guard. Duty came first.

"We don't even know what it is. It might be nothing. We all know how important Namragan is to you. If there was something that needed to be done, you'd be the first to know. Let Bremin do his job."

Papan's jaw relaxed a fraction and the hints of outrage Katira detected through his wall died back. She didn't want to fan that fire to life again, but one question remained unanswered.

"What about the hounds?" she asked. "Bremin can't safely handle them on his own. Can the companionship there fight them if needed?"

Papan's jaw went tight again. "Are there hounds, Alystra?" he asked in a voice that was too quiet compared to the fresh torrent of anger coursing through him. Katira had never seen him address the High Lady directly like this before.

Lady Alystra's head lowered. "We need to talk. In private. Leandra, escort the apprentices out and assign them whatever punishment you see fit for the wrong committed to you."

Leandra gave a curt nod. If she was pleased with getting her way, she didn't show it.

Katira stood frozen. Lady Alystra couldn't be sending her away. Namragan was her home too. This involved her as much is it did Papan.

Isben slipped his hand into hers. "Come on. There's nothing more you can do here. Let them sort things out."

At his, Katira let him lead her from the room.

Jarand followed Lady Alystra into her private study, a comfortable affair filled with a long low couch and several deep upholstered chairs arranged around an unlit fireplace. This late in the evening, the power-fueled globe in the center of the low table and those on either side of the two doors made the room glow with warm rose-colored light. Issa entered last, closing the door behind her with a soft click.

Between finding the best way to handle Katira's lack of judgment and learning that Namragan might be in danger, Jarand's head spun with different needs to address. He needed to speak with Katira and learn for himself why she had left the Tower when he'd asked her not to. He needed to know that the situation in Namragan was being taken seriously. More than anything, he needed to know if Wrothe, that conniving monster, was behind any of it.

He didn't wait for the High Lady to take her customary seat next to the fireplace before the first question flew off his tongue. "Have you sensed anything that might give us a clue?"

Bremin was their best bet at unraveling the truth of the situation. As Lady Alystra's companion, she'd know if he was experiencing unusual stress or fear. It would be foolish to jump to assumptions and conclusions without considering all the facts.

"Nothing useful. I expect news from him any day now. He's been there long enough." Lady Alystra held out her hand. "May I see the locket again?"

Jarand handed it to her and she flicked it open.

"Please, sit." She motioned for both him and Issa to join her. It took a pointed glare before Jarand complied.

"Like I said, it was only a few days ago when we first heard there was a problem," Lady Alystra began. "It seems hounds continue to slip into the village regardless of all efforts to reinforce it by the companionship stationed there. Bremin helped you with that particular ward, so he felt it best that he go assess it. I have every confidence that he'll be able to take care of the problem."

Jarand wanted to agree with her. Bremin was more than qualified to do what was needed, but the uneasy roiling of his gut said they were missing something.

"The boy appears as if he's been through a war." He gestured toward the locket. "If things were under control, if Bremin's intervention was successful, there's no reason why he should look like that."

Lady Alystra's brow wrinkled. She laced her fingers together in her lap around the locket. Wrothe's recent threats to Stonebearer Society had aged her more in the last few months than in the previous hundred years. Jarand noted the hollows in her cheeks and the tremors in her hands. It wasn't fair to demand answers like this, but if it made a difference, if it saved even one life, it was worth it.

"I'd hoped it was nothing. Wanted it to be nothing. After all you've been through, I worried that having your home threatened would be more than you could bear. It's clear now that whatever is going on in Namragan is worse than expected. I'm sorry."

The sentiment warmed him. "You're still protective of me even after all these years."

"What can I say? You've always been a favorite."

Issa leaned forward and rested her elbows on her knees, eager to return to the problem at hand. "For Bremin's sake, help needs to be sent. Even if he thinks he has things under control, I'd feel better with another set of eyes on his back."

Jarand was keenly aware how every time Bremin stepped out of the Tower and into the world, he risked his life. His only assurance of safety was his uncanny ability to make people like him, his wealth of knowledge, and should it come down to it, the knives he kept tucked under his coat.

"Agreed," Jarand said. "The townspeople are stubborn at best and downright willful at worst. They could be making trouble for him."

Lady Alystra handed back the locket, which he tucked safely into his pocket. "Is there any way this could be connected to Wrothe?"

At the mention of her name, Lady Alystra's sharp focus returned. "It is a possibility that must be explored. She has slipped past our protections before. I can promise you that if she is plotting something, I will do everything in my power to stop her. Issa, inform the Council that we'll meet at first light."

Issa gave a short bow with her fist over her chest before excusing herself from the room.

Jarand straightened from his chair. The spot he'd taken the blade in his back all those months ago pinched and ached. Long days and trouble always made it worse. He gave his own bow. "By your leave, my Lady."

Namragan was his town, and Bremin his friend. He'd do whatever he could to safeguard them both. But, returning to Namragan meant returning to the home he and Mirelle had built together. It would force him to face the pain of losing her once again. If Mirelle were alive, she would remind him that facing this kind of pain, while hard, would help heal up the empty spaces she'd left behind. Maybe it was for the best.

CHAPTER 3

*L*eandra moved with the swift graceful steps of someone whose life revolved around training and fighting. Katira and Isben, armed with rags and water buckets, struggled to keep up as she turned down one hallway after another until they'd made their way to the part of the Keep dug deep into the side of the mountain. When she finally stopped, they stood in front of one of dozens of storage rooms.

The door squealed in protest as Leandra pushed it open. "These rooms have needed attention for ages. Your job is to wipe down the centuries of dust that has gathered, sweep away the cobwebs, and scrub the floors."

With each detail she listed, Katira swore she spotted a hint of joy cross the woman's face, but it might have been a trick of the light. Katira had never seen the woman pleased at anything.

"Any questions?" she asked.

The light from the hall spilled into the room and over the crates, bags, and boxes lining each wall. Isben entered the room, looking around as if trying to figure out just how much work cleaning it would take. Dust swirled around him, triggering a loud sneeze.

"How long will you have us working down here?" he asked.

"I haven't decided yet. Long enough for you to learn your lesson." She tapped her lip in thought. "Perhaps as long as it takes to find a replacement for the hound you destroyed."

"And how long will that take?" Katira wasn't sure she wanted to hear the answer. She started to regret joking about not liking doing laundry.

"The last one took nearly a month to find and capture successfully. Even if we find one right away, it might take weeks to trap it." She made a sour face at the thought. "Get comfortable. You two might be at this for a while." With that, she turned and left.

Isben removed his apprentice robe and dropped it on the relatively clean floor outside of the storage room before pushing the door the rest of the way open and using a smaller crate to pin it in place. He then turned his attention to the nearest wall running his fingers lightly along the surface as he looked for the focal point that would activate the power-fueled glowing sphere embedded in the ceiling.

"Got it." Isben cheered as the room filled with light. Something squeaked and scurried away beneath the rubble.

Katira slid off her heavy formal robe, folded it, and set it down outside the room next to Isben's. "Do I want to know what that was?"

"No. No, you don't." Isben rubbed his already soiled hands against each other in disgust. "But it's probably rats. They shouldn't bother us as long as we don't bother them."

"That's just great."

Katira tied up her hair, rolled up her sleeves, and tried to ignore how her stomach gurgled. With all that had happened, they'd missed the evening meal. She poked at the settled dust on the nearest shelf and found it had hardened into a thick shell. This was going to be even worse than she thought. *The only way to finish a task was to get started*, Mamar had always said. Katira removed the items from the nearest shelf and carefully set them on the floor before scrubbing at the uneven lines of built-up grime with her washrag.

"I'm guessing there isn't a nice little piece of glyph work you could use to remove this, is there?"

Isben slapped his washrag into the water bucket. "I have a feeling Leandra wouldn't approve of that."

"That's the understatement of the century." Katira rinsed her rag into her own bucket and made a face. At this rate they'd need to get fresh water after finishing each shelf.

"Hey, at least it's not the laundry room. Matron Nelly isn't here to tell us how are doing everything wrong."

"Could you do it if you wanted to?" She poked at the dust with a fingernail and wondered how many centuries had passed since the last unfortunate apprentice had been tasked with cleaning it.

"Maybe. I'd have to change the structure of the dust itself, make the connections between each particle brittle. I've never tried or even seen anything like that done before." He swiped a finger along the next dirty shelf and studied what collected on his fingertip. "Truth is, it would most likely be more difficult and take longer than the cleaning we're doing. With the amount of dust in here, using the power is more likely to suck me dry before clearing even a fraction of this room."

"Pity."

"I'm not dying over a pile of dust, thank you very much."

"I'm not asking you to. At least, not anymore." She rinsed out her rag again and scowled at the dirty water. "What about separating the dirt and grime from the clean water? That would be handy."

Isben laughed through his nose. "Would you stop? Moving one thing away from another? That would be better handled by a Traveler, wouldn't it? Even a Healer would be better at it than a Bender. You're trained to remove sick tissue away from the healthy, and this water is sick."

"Okay. You've made your point. No power-aided cleaning. Got it."

Hours passed as they scrubbed, fetched fresh water, and scrubbed some more. Just when Katira thought they were making good progress, she'd see the dozens of other shelves waiting for attention. Her back ached with all the reaching and bending. At least she had Isben to talk to, it made the process that much more tolerable.

She lifted a bag no longer than her forearm and set it on the floor with a crystalline ping.

Isben stop scrubbing and set down his rag. "Wait, what was that?" He picked up the bag and carefully opened it. An ivory-colored rod slid out into his palm.

The sight of it sparked something from Katira's memory. Master Aro had used a rod like this to make the barrier visible between the real world and the mirror realm when they were working with the Occulus Seat.

"That looks just like ..." she started but trailed off, not ready to relive the memory.

Isben peered closer at it. "Glyph rods are usually stored in the Bender's workshop for decades before getting carted to storage." He glanced at the discarded bag. "But it's cleaner than the rest of the stuff in here. Maybe once Master Aro was finished with it, he didn't want anyone messing with it and stuck it in here instead. Weirder things have happened."

"Is there a way to find out?" Katira's thoughts drifted to her worries about the shadow hounds appearing in Namragan. If it was a problem with the barrier, a glyph rod like that would come in handy.

Isben nodded. "All glyph rods have an identifier for exactly that reason. It helps Benders to not accidentally blow anything up." The lines on his arms glowed to life as he summoned the power with a wince. Several small glyphs appeared in the air, combined, and flowed into the rod. In response, a series of symbols and words appeared on the rod's surface.

He let his power fade. "There's your answer. It's the same one."

The sound of footsteps echoed toward them from the end of the hallway. While Katira knew she should put the rod back onto one of the already-cleaned shelves behind her, something urged her to keep hold of it. She slipped it into one of her dress's deep pockets instead.

Papan stuck his head through the doorway. "All right, you two, it's time to be done for tonight. I promised Leandra you'd report to her first thing in the morning."

Katira tossed her rag into the bucket and scooped up her robe, very aware of each time the glyph rod bumped against her leg. If she could keep it hidden, no one would get in trouble.

~

Back in their rooms, Katira tucked the small Bender's rod into the pocket of the simple linen work smock she set out to wear the next day. Her skin itched with the dust that still stuck to it. Had it not been so late, she would have drawn up a bath instead of making do with a damp cloth.

When she returned to the sitting room of their apartment, Papan stood at the window and gazed out at the star-filled sky and the surrounding mountains. Hours had passed since he'd first put up the wall between them, and there was no sign of him being ready to take it down. Between her disobedience and what he'd learned about Namragan, there couldn't have been a more effective way to shut him down.

She found her locket waiting for her on the table and returned it to lie around her neck before curling up into one of the armchairs near him, unsure of what to do. Papan had promised her he'd never shut her out again, not after what they been through together. She understood why he did it, there was trouble on the horizon and it involved a place that was dear to him, but it still hurt.

Back in the early days after Mamar had died, he'd worried that the pain of his loss was too strong and would overwhelm her, so he'd chosen to bear it alone. Faced with this new threat, it was natural for him to fall into the same pattern of trying to protect her from the intensity of his feelings.

But it didn't mean it was the right choice. If the two of them had learned anything over the past few months, it was that suffering alone only made things worse. She pulled the apprentice stone into her palm and nudged at the wall with her own worries and fears.

At the window, he released a slow breath and let his head fall to his chest. Slowly, brick by brick, he pulled the wall down and let her in. The worry that flowed through the cracks was expected. What was happening at Namragan was indeed something to worry about. His frustration made sense as well, there was so much they didn't know. It made it impossible to know how to think, what decisions to make. Thankfully, she felt neither the spiky barbs of anger nor the hard chill of disappointment. He'd either forgiven her or pushed that situation aside for later.

"You want to go, don't you?" he asked without turning from the window.

Katira considered the question carefully before answering. If they went back, even for the right reasons, they flirted with danger. The people of Namragan, like those of many small towns, clung tightly to their beliefs. Most saw Stonebearers as unnatural abominations, monsters capable of causing everything from crop failure to plagues. They knew about her, about Papan. Elan had been back long enough to have shared everything he had seen. With them gone, he had no reason to keep their secret.

"Namragan is dear to both of us. If we don't go, if anything goes wrong, we will never forgive ourselves."

He pushed himself away from the window and sat in the chair next to hers. "If we do go, things might still go wrong. People we care for may get hurt or killed despite our best intentions. Regardless of what happens, we will carry the blame." He ran a hand over his face and winced as if remembering something awful. "Will you still be able to forgive yourself then?"

"We lose regardless of what we decide." She hugged her arms around herself. "If we go, we will know with a surety that every effort was made to protect our friends. There won't be any doubts."

"What about facing Elan? I know you two parted on good terms, but he has always been uneasy about Stonebearers. This whole business with the shadow hounds could make him bitter. He might take his anger out on you. Are you prepared to face something like that?"

"He wouldn't." The words came out without thinking. Elan would never be angry with her for what she was, would he? Then again, she'd never seen him as furious as on the day they'd discovered Papan was a Stonebearer.

"All the same, it would be wise to prepare your heart."

As he spoke, Katira had the impression that he'd gone through something similar, possibly more than once. He'd lived long enough and in enough places that this advice came from his own hard experiences. She thought about asking him about it but changed her mind. It would be cruel to make him dredge up unpleasantness from his past.

"What happens now?"

"The Council meets first thing tomorrow morning. They will weigh the facts of the situation and decide on the best course of action."

Katira straightened as a thought struck her. "You sit on the Council. They'll listen to you, won't they?"

"I'm one of many voices." He held out his hands in a gesture that said anything could happen. "That said, I know them. I've been on that Council and debated more issues like this than I can count. Odds are that they will decide in favor of me going. I have experience with the area and have allies there."

"What if they question your ability to do so?" This was the one thing they avoided talking about. He wasn't the same man as he had been before Wrothe's minions stabbed him in the back. It still hurt him, a deep persistent ache that occasionally blossomed into something more. The strength in his left leg had never fully returned.

Worse still was the damage he'd sustained to his heart when Wrothe had dug her roots into him. Katira's healing had saved his life, but even the most skilled healer couldn't prevent scarring. His stamina wasn't half of what it was before. Often, simple tasks left him winded.

"Like I said, I have allies there. Friends. That alone makes me a valuable asset, even if I can't fight like I used to. If they believe someone else would have a greater chance at resolving this, that person has my blessing. But I doubt they will." He let out a pent-up breath. "If I am chosen, I don't want you to go. Facing rejection by the people you loved is hard, harder than you would think. Stay here, protect your heart."

"I refuse." The strength of her conviction surprised even her and left her breathless. "I don't care if it's hard. I refuse to avoid pain simply because hiding is easier. I never got to say goodbye to the home I loved. You owe me that much."

Papan's brow creased. "You'll hate me for it. It won't turn out well, I can promise you that."

"This is my pain. I have the right to choose where it comes from, and right now it's either from them or from you. I'd rather it be from them." She stood, unwilling to continue the discussion, and left the room.

CHAPTER 4

When Katira awoke, Papan had already left to attend the Council meeting. She busied herself with the morning chores and tried to lose herself in the repetitive motions, anything to keep herself from thinking about Namragan. Leandra expected both her and Isben to return to their punishment at the morning bell. If she didn't finish her usual apprentice chores quick enough, she wouldn't have time to get breakfast.

In the past, Katira had used work as a distraction from anything bothering her. Moving from task to task kept her hands busy and mind quiet. This worry was different. With every breath, with every task, it dredged up another reason about why she should be allowed to go.

Every worry Papan had voiced the night before, every possibility of what could happen both good and ill, every horrible thing she could think of, paraded in an endless loop through her mind. She couldn't focus on even the simplest chore and caught herself pacing from the bookshelves to the doors leading to the two bedrooms, and back.

A cloud passed over the sun, causing a shadow to flick across the floor. Worrying had eaten up what little time she had. Papan would have to forgive her for not finishing her work. She tugged on the work smock and tied it over her kirtle. The rod bumped her leg from where it hid inside the pocket, its solid weight hard to ignore.

With everything in place, she hurried down to the dining hall. Knowing Isben's endless appetite, he was sure to be there, or would get there soon. He wouldn't miss breakfast, especially with a hard day of labor before him. She passed through the double doors and searched the room, hoping to see his disheveled blonde mop of hair bent over a bowl of porridge or plate of eggs.

A dozen or so people dotted the long tables in pairs in trios and talked quietly as they ate. Judging by the hushed voices and sideways glances, news of what the two of them had done at the quarry had spread.

"There you are," said a familiar voice from behind her. Isben walked past carrying a simple breakfast of cooked oats and berries. "We better hurry. I can't imagine Leandra will be any nicer if we get there late."

Following his lead, Katira scooped up her own cereal from the large black cooking pot and topped it with a handful of berries and a splash of fresh cream before hurrying to catch up. When she reached the table, she sat down the bowl harder than necessary.

"She can be mad all she wants. This punishment is a stupid waste of time."

"Whoa. You're feisty this morning. What's going on?"

Katira stared at him, spoon halfway to her mouth.

"You can't be that upset about having to clean storage rooms. I mean, it's bad. But it's not *that* bad." He shoveled another bite of breakfast into his mouth. After a moment of thought, his eyes widened. "Wait. This isn't about that at all. I'm sorry. After everything that happened last night, I almost forgot. Are they in Council right now?"

She nodded and swallowed a bite of her berry-studded oats down past the lump in her throat. "Papan's in the meeting. There's a good chance they'll send him back to Namragan to help figure out what's going on."

"Will you go with him?"

"I'll have to, won't I? I mean, I'm bonded to him as his apprentice, so I need to go with him, just like you went with Master Regulus to Khanrosh. It's part of my duty as apprentice to help him with his work, regardless of where that work takes him."

"Do you want to go?" Isben asked, his voice quieter than before.

"That's the thing. I never had a chance to say goodbye. I'd like to be able to do that. And, I'd like to collect a few of my mother's things that were left behind." That alone was reason enough to compel her to go, even considering all the complications she was destined to face.

"What about Elan?"

Katira slid her bowl away, appetite gone. "What if he hates me? Or worse — what if he still loves me?"

Isben placed his hand over hers. Even without joining with the power, this small touch communicated his trust and devotion. "It's okay to worry. The best you can do is have a plan in place should either of those things happen."

She lifted out the locket to study it in the morning light which streamed through the high windows dotting one side of the dining hall. Elan had washed his face and the wound on his forehead had been cared for. Like before, his eyes bothered her the most. They spoke of exhaustion and desperation she'd only seen in those in the Tower when Wrothe's attack had reached its worst point.

The pull to go home tugged stronger. "There's something more going on. Something beyond the shadow hounds, beyond simple unrest. I can't explain it. I need to be there."

Isben pointed to the locket. "I can. You still care about them. You want to protect them from all this darkness. Knowing you, you've somehow managed to find a way to feel responsible."

"You think it's foolish for me to go, don't you?" It was a statement more than a question.

"It's not that. I think you need it." He paused, and his brow creased. "When I was taken from my home, I never got to return. I still have a family, including a sister who I miss terribly. I've never had a chance to find closure." He gave her hand a small squeeze. "You need closure as much as anyone in your situation. But facing the past after all you've been through is going to be harder than you imagine. I hate seeing you hurt, even when it's for the best."

Katira poked at the berries in her bowl. "Look at us, getting all worked up about something that's not decided yet. There's still a chance that the Council will send someone else. Then all this worry will be for nothing."

Isben looked up and his eyes went wide. "Especially when we have a whole new worry to deal with."

Katira turned and found Leandra standing directly behind her, shoulders squared, and hands clasped behind her back. The first bell must have rung, and they'd missed it. If her face was stern before, it was absolutely stony now.

"Get up. Get moving," she ordered. "I have better things to do than shepherd children."

Katira's opinion of the dusty storage room didn't improve after a troubled night's sleep. If anything, now that she knew what to expect, the job seemed worse. Her shoulders already complained from their work the day before. She could only imagine how much worse that ache would get before their punishment was complete.

At least when she trained with Issa, every bruise and strained muscle meant she was making progress toward greater skill and strength. Discomfort from cleaning the storage room was meaningless.

Isben leaned his weight against the open doorway. "Working in the laundry is sounding better by the minute."

Katira set the bucket and stack of washrags inside the room. "No. They're both horrible."

As they set to work, the process of cleaning took on its own rhythm. Remove the items from a shelf, scrub it down, wipe each item, put it back. Over and over. Something about working alongside Isben helped her find that ease of mind she so desperately sought earlier that morning. The Council's decision would be made, and she would have to abide by it regardless of what it was. Until then, she would find momentary peace and calm in the work before her.

"I've been thinking ..." Isben started.

"That's dangerous. What about?" Katira set down her rag and leaned against the crate lining the nearby wall. The rod in her pocket bumped against her leg. She should just put it back, but something made her want to wait a bit longer.

"If you do go, do you think they'd let me come as well?" He wiped clean a stoppered bottle with amber colored glass and set it back. "Then, maybe on the way back, we could take a few days to visit where I grew up. You've never seen a place as beautiful as Dunlin with its leagues of vineyards."

She closed her eyes to imagine it. His childhood, or at least the parts he had shared with her, was full of days working in the vineyard hauling water and dunging the crops. It was labor he'd been born into, as were his parents, and their parents. They were proud people who worked the land. Katira reasoned it was why even now, Isben never shied back from hard monotonous work.

"I'd like that," she said. "Then we'd both get what we want."

The familiar cadence of Papan's uneven footsteps echoed down the empty hallway. The Council must have concluded.

Isben gave him a respectful nod as he stepped into the room.

"It is decided," he said, his voice low and serious.

Katira's stomach twisted violently and pinned itself tightly to her chest, making it hard to breathe. No matter what he said, there would be serious repercussions. Going meant finding closure, but also facing a slew of dangers once again. Staying meant she could do nothing to help the people she cared for.

"Well?" Her efforts to not sound anxious were betrayed by the squeak in her voice.

He touched the edge of a shelf they hadn't cleaned yet and rubbed the dust between his fingers. "The good news is you won't be stuck down here cleaning any longer. Leandra will not be happy, but she has to abide by Lady Alystra's decision. You and I are going to Namragan along with Issa and Cassim."

A rush of relief wash over Katira, and for a moment she sat

there, dumbfounded. She wanted, no, needed to go, and now she was. Papan's face remained unreadable and the sensation through their bond was a muddy mix of different emotions.

"Are you okay with this?" she asked.

"I'll have to be. The High Lady's ordered it, and I go where she commands."

"That's not what I asked."

Lines of worry marked his face and tightened his jaw. "After considering everything, going is better than not going. Namragan was good to me for all those years. I owe them."

"What about me?" Isben set down his rag and stepped forward. "Is there any way I could come along?"

Katira wanted him to come more than anything. With him there, it wouldn't matter how Elan reacted to seeing her again, she would have someone to lean on.

Papan regarded Isben carefully before answering. "It wasn't discussed. It would be best if you stayed here."

"I disagree." Isben let his hand brush against Katira's. "Neither Cassim, Issa, or Bremin for that matter, have an apprentice to handle their more mundane tasks. If I'm there, they'll have more time to devote to the problem you are trying to solve. I did it for Master Regulus. I'm already accustomed to the work."

Papan's gaze shifted back to Katira and she prayed he'd see how much she needed Isben with her.

He narrowed his eyes and studied Isben in light of this new information before giving a slight nod. "Allow me the afternoon to see what I can arrange. Until then, Isben, your job is to make sure Katira has what she needs for the journey. Only the essentials. We leave tomorrow morning."

Isben gave a crisp bow with his fist over his heart. "Yes, sir."

As Papan turned to leave, Katira realized there was still one loose end that needed to be taken care of.

"Wait. Has Leandra been told about any of this?"

He stopped mid-step. Katira swore she saw him shudder. "I'll take care of it."

CHAPTER 5

The morning brought with it clear skies and a warm teasing breeze that tossed Katira's hair into her face. She hefted her bag over her shoulder and let its solid weight settle on her back. Ever since Papan had told her she was accompanying him to Namragan, her stomach had tied itself into a solid knot that refused to loosen. Isben stood beside her, shouldering his own pack as they waited for everyone to gather.

Despite Papan's initial misgivings about Isben joining them, in the end, he'd been the one who convinced Lady Alystra that he should come. Katira was glad for it. Isben gave her the courage to face whatever might happen.

The large double doors leading out from the main hall into the courtyard swung open. Issa and Cassim stepped down the handful of stairs dressed in drab traveling clothes. Katira wasn't used to seeing Issa without the usual blues and yellows of her Tower livery. The woman sported well-fitted leathers and an unremarkable scabbard holding her impressive sword. Even in disguise, there was no mistaking that she was dangerous.

Cassim, on the other hand, could have been mistaken for a farmer or goatherd. His simple tan tunic hung over dark baggy pants drawn in over scuffed boots. Over the tunic he wore a shabby vest the color of mud that seemed to shift on its own. Katira swore she spotted a tail feather before it tucked itself back in.

Papan and Lady Alystra followed behind them. Walking side by side, she stood no taller than his shoulder. Her cornflower blue dress made her stand out like a bright jewel among their unremarkable clothes. Seeing Papan wearing the same simple lace-up shirt and dark practical pants he wore back in Namragan summoned up all the memories of home Katira had been determined to push down. If it wasn't for the cane in his hand, she could have let herself believe that all had happened over the past six months was just a dream.

"I guess this is it." Isben straightened from where he leaned against the low wall surrounding the traveling post. "You ready?"

"Ready enough, I suppose." Katira shifted the pack once more and tried to ignore the small ache forming between her shoulder blades.

Papan gestured for her to walk with him as he crossed the last half of the Tower's looming courtyard. When she matched his stride, he leaned closer. "Are you doing okay?"

Katira answered with a nod. It was the truth, or at least something close to it. "I just want the waiting part to be over. It's making me crazy to not know what's happening. The sooner we get there the better."

"I agree. Had it been up to me, we would have left the first moment you spotted trouble." He stepped through the opening in the short wall and up onto the circular platform inside. "But then these two would have been tasked to go after us." He tilted his head toward Cassim and Issa. "It's best not to start something like this with your best teammates wanting to throw you in the nearest lake."

"I wouldn't!" Cassim protested.

"I would." Issa smirked.

Lady Alystra took her place at the pedestal with her stone in hand, and their smiles faded back to seriousness.

"You know what needs to be done," she said. "Take care of the problem. Stay true to your oath. Return when you are finished."

She turned to Papan. "And if Bremin's gotten himself into some sort of trouble, please be so kind as to sort it out."

Papan gave a nod. "Without hesitation, my Lady."

The High Lady turned her attention to Katira and Isben. "I know you've both used a traveling post before, but it's good practice to remind you what must be done."

Katira reached for Isben's hand. The one time she had traveled this way, she was still dazed and half-conscious from surviving Wrothe's death oath. The little she remembered, she didn't like.

"It's simple," The High Lady continued. "You must stay calm, breathe slowly and evenly, and most importantly, remain still."

"Yes, my Lady." Katira hoped she sounded braver than she felt.

"If you can do that, I can guarantee your safe passage. When there are this many of you, I need all the help I can get."

Without another word, Lady Alystra set her hand on top of the pedestal with her stone nested in her palm. Three distinct glyphs formed in the air, and she guided them into the traveling post. As soon as they touched its surface, tendrils of light sprang across the top and down its sides to the platform below.

Isben gave Katira's hand one more squeeze before releasing it and hugging his arms to his chest. On seeing that, Katira did the same, grasping the straps of her pack so she had something to hold onto. It would make it that much harder to jerk back should something catch her by surprise.

The surface beneath her feet rippled like water and edged up the sides of her boots. Katira's pulse quickened.

Stay calm.

Her fingers ached from clenching the straps. The High Lady's words echoed through her head like a mantra. *Breathe evenly, don't move.* The water-like power wrapped up her calves, her knees, her thighs, and pressed against her like a warm blanket as it crawled higher and higher.

Stay calm, don't move, breathe steadily.

Stay calm, don't move, breathe steadily.

It passed over her chest, her shoulders, her neck. She continued to repeat the words to herself, using them as a lifeline. The power leapt up and over her head, plunging her into a suffocating darkness. When her eyes adjusted, Lady Alystra's gentle swirling ribbons of power came into view along with another, much older, flow of power.

Something about this older flow felt familiar. Katira was sure this was the same presence that had guided her in her most desperate moments. It had helped her when all other hope was lost. This was the intelligence held within the Khandashii and perfected in the motherstone.

She couldn't appreciate it for what it was for very long. Without warning, the flows pressed in tighter, squeezing the air from her lungs and making it harder to breathe as she'd been instructed. She couldn't panic, not now. She had to trust that Lady Alystra would deliver them safely. Stars burst at the edge of her vision as the crushing pressure tightened once more. Breath refused to come. Her pulse pounded in her head.

Then, the pressure disappeared. The darkness and the dancing flows of power faded to greens and browns. The air filled with the smell of pine. A different circular platform glowed beneath her feet, and at its center, another pedestal. One by one, Isben, Papan, Issa, and Cassim appeared. Their forms shifted from ghostlike to solid before her eyes. The light receded in the same rippling tide as it had come.

Don't move, stay calm, breathe slowly and evenly.

Katira's head continued to pound. Papan set his hands on her shoulders.

"It's okay, Katira. You're here now. Do you need to sit down?"

The shaking in her knees turned to full-fledged tremors, and she sucked in a breath of fresh air. He guided her to the trunk of a fallen tree. When she sat down, the weight of the glyph rod shifted against her leg. Again, she couldn't shake the feeling that it needed to be with her. The real problem would be how to explain its presence to Papan.

Isben joined her and rested his head in his hands with a moan. "That is just as uncomfortable as the last time I tried it. I think I'm going to be sick."

As Katira waited for the world to stop spinning, Issa, Cassim, and Papan clustered at the other side of the small clearing, speaking quietly to each other. She could only make out bits of the conversation here and there, but she swore she heard Issa scold Cassim for bringing Onyx with him. Unfazed by the scolding, the raven marched happy circles across the top of Cassim's shoulders.

"Is this Namragan? Are we here?" Isben asked. The color had returned to his face, and he'd released his grip on his head to look around.

Katira looked up. The tall pines blocked most of the view, making it hard to say where they were for certain. She breathed in the smell of the forest, taking in the sharp green notes of creeper vine and the sweetness of the pine. It certainly smelled like home. Off to her left came the familiar burble of the Kanth river.

"We're close, I can feel it."

"You were right. It's beautiful here." Isben plucked a leaf from the vine at his feet and twirled it between his fingers. "Not as beautiful as Dunlin, but it'll do."

Papan loosened the ties on his water skin and offered it to Katira, who took it gladly. "From here forward, I expect both of you to keep up and do as you are asked immediately and without question. We still don't know what kind of situation were walking into, so stay aware of your surroundings." He took the water skin from Katira and offered it to Isben.

"When do you think we'll get there?" Isben took a drink and handed it back.

Papan glanced up to the cloudless sky and squinted against the brightness. "Depending on the condition of the road, we should get there around nightfall."

Katira had wanted to return home for so long that the idea had turned into something that felt more like a dream. Now that they were there, Papan's warnings rang far more real in her mind. All her worries about returning, about Elan, about facing what she left behind, would be confirmed or dismissed that very night. She hoped she was strong enough to face them.

With each passing league, the steep-sided canyon grew more familiar. Katira ran her fingers along the exposed granite outcroppings and breathed in the sweetness of the flowers growing along the river, the gentle green of pine, and the tang of sheep grazing along the narrow road. Ahead, nestled in the grass, a spot of bright red caught her attention. She bent and plucked a sanaresina blossom and rubbed its petals between her fingers to release its scent.

The smell of camphor and pepper filled her with memories of Mamar and long afternoons grinding the healing herb to powder that would stain her fingertips red. Tears pricked at the corners of her eyes. She kept telling herself that she'd made peace with her mother's death. Perhaps if she'd said it enough times, it would make it true.

Isben, who had been taking in the scenery as he walked quietly alongside her, took notice. "We both knew this would be hard. Do you want to talk about it?"

Katira shook her head. "No, I'm okay. There are lots of memories here, that's all." She opened her hand and showed him the bundle of petals. "This sanaresina is different than what we are trying to grow at the tower. It smells stronger."

He picked up one of the petals, cupped it to his face, and inhaled deeply. "You're right. Does that mean it's more potent?"

"Hard to say. I suppose so."

They walked along in a pleasant silence for several minutes before he spoke again. "You'll tell me if it gets to be too much, won't you?"

She took another deep breath of the petals in her hand. If this one smell of home was enough to tighten her throat, she didn't want to think about what being surrounded by all the other sights and sounds would do. "Even if it did, there's nothing I could do about it. I'm committed to seeing this through."

"That's exactly what I'm worried about. You're going to convince yourself that it's okay to struggle alone because you don't think anyone can help. I can help you, the same way you know you can help me." He ducked under a low hanging branch. "Promise you won't shut me out?"

Katira wrapped her fingers around the petals gently, the same way as one would hold a butterfly. In a way, Isben was doing the same thing with her, caring for her as if she were something delicate and likely to break. As much as she wanted to be angry at him, she appreciated how hard he tried to support her, even when it made her want to prove him wrong.

She breathed in the scent of the petals one more time before letting them fall to the ground. "I'll do my best."

They walked on, stopping only for a quick meal after a few hours. Thanks to Issa's training, the long walk felt good. Cassim, on the other hand, stayed at the rear of the group and clutched a soaked handkerchief which he used to mop the sweat from his brow. Onyx perched on his shoulder and scanned the surrounding forest with her beady black eyes.

Issa stayed with him, making small talk to keep his mind off the walk while serving as rearguard for the group. If something crept up behind them, she'd be the first line of defense. Papan insisted on walking at the head of the group for the same reason.

As they drew closer to Namragan, Katira's worry and excitement only grew worse. Every familiar sight brought a strange mix of joy paired with sadness. The happy bubble of the Kanth River, the tall pines swaying in the breeze, and the dramatic rise of the mountains on either side all summoned memories of things she loved but could no longer have.

At last, the sun dipped behind the ridge of the saw-toothed mountains and plunged the road into purple dusk. A cool breeze teased them from the road ahead as if welcoming them. On that breeze, Katira caught hints of wood smoke and roasting meat. Not long after, the narrow canyon opened into the bowl of Namragan Valley where light from dozens of lanterns gave them a cheery welcome.

Instead of continuing along the road that led up to the main gate, Papan turned to follow a narrow trail that skirted around the edge of the valley.

"What are you doing?" Katira asked. "I thought we were supposed to go straight to the town and find out what was going on."

Papan gripped his cane tighter. Across the bond, Katira sensed how the long walk had aggravated the muscles around the knotted scar in his back.

"Only a fool would walk straight into an enemy's camp. Bremin is lurking around here somewhere. The moment he senses we're here, he'll seek us out and tell us exactly what we need to know. Until then, we need to lay low." He turned away from her and continued walking along the trail, using the forest and the darkening night to hide their approach.

"But what if they need us now?" Katira pressed. "What if they are struggling with shadow hounds getting into the town itself? We should be there to help them."

Onyx, who had been dozing on Cassim's shoulder, flapped her wings and sounded a throaty alarm. Steel whispered against leather as Issa drew her sword.

Papan turned toward Issa. "What is it?"

She had turned her attention to the deepening shadows along the trail. "Movement in the undergrowth. Something spooked Onyx. We best be wary."

Katira bound her stone into her hand and loosened the knife hanging at her belt. Onyx's attention fixed on the tree line, and she squawked another alarm before launching herself into the air.

Papan set down his cane and drew his sword. "I didn't think they'd find us this fast. Issa, flanking positions. Nothing gets past us."

A wash of blue glyphs chased down his blade as the first hound stepped into view. Behind Katira, Issa's blade glowed to life as well. The hounds didn't hesitate. They darted forward and snapped at anything that moved. Katira counted four, but they were moving so quickly she couldn't be sure. Papan and Issa worked together seamlessly, creating a wall of flashing steel around Cassim, Katira, and Isben. As soon as the attack had started, it was over.

"Is that all of them?" Cassim asked.

Issa scanned the surrounding forest before releasing her power and giving a curt nod. Papan looked at his blade with disgust, wiped it clean, and replaced it back into its scabbard before snatching up his cane. Prior to leaving, Katira had heard Master Firen giving him a stern warning about overexerting himself, about how his damaged heart wasn't as strong as it used to be. Even now, Cassim watched him carefully as he whistled for Onyx to return.

"I believe so." Issa nodded. "We best find a defensible place to make camp. I'd rather fight these things on my terms, not theirs."

"But what about the town?" Katira asked again as she gestured toward the flickering dots of lantern light. "How can you be so sure that they're safe tonight?"

"Don't fret." Papan leaned heavily on his cane, that spot in his back angrier than before. "Hounds tend to be drawn to those with power. With the five of us here, eight if you count Bremin and the other companionship, we make an irresistible target."

Over the course of thousands of years, the Kanth River had cut its way through the softer layers of stone, creating a winding passageway that flowed from the north to the south. Papan led Katira and the others along the river until they reached a sheltered alcove where a deep swath of grey sand had accumulated, making it a good spot to camp.

As apprentices, setting up the camp fell largely to them. Katira set herself to organizing all the different supplies as Isben built a firepit from the smooth river rocks dotting the camp. When no one was looking, she slipped the glyph rod into the bottom of her pack and hid it beneath a spare set of clothes. She planned to tell Papan about it later that evening, after he'd had a chance to recover from the day's events.

They hadn't been at the campsite for more than a half an hour when a familiar lanky man with a ratty red scarf wandered up the same trail they'd taken.

Papan stood from where he and Issa had been discussing the camp's defenses to greet him. "You're quicker than I thought you'd be. Either you're bored, or you're desperate."

"I'm glad you're here." Bremin pulled Papan into a backslapping hug. "You have no idea how relieved I was to sense that ripple of power earlier. It's been madness ever since I arrived."

Issa didn't bother getting up and gave a halfhearted wave instead.

"It's good to see you too, Issa. Miss me?" Bremin set down his pack and rolled the stiffness from his shoulders.

"Hasn't been long enough for that. Seeing you sooner usually means there's trouble," Issa said with a hint of amusement. "Just what kind of trouble are we getting into?"

Katira stopped her work of chopping up the dinner vegetables, eager to hear what the man had to say.

"Come, sit. All of you. We might as well be comfortable." Bremin dragged his pack to where Isben busied himself with readying a cooking fire.

By the time everyone had gathered, all the questions Katira had been holding inside pressed against her as if she were a bottle and her lips were the cork. Any sudden motion might make her pop. Judging from the stream of frustration flowing across her bond with Papan, he felt the same way.

Isben set flint to the nest of kindling, and soon a merry blaze lapped up around the lengths of driftwood. Satisfied, he sat next to her and leaned in close. "Whatever he says, try not to get upset. From the looks of it, he's had a hard few days."

She'd been so absorbed in her own worrying that she hadn't noticed the stains on Bremin's normally tidy clothes and the hollowness of his cheeks.

Papan settled on one of the larger rocks around the firepit and rested his arms on his knees. "All right, out with it. What are we up against?"

"The companionship stationed here, Felix and Tiala, initially thought the warding wall had some sort of breach. They did what they could to reinforce it, but hounds kept showing up within the town." Bremin's gaze flicked toward where Katira had been preparing the meal and his stomach growled.

"That doesn't make sense. We've been using warding walls like that here for ages." Papan picked up one of the sticks that Isben collected earlier and pressed it between his hands. "They've never failed before."

Issa crossed her arms over her chest. "If we learned anything last winter, it's that hounds can slip into our world several different ways. What do we know about the shadow barrier here?"

"I'm getting there, let me finish." Bremin shot her an annoyed glance. "Felix is a Bender and studied some of Master Aro's notes. His understanding of the barrier is limited, but he believes it might now be thin enough that the hounds can simply pass through."

"Are they slipping through on their own, or is someone helping them?" While Papan's question was simple, Katira knew the answer most certainly would not be.

Bremin took his time considering his answer, and the strain of it showed in the rugged lines on his face. Cassim, who had been observing him with some amount of concern, rummaged through his pack and pulled out a wedge of cheese and a small roll. Bremin accepted the food with a resigned sigh and immediately broke off a piece of the cheese to eat.

"Even with Felix helping me, I couldn't find evidence either way. We should suspect the worst. That way we can be prepared."

A wave of dread echoed through the bond, and the stick in Papan's hands snapped in half. He tossed the resulting pieces into the fire. "We'll do what we can and pray it's enough. How about the town? How are they faring?"

"They're scared. When the first hounds came through, Felix and Tiala did an admirable job dispatching them in secret, but they were fighting a losing battle from the beginning. Too many came through too often." After finishing the cheese, Bremin started in on the bread. He ate as if he hadn't seen food in several days. "Rumors of dark ghosts cropped up in the marketplace. Eventually, Felix was caught using the power."

"I imagine that didn't go over well." Issa took out one of her smaller knives and methodically sliced the bark from one of the larger branches she'd selected from the stack of firewood.

"About as well as you would expect." Bremin gestured toward Papan. "Your friend, Master Lucan, is a good one. Convinced the angry crowd to throw them both into that basement they call a prison instead of killing them, and he took Felix's advice to put out more lanterns. I wish I could say it was enough."

Katira returned to preparing the evening meal as she listened to the discussion. Sooner or later, Papan would bring up the matter of the locket. At mention of Master Lucan, she had to speak up. If Elan had somehow gotten hurt in the middle of this mess, Bremin was sure to know something about it.

"Is Elan okay?" she blurted out before she could stop herself.

She immediately wanted to take the question back, to wait for when it was a better time. Now that the question was out in the open, the worst he could do was refuse to answer.

Papan turned to Bremin to explain. "That's the reason we are here. Before the boy left, Katira had the Benders make a pair of lockets, each with an enchanted picture of the other. When she opened it two days ago, she saw hounds lurking behind him."

"How romantic," Bremin stated flatly. "I suppose I should be grateful. If things continue the same way for much longer, the town will be in real trouble." His serious expression softened as he turned to Katira.

"Elan took a nasty fall running from the shadow hounds and knocked himself out cold. Cut his head something awful. His mother patched him up the best she could, but I have my worries."

Cassim shifted on the blanket he was using as an improvised seat. Onyx had tired of exploring the camp and had nodded off on his shoulder. "Can we go to him without attracting the town's notice?"

Bremin shook his head. "They're on their guard now. If we're caught sneaking around, it will confirm their suspicions that this hound business is our fault."

Katira couldn't stand the thought of someone needing help and not being able to give it to them. With that someone being Elan, it bothered her even more. She'd watched him take a blade months ago and the shock of it still lingered with her. With it happening again, all of those painful memories pressed their sharp edges against her skin.

"Then we don't sneak," Papan said, much to Katira's surprise. "While you were prowling around, did you catch any rumor of the town knowing the truth about Katira and me?"

Bremin itched at a spot on his neck as he thought. "Now that you say it, nothing like that has come up. Something that big would have been the talk of the town for years, especially considering the current situation."

Papan gave a relieved laugh. "I don't believe it. The kid kept his word. I knew Lucan would, but Elan had no reason to. That makes things a bit easier."

"He's a good lad. Showed real quality during his time with me. What do you propose?"

"If we are to help, trying to do so in secret will make our job harder and take longer. Each delay increases the likelihood of shadow hounds making more kills. I won't take that risk. If the town doesn't see me as a threat, we can use that to our advantage. But we need Master Lucan's cooperation first. I need to speak with him."

Bremin chewed his last bit of bread. "You of all people understand how stubborn Northerners can be. But these are your Northerners. Maybe we can use that stubbornness to our advantage."

CHAPTER 6

As they approached the low sheep wall surrounding the town, Katira caught the edge of a whispered conversation between Papan, Cassim, and Bremin. The next time she glanced up, Bremin had disappeared into the night.

Papan insisted they keep the group small to visit Lucan and Katira agreed. Master Lucan was slow to trust, even under the best circumstances. Showing up with a small army of Stonebearers would only make the man defensive, and they needed his cooperation. That said, she still would have much rather had Isben at her side when she saw Elan, instead of leaving him up at the camp helping Issa.

A lantern hung from a weathered hook on the back of Master Lucan's leather goods store, forming a dull circle of light that barely reached the first of the many tanning vats dotting the yard.

Cassim coaxed a sleepy Onyx onto the top of the lantern hook and scratched the feathers on her head. "If you see any of those nasty shadow hounds, you sound the alarm, okay?" Onyx fluttered her wings and responded with a throaty chirp.

Jarand rapped lightly on the back door. When Master Lucan

opened it, he was wielding a large paddle as if he had every intention of using it.

"What's the meaning of this?" he blinked into the darkness.

Papan stepped further into the light. "Good to see you too, old friend."

"Jarand?" Lucan straightened abruptly, seeking Papan's face. "Is it really you? I thought I'd never see you again." He pulled Papan into a bearlike embrace. "What are you doing here?"

"Heard of the recent problems you've had, and thought I could help."

"Is that so?" Master Lucan took a moment to study Cassim before his gaze settled on Katira. "Best you come in then. We've got some catching up to do."

Inside the shop, Katira breathed in the scent of leather polish and wax paired with fresh cured hide. It was a smell she associated as much with comfort and home as she did sanaresina. Master Lucan ushered them into the comfortable sitting room that adjoined the kitchen where Master Lucan's wife, Nora, sat busily knitting in a chair. Her needles stopped when she saw them.

She dropped her handiwork into the basket at her feet. "Of all the miracles, is it really you?"

"I didn't quite believe it myself." Master Lucan cleared the stack of rolled calfskin off the kitchen table to a nearby shelf.

"But, how? I mean, I thought he'd gone back?" She stopped short when she saw Katira, her next thought hanging unsaid. She rushed across the room and wrapped Katira in a motherly embrace that felt so right, so welcome, that Katira didn't want her to let go. After a long moment, she released her embrace with a sniff.

"Goodness, child. I've been so worried about you."

"I've missed you too. I'm fine, really."

"After everything I'd heard, I couldn't help but think the worst. I'm so glad to see you again." She pulled out a handkerchief from her sleeve and dabbed at her eyes. "Stay right here, I'll make us some nice tea."

"No need, Nora, we won't be staying long," Papan called to her as she hurried into the kitchen.

"Nonsense." Master Lucan sat at the table and gestured for them to join him. "I don't know how you managed to hear about our troubles, but I'm glad you came. First, an introduction is in order. Who's this?"

Cassim offered his hand. "I'm an old friend of Jarand's. Mirelle and I studied the healing arts together."

Master Lucan's eyebrows raised at that. "Just how old are we talking?" Suspicion crept into his voice.

Cassim drew up the edge of his sleeve, revealing the marks on his wrist. "Old enough."

Master Lucan sucked in air through his teeth. "Jarand, you've proven your trustworthiness over the years. I know you'll do what's needed to protect this town. But I can't extend that same level of trust to just anyone."

"I don't expect you to. Like you said, that kind of trust is earned. Cassim here has earned my trust, as have the others I've brought to help you."

"He's got my trust too, if that means anything." Katira added. "He's been my teacher these past months."

Cassim gave Katira a warm smile and mouthed a silent *thank you.*

Master Lucan continued, undeterred. "Those other friends of yours, the ones that Elan brought home with him, were caught using magic right here in town. Scared a whole lot of people. I managed to convince the council that it would be best to lock them up and keep them out of sight until we figure something out. They're not safe here."

Nora brought a tray with several steaming cups of tea along with a tray holding slices of bread and fruit.

"It's already taken care of," Papan said.

She handed a cup to him. "What's already taken care of? The monsters? I don't believe it."

Before he could reply, the front door of the leather shop whipped open and Andril, Elan's older brother, charged in. "They're gone. Escaped somehow. We must find them before they can cause trouble."

When he saw the group gathered, he stopped short. The urgency that had brought him there drained away, leaving him standing there with his mouth hanging open. "Master Jarand, what are you doing here?"

Master Lucan rounded on Papan, his hand curled into a fist. "You freed them?"

"Technically, a friend of mine did. He's got a certain set of skills that come in handy. They'll be long gone by now."

Andril became more flustered by the second as he tried to inter-ject himself back into the conversation. "Pa, what do you want me to tell the others?"

Master Lucan reluctantly let his attention shift. "We know noth-ing. Don't bother with starting a search. Let them believe what they will for now. Go."

The moment Andril was gone, Master Lucan poked Papan in the chest. "You had no right to interfere. All you've done is made the townspeople more frightened. They'll think you people can vanish and reappear at will. It makes you no better than those monsters."

Papan kept his face passive, as if unwilling to rise to the man's anger. "I assure you it was a tactical choice. When it comes to protecting our own, we will do what's necessary. The only outlet for the town's fear was an execution. While we respect your laws and justice, we won't die for them."

Master Lucan had the grace to look ashamed. "I did what was best for the town. I don't regret my choices."

"And I don't regret mine."

A soft shuffle drew their attention to the side of the room where Elan held onto the doorway as if it were the only thing keeping him standing. The cut on his forehead was swollen and purple as was the side of his face. Whatever had hit him, must have hit hard.

He squinted into the brighter light of the kitchen. "I heard raised voices. What's going on?"

∾

Katira watched with ever-growing concern as Elan took a few unsteady steps into the sitting room. Even walking that short distance seemed to be too much. He swayed on his feet and gripped the back of the nearest chair, pressing his eyes shut against the light. Bremin was right, there was definitely something wrong with him.

Master Lucan hurried across the room. "You should be in bed, boy. You're clearly not well enough to be up."

Elan didn't answer and instead scanned the room with narrowed eyes. When his gaze fell on Katira, he lost his grip on the chair and nearly fell before catching himself. "When I heard your voice, I thought I was imagining things."

She was on her feet in an instant, worried that at any moment he might faint. Everyone told her seeing him again was going to be hard, that the same tearing sense of loss would hurt her as when they said goodbye. They were wrong. Yes, she'd missed him, but with Isben in her life, the hole in her heart left by his loss had been filled.

"What happened to you?"

Elan chuckled softly and looked away. "Tripped running from a hound and ran headlong into a gate." He pressed his eyes shut and his grip tightened on the chair. "Looked horrible when it happened. I think I made someone faint."

Cassim pushed himself up from the table and brushed the breadcrumbs from his shirt. The only reason he'd accompanied them was to tend to Elan, and this was his chance.

"Come now, let's get you back to bed." Master Lucan hooked his hand under Elan's shoulder. "You and Katira can talk in the morning after a good night's rest."

Standing closer, Katira saw how Elan's hands shook. He couldn't fix his gaze at any one place for longer than a few seconds. She reached for the stone under her shirt.

Cassim arched an eyebrow. "I know that look, Katira. Don't even think about it." He stepped around her and turned to Master Lucan with that friendly yet businesslike smile he used when working with patients. "As Jarand said, Mirelle and I worked as healers together before she came here. I would feel much better if I were allowed to check your son for injuries that aren't immediately obvious. Ones that can disable or even kill."

When Master Lucan hesitated, Papan spoke up. "I trust him, Lucan. If he believes Elan needs care, you best let him."

Lucan shook his head and guided Elan back toward the darkened room. "Nora's got a steady hand. She was able to stitch up the cut well enough. The rest simply needs time, that's all."

Katira put herself between Elan and the doorway. "I understand how hard this must be. You've all faced so much these past few days and even with your best efforts nothing feels like it's getting better. Having someone you love hurting is probably the hardest thing you'll ever have to endure. Cassim can help him, just like Mamar helped him before."

Master Lucan's squared his shoulders and addressed not only Katira, but everyone in the room. "I know your intentions are good, but it was your kind that caused this trouble in the first place. I'm not willing to risk making it worse by involving you in trying to solve it, starting with Elan. I appreciate the offer, but we've always taken care of our own needs."

Nora set down the cup she'd been clutching. "I want them to try."

Elan pressed his palm against his temple, eyes closed tight with the pain. "I'm fine. Really. I just need some sleep."

Katira lowered her voice. What she had to say was between just the two of them. "I think you hurt yourself worse than you believe. Let him use his skill to find out for sure. If there's nothing wrong, then at least we know." She set her hands on Elan's shoulders and forced him to meet her gaze. "But if he does find something, promise me you'll let him fix it. Your poor mother needs to know you're okay."

"Let him be, Katira." Master Lucan's voice came soft and low. "I know you mean well, but you must respect our wishes."

Papan rose from the table and stepped closer. "Lucan, please. Look at him. He needs help."

On hearing Papan's voice, Elan turned, perhaps too quickly, as if to give an angry reply. Before he could utter a word, his eyes rolled back in his head and his legs gave out from under him. If Master Lucan hadn't had hold of him, he would've collapsed. As it was, the man had to half-carry, half-drag him into a nearby chair, where he sat drifting on the edge of consciousness.

Katira pressed a hand to Elan's cheek and found it cold and clammy. He didn't respond to her touch. Master Lucan's brow pinched tight, his eyes darting from Elan's face to the stone held in Cassim's outstretched hand.

He gave a reluctant nod. "Do it."

Katira moved out of the way to make room for Cassim, who stepped up quickly. He set his fingertips against the side of Elan's neck. The lines running down his wrist and palm glowed to life.

"This part will feel warm, nothing more."

As Cassim worked, the furrow in Elan's brow smoothed. "Feels nice."

"That's the easy part." After a few minutes, the glow faded and Cassim withdrew his touch. "The good news is that there is no permanent damage, yet."

"What's the bad news?" Master Lucan asked, still standing so close to Elan that their knees touched.

"There are a few things that must be fixed immediately. It will be uncomfortable, but I assure you, it will be quick."

Elan's eyes, which had drifted mostly closed, sprung open. "Like, how uncomfortable?"

"Like, you'd best hang onto something so you don't hit me, uncomfortable. Which is leagues better than needing to be held down, uncomfortable. Although I'm sure Jarand wouldn't mind helping me with that, should you want it."

Papan gave a curt nod as the healer continued. "Regardless, you'll feel loads better than you do now. Best not to think about it too hard."

Elan exchanged a glance with Katira before gripping the edge of the chair with both hands. "Okay."

With that, Cassim set his fingertips along the bones of Elan's neck. The lines at his wrist glowed back to life and with a pulse of power, he urged the bones to shift back into alignment with a series of sharp cracks. Katira pressed her hands over Elan's, pinning them to the chair.

"Don't hold your breath, it makes it worse. I'm nearly done." Cassim's voice remained calm and detached as he worked.

After another minute, the color returned to Elan's face and his hands relaxed. Katira made a mental note to ask Cassim about what he had done the next time she studied with him.

"That should do it." Cassim pulled back his hands and tucked his stone under his shirt. "Gently move your head. You should feel a big difference."

Elan did as he was told, carefully at first, then with bigger and more deliberate movements. "That's amazing."

"You'll want to be careful the next few days. I put everything back where it should be, but your body needs time to adjust. The best thing you can do right now is get something to eat and then a good night's rest."

Master Lucan studied Elan's face for a moment longer, as if waiting for something awful to happen. When it didn't, he released an unsteady breath. "Thank you. I'm sorry I didn't trust you before."

Cassim acknowledged the apology with a dip of his head. "You're not the first stubborn person I've come across. Won't be the last either."

"Before we leave," Papan moved out of the way as Nora fetched a plate of food from the kitchen for Elan, "there are a handful of things I'd like to discuss with you."

Master Lucan grimaced at the request, but returned to the table and gestured for Papan and Cassim to do the same. Katira sat in the chair closest to Elan and waited for him to break the silence. She didn't have to wait long.

"I've been worried about you, about if they're treating you okay in that strange place. Are they?"

"It's about the same as living here, if you can believe it. I've got hordes of chores and work to do. If I do my work well, I earn their respect. If I don't, the punishments are fair. The only real difference is that I finally feel I'm where I belong." Katira fought back the urge to touch his arm like she used to, an unconscious gesture spurred by her new life colliding with the old. "And you? I imagine you were quite the sensation around here after you came back."

"It was ridiculous." Elan shook his head with a smile. "It was the closest thing to a storybook adventure anyone here had ever heard of. After a few days of way too much attention, I was happy to hide out back working the vats to avoid talking about it again and again."

Elan eagerly shared all the fun and gossip that had happened in Namragan since she'd left. In the past, she'd loved listening to him talk about anything and everything. But after all she'd been through, his stories came across as trivial, petty even, in comparison.

When Papan stood to leave, Katira was secretly relieved that she wouldn't have to try to explain all that had happened in her life since they parted. Elan still cared about her, but that wasn't enough to help him understand.

Master Lucan tapped Elan on the shoulder. "That's enough excitement for one night. We best get this one back to bed. I'm sure there will be opportunities for the two of you to talk more in the days ahead."

CHAPTER 7

When Katira returned to camp, she found Isben sprawled out on his bedroll still wearing his boots. Bremin and Issa talked quietly over the embers of the dying fire.

Papan gave her a nudge when he caught her yawning. "Looks like Isben has everything prepared. Go ahead and turn in for the night."

She looked over the camp, taking in the tidy stack of supplies, the neatly stored packs, the prepared bedrolls, and the healthy supply of firewood. He really had thought of everything. He'd even gone as far as preparing her bedroll not far from his. After the long day, Katira welcomed the chance to take off her boots and rest.

Sleep did not come easily. The events of the evening played in her head on repeat, each time exploring a new and terrible outcome of what could have happened. Eventually, the gentle hush of the trees and whisper of the nearby river pulled her eyes closed.

It wasn't a restful sleep; nightmares stalked her at every turn. In one, they had arrived at Master Lucan's cottage only for Elan to fall dead at her feet. When she reached for him, he was bleeding on the forest floor with Surasio's knife sticking out of his chest. She woke with a start, her heart pounding in her throat. To her relief, none of the other sleepers stirred.

Over the past months, Papan had taught her meditative breathing exercises to calm her mind. With each breath, she released the nightmarish thoughts of what might have happened like feathers on a breeze and imagined them floating away. Yes, things could have gone wrong. But they didn't. There was no use fretting about it.

A soft rustle of clothes signaled the change in the watch. Issa made herself comfortable next to Cassim while Bremin took up her place next to the fire. Onyx ruffled her feathers in her sleep where she'd cuddled up to Cassim for the night.

It wasn't until someone shook her shoulder that Katira realized she'd slipped back to sleep. The light of the new morning shone surprisingly bright and wreathed Isben's head as he crouched next to her.

"Duty calls. We best fetch some water and get breakfast started. It looks like Master Jarand and Issa want to head out early."

Sure enough, Papan sat buckling his boot on one of the rocks near the campfire. Nearby, Issa paced and absently checked the collection of knives she kept on her person. Cassim, who had never been a morning person, sat hunched and bleary-eyed by the fire with a steaming mug resting on his thigh. At his feet, Onyx tapped her beak on pebbles and nibbled at blades of grass. Bremin was nowhere to be seen.

Papan fastened the last buckle with a tug. "Strange to be back, isn't it? Do you feel better now that you've seen Elan?" He adjusted the baldric crossing his chest and the scabbard attached to it.

"Yes and no. I mean, I'm glad Elan's okay, but that's not the real reason we're here." She looked through their supplies and selected a wedge of cheese and some dried fruit. Onyx wandered over to examine her fingers, hoping for treats. "Where are you two going this early?"

"To check the warding wall. Bremin wants to rule out any possibility of the hounds breaking through that way before we do anything else."

"That sounds like it will take a long time. Did you eat?" She waved the piece of cheese at him.

Issa held up a parcel. "Already taken care of, but thanks. We should be off. The sooner we finish, the sooner we'll know what kind of problem we're dealing with."

Papan gave Katira a pat on the shoulder as he turned to leave. "Don't give Cassim a hard time while I'm gone. He hates camping."

"Wait." If he was going to wander around the outskirts of the town, she wanted to go with him. "You'll need a runner." She tried not to sound desperate. "Just in case there are any issues."

Impatience put an edge to his voice. "Your responsibility lies with the needs of the camp and assisting Cassim and Bremin."

"You don't understand." Katira grabbed her belt, needing him to change his mind. "I'm coming with you."

Issa ran a thumb over the edge of her blade, checking its edge. "No, you're not. That's an order."

The finality in Issa's voice caused the belt to slip from Katira's hand and clatter against the rocks lining the trail.

"Don't go getting yourself all worked up, Katira." Cassim took a sip from his mug. "That type of work is deadly boring. The fewer distractions they have, the faster they can get it done. No offence, but you're a distraction." His gaze flicked towards Papan. "Once they're done, I'm sure there will be something more interesting you can help with."

Papan's eyes tightened as if he wasn't prepared to promise anything of the sort.

"Sometimes a little compromise is good," Cassim explained with a shrug. "You both get what you want. You and Issa can work without interruption and Katira will go with Isben to gather whatever supplies and foodstuffs we'll need over the coming days. And, if there's time, I would like her to teach me about the unique medicinal herbs found here." A mischievous smile spread across his face. "I get what I want, so I can't complain."

Papan pursed his lips as he considered the options. "It's a good compromise. Do you agree, Katira?"

"I suppose I must." She pinched at her sleeve. "Will you teach me more about the warding wall when you return?"

"I will. Behave while I'm gone." Without another word, he hurried to catch up with Issa.

Katira had the most bizarre temptation to stick out her tongue at him. It seemed that being back in Namragan brought with it several of her old vices.

That small taste of home the night before wasn't enough; she wanted more. She wanted to see the town square bustling with life and sound. She wanted bread from Mama Thanes' bakery with wildberry jelly. She wanted to visit the cottage and pretend she'd never left.

It only took a moment to gather up the things needed for shopping in the market square. No doubt, the news of her and Papan's return had spread. If she didn't make an appearance, rumors would spread as well. If the wrong rumor got started, it could spell trouble.

"Where do you think you're going?" Cassim asked with an amused smile.

Katira had been so lost in her own thoughts that the question startled her. "To market. The best produce and meats sell quickly, so I thought it best to grab what we need earlier rather than later."

The healer grimaced as he tested a bite of the porridge Isben had prepared and gave the rest of the spoonful to Onyx, who attacked the spoon as if it were a mouse. "Not alone, you're not. Besides, you haven't eaten any breakfast."

She weighed her coin pouch in her palm and tied it to her belt next to her knife. "If this is about the shadow hounds, I'm prepared to handle them."

"It's not that. Honestly. Although I'd rather not have you face hounds alone either." He rummaged through their supplies and extracted a box of salt. "It's the villagers. I don't trust them. While Master Lucan managed to keep Jarand's and your true identity secret, Stonebearer bless the man, he specifically instructed us to be careful."

Katira crossed her arms, and her stubborn streak nudged against her restraint. "You said it yourself, we need food for while we're here. The town knows me, so there's no reason they should cause me any problems."

"I'm with Cassim on this one. You definitely shouldn't go alone." Isben smirked. "So, if you go, I go."

Cassim grumbled something under his breath about troublesome youth as he added a pinch of salt to the pot and stirred it in. "Well, I suppose I did say something about getting more food, although I meant scavenging here in the forest. All the same, I'd much rather have some nice sausage and fresh bread than bark mushrooms and rabbit." He tasted the porridge again and gave a curt nod of approval. "Eat some breakfast first and then you both can go. I'll draft up a list."

~

Unlike the night before, this homecoming felt far more real to Katira. Ahead of her, laid out like a picture, was one of the winding lanes that cut the town into pieces. To the left, the colorful flags and banners on the market tables swayed in a rainbow. The rank sour smell of Master Lucan's tanning vats wandered in on the morning breeze. The cottage, her home, sat off to the right, close enough that she could see the wall Mamar had built to protect the herb garden that grew just outside the front door.

It wasn't until Isben set a warm hand on her shoulder that she realized she'd stopped walking.

"Whatever is going through your head, know that I'm right here. You're not alone."

"What if Master Lucan is wrong? What if they know the truth about me? What if something happens?" Another dozen questions popped up behind her tongue and fought to escape. She bit them back.

"Then it's best we find out sooner than later." He urged her to keep walking. "The only way to rid yourself of these doubts is to find out the truth."

When they reached the town square, Katira took a moment to breathe in the familiarity of it and let it soothe her. She'd missed this the most, the smell of fresh breads and spices, the pleasant noise of people going about their business, and the weight of a bag or basket yet to be filled on her arm.

She fished out Cassim's list. He'd jotted down more than a dozen items, including the expected things, root vegetables and grains and the like, but also several items that she suspected were foods the healer was craving.

"Oh, honestly, if he thinks I can find candies at this time of year, he's going to be disappointed." Katira handed the list to Isben.

He studied the other items before handing it back. "It's wishful thinking. If we can't find him some candies, we should find some other kind of treat. I think he's earned it."

It wasn't long before people noticed she was there and greeted her with smiling faces and hearty handshakes. It was every bit the warm welcome she hoped it would be. The novelty of it wore off quickly, and she understood why Elan felt like hiding. She had expected questions. What she didn't expect was how fast and thick they would come, and how each of her answers risked revealing more about her life after she'd left than what was safe.

"Is it true you were kidnapped?"

"Did you see the ocean?"

"Is it true about those wielders? Were they involved?"

"Why have you come back? Are you going to stay?"

With each question, her answers grew shorter and less detailed. It didn't help that the ripples of Papan and Issa both using their power kept catching her off guard. Each time she felt it, she couldn't help but think there was trouble. After an hour, she was more than ready to be done. With a smile and a wave, she promised she'd answer more questions later.

When it was clear she wasn't going to change her mind, the curious crowd thinned down to a handful of children that dogged her and Isben's steps.

"For all Cassim's worrying, they seem nice enough," Isben said as he arranged several of their purchased items into his pack.

"A bear might look nice until it's threatened. Don't make assumptions." Katira scanned down the last of the list, thankful that

Cassim had mostly chosen practical, easy-to-find items. They didn't find candies, but she found the next best thing — a roll from Mama Thanes' bakery slathered in wildberry jelly.

"Okay, point made. Is that why it's so hard to wake you up in the morning? Are you secretly a bear in disguise?"

Katira gave him a playful shove. "Better watch out, I might eat you."

Isben continued to laugh and joke with her as they found the last few items and tucked them away in their packs. Even with all the questions and attention from the townspeople, they made an efficient team. The sun had only crept halfway up the sky. If they returned this early, Cassim was sure to find plenty of things for them to do, none of them pleasant. From the sound of it, Papan and Issa might be away from the camp for hours more, if not the entire day. It was time enough to visit the cottage.

She led Isben back through the market stalls and toward the fountain where she stopped at its edge and leaned forward to gaze into the water. Away from the crowd and the noise of the market, the poignant stab of being home finally hit its mark. This one place held so much memory. It was there that Bremin had comforted her when she was upset about the prospect of leaving. It was there where her last Harvest Festival had begun. It was there that she'd let Elan see her cry.

Isben sat on the edge of the fountain next to her and set one hand over hers. It was an invitation, a soft one, asking if she wanted to share what she was going through. Had they been somewhere more private, she would have been more than willing to open herself to the power and let their emotions mingle.

Her worries about the town, about its people, surfaced again. What if they couldn't protect them? What if by simply being there, they brought an even greater evil? How would she forgive herself if her worst worries came true?

"You're a Bender. Do you think that fixing the warding wall will work?" She kept her own suspicions in check, needing to hear what he had to say before voicing her own concerns. Deep in her gut she knew there was something much, much bigger going on. If fate played its hand with her again, she would end up right in the center of it.

"I think it's a good place to start. But if the other companionship couldn't find anything wrong with it, then it has to be the barrier. Something has to have changed. Nothing else explains it." He got that far off look that told Katira he was lost in his own thoughts. After a moment, his brow furrowed and he turned to her abruptly. "What happened to that glyph rod?"

Katira's mouth went dry. She'd meant to come clean with Papan the night before and hadn't found the right moment.

"You still have it, don't you?" An eager excitement put a twinkle in his eye.

"I meant to put it away, I really did. It's just that ..."

"You don't need to apologize. Don't you see? You may have solved this whole thing for everyone. With the glyph rod, we can assess the barrier far more accurately. We will be able to see exactly how the hounds are coming in." He reached for her hand. "Come on. Let's get back to camp. The sooner we can check this out, the better."

She took his hand, but didn't move from the fountain. The whole reason she wanted to come down to the town was to visit the cottage and collect a few special things. The glyph rod could wait for her to take this moment.

"There's one thing I need to do first."

Katira wasn't sure what to expect when she reached her home. Felix and Tiala hadn't lived there long enough to have made any drastic changes, but it would be unreasonable to expect everything to be the same. Isben checked the front door and found it unlocked. With a grand gesture, he ushered her into the comfortable coolness inside. Much of the furniture had been left where it was. Mamar's large worktable still rested under the window that looked out into her herb garden. The sturdy round kitchen table still sat with its collection of chairs in the center of the room. All of the bundles of medicinal herbs still hung from the rafters.

Then there were the differences. An unfamiliar coat hung from the peg on the wall that had always held Papan's leather work apron. The baskets lining the shelf in the kitchen had been organized differently. The acrid smell of ash and metal from the forge had faded, replaced by the astringent smell of pine. At least the smell that lulled her to sleep at night, the pepper and camphor of the sanaresina, stayed.

Isben wandered to the cold fireplace and studied the items on the mantle. "You said something about collecting a few things to take back to Amul Dun. Do you know what you are looking for? Maybe I can help."

"Not exactly. But I'll know when I see it." She joined him to look at what he had found. Seeing one of the items, a small wooden rabbit, surprised her. Papan had carved it for her when she was a baby and she thought it had been lost. She picked it up and marveled how it still felt so right in the palm of her hand.

The rabbit and a handful of other items found their way into the safety of her pockets, each holding a prized memory of her past. She was hefting the heavy mortar when the front door quietly opened and Elan slipped inside. Compared to the night before, his hands were steady and he stood straight and tall.

"Andril spotted you in the marketplace. When I couldn't find you, I figured you might come here."

Katira let the solid weight of the mortar ground her. "I wanted to collect a few things. Memories, you know."

"Everything happened so fast that night. I still have a hard time believing it, and I lived part of it." Elan wandered further into the room but stopped when he spotted Isben standing next to the fireplace. "I have so many questions. I don't know what to ask you first."

"Maybe I should start then." Katira returned the mortar to its place on the shelf. It was too heavy to bring back with her to the Tower. "How are you feeling today?"

"You know that's not what I meant. I'm fine. Whatever it was that Cassim did worked wonders." His gaze flicked to Isben again as if trying to figure out where he fit in this new equation. "I know you said you were fine last night, but I know how you hide things. Are you really?"

If there was ever a question that was doomed from the start, it was that one. "I know it's hard to believe, but I was telling the truth. Papan has taken good care of me at Amul Dun and my training is going well."

"I guess what I'm trying to ask is, are you happy?"

Isben must have seen the need in her eyes. He crossed the room to stand by her side. Happy wasn't the right word, not by a long shot. What she had was more lasting, more secure. She was content, purposeful.

"I've found where I am meant to be, what I meant to do." She paused and exchanged another glance with Isben. "Who I am meant to be with. So yes, you could say that I am happy. What about you?"

Elan gave an unexpected sigh of relief. "I worried about you, you know? I worry that if I moved on it would somehow hurt you. But, from the looks of it, maybe I shouldn't have worried so much."

"Are you trying to tell me you found someone?" Katira ignored the tiny bittersweet lump in her throat.

"I did. And what's strange is she's nothing like you, and yet we fit together perfectly. Fate is funny like that." He looked away and rubbed his nose as if he was suddenly uncomfortable to be there. "Well, I'm glad that's settled."

Isben shifted at Katira's side. "We should be going soon. If Cassim thinks we are up to something, we'll never hear the end of it."

Elan stepped in front of the door, blocking their path. "One last thing, I promise. Can you tell me the truth about those monsters? Was it Stonebearers who summoned them here?"

"No. I can assure you of that. They're as much as a nuisance to us as they are to everyone else," Katira answered, glad that part of the question was easy. "As for why they've suddenly started causing problems, that's what we intend to find out."

CHAPTER 8

When Katira and Isben returned to the camp, they found Cassim sitting next to the long dead fire and stripping the leaves from a pile of slender willow branches. Onyx snatched up a falling leaf and paraded around with it before tucking it beneath one of her wing feathers. Judging by the healer's steady rhythm, he'd been working like this for a while.

Mama Thanes' roll with wildberry jelly, the one they'd got just for him, was tucked safely on the top of her pack. A surprise like that was sure to make the man smile. Katira held a finger to her lips and gestured something she hoped looked like sneaking to Isben who gave his enthusiastic agreement. Together, they skirted around the edge of the camp, staying just out of sight. When they got close, she removed the carefully wrapped roll and reached to grab Cassim's shoulder. Right before she touched him, Onyx spotted her and warbled a happy sound.

"Traitor," Katira hissed at the bird, who squawked right back at her.

"You know I spotted you the moment you entered camp, right?" Cassim set down his small knife. "That took longer than expected. Did everything go okay?"

"We got pretty much everything on the list." Isben set down his pack to unload the series of parcels they had collected.

Katira held out the roll to Cassim. "Here, this is for you. Couldn't find any candies, but this is so much better."

At the site of it, Cassim's eyes lit up. "Why, thank you." He immediately took a bite. After a moment of chewing, his eyes rolled back, and a contented smile spread across his face. "You're right. This is divine." He took another bite and licked the stray jelly from his fingers. Onyx poked at his knee, her keen beady eyes fixed on the pastry. He pinched off a crumb and offered it to her, which she accepted with a bob of her head. "Don't think this gets you out of explaining what took you so long. How's Elan?"

"He said whatever you did worked wonders, so that's good," Isben said before realizing his mistake and biting his lip.

"Ha! I thought you might go check on him. I'm glad you did, because now I don't have to go later." Cassim ate the last bite of the roll and looked surprised to see it was gone. He laid out the square of fabric and let Onyx snatch up the remaining crumbs.

"Any word from Issa and Jarand?" Isben finished emptying his pack and reached for Katira's in an offer to take care of hers as well. She pulled it closer and shook her head.

Cassim brushed his hands clean and retrieved his knife to resume his work. When his back was turned, Isben pointed to her bag and whispered. "Is it in there?"

Katira gave a subtle nod as she removed the items from the market.

"They haven't returned yet, but it shouldn't be long. Namragan isn't that big." With a practiced hand, he peeled away the bark from the first switch and picked up the next one. "I hope for all our sakes they find something that needs fixing. Then we'll be done here and can return to the Tower and all its comforts."

The sour taste of bile rose up in the back of her throat. "It won't. This is part of something bigger. I know it, but I can't explain it."

Cassim deflated a touch and scowled at her. "Well, aren't you a ray of sunshine?" He took up another switch and waved it at her before putting it to his knife. "If I believe hard enough that a simple fix will be successful, then perhaps somehow it will. It's silly, but it makes me feel better. Don't go fretting about things we don't know for certain yet."

He collected the pile of bark from off his knee and set it neatly on a flat river stone in preparation for the next step of preparing the tincture. Onyx immediately stole a piece and ran away. Her squawks of delight sounded like laughter.

With the last of the items from the market organized with the other supplies, the only thing left inside Katira's pack was the glyph rod. Telling Papan about it meant facing his judgment. She'd do it eventually, but she didn't relish the idea. Telling Cassim, on the other hand, felt so much safer. Perhaps he'd see having it the same way Isben did and help defend her.

"I've seen that look before." Cassim selected two small vials from a box and worked their corks free. "There's something bothering you."

Her hand rested on the rod as she deliberated on the best way to proceed. "If the warding wall isn't the problem, then it has to be the barrier itself, right?"

"Obviously. There's not anything else to consider."

"What would it take for us to check it, and if needs be, to fix it?" She let her fingers wrap around the rod as she built up the courage to show it to him.

"What are you getting at?" Cassim set down the vial and turned his full attention toward her.

Isben looked up from where he worked to fill the drinking skins at the river's edge. Unlike Cassim, he knew where she was going with her line of questions.

"Master Aro is one of the best Benders in the Tower. Even he needed help to see the barrier so we could understand what was going on. What chance do we have of doing anything like that here?"

"Bremin's confident that we can find a solution. I trust him, and you should too." A warning darkened Cassim's voice. Onyx crept back and set down the piece of bark she stole.

"Answer me, please. We have no way of seeing it. Do we?"

He tossed up a hand in frustration. "Are you being difficult on purpose? We are doing the best we can with the resources we have. It's what we've done for centuries."

Isben returned carrying the filled and dripping water skins and set them with the other supplies. "Enough, Katira, just show him."

Cassim's eyes narrowed, then widened as if an unpleasant thought slapped him across the face. "I'm missing something, aren't I?"

Katira pulled the cloth-wrapped rod from her pack and held it over her crossed legs. Onyx paraded over to inspect it, nibbling at its corner before being shooed away.

Cassim's mouth opened and shut several times before he managed to form words. "Is that what I think it is?"

"It was in that storage room Isben and I were cleaning. At first I stuck it in my pocket to keep it safe, but when I got the chance to put it back, it seemed a better idea to hold onto it." Her explanation sounded like a stupid excuse as soon as she said it.

Cassim lifted the rod from her hands with reverence, peeling back the cloth to reveal its milky motherstone surface. The lines along the backs of his hands glowed to life briefly as he touched it with a spark. The rod's identifying symbols ran across its surface, just as they had back in the storage room.

"Well, isn't that something?" he said in awe.

What they were doing was clearly more interesting than any apprentice work Isben could come up with. He sat next to Katira. "Master Aro taught me a bit more about the glyphs he used to make it. It really is a masterful piece. We could check the barrier right now if we wanted to, see if there is anything going on that is causing problems."

As they'd been talking, that pull, that draw to use the rod grew stronger. Katira couldn't shake the feeling that something just out of reach was calling to her. "No amount of warding will help the town if the problem lies within the barrier. We should check it as soon as possible, right now even, and find out."

That earned her a raised eyebrow from Cassim. "Absolutely not. We wait for Jarand and Issa to return. I'd hate them to think we'd gotten ourselves into some sort of trouble and need to check in on us before finishing their work." He rolled the rod back into its cloth and tucked it into one of his deep pockets. Katira itched to take it back from him as she watched it disappear.

It wasn't until deep in the afternoon when Papan, Issa, and Bremin returned to the campsite. Remembering her duties, Katira offered one of the waterskins to Papan as Isben did the same for Issa and Bremin.

"It leaves us very little to work with, that's all." Bremin ignored the offered water. Whatever they were arguing about, they must have been at it for a while.

"It comes down to strategy, that's all. Issa and I will track where we spot them and keep narrowing down possibilities until we know where they're slipping through." Papan unbuckled his sword belt and slid free from the baldric, handing them both to Katira.

"The warding wall is fine then? " Katira asked as she stored the items with the other gear.

"As much as we can hope it to be, yes."

Papan took another swig of the water and limped back to where Cassim was sealing the vials of willow bark tincture with wax. Onyx had snuck into the shade of one of the nearby trees to nap away from the heat of the early evening.

"That sounds an awful lot like we're not done here." Cassim cast a cautious glance toward Issa as if hoping for more information.

She shrugged free of the leather chest plate with a relieved sigh and handed it to Isben before joining them. "This possibility was always on the table. But the fact stands, the hounds didn't cross the wall. They entered the town from somewhere inside it."

Bremin loosened the ratty red scarf at his neck and ran his

fingers through his short salt-and-pepper hair. "We can't defend the town from here. Even if the hounds are drawn to us, they won't be able to cross the warding wall. They'll make do with the nearest target instead. When you killed the hounds making trouble last night, it bought us some time. They're sure to be back tonight."

Papan studied the lowering sun, gauging its distance to the horizon with upheld fingers. "We should plan on moving out within the next two hours if we want to make it to the cottage by nightfall."

"There's something you three need to know." Cassim looked decidedly uncomfortable as he gestured toward Katira.

All three sets of eyes fixed on her, making her yelp at the sudden attention. She'd assumed Cassim would be the one to do the explaining. By making her tell them about the rod, it also forced her to admit to stealing it from the Tower.

Katira wrung the strap of her pack between her hands, needing to paint a picture that transformed her accidental theft into an unexpected advantage. "You have proof now that the hounds have been passing through the barrier somewhere inside the town." She took a breath around the foul thought that wouldn't free itself from her mind. "Don't you see, it's Wrothe. She's targeting us. She knows this is our home. Somehow she's trying to bait us. It's a trap."

"Wait, that's not what we discussed before." Cassim screwed up his face in confusion. "Where are you going with this?"

"I have no doubt that she's behind this," Bremin stated simply.

The casualness of his remark caught Katira off guard. "I don't understand. If you knew, why aren't we gathering reinforcements? You don't intend for us to face her like this, do you?"

"She can't break through on her own." Bremin stowed his handful of belongings back into his pack. "All of her ties have been severed from this world. I have no intention of facing her. Our task is to shield and protect the town, much like what we've done for the Tower. Nothing more."

"On the Stonemother's throne itself, Katira, tell them already," Cassim cursed.

Issa jerked up her head from tying her bedroll to the base of her pack, her attention snapping back to the conversation.

Katira stopped twisting the strap of her own pack and set it down. With everyone's attention locked on her like this she hoped telling the truth was enough to protect her from the anger that was sure to come. She held out her hand to Cassim and he deposited the cloth wrapped parcel into it.

"This is Master Aro's glyph rod." Katira unwrapped it and held it out. "When Isben and I found it in the Tower, I was drawn to it. I didn't know why, but now I do. It will help us find the breach in the barrier that much faster, make Namragan safe that much sooner."

Papan sucked in an involuntary breath. "Do I even want to know how you got this?"

"It was an innocent mistake." Cassim interjected. As it was his fault she had to take responsibility like this, it was kind of him to attempt to deflect Papan's anger. "She found it while cleaning out that storage room. We left so quickly she didn't have a chance to put it back."

"She can speak for herself, Cassim." Papan's voice grew low and dangerous.

Cassim snapped his mouth shut. Onyx, awakened by the noise, flapped back to his shoulder and gave a short squawk before hiding behind his head.

Had she been younger, she'd have lied about it and tried to diffuse Papan's anger. Not anymore. She wasn't that young girl who used to carry water until her fingers bled as a punishment. It didn't matter where the rod came from, it was a useful tool.

"I know what I did was wrong, and I'll accept whatever punishment you choose to give, but only after Namragan is safe." She handed the rod to Papan. "Like you said, the sooner we can get to the bottom of this, the less likely anyone will get hurt."

"She's got a point." Issa rested her elbows on her knees. "I say we use it. "

"Really?" Of everyone gathered, Katira didn't expect Issa to agree so easily.

Papan didn't look pleased, but the anger she'd sensed from him earlier had faded. She'd once again put him in a position where he had to choose between dealing with her disobedience and his duty to a much larger cause.

Before he had a chance to agree or disagree, Bremin lifted the rod from his hand.

"This changes everything."

CHAPTER 9

The argument over whether it would be better to study the barrier at the camp against doing it in the town came down to visibility and safety. Bremin argued that at the camp, they were less likely to be seen and, should something go wrong, less likely to accidentally blow anything up. Papan argued that the only place that made any sense to check the barrier was the place they were trying to protect, and with the threat of hounds looming on the edge of night, they were wasting time.

Katira listened on as she helped break down the camp and sorted everything back into their packs. The second it was decided that they would go back, she didn't want a single delay.

"We try it here first. It's useless to get our hopes up if we can't make heads or tails of what it shows us." Bremin's tone left no room for argument. "We'll make it quick. I promise."

Papan picked up his cane and followed Bremin as he carried the rod away from the fire and closer to the river's edge.

"This should do nicely, plenty of room." He handed the rod, still wrapped in its protective cloth, to Papan. "For this, I defer to you."

Katira had no intention of missing the test. Even with her limited experience, she'd seen more of the barrier than most. If they wanted her to leave, they'd have to care enough to make her. When Isben spotted her joining the circle, he hurried to stand by her side.

Papan slid the rod from its pouch, handling it as if it were as delicate as a butterfly wing. "Any ideas of what we should be looking for?"

When no one answered, Isben, who had worked with Master Aro more than anyone, stepped forward. "It has everything to do with density. The barrier's threads should be tightly knit, like a thick carpet. I imagine if there are weaknesses here, the threats will appear thinner, as if they were moth-eaten."

Papan rotated the rod between his palms as he considered the information. "Does that sound about right, Bremin?"

"It's what I've been led to believe as well. The analysis of the barrier itself might be more subtle than that. But we have to start somewhere."

"Seems straightforward enough to make an attempt." Papan straightened and rolled the stiffness from his shoulders as he took charge of the situation. "Issa, keep watch of the perimeter. I don't want any surprises. Cassim and Bremin, I want your full attention on the barrier. Katira and Isben, you watch closely as well. Any and all insights will be helpful. Everybody ready?" He glanced around the group, taking in the nods of agreement before the lines on his arms glowed to life.

With a gentle pulse, he activated the rod and fed in a thin stream of power. Just like before, the glyphs embedded into the rod leapt into action and formed elaborate patterns in the air. Ever so slowly, the barrier's threads came into view. Isben inched closer, his eyes gleaming with an intense interest that rivaled that of when she'd watched him work with Master Aro.

The barrier did appear weaker. Instead of a thick vibrant mass of color and life, such as they saw at the Tower, the threads moved in lethargic jerks, reminding Katira of death throes. If this was some kind of sickness, perhaps there was something she could do to bring it back to health. She bound her apprentice stone to her palm, the motion practiced and automatic.

Isben set a hand on her shoulder. "Wait. Don't do anything until they've had a chance to discuss their findings."

She sensed tension in that gentle touch and lowered her bound palm. Their last experience working with the barrier had brought Amul Dun to its knees and nearly killed the High Lady Alystra. If anything like that happened here, Katira could never forgive herself. Wrothe had pulled strings, manipulated trusted leaders, and twisted their plans to suit her needs at the Tower. Katira squinted, seeking out anything that looked like the woman's tethering lines. If she'd sunk her claws into a poor soul there in Namragan, their job would be that much harder.

Bremin stood close to Papan's shoulder and examined the opening with the same intensity he displayed whenever tasked to solve a problem. "Are you seeing what I'm seeing here?"

Cassim stepped closer and squinted at the writhing mass of threads. "It's definitely different. But who's to say that it hasn't always been that way here? Maybe different areas have different looking barriers."

Katira studied several of the individual threads, convinced that there was another explanation. The longer she watched them shift around each other, the stronger her impression became. "No, it's not that. Something about it feels wrong. Like it's sick or broken somehow. I can't explain it."

Papan held the rod steady and continued to feed in a thread of energy. "I feel it too. Something isn't right, but I can't put my finger on what."

"Well," Katira began cautiously. She'd stepped out of line before by putting herself into situations where she didn't belong. "If it's sick, maybe fixing it is a matter of finding a way to heal it."

At the mention of healing, Cassim's head snapped up. "This isn't a person. It's not even technically alive, as far as I can tell. There's no telling what might happen if we use healing glyphs on it."

Issa scanned the perimeter of the campsite, vigilant as always. "She might be onto something. When Jarand and I tried to close the rips in the barrier back at Amul Dun, the severed threads certainly acted as if they were alive. The barrier might not be a living creature, but it's not dead either. Do you think you could delve it?"

Cassim shrank back, horror shining in his eyes. "Touch that? With the power? I wouldn't know where to start. There are no organized systems, no pathways of health. It's a jumbled mess of string, for crying out loud."

"I can do it," Katira offered before she could stop the words from leaving her mouth. Once again, something about the barrier drew her in, made her want to learn more. It had been the same back at Amul Dun where dealings with the barrier drew her in like a magnet to steal. "I might not find anything, but then again, I might. It couldn't hurt anyway."

"Cassim, do you object to Katira trying?" Papan's gaze pierced through the barrier to where she was standing.

The healer kneaded his hands together and chewed at the corner of his lip. "I suppose not. Delving doesn't actually touch anything, so it should be safe enough."

Isben sucked in a tiny breath, as if he hoped that the healer would object. If anyone was more protective of her than her father, it was him. He wouldn't want her doing this; there were too many things about it they didn't understand.

"I say no," he said. "And, I don't think anyone else should either. This barrier looks far different than in the Tower. It's not just thinner or sick, there's something else there that I can't put a finger on. I'd prefer we not meddle with it at all." He ignored the pointed look Katira shot at him. "What would it take to reinforce the town the same way that the Tower is reinforced? If we do that, we avoid all of this uncertainty."

"That would be the safer choice, I agree." A warm breeze tugged at Bremin's scarf. He glanced at the setting sun. "But time isn't on our side. The warding protecting the Tower took years to put in place and decades to perfect. I can only imagine how long it might take for an entire town. We can do it if we have to, but it would be wise to explore other options first."

"Then I should try delving the barrier." Katira set her hand on top of Isben's, needing him to be okay with her trying, needing him to understand that she would be careful. The tightness in his jaw relaxed a fraction, but the unease remained.

Papan pursed his lips. The undercurrent of fear he'd been trying to repress surfaced again. With it, came something unexpected across the bond, trust. "Whenever you're ready, Katira. Everyone else, stay alert."

She didn't waste a second. She welcomed the harsh burn as she opened herself to the power. After so many months of practice under both Cassim and Master Firen's tutelage, the eye-shaped delving glyph formed easily. She guided it forward, allowing her awareness to flow into the weave of the barrier the same way she would a patient. Instead of the familiar rhythms and pathways found in a body, her senses sang with each thread's distinct vibration. The steady thrum of a heart was replaced with something that reminded her of music. It thrilled her. The further she moved within the threads, the more of these melodies collected around her, speaking to her, guiding her.

With each touch of her glyphs, the strands shifted and twisted. Katira sensed a deeper thrum of power gathering around her in an aura of warmth and need. Together, the aura and the strands, the weave and the wild, all clashed together into a symphony of beautiful chaos.

The intelligence within the power awoke and formed a series of new glyphs which flowed from her to join in the dance. The strands of the barrier danced back, floating around her and through her, creating a sensation of belonging more intense than she'd experienced before. It overshadowed her apprentice link to Papan and even the sense of completion when she and Isben touched while holding the power.

Nothing could compare to becoming one with the familiar strangeness of the barrier. What she was doing had moved past delving into something more. She was being guided, as she had been guided before. She trusted that ancient wisdom.

Her awareness of the campsite, the sand beneath her feet, of those gathered around her, faded to a single pinprick.

"Is this normal?" Isben sounded far away.

If there was a reply, she didn't hear it. Isben set a hand on her shoulder, and she welcomed the connection between them as it opened. It felt right. The welcoming aura held her as close as any embrace. Its warm waves expanded to include him as well. Isben's grip tightened. His heart beat faster.

"Stop what you're doing. Come back to us," he urged, fear straining his voice higher.

It didn't make sense. Why was he afraid when he was surrounded by something so beautiful? She extended her calm toward him with the hope he'd stop fretting and let himself experience the barrier as she did. Strange glyphs continued to run freely from her fingertips. She hummed with the music filling her head. The real world wavered and flickered around her.

Papan's large, callused hand gripped the back of her neck. "Let go. Whatever you're doing, stop," he ordered.

Through the apprentice bond, she felt his words rather than heard them. Papan wasn't one to be fearful, not when there was something to be done. In the short span of time they had been bonded, she'd only felt fear of this magnitude from him a handful of times. It was almost enough to convince her to pull back and let the music fade.

Almost.

If she could help him hear the music, then he'd understand. She clung tighter to the melodies, needing him to pay attention so he could feel how the barrier's aura brought bliss and contentment. He didn't need to be afraid.

Jarand fought to keep hold of Katira even as the strange light flowed from the barrier and wrapped tighter around her. Lady

Alystra had warned him that her power would continue to take control and could do so at any moment. Her destiny as an Innate meant she would be drawn to complete the task she was born to accomplish, a destiny that would most likely result in her death. He wasn't prepared to let that happen for something as trivial as delving the shadow barrier.

He cut off the flow of power from the rod, hoping that if the view of the barrier was closed, it would sever whatever had trapped her.

"What are you doing?" Bremin shouted over the growing angry buzz.

"She's not coming willingly. I have to force her out." He extended a ribbon of power into the maelstrom, seeking a crack in the envelope of energy which wrapped around both her and Isben. The flows holding them batted his power away like a feather in the breeze.

"By rock and ruin, she's fading. Isben too." Issa set her flows alongside his, lending her strength. "Whatever you're doing, do it faster."

"I can't get close enough. It's stopping me." He pressed forward several more lines of power, wrapping them tightly together like a spear to keep them from blowing apart.

"Cassim, pull Isben away," Issa ordered. "It might only be holding her."

Cassim hurried forward, his power leaping to life and his own set of seeking strands moving into action. Together, they frantically worked to gain purchase.

"I can't touch him either. Can you sense if she's in trouble?"

Jarand plunged a second, stronger spear of power into the expanding storm, hoping to get close enough so he could get hold of her. "She's calm, happy even. But our connection feels as if it's stretching, as if she's being pulled somewhere far away." His words came out bowstring-tight. This was not how he was going to lose his daughter.

"To where? You don't think ...?" Issa trailed off as the only answer to that question took hold. The color disappeared from her already pale skin. She squared her shoulders and pressed even harder.

Bremin sprung to action. "Jarand, stand aside. Issa and Cassim, join together and use your combined strength to untangle them from this mess."

Jarand only hesitated a moment before giving the pair space. While not done often, a companionship working together could perform feats above and beyond what any two Stonebearers could do alone. With Issa's skill at finding weaknesses and Cassim's ability to make things whole, it was their best chance.

They slammed their combined glyphs into the thickening layers surrounding Katira and Isben like an arrow punching through a sack of grain. The light, already star bright, intensified until Jarand was forced to look away. The buzz filling the campsite grew to a roar so loud it felt as if it would crush his head.

Blinded and deafened, Jarand threw one last desperate glyph in the direction of the barrier. If he weakened it, it might be enough to give Issa and Cassim a chance. Instead, the light shattered like a pane of glass. The roar quieted into an unearthly silence. When Jarand's vision finally cleared, the circle stood empty. Katira and Isben were gone.

A guttural cry ripped from his throat and he lashed out with the power, sending a wave of the small river rocks at his feet flying in all directions. It wasn't possible. She couldn't just be gone. The flash of Issa's shield flared at the edge of his vision, and several particularly creative curses escaped her lips before she regained her usual calm.

Something wet dripped down the side of Jarand's face. When he touched it, his fingers came away red.

Cassim approached him slowly, the same way one would approach a skittish horse. "May I?" He didn't come closer until Jarand took a breath to calm himself. Cassim knew warriors well enough, being a companion to one, and understood when it was best to give them some space.

He pulled out a handkerchief from his pocket. "A rock nicked you."

Jarand took the cloth and pressed it to the stinging line, grateful he wasn't alone facing this new overwhelming challenge. Every fiber of his body was being pulled in a different direction and only his determination kept him from splitting apart. He needed to sit, to think, to plan.

"Can you still feel her?" Bremin's question was so cautious and held so much worry that Jarand didn't dare look at the man's face for fear of what he might see.

He pinched his stone between his fingers and sought out the space in his mind where he felt Katira the clearest. The apprentice bond had always been a mixed blessing between them, but, in that moment, when he sensed her alive and unharmed, it was the sweetest thing he'd ever felt.

He released a pent-up breath. "Yes. Wherever she is, the bond still holds." He scooped up the rod from where he'd set it and handed it to Bremin, trusting him to keep it safe while they figured out what to do.

Issa folded her arms over her chest. "How long do you think the two of them can last on the other side?"

The other side. The mirror realm. The place they had condemned Wrothe to rot for eternity after she tried to destroy Amul Dun. Jarand swallowed back the bitterness that coated his tongue. Katira couldn't be there. Shouldn't be there. And yet there was no other place she could be.

"If Wrothe finds them, not nearly long enough." Bremin raked a hand through his hair. "But if by some miracle they manage to not attract her notice, they should be okay for a few days."

Behind them, the sun touched the horizon, signaling the swift arrival of night. A terrible choice had to be made. If they left now, they could protect the town from the hounds that were sure to come, but it came at the cost of abandoning Katira and Isben to an unknown fate.

Judging how Bremin kept glancing toward the town, he was thinking the same thing. When he spoke, his voice was full of determined resignation. "You three stay here. Do whatever you can to try to force an opening through the barrier and get them back. I'll return to the town, draw the hounds to me, keep the people there safe."

Jarand had often heard it said that the hardest choices tended to be the right ones. This was a hard choice. "Absolutely not." He picked up his sword belt and fastened it on, ignoring how the pain flared in his back. "I'll go. The people trust me, just as I trust all three of you to get my daughter and Isben back."

CHAPTER 10

Given the choice, Katira would have stayed within the threads of the barrier forever. Its embrace filled her with a peace and warmth she didn't imagine possible. The world faded away, and she felt as if she were floating while surrounded by the most beautiful music.

When that embrace began to loosen, when the warmth began to cool, she fought to hold on to that peace as the threads of the barrier released their grip. One by one, they slipped away and returned to their place.

"What was that?" Isben's breath hitched as he loosened his fingers from the fabric of her shirt. "What did you do?"

When Katira opened her eyes, instead of the vibrant green array of pines and aspens in the heat of summer they were surrounded by a riot of reds, pinks, and purples. The sky burned in an unhealthy smear of muddy black. An overwhelming silence pressed against her ears. The wrongness of it all assaulted her. She rubbed her face and blinked, hoping it was a temporary effect of being within the barrier, but nothing changed.

"Are you seeing this?"

"I am, but I don't think I believe it." Isben bent to study the odd orange of the river.

It had to be a dream. Something unexpected must've happened when she delved the barrier, big enough to knock her out, and she was imagining this bizarre world. She pinched the skin of her arm and was rewarded with a very un-dreamlike pain. Whatever this was, it was real.

"Where did Papan go? He was here a few seconds ago. They all were."

Isben paced the length of the camp, observing each detail, each change. "If I tell you where we are, will you promise not to panic?"

"Not when you say it like that, I won't." Despite her best efforts to stay calm, her breath pressed tight inside her chest. "Besides, I think I know. This is the mirror realm, isn't it?"

It shouldn't have been possible. The mirror realm was a place of shadows; people weren't meant to exist here. She fought the urge to pinch her arm again to see if she'd been mistaken the first time.

"We need to get out of here, it's not safe." Isben checked the chain that bound his apprentice stone to his palm. "What did you do to get us here?"

She touched her own stone, trying to think back through each step as it happened. Most of the memory had smeared into an unhelpful blur. "It wasn't me. I think something else wanted us here, pulled us through."

"What do you mean, *something*? Like what?" A note of worry filled his voice. "There's nothing here that we want anything to do with." He scanned the empty campsite, peering through the breaks in the red leaves of the unnatural trees before continuing in an exaggerated whisper. "In case you forgot, this is where Wrothe lives. Where shadow hounds come from. If dragging us here was her doing, she'll kill us both."

"It wasn't her." Katira couldn't explain how she knew it, but she was certain that what she experienced as they were being pulled through the barrier contained no trace of the madwoman's malice. "If it was, she'd be on us already. I know it sounds strange, but I feel as if I'm meant to be here."

She scanned the surrounding area, seeking motion and leaning on her intuition as Papan had shown her. For the moment, nothing gave her cause for alarm. "We're safe enough for now. One problem at a time, right?"

Isben arched an eyebrow at her. "To do nothing is death."

"Stop it. I'm not doing nothing. I'm assessing the situation. What are you doing that's helpful?"

He poked her shoulder. "I'm questioning the only person that might know more about what happened than I do. You."

"We both know how helpful that's going to be." Katira plucked a pink pine needle from one of the surrounding trees. "If there was anything else I could tell you, I already would have. Still, I'd feel better if we knew we could leave. Like you said, there are dangers here. Good thing you know more about the mirror realm than most people, right?"

He pressed his eyes shut and pinched the bridge of his nose. "Clearly not as much as I thought. I swear, no tree or sky should look like that. This place is giving me a headache. How is it possible for quiet to feel so loud?"

"Come on, it's not that bad. Just different. I kind of like it." She opened herself to the power again, needing the sharpened focus it brought with its tide of intense heat. Instead, a wave of cold filled her veins with ice. She gasped at the shock of it and lost her focus. The power retreated as quickly as it had surfaced.

Isben was back at her side in the space of a heartbeat. "What? What is it?"

Katira hugged her arms around herself as she waited for the last of the chill to disappear. "It's cold. Must have something to do with being here. Ugh, and I thought the power being hot was awful."

He pulled her close and rubbed her back until she melted into the welcome heat. He didn't let go until she stopped shivering.

"I want to try again."

"Are you sure?"

"Like you said, it's not safe here." Knowing the cold was coming helped, but she still shuddered as it filled her. If her need to leave was strong enough, it might trigger the intelligence within the power to wake. Several glyphs flew from her fingers, but the barrier didn't reappear.

When nothing happened, Isben broke the silence. "Talk to me. I can help."

Katira lowered her stone. "It's no use. Without seeing the barrier, there's nothing for me to anchor my focus on."

"You started with a delving glyph before. Perhaps if you formed one again you might be able to sense the threads."

"If you're so smart, why don't you try?" Katira snapped without thinking. She heaved a sigh of frustration. Using the power wasn't easy at the best of times. She had no control over when the intelligence took over.

He ignored her outburst and instead began to pace, head lowered, eyes closed. "No, you were successful the first time. Our best chance is if you can repeat what you did."

Katira squashed down the irritation marching circles inside of her head. For some insane reason, she wanted him to be angry with her. If he was, it would give her a reason to justify the anger that piled up inside her chest.

She grimaced at the fresh rush of cold as she drew on her power again to form a delving glyph. It was so simple compared to the more complex patterns she'd worked up to in her trainings with Papan that she worried it wasn't enough. As it was, without the barrier visible, there was nowhere for it to go, no patient for it to assess. She couldn't sense even a hint of the threads.

She released her flows with a huff and marched back to the abandoned firepit, looping her stone back around her neck as she went.

"It's okay." Isben followed her. "We'll keep thinking of new ideas to try. I promise." He touched where her stone dangled over her shirt. "What about your father? Can you still feel him?"

Katira cursed at herself. Papan was probably frantic trying to figure out where they'd gone. She drew her focus inward to where she usually felt him, how she usually felt him. While his presence was still there, it was tiny, almost too small to notice. She heaved a sigh of relief.

"Yes, barely. It's enough for him to know I'm safe. That we are safe, at least for now."

The setting of the sun stirred up a welcome breeze that brushed whispers from the tall pines scattered along the edges of the narrow canyon. Jarand breathed it in as he walked down the trail, trying to calm the thoughts that raced through his head. Leaving the campsite, leaving Katira, went against his every instinct.

Back when Mirelle was alive, she would remind him how much he trusted Bremin for his wisdom and Issa and Cassim for their skills. He wasn't lying when he said they were the best team he could assemble. But when it came to protecting Katira, he never felt like he was doing enough. He leaned on his cane, needing it more after the long day and what was promising to be an even longer night.

When he reached Namragan, a pair of smoking oil lanterns hung on either side of the northern gate. Master Thanes, the baker, sat on a three-legged stool with a makeshift spear resting against the broad expanse of his belly. Beyond the gate, a lamplighter worked hang more lanterns down the street. Good. More light would make it that much easier to spot any shadows misbehaving.

"Cutting it a bit fine, aren't we?" The baker squinted into the dark. "Get somewhere safe. There's no telling where those demons might appear." As if to emphasize his point, he made a face that was meant to be fierce, but instead looked like he had gas.

"Where can I find Master Lucan? I need to speak with him." As Jarand asked, a ripple of power pressed through him from the direction of the campsite. He clenched his hand around the stone still bound to his palm and fought the urge to open himself to the power and sense better what was happening.

"At the inn, no doubt. Giving orders for the night. Best not get in his way, he's awful busy." The baker lifted one of the lanterns to see better and a spark of recognition finally touched his eyes. "Ah, Master Jarand. I'd heard you'd come back. Good to see you. Ignore what I just said, Lucan wants to talk to you." He reached for the pewter mug at his feet and was disappointed to find it empty. "And while you're there, perhaps you can have someone bring me another ale. As volunteer for the first watch, I deserve it."

If Issa were there, she would've had a word or two to share with the man about drinking on duty. Perhaps it was for the best she wasn't. The surge of power rippling through the air remained consistent but cautious. If it were him, he would have been far more aggressive.

"We'll see. Best to stay sharp with these things. Like you said, they come out of nowhere." Jarand gave a knowing smile and hurried through the gate before the man spotted the sword hanging at his hip. Best not to raise any questions in the man's mind if he could avoid it.

Jarand's plan to deal with the hounds required Lucan's cooperation, and even with it, it wasn't one of his better ideas. He would have much rather stayed hidden and let the hounds come to him than to face the crowd that had most likely gathered at the inn.

The Mad Rabbit Inn sat in a prominent place at the top of the town square. As the sole building in all Namragan with a second story, it served as both command central and watchtower. Two men stood on the balcony armed with signaling lanterns and longbows. Lucan might not have fought in an actual war, but as an experienced hunter, he certainly had a good sense of how to assess his prey.

Jarand was greeted with smiles and hearty welcomes when he pushed through the doors of the inn. On any other day, he would have rejoiced in making up for lost time, but right then he needed to talk to Lucan.

He found the wide-shouldered tanner at one of the larger tables near the fire with a crudely drawn map of the town splayed out before him. Andril stood to one side of him, but thankfully Elan was nowhere to be seen. He wasn't ready to share what had happened with Katira yet, not when he had a job to do. Several of the other townsmen clustered around him pointing to the map and murmuring suggestions.

Jarand sat across from Lucan and tucked the sword out of sight under the table. A mug of ale appeared at his elbow.

"Welcome back, Master Jarand. It's good to see you. This one's on the house." Madame Duvall, the proprietress of the inn, gave him a wink before tossing her mass of ebony curls over her shoulder and moving on to her next customer.

When Lucan took no notice of his arrival, Jarand slapped a hand onto the map. "Master Thanes is nursing a pint over at the northernmost gate. Is that what you call discipline?" he said with mock severity.

Lucan didn't look up. "Master Thanes can do what he wants if he guards that gate for a few more hours." It took a few moments for him to register Jarand's voice. When he did, a big smile split his weather-wrinkled face. "Where have you been all afternoon? I was hoping you'd help me to organize our defenses. Everyone keeps telling me how much I desperately need it."

When Jarand didn't return the smile, Lucan's face fell. "Something's wrong, isn't it? I got my hopes up that nights like this would be numbered. Speak up, what's happened?"

Jarand touched the back of his hand, a subtle reminder about who he was. "This isn't the place."

Lucan looked Jarand over as if trying to read him. "Of course not. What was I thinking? Come with me. Andril, you manage the men for a bit."

Madame Duvall's private office was tucked off to the side of the bar that stretched along the far end of the common room. Lucan ushered Jarand inside and closed the door behind them. The room was barely large enough to hold the wide desk that divided it into two narrow spaces. A lantern hanging from the ceiling filled the room with dim light. Several stacks of paper, all weighed down with various odd objects, were lined up in a row awaiting the proprietress's attention. Lucan rounded the desk and rested his weight on his fists. "I know you. Know that face. What's going on?"

Jarand had brought the mug of ale with him and took a long drink before settling himself in one of the chairs in front of the desk. While the ale at Amul Dun was considerably better, especially considering the ale master there had spent several centuries perfecting his craft, Jarand had missed this local brew with its unique bitterness and notes of honey.

"I'll start with the good news. We've ensured that the warding wall ringing the town is intact. Hounds prowling around outside the wall can't enter."

"If that's the good news, then dare I ask what's the bad?"

The steady ripple of power coming from the campsite jolted into an unexpected surge. Jarand found himself reflexively clenching the stone in his fist. Either it meant they were making the final push to bring Katira and Isben back, or something unanticipated had happened. The only thing keeping him from bolting out the door was the cast-iron emotionless control he'd learned as a General.

"The shadow hounds that have been bothering you didn't cross the original warding wall. They are slipping into the world some-where inside the town."

Lucan sagged back into the chair. "Is that as bad as it sounds? Because it sounds bad."

"It complicates things, nothing more." Jarand chose against sharing more than necessary. This wasn't the time. "I can protect the town tonight, but I need your help."

Lucan didn't even blink at the request. "Anything. Name it."

"Keep everyone out of the town square. The men can remain at their posts on the walls, but no watchers from the top of the inn." Jarand tapped his finger against the desk with each point.

Lucan's forehead drew into a concerned wrinkle. "I don't under-stand. How is that going to help?"

"The hounds are attracted to the power. To me. If they enter the town anywhere, they will come after me first."

Lucan sucked in air through his teeth. "So, you're using yourself as bait? I don't like it. Those things can't be killed. Anything they manage to scratch or get their fangs into dies a horrible death. I can't risk you like that. You're too valuable."

Jarand unsheathed his sword and laid it on the desk between them. Lucan's eyes grew wide with wonder, and he stood to get a better look. Another surge of power rippled through the air and pulsed against Jarand's temples. This time, when it faded, it faded completely. His sense of Katira through the bond didn't change. They had failed.

"You know what I am, but you still don't understand what I am capable of. You've heard all of the legends about us, about Stonebearers. Well, they're mostly true. I'll be fine." He opened himself to the power and woke the glyphs embedded in the blade. Bright blue light spilled from its edge. "Can you keep the town square clear for me tonight?"

It took a moment for Lucan to work the moisture back into his mouth. "Of course I can."

CHAPTER 11

The act of sitting and trying to think of a new idea seemed about as effective to Katira as staring at a blank piece of paper with the belief that words might magically appear. For her, the best ideas always came as a result of considering everything she already knew and then combining that knowledge in a different way. Thanks to Wrothe and her recent efforts at Amul Dun, they had learned plenty about the barrier but pitifully little about the world that existed on the other side. She pressed her eyes shut and tried to recall every last sliver of information, anything that might be useful.

Isben, on the other hand, paced back and forth with his head down, moving from the edge of the strangely silent river to the wall of rock at the back of the campsite. He still avoided looking anywhere beyond the tips of his own shoes. On his sixth or seventh pass, a low buzz grew from where they'd viewed the barrier earlier. The noise of it was startlingly loud compared to the unearthly quiet of the rest of the world.

He stopped midstep. "Are you doing that?"

She pushed herself to her feet. "I was about to ask you the same thing. They must be trying to break through."

Isben moved closer to where a patch of air started to glow. The barrier strands didn't come into view as they had before, but clearly the same forces were at work.

Katira took hold of her power and grit her teeth against the shock of cold. With the view opened, she'd have a much better chance to pull herself and Isben back through. She sent the delving glyph into the strands just like before, sensing, seeking, pressing to find something, anything that would trigger those strange glyphs that blossomed from the tips of her fingers. If her need was strong enough, then they should appear. She pushed harder, growing frantic. What was the use of having a special gift if it disappeared when she needed it most?

"There was more last time, and you used different patterns. Can you bring those back?"

Katira gripped her stone tighter. Couldn't he see she was trying her best? "Something triggered them, something in the barrier itself. I can't find it."

"Keep looking. It has to be there."

One of the barrier threads cracked through the air with an angry hiss, missing the side of Isben's head by inches. It was as if the barrier itself didn't want them meddling with it. Isben pulled Katira out of reach as several more threads whipped into the space where she was standing.

Undeterred, Katira extended her delving glyph deeper into the threads. If she could find what gripped them before, she could pull them both back into the real world. Isben flung up a shield as another assault of whipping threads came too close. Then, as quickly as the barrier had appeared, it faded back into nothingness.

He released the shield. "Why are they stopping? We're still here. They can't just give up like that."

"They can." Katira curled in on herself, teeth chattering with the cold. Holding the power that long had chilled her to the bone. "They have Bremin with them. No doubt they tried everything he could think of. When he thinks of something new, they'll try again."

She refused to tell Isben that part of her was glad it failed. The sense that she was meant to be in the mirror realm grew more intense the longer she stayed there.

Isben, on the other hand, grew more agitated. "What does that mean? Do we simply stay here and wait? There has to be something else."

To do nothing is death. The thought came unbidden, bringing her back to that desperate time when Papan lay bleeding in the dungeons of Khanrosh, and she could do nothing but wait. Isben had been by her side, guiding her, encouraging her to stay ahead of her fears, and not let panic win. Here, in the strangeness of the mirror realm, it was her turn to be the strong one.

She clutched her stone and allowed the vessel of her power to tip again and fill her despite the cold. There had to be a way to force that intelligence hiding within the power to act. If she could puzzle it out, if she could wake up that ability at will, then they'd be that much closer to leaving.

Are you calm? An echo of her father's teachings filled her head. *Nothing will happen if you force it. The Khandashii is a partnership.*

Even here, even now, he managed to watch over her. But how could she be calm when her failure put them in danger of shadow hounds and an untold number of other deadly things they hadn't discovered yet? They'd fought a single hound off before. Thanks to Issa's teachings, both she and Isben were far from defenseless. Fighting off several at once shouldn't be that much harder, right? She squirmed at the thought. Maybe if she told herself enough times, she'd believe it.

The burnt tarlike darkness of the sky lightened as the unnatural day shifted into an even more unnatural night. The weird stillness of the mirror realm did nothing to calm Katira's imagination, which was intent on making her believe all manner of monsters prowled just out of sight, waiting to cause trouble.

Isben came closer, and his familiar smell of aged paper and ink washed over her. "I'm sorry about what I said earlier. None of this is your fault. Don't let my foolishness be the reason you try something that perhaps you're not ready for." He touched her arm, and his hand felt wonderfully warm against her power chilled skin. "You don't have to prove anything to me."

The only thing worse than having Isben upset with her was for him to feel he needed to ask her forgiveness. It meant something she did made him feel bad. The biggest reason she was trying to get back through the barrier was for him.

"This?" She held up her arm where her lines were glowing. "I figured it wouldn't hurt to keep trying while we wait. The right combination of glyphs and intention has to exist. If I keep trying, something might click."

He opened his bag and fetched out the flat wooden box he used as a writing desk. "Do you mind if I join you? I have some thoughts I'd like to jot down, see if I can make any sense of what I saw."

She patted the sand next to her. "Not at all."

Having him that close usually distracted her, but with the situation as it was, having him near helped calm the fears that kept sneaking up on her. She knelt in the meditative posture Papan had taught her: toes together, knees apart, weight centered, fingertips touching. A complete circuit for energy. Mind the breath, let the energy within flow, let it connect with the breath. Let all awareness of the world dim, observe and release thoughts as if they were flower petals in the wind.

With each measured breath, Katira's racing thoughts slowed their frantic twisting enough to where she could make sense of them. She'd been brought to the mirror realm for a reason. The fragments of knowledge that would help her understand why hid somewhere deep inside her, either in her own memories, or within the cryptic flows of the Khandashii. Finding the answer was a matter of picking up the proper pieces and putting them together.

Within that calm bubble of space, she revisited the experience of being pulled through the barrier and watched for details she'd missed while its music enthralled her. While the barrier might have behaved like a living thing, she never had the impression that it could act on its own. The more she considered this, the more it was clear that the barrier couldn't have created the glyph sequence that trapped her. The real question was how did those patterns get there? Were similar patterns woven into the barrier's threads in other places? If so, why hadn't she heard of anyone else being sucked in?

She and Isben had been pulled through the barrier because

someone, or something, had placed glyphs there that woke the intelligence inside her. The glyphs she found were strange in a way she couldn't quite place, but she'd seen them before.

Katira's stomach dropped when she remembered. Wrothe had used glyphs just like them. She was certain she'd sensed none of the madwoman's malice in the sequence, but the woman had to be involved somehow.

A noise caught her attention from farther down the trail. Katira checked the stone bound to her palm, knowing full well they weren't capable of facing Wrothe, not now, not ever. Fully trained Stonebearers at the Tower were no match for her.

Isben was so engrossed in his writing that he hadn't noticed the noise or the change in her.

She nudged his shoulder. "Something's coming."

He jolted from his work, ink splatting on the page as he accidentally stabbed it with the pen. Normally he would have scowled at her for messing up his tidy work, but when he noticed her gripping her knife, he set aside the desk and bound his stone to his palm.

"Hello?" A man's voice called. "I know you are there. No need to be frightened."

She shifted her grip on the knife, suddenly unsure if this man presented a threat or not. He sounded friendly enough, but then again, Wrothe could sound friendly if it helped her get what she wanted.

When the man entered the clearing, Isben sucked in a surprised gasp and the knife fell from his hand. He knelt, head low, his fist pressed to his chest. Something about this stranger struck Katira as familiar, like she'd seen him somewhere before.

He walked with a spring in his step and wore a pleasant smile. His clothes appeared too fine for walking in the woods, all expertly crafted from expensive materials that Katira had only seen on royalty — and Stonebearers. A wealth of shining silver buttons marched down his deep green doublet. Its low collar revealed white Khandashiian lines branching up the sides of his neck.

"Ah, there you are. Wasn't sure where around here you'd end up. My beacons are informative, but not terribly accurate. Let me take a look at you." The gentleman walked closer and looked over both Katira and Isben in turn. "Now, tell me. Which one of you activated the sequence nestled in the barrier?"

It wasn't until he turned to look at Isben, who hadn't dared to move, that Katira remembered seeing that same distinct nose on a bust in Lady Alystra's study. It was impossible. It couldn't be the same man. He'd been dead for centuries.

Katira hesitated to answer and pinched her arm again, worried that maybe she was beginning to lose her mind.

"That was me," she stammered, still not believing what she was seeing. The only thing missing from the man was the simple circlet of gold that should've rested over his tightly curled short dark hair. "Are you who I think you are?"

He laid a finger on the side of his nose and smiled. "That depends on who you think I am." He held out a hand to Isben. "That's quite enough of that, you can get up now."

Isben brushed the sand from his knees and found his voice again. "You're King Darius," he finally managed to say. "The man who brought order to those with the power, the one who organized the first Tower, one who discovered the use of motherstone, the list goes on and on." He took hold of the man's hand and kissed it. "It's an honor to meet you, your Majesty."

King Darius laughed and clapped Isben on the shoulder. "No one calls me that these days. You two certainly won't, I insist. It's only been a few centuries since the shadows stopped cursing my name. No matter. All will be made right now that you're here." He turned and waved a hand for them to follow. "I imagine you have lots of questions. Come with me, I have a place where we can speak comfortably."

Katira hesitated, unwilling to leave the clearing and not yet ready to trust the stranger, regardless of who he appeared to be. "We can't leave. Not yet at least. There are people on the other side of the barrier trying to reach us."

"You don't question a king's orders," Isben said through his teeth. "Come on."

Katira folded her arms. "We're not even sure if he's real. What if this is one of Wrothe's tricks?"

Darius stopped at the edge of the campsite, his cheer replaced by something that looked more like pain. "Like I said, I'm sure you have plenty of questions, including ones centered around her. Your friends on the other side don't have the right keys to pass through, much less open the door. They won't succeed. You'd best come with me, because there's plenty of things that need discussing, including why you're here."

Doubts or no doubts, if he could explain why they were there, Katira was that much more willing to listen to the man. She gathered up a few things and stuck them in her pack while Isben carefully corked his inkwell and replaced it into the small box along with his pen. When it was time to leave the familiar safety of their camp and the chance of Papan finding a way to open the barrier for them, she hesitated.

Isben reached out a hand. "I don't know about you, but I'd rather be with him then deal with the hounds alone."

With the last of the stragglers finally wandering out of the town square and back home, the space felt strangely lonely. Jarand had never been there with it empty like that. He didn't like it, even if it was for the best. It felt like ages since the last ripple of power from the campsite had coursed through the air. He needed answers. The sooner Bremin and the others joined him, the sooner they could construct a new plan.

Jarand wasn't sure if he was grateful or annoyed that no hounds had come yet. The whole reason he'd left camp, left Katira, was to ensure that the town was protected. The longer the hounds delayed, the more bitter he became. He could have stayed and helped Bremin. His added strength might have made the difference between success and failure.

He relaxed his white-knuckled grip on the head of his cane. Thinking of what might have happened only served to make him more agitated, and he needed to stay focused on the task at hand. He forced himself back into a wary calm. Protecting the town was the right choice. Besides, no amount of wishing would change the situation now. He had a duty to perform, and he wasn't going to fail.

He checked to make sure no one had wandered into the town square before opening himself to the power and forming a specialized set of glyphs meant to detect the presence of shadow hounds. With a spark of power, he sent it rushing over the ground in all directions like a massive spider's web.

Someone behind him let out a low whistle. Jarand yanked the detection net back faster than he should have and winced at the sting of it. Whatever they'd witnessed him do, he could explain, or at least he'd try.

Issa sauntered out of one of the darker shadows with Cassim and Bremin in tow. Cassim had that ridiculous bird of his tucked under the fabric of his vest.

"I don't know if I've seen that pattern before," she said, "You're going to have to show me how you made it."

Jarand unwrapped his fingers from where he had unconsciously gripped the hilt of his dagger. "Of all people, you know better than to sneak up on me."

"Of all people, I think I can defend myself should you try anything. You see any action?"

Jarand urged his heart to slow, ignoring how it lurched in an unsteady rhythm before righting itself. "Not yet. The night is still young. It's not even fully dark yet." The last thing he wanted to discuss was fighting shadow hounds, especially when there were more pressing things on his mind. "What happened up there?"

"I'm sorry," Bremin said. "I thought whatever force pulled Katira and Isben through might still be present, that we might be able to trigger it and either pull them back, or have one of us pulled in with them. Then at least they wouldn't be alone."

Jarand voiced the suspicion he'd been holding all evening. "It was a trap, wasn't it?"

Bremin looked away, something he often did when he had to share bad news. "We wouldn't have spotted it, if that's what you're asking. It was well concealed with its pattern inverted in on itself, making it practically invisible until awakened. There was no way we could have known. The remnants we found were spent and broken. It was only meant to be used once."

"You took notes on what you saw?"

"Of course." Bremin tapped one of the many pockets of his coat. "Might hold a few clues to help us figure out what happened and put together a plan."

Issa shifted her weight on the balls of her feet. "What we did up there should have attracted any hounds roaming the area like moths to flame. For them not to show up anywhere tonight is concerning."

Bremin tugged at his scarf. "It might be that it's not dark enough, although the time of day didn't seem to matter back in the Tower. Then again, that was when they were being forced to attack. They might not hunt naturally until true dark falls. Master Lucan only reported attacks at night, so I don't think we can read too much into it yet. I'm sure they'll show up one way or another. With all four of us here, I can't imagine a juicier target."

"It's not surprising that they haven't shown themselves yet." Cassim sounded more morose than Jarand had ever heard him before. "If *you know who* is behind this, she already has what she wants. There's no reason for her to keep sending them in. Katira and Isben are in serious danger, and there's nothing we can do about it."

Issa set a hand on his shoulder and he leaned into it. "We're all worried. Don't think for a minute that we've given up. We have to assume that this isn't an end but a beginning. Every time we've faced *her* before, she's used Katira as a way to get to Jarand, and I don't imagine that's changed. They might be safer than you think "

"She's had no problem hurting me, that's for sure," Jarand grumbled under his breath. "Although during one of my last fights with her, she came very close to claiming Katira as her new host. That goes a step beyond harming if you ask me. We can't assume her or Isben's safety."

Bremin snapped his fingers. "No, we assume nothing. That's what gets us in trouble. We all saw how hard she fought to break into our world at the Tower, what she was willing to risk. We'll learn as much as we can and see if we might use the patterns we found, in combination with the Master Aro's glyph rod, to create an opening of sorts. "

"Good. We start there." Jarand leaned his weight against the edge of the fountain. "With true dark upon us, we best set a watch for the hounds as well."

"I was just thinking about that." Issa tapped her fingertips on her sword's pommel. "Show me what you were doing right as we got here. I have an idea."

CHAPTER 12

Katira followed Darius down the trail toward the small valley below, taking in the reds and pinks of the pine forest and squinting through the surreal white striped tree trunks of the mirror realm as she tried to catch a glimpse of the town she once called home. As they turned the final bend, she expected to see the square with its cheerful fountain and its ring of shops. Instead, a large empty meadow stretched before her dotted with dozens of black and white sheep. A tiny cabin sat in the shelter of the trees near a bend in the Kanth river. A dark tendril of smoke rose from its chimney.

"It's gone. How can it all be gone?" She instinctively reached for Isben, seeking reassurance in the familiar warmth of his hand.

Until that point, he'd walked in silence behind and avoided looking at the riot of wrong colors. This unexpected change caught his attention. "It's okay. There has to be an explanation for it."

Darius tucked his hands into the pockets of his coat. "There is, don't fret. I imagine this valley looks different from what you're used to. Time, among other things, doesn't work the same here."

"I thought the mirror realm was a reflection of the real world. Shouldn't that which exists there exist here as well?" Isben asked.

"Like I said, I have a lot of explaining to do." His attention shifted ever so slightly toward the mouth of the valley, and he touched the motherstone hanging over his chest. "Come along, we must get you two to the comfort of the cabin."

Darius's casual pace shifted into a quick purposeful walk that bordered on a jog. As much as Katira ached to find anything familiar as they hurried through the meadow, it seemed unwise to slow down. She found comfort in the unchanged sharp edges of the surrounding mountains and the graceful bends of the river. Even with the buildings gone, this was still her home.

Inside the cabin, a fire burned in an array of blues, reminding Katira of the first time she saw the ocean and its crashing waves. A neatly made bed rested in one corner, and in the other a simple table with a single chair. One plate and one tin cup nested on top of each other in the center of the table next to a lone candle stuck in a circle of its own wax. A small pot hung from a hook near the fire. Katira held her hands out toward the fire, still chilled from holding the power, only to find it made no heat.

Darius closed the door behind them and set his palm against it. The lines on his hands and neck glowed to life, not with the bright whites Katira expected, but with the same oily darkness she'd seen on Wrothe's skin. She drew back, the sight of this dark power summoning up fear after fear.

"I knew it, this is a trap." She clenched her fist around her stone and woke her power. The last time she faced Wrothe, she was unprepared. Had it not been for the intelligence hiding within her, neither she nor Isben would have survived. This time would be different. With all she'd learned, she stood at least a sliver of a chance.

"Katira, wait." Isben pushed down her extended arm as he watched the web of glyphs fly from Darius's palm and up around the cabin. "Those look like shielding flows. He's trying to protect us, I think."

"But his lines, they're dark. That makes him just like Wrothe. We have to get out of here."

"No, we need to understand what's going on. Master Regulus's lines were dark too, remember? That didn't make him evil. All it meant is that Wrothe got her hands on him."

Katira struggled to get this fresh onslaught of panic under control. Darius had done nothing that gave cause for alarm, just as the weaves in the flow that pulled them through the barrier reflected none of Wrothe's malice. She calmed herself enough to pay attention to the flows of Darius's power. If he had any part in creating those glyphs in the barrier, she'd see similarities to what he was using to seal the door.

It wasn't a perfect match, but it was close. Close enough to believe he'd been involved.

Darius's flows locked into place, creating a bubble of security around the cottage before fading from view. He struggled to catch his breath as he sat in the lone chair with a thump.

"Oh, be sure to keep your packs either next to you or at your feet. As long as you're still touching them, they shouldn't disappear." He patted a small pouch attached to his belt as if checking if it were still there. "Things tend to return to the place they started. Should you set those down and not think about them for a while, they'll most likely return to your campsite, but there's a chance they'll disappear entirely."

Katira shook her head and took a seat on the bed next to the unnatural fire and Isben joined her. While she'd come to terms with the bizarre reds and purples of the world outside, inside the cottage she found herself struggling to make sense of the overwhelming riot of whites and greys.

He watched them as they took in the small space. "It's not what you expected, is it?"

"I didn't know what to expect. Coming here wasn't my idea."

"It's worse." Isben pressed his face into his hands.

"You okay?" she asked him in a whisper.

"Something about the colors, the silence, it's making my head pound."

Back in the clearing, he'd said something similar, but she hadn't given it a second thought. The sudden change was enough to give anyone a headache until their eyes adjusted. The fact that he was still hurting meant he'd been growing this headache for hours. It wasn't a good sign.

"If he needs food, feel free to help yourself to the mush in the pot. It might help."

Isben swallowed and looked like he was going to be sick. "No, thanks. I don't think I could eat even if I wanted to."

"Hang on, I have something that should help." She rummaged in her pack seeking out the leather-bound roll of tinctures and other medicines she kept stashed inside. She fished out a small vial of willow bark tincture and held it out to him. "Here."

"Does it taste horrible?"

"Do you want that headache to go away?"

He plucked it from her hand. "The whole thing?"

"The whole thing."

Isben downed the vial with a grimace and handed it back. "Thanks. I think."

Darius cast a wary glance out the tiny window beside the door. "We can stay here for a while, but eventually we'll have to move on. This cottage will only provide temporary protection."

"So, I was right. It is dangerous here." Isben had lain back on the narrow bed and flung an arm over his eyes.

"Yes, but probably not in the way you assume. There's only one thing for you to worry about here, and once she catches your scent, she'll be relentless trying to get you." He made a vague gesture toward the door. "Thus, the elaborate warding."

"It's Wrothe, isn't it?" Katira hesitated to ask, but who else could it be?

Darius's face fell. "Please, don't call her that. But, yes. She's ..." he ran a hand over his mouth, clearly troubled. "I stopped trying to understand her ages ago. She's dangerous. Unpredictable. Her trap was designed to bring you in, and I need to figure out why." He shuddered and looked out the window again. "If you're here, you have a right to know. That woman, in all her terribleness, is my bonded companion. Her name is Rose." His voice broke. "She wasn't always this way. "

That caught Isben's attention. He sat up with a jerk. "You're right. You have a lot of explaining to do."

"You must understand, this is a story that is centuries in the making." Darius ladled two servings from the pot over the fire and placed them in front of Katira and Isben with a nod. "The short of it is that I broke something a very long time ago and I've been working ever since to fix it. Please, eat. I insist. The long of it will take more time than we have, but I'll do my best."

Despite her reluctance to eat anything from this world, Katira found herself picking up the offered bowl. When she sniffed at the contents she smelled nothing. The food sent a curl of steam into the air, yet the bowl felt neither cold nor hot. The mush, as Darius called it, looked like something Mamar made during the deepest part of winter when food was scarce. Each day, she'd add more water and a few handfuls of whatever grains they had available, sometimes wheat, sometimes barley or oats. Whatever else joined the pot was determined by what was about to spoil first and ranged from leathery potatoes, tough-skinned winter squashes, and the occasional cut of salted, dried, or smoked meat. All the flavors slowly blended together as it simmered into something oddly comforting.

From the corner of her eye, Katira caught Isben scooping up a small bite and cautiously tasting it. Darius was right. If he could get some food in him, he would feel better. Katira took a bite and was surprised to find that while flavorful, the mush held no warmth. Coming straight from the pot, it should have been wonderfully hot, and it simply wasn't.

"Another quirk of this world, I'm afraid. We can't make things hot or cold." Darius wrinkled his nose. "You almost get used to it. Now that you're more settled, we can all start getting answers. First things first. Which of you triggered her trap?"

Katira swallowed down the spoonful of mush, unprepared for him to ask such a direct question so quickly. "It was me. We wanted to see if the barrier was weaker here, see if it had anything to do with the shadow hounds that have been plaguing the area."

Darius gave an unexpected laugh. "Is that what you call them? Interesting. Rose's pets are definitely a nuisance. We originally created them to help us find a way to return to the real world, an effort that clearly failed. Now, she keeps them for their company. You say they have been plaguing this valley lately? Interesting."

While Darius had been open and straight forward with all he shared so far, Katira couldn't shake the feeling that he wasn't telling them the whole truth. If she could keep him talking, then perhaps that feeling would fade.

"You know more about all this than anyone. Do you know why?"

"I suppose I can make an educated guess." He picked up the tin cup from the table and rolled it between his hands. "This place, the mirror realm as you call it, extends only as far as Stonebearers have traveled in the real world. As few have been this far north in this particular canyon, the barrier is indeed thinner here. It makes it an ideal location for us to test our theories and perform our experiments. Lately, Rose's been meddling with something new and the hounds are part of it. It worries me."

"Why?" Isben set down his fork after eating only a few bites.

"After you've lived with her as long as I have, worry becomes second nature. I've made it a habit to examine anything she's done with the barrier, as her efforts often jeopardize my own. When I saw her intention was to draw someone in from the real world, to use them, I had to act. No one deserves that." His brow furrowed and he pressed his stone between his palms. "So, I changed it. She'll be so angry when she finds out. I couldn't stand the thought of her hurting anyone else."

The distrust Katira couldn't shake from earlier flared up again. "But we're still here, still trapped. What do you want from us?"

Isben took hold of Katira's knee and gave it a warning squeeze. "Stop it, Katira. He's done nothing wrong. He could have left it alone and let her have us."

"And he could have disabled it entirely and left *us* alone." Katira's blood was running hot. If she didn't get answers and soon, she might just burst. "You said you had a lot of explaining. You'd better start."

"Your anger is understandable. I'm no better than a kidnapper in your eyes, and that's fair." Darius held up his hands as if showing he had nothing to hide. "You want the truth, here's the truth. Rose intends to break her way back into the real world, this time for good. I've listened to enough rage-fueled screaming to know just how angry she is about how you took away a victory she'd been planning for centuries. She knew enough about you, Katira, and about your father that she believed if she tormented this area enough, it would draw the two of you to where the barrier was thinner, making it that much easier for her trap to work."

Katira shook off Isben's grip and stood, needing to move, needing space to think. None of what Darius had shared surprised her; in fact, it supported what she'd already believed was happening. What did surprise her was Darius's deliberate sabotage of Wrothe's work knowing he risked her anger. The man was Wrothe's companion, someone who at one point had loved her and would have done anything to support and protect her. For him to act against her meant there were still forces at play Katira didn't understand.

"Why risk yourself for us? There must have been dozens of times in the past you could have stopped her, so why now?"

To Darius's credit, he remained calm in the face of Katira's rage. When he finally spoke, his voice was filled with something that sounded an awful lot like hope. "Because for the first time in hundreds of years, I think I can finally put an end to this misery once and for all, not by fighting against it, but by restoring what was broken." He turned his gaze away from Katira and directed it down to the tips of his fingers. "You must forgive me. Old dreams, they're hard to kill, you know. If I can heal the mistake that created this place, then I can finally make things right."

Katira sat on the stiff bed with a thump. Healing his mistake? What did that even mean? She'd talked about the idea of healing the barrier with Cassim, but always as a way of making it stronger to prevent hounds from passing through. The way Darius spoke of healing seemed much bigger, as if it might put an end to the mirror realm itself. Was that even possible?

"Assuming that what you speak of can be done, why me? Why not any of the other Stonebearers Wrothe sank her claws into before this? If she could get her hands on them, why couldn't you?"

Katira ignored how he flinched when she used the incorrect name. Good. From what he'd shared, he was partly responsible for the pain that madwoman had caused in her life. Causing him some discomfort might help him understand her reluctance to bow down to his every whim.

He turned his full attention on her, enough that it made her squirm. "Let me answer your question with another question. Has your power ever taken control? Formed glyphs you hadn't been taught? Did things you didn't think possible?"

Katira's hands went cold. This was something she'd only discussed with a rare few. "How did you know?"

"You fought against Rose and pulled her influence away from your father. No one has ever done that and kept their life. She said you'd only been training a handful of weeks." He held up his stone with a sympathetic smile. "It means you and the power have a special relationship. It works through you and uses you as a conduit so it can perform miracles, just as it works through me. You're an Innate."

An Innate. Katira had only heard of the term in Stonebearer legend, and then it was only used to describe one person — King Darius himself. For him to use it when speaking about her was wrong. She was just a girl who wanted to follow in her mother's footsteps, but everything he said, about her power taking control, about it working through her, was true. It was too much. The need to get away, to find somewhere where she could sit in silence and listen to the endless parade of her own thoughts, rose up in her throat and threatened to choke her.

Isben leaned in close and spoke in a quiet, reassuring voice. "I've been with you ever since your power woke, seen what you can do. If Darius believes that you are meant to do something great, then maybe you are."

While she knew he was trying to reassure her, the hugeness of what they were both saying couldn't fit inside her skull. She pressed her hands against either side of her head in a desperate attempt to keep it from breaking apart.

Isben rubbed small circles on her back. "It's okay. Take the time you need to think about it." He turned his attention back to Darius and thankfully changed the subject. "You must forgive me if I've been staring at you all evening. You've been dead for centuries. How is this possible?"

"I suppose this is as good of time as any to talk about the reality that is this world." He dragged the tin cup across the table before helping himself to a drink from a bucket near the hearth. "As you've noticed, there's nothing natural about this place. Time itself is stuck in a perpetual circle locked around the day it came into existence. Which means I can't age, can't die, and am trapped reliving the same day for eternity."

Isben's gentle stroking over Katira's back stopped. "But that's crazy. You'd lose your mind."

"If it weren't for Rose keeping me constantly alert, it would have been so easy to do just that. This kind of existence has its challenges. You've already noted the strange absence of sound, smell, and temperature. It's easy to fall into a state where you are numb to everything and simply sit and stare for hours. It makes you feel empty and stupid, and that's not the worst of it."

Isben made a pained sound deep in his throat. "It gets worse? I'm not sure I want to know."

"You need to know so you'll be prepared." Darius laced his fingers and rested them on the edge of the table. "When I fall asleep, the cycle restarts. It doesn't matter where I am or what I've been doing, even if I nod off for a moment, I reappear in the place where the split happened. It takes a while to remember that I've done it before, woke up in this strange place before. My best guess is something similar will happen to you. If you fall asleep, you'll most likely return to the campsite where I found you. At first you won't remember how you got there or what you were doing before you fell asleep." He gestured to their packs. "The same goes with objects. As long as someone is paying even the tiniest amount of attention to them, touching them is usually enough, then they'll stay, but had you set them by the door, they would have disappeared during the course of our conversation."

"You can't sleep without starting over?" Isben nudged his plate away. "That's insane."

"Agreed. While there is one way to prevent the cycle from restarting, it presents its own difficulties. If someone stays awake with you while you sleep, it prevents the sleeper from being reset."

As strange as it was, listening to Darius explain more about the mirror realm proved enough distraction for Katira to regain her sense of calm once more. Isben's hand remained on her back, a warm presence that kept her together when she felt as if she were flying apart.

Without warning, Darius jerked upright and touched the motherstone resting on his chest.

"What is it—" Katira started to ask only to be shushed by his upheld hand.

"Be very quiet and very still. And if you know what's good for you, definitely don't open yourselves to the power," he whispered as he peered through the small window by the front door. "Something crossed one of my wards."

Outside the window, a pair of hounds stalked through a world turned nearly white as true night fell. The grey sheep, who had been silent all this time, bleated in terror and ran to the far side of the meadow, where they stood huddled in a giant knot. Behind the blur of shapes, the distinct outline of a woman came into view. As she drew closer, Katira caught sight of the blood red dress which clung to her every curve, just as she'd seen it back at Amul Dun and Khanrosh.

Darius hadn't moved from his place near the window. "With any luck, she'll only stay a few moments and then be on her way. With the changes I made to her trap, she wouldn't have felt it triggered.

She has no reason to check it or this cabin." He sounded as if he were trying to convince himself.

Isben's hand fell away from Katira's back and he stood, slapping his hands on the table. "If she's bonded to you, that means she can sense you. If anything, you've led her straight to us."

"You don't live hundreds of years without learning a few tricks." Darius waved a hand as if to tell Isben to sit back down. "The moment I felt her trap spring, I created an illusion of myself and came as quickly as I could. If she tried to find me, our bond would direct her to the library in Khanrosh. To her, I never left. Should she try to touch the illusion, she'd find it nothing more than twisted light. But she won't. She's much too focused on her own plans to bother with me."

Katira's mouth suddenly went dry. "Both of us used the power when we first arrived. The residue would still be in the air. What's to keep her from sensing that?"

"She'd need a reason to want to, and we haven't given her much of one. Like I said before, she was trying to entice you back to your hometown. She brings the hounds here so they can pass through the barrier to feed."

"That explains why they've been a bigger problem than usual."

Darius nodded his agreement before continuing. "If she follows her familiar pattern, she won't even open herself to the power. Even if she did, any residue would be pretty thin, hard to read." He finally turned away from the window. The tight line of his jaw relaxed a fraction. "As soon as she's gone, we best be heading on our way as well."

"But ..." Katira started, not wanting to leave the relative safety of the cabin.

"I can't maintain the illusion for much longer. The second it fails, I intend to wall her off, and I'd prefer to be somewhere she won't come looking when I do."

CHAPTER 13

$\mathcal{J}$arand wasted no time explaining what Issa wanted to know, drawing the glyphs he'd used to create the sensing net in the dust at his feet with his cane. Issa tapped her finger on her lip as she studied the pattern with a trained eye.

The last of the day's heat finally faded into the pleasant warmth of a summer's night, filled with the song of crickets, the burble of the nearby fountain, and the comforting scent of cooking fires mixed with the smell of warm earth. Had the situation been anything other than what they were facing, Jarand would have enjoyed sitting and soaking in the rare peace. It was one of the reasons he was drawn to Namragan in the first place.

Issa pointed to one section. "It looks like this part here controls the expanding net. Is it just to detect shadow hounds, or can it detect other things?"

"Just the hounds." Jarand straightened from his work and leaned on the raised edge of the fountain. "I might have borrowed an idea or two from Bremin's design of the warding wall. Instead of deterring them, it sends a signal to whoever holds the net."

She raised an eyebrow as if surprised. "Clever. How precise is that signal? Let's say you were holding it at the cottage, how accurate would your guess be if it is activated?"

"It's accurate enough for what we need it to do. The problem is the amount of power required to use it. The fountain is roughly at the center of the town, so the net doesn't have to stretch as far, but it's still too draining to hold it for longer than a few minutes."

"That's where I think I can help. Lady Alystra had me change a few of the wardings at the Tower so if anything from the mirror realm broke through our defenses again, we'd know about it immediately." Issa crouched to trace a few symbols in the dirt. "I found the same problem, too draining. Thankfully, Bremin and Master Aro had a few ideas that seemed to do the trick." She added a larger circle around the smaller groupings and inscribed a new set of glyphs. "I'd much prefer to lay something like this in place with the help of a Bender, but between the two of us, we should be able to manage."

Jarand studied the new smaller groupings as well as the large all-encompassing one that Issa laid out on the ground. It was a masterful pattern, something that he'd never have come up with himself.

He pointed to an unfamiliar pattern. "What does that one do?"

"It inverts the flows so that they don't glow. Once set, they won't be detectable by normal folk. I thought it might be useful here as we are trying to avoid notice. As it is, it will still glow plenty as the net is placed into position, so we'll need to be careful with the timing."

She brushed the dust from her knees and joined Jarand at the edge of the fountain. "I can see why you wanted to stay here all these years. It's got a lot to offer, things that the Tower can't provide." She released a pent-up breath. "If it wasn't for my duty to Lady Alystra, I'd consider finding a place like this of my own. Stonemother knows, Cassim would be overjoyed to have a change in scenery. I can't tell you how tired he is of spending endless days in either the infirmary or the library."

"She'd be hard pressed to replace you. But if that's what you want, she can be reasonable." In a way, he'd been lucky. The High Lady had practically insisted for him to leave all those years ago. "It would be good for both of you to have a break from all that."

Issa gave a small shake of her head as if to clear it. "No use dreaming when we've got work to do. We should have Bremin take a look at this, make sure we don't blow anything up."

"We don't have time for his perfectionism. You know him, he'd want us to diagram it on paper so he could study it in the cottage — preferably with a mug of ale in his hand. I want this in place as soon as possible." Jarand pressed his fists against the small of his back, trying to relieve some of the ache gathered there. "I'd rather have him doing what he's doing, because those notes he gathered from the barrier might be our only clue to figuring out our next step."

"You're being rash," she flung back. "If either of us made a mistake anywhere, we'll lose far more than time, we'll risk losing the trust of your friend Lucan and gaining the suspicion of everyone in town."

Jarand wasn't used to being corrected. He grit his teeth. Issa knew him better than most, he'd be a fool not to listen to her.

"Fine, we'll get him to take a look. But before that, I best check if we have company or not. I seem to recall that someone interrupted me last time."

She grinned and stood out of his way. "Admit it, even after all these years I haven't lost my touch."

"You've certainly had long enough to practice."

After a final check to see if the square was empty, he summoned his power and brought the pattern into being. The temptation to weave in several of her more subtle groups lingered just within reach. In the end, he chose not to. He'd never hear the end of it if it failed while she was watching.

As he worked, he was haunted by the uneasy thought of what might have happened if someone different than Issa had snuck up on him. He'd been distracted, true. He had good reason to be. But it was no excuse. He was a seasoned warrior, and that kind of distraction would have gotten him killed on a battlefield.

"Wait." Issa's hand went to her sword. "Damn it, they found us first."

Jarand let the unused glyphs fall apart and set down his cane. "What direction?"

"South-east. There's a pair prowling at the edge of the bakery behind the lamppost. Good cover there."

"Keep them here in the square. End it quickly." He drew his sword and brought its glyphs to life.

She woke her blade and held it away from her face with a squint. "So much for being subtle."

With a silent cue, they separated, each taking a different direction to flank the pair of hounds. Two sets of yellow eyes flashed in the flickering lantern light, followed by two mouths full of needle-like teeth.

Jarand paused at the edge of the light to see if they'd attempt an attack or retreat. He didn't have to wait long. One hound lunged at Issa the moment she crossed into the darkness. She dealt a vicious slice down its hindquarters. Its shrill whine filled the quiet of the square as it fled toward the inn. Issa pursued at a run.

He targeted the other hound as it backed deeper into the shadow, crouching low and trying to get away from him. If it managed to slip down the narrow alley and behind the bakery, it would be nearly impossible to find again. He formed a small missile and shot it at the stone foundation of the baker's shop in a bright snap of light. The hound bolted into the open, making for the shelter of the fountain. The last thing Jarand wanted to do was give chase. From the corner of his eye, he spotted Issa strike a killing blow.

It was time to end it. He formed a cutting glyph over his palm.

"That," Issa called out from across the square, "is cheating."

"Not cheating if it gets the job done. Anyone who might have seen us, already has." The remaining hound darted out into the open, presenting the perfect shot. He released his glyph. It soared through the air and struck the hound behind the shoulder blade, and it dropped soundlessly to the ground. A clean kill.

Instead of releasing the power as Issa had, Jarand formed a new sensing net and pressed it into the ground. If there were more hounds in the town, he needed to know.

The net shot along the ground, shining in the pale moonlight as it crossed the square and wove itself between buildings. The harsh pull on his reserves darkened his sight as the net stretched further and further until he reached the warding wall itself. He held it there, again ignoring how his heart struggled to keep up, until he was confident that the threat had been eliminated.

"And?"

"They're gone. At least for now." Jarand looked down to find that their diagram had been spoiled by the fighting. "Sorry about that. I suppose Bremin gets what he wants after all. There's paper in the cottage."

As Issa cleaned her blade and slid it back into its scabbard at her hip, something caught her attention on the other side of the square. The lines glowing at her neck faded.

"There's a different problem we better face first." She jerked her nose toward the other edge of the square where a young man stood staring. "Do you know him?"

Jarand allowed his power to fall dormant as he squinted through the dark, comparing the lad's silhouetted outline to those he knew in the town. This one appeared to be a sturdy chap who held his head at an angle, which made him look as if he wanted to ask a question.

"We're in luck. That's Gonal, my old apprentice. He's about the same age as Katira, she went to school with him."

"Is he going to cause a problem?" Issa's voice fell to a hush that wouldn't carry. She hadn't taken her hand from the hilt of her sword.

"He's a good lad. I don't think so. But he won't keep what he saw a secret either." Jarand returned his stone back around his neck, replaced his sword into its scabbard with a snick, and sought out his cane from where he'd set it down when the fight began. "That said, I've found this age to be unpredictable at best. Stay alert." He turned toward the lad with his hands outstretched, showing that he held no weapon.

"Master Jarand? Is that you?" The voice came out an octave higher than expected before the lad cleared his throat. He didn't run, proving he was braver than most. "I saw the light, heard a ridiculous story I didn't want to believe ..." He trailed off as he struggled to put whatever was in his head into words. "Is it true?"

"There goes your theory about rumors not spreading yet." Issa stepped closer to the puddle of lamplight where Gonal stood, and the lad shrank back. "It was good while it lasted."

Jarand gave Gonal what he hoped was his friendliest smile. "That depends on what you're asking."

Gonal fidgeted with the hem of his sleeve. "They say that you're one of them. That you can save us. Can you?"

He wasn't expecting that. Normally rumors named him a devil and promised trouble. He pressed his fist over his heart. "I will do everything I can to make this town safe. This I swear."

When it was time to leave the cabin, the bizarre burnt black of the sky had lightened through deep rusty reds then to copper with hints of green. The world continued to fade down to its barest details as they walked; a hint of lavender where moonlight spilled over a branch and watery blues and greys where it splashed up on the edges of boulders.

It reminded Katira of waking on cold mornings to find everything covered in a thick blanket of frost. The moon itself shone as a dark crescent in a sea of buttermilk, a sight that was both bizarre and beautiful. Ahead, Darius carried a lantern that brought detail and color back to the ground beneath him.

With all that they'd discussed in the cabin, Katira was grateful that neither Darius nor Isben broke the strange silence. It gave her time to finally piece apart what Darius meant by telling her she was an Innate, and what she needed to do as a result of it.

They picked their way down the trail for the better part of an hour before Darius stopped at a secluded glade near the river and set his lantern on the edge of an old firepit. The trunk of a large fallen tree hemmed in one side of the clearing. At Darius's insistence, they settled in next to it while he busied himself with lighting the fire.

"I know Rose caused a lot of pain in your world." He snapped off a dead branch from the fallen tree and proceeded to break it into smaller pieces over his knee. "She told me enough about her exploits that it makes me ill to think about it. Knowing what's she's done, what she's capable of doing, makes it all the more important to correct my mistake and make it so she can never influence your world again." He carried the lantern back to the edge of the clearing and collected another branch. "But first, you deserve to know the truth about how the mirror realm came to be."

When he returned with the lantern, the light bobbed and danced around the clearing, throwing up wild splashes of color as it went. Isben pressed his hands to his eyes with a soft groan. If the effects of the first dose of willow bark were already wearing off, either it wasn't as effective as Katira had hoped, or the pain was simply too great. She considered giving him the remaining vial in her pack. It might prevent the headache from getting worse and keep him alert. But doing so would leave her with nothing left to give him when the pain invariably returned later.

Darius arranged a few of the smaller sticks in the pit before looking up. "Is he okay?"

She set a hand on Isben's knee and took note of how pale he'd become. "The light and color of this place is giving him a horrible headache. Sleep might help."

Isben gave an irritated huff. "It's only a headache. I can speak for myself. Darius was about to explain how this world came to be. I'd still like to hear it." He changed the subject before she could dig in further or ask questions.

"Ah, yes." Darius drew a small knife that had been concealed beneath his coat and proceeded to peel thin strips of bark from the branches for kindling. "Nearly a century had passed since the completion of our stronghold, Khanrosh. The more connections we made with the people of the world and the further our influence traveled, the more it became clear that we needed a much better way to communicate. Sending a message or aid between different regions took far too long, and people suffered because of it."

He arranged the kindling in the center of the firepit and pulled out flint and steel to light it. "Tell me, are the traveling posts still in use?"

"Yes. The histories say that was Rose's accomplishment, is that true?" Isben's hand fell away from his eyes, his interest piqued.

It took several strikes before the nest of bark caught a spark. Darius nursed it to life and added the smallest twigs from his gathered branches until they caught and grew into a sky-blue fire laced with violet.

"Rose is a talented Bender. It was her talent and hard work that made the traveling posts possible. When it was clear they were a success, a world of new possibilities opened up for us."

With the fire built up and lighting the small glade, it was easier to forget how they were surrounded with a world as blank as a sheet of fresh parchment. Katira shifted closer to Isben and leaned against his shoulder.

"This success turned into her downfall. The posts had too many drawbacks, too many dangers. People still suffered because we couldn't get aid to them fast enough. Each death, each conflict proved to Rose that she'd still failed somehow.

This part of the story hadn't made it into the history books. It caught Isben's attention as sure as a cat spotting a mouse.

"I tried to calm her fears, tried to convince her that our efforts were making a difference for good, that our brothers and sisters had prevented far more misery, had staved off far more wars, than ever before. But it wasn't enough." He fed another branch into the fire, sending a cascade of dark sparks flying into the milky sky.

"I should have seen it coming. Should have known her wild musings were growing from something bigger. She kept talking about how much easier everything would be, how much faster, if we could simply compel our people to act, instead of discussing the matter in council first. The very idea of it went against everything we stand for. Compulsion of any kind is forbidden, always has been." Darius tucked his knees up against his chest and hugged his arms around them.

"She knew I didn't agree, that I wouldn't help her when it came to something like that. So, she tried to do it on her own." He cleared his throat and raised his gaze to the heavens as if pleading for strength. "Her plan was as ambitious as it was awful. She'd tied herself directly to the rich system of motherstone she'd become so familiar with while constructing the traveling posts. With that as her anchor, it gave her a way of linking herself to anyone who wore the stone. Her goal was to bond herself to all who possessed the power. That way she could force them to act when the situation called for it, regardless of if they agreed or not."

Isben flinched and touched the stone hanging around his neck. Katira set her hand over his, hoping to calm how it trembled.

"How could she even consider it?" she asked.

Darius picked up another stick and proceeded to break it into small pieces, one snap at a time. "That wasn't the worst part, if you can believe it. Those binding anchors didn't just seek out fellow Stonebearers, it grabbed hold of innocent bystanders as well. She'd take control of the whole world if she thought it would make it a safer place."

He gripped the pieces in his fist before dumping them in the fire with a sigh. "We fought, her power against mine. Her convictions against mine. She knew better than to draw strength from the well of motherstone beneath Khanrosh, had seen others lose their minds or be killed outright when they tried, but she did it anyway. It broke something inside of her, turned her unpredictable, and warped her judgment."

The pieces burned quickly and fell out of sight. Katira ached for him. This was someone he loved, and he'd watched her descend into madness. She let him continue. Maybe he'd find some relief in sharing his pain.

"It wasn't until she tried to dig her anchors into me that everything went wrong. If Hannah wasn't there, she would have had me. As it was, the combination of all the different powers thrown together amplified each other and warped into something new." He swirled his hands to show the chaos of it. "I drew on everything I had to stop it. I pulled on every last resource, every last thread down to that of my life force itself, but it wasn't enough."

His hands clasped around his knees once more. "All those

connections Rose had made, all those people, all those threads tore apart, and the world tore with it." His gaze fell to the strange blues of the fire. "We tore with it."

CHAPTER 14

As Darius finished sharing the last of his story, the pieces of information that refused to fit together in Katira's mind before, finally snapped into clarity. Wrothe's unnatural strength, how she'd lost her humanity, it all started to make sense. Darius had spent centuries seeking out someone else who could help him subdue that force. No ordinary Stonebearer could do it. It had to be someone with the same unique connection to the power as he had, someone with the same gift.

"Do you think it can be done?" Katira asked carefully. "That somehow we can undo what happened?"

"After a few hundred years of testing and trying different theories, I believe I've found a way." Darius tapped the side of his head. "But I can't do it alone. When the world was broken, it didn't snap apart like a stick. Instead, it peeled away from itself into two opposite parts, the real and the mirror. That's where you come in. You see, I can't handle the threads of the barrier that are rooted in the real world. I imagine the same to be true of you and the threads from this realm. Should we work together, we can reunite each thread with its broken half." As he spoke, he laced his fingers together as if to demonstrate the two worlds fusing into one.

As much as Katira wanted Wrothe gone for good, there was a giant hole in Darius's plan. "The Rose we know would never agree to this. She was part of the breaking, so she'll have to be part of the healing for it to succeed. Does she know what you intend to do?"

A shadow hound howled, its call breaking the night. In the distance, another answered. With all three of them together, it would be hard for any hound to resist the temptation. Darius didn't give the sound any attention, as if hearing those monsters was so ordinary that he didn't notice it.

"Will they seek us out?" Isben asked.

"Will what?" Darius furrowed his brow at the interruption. "The hounds? I doubt it. I imagine they are making their way back to Rose."

"What if they aren't? What's stopping them from hunting us?"

"This world makes hunting harder as there's no scent for them to follow. They won't come after you unless they come upon you by accident, or if they're protecting Rose. And yes, she knows full well about my plan. I wasn't joking when I said I've been working on it for several hundred years. She knows mine, just as I know hers. The difference is, she believes it impossible for me to find the last key piece, an Innate like myself."

Katira touched the small apprentice stone hanging around her neck at the use of that title, *an Innate*. The idea that she could be anything like Darius, the immensity of it, scared her. She didn't know what he expected her to do, but it sounded far too big for an apprentice like herself.

"Just how exactly do I fit into all this? You must have been expecting someone with more experience. Someone older." *Someone like Lady Alystra or Papan.*

He tapped the side of his head. "That's a discussion full of details and explanations. I'd prefer you both to be rested and alert for it. I imagine it's been a long trying day." Darius stood and straightened his fine coat. "If you'll give me a moment, I'll go fetch a few things to make the evening more comfortable."

Isben craned his neck toward the sky, where dark flecks of stars floated in an expanse of white. "How do you tell time in this place? I can't make any sense of it."

Darius glanced toward the moon. "The sun set a little more than an hour ago. You'll be safe here for the time being. I won't be very long. Katira, if you would kindly stay awake until I return, it will make things easier."

She agreed with a nod. It wasn't like she'd be able to sleep anyway, not with Darius's story and her part in it to consider. He swept up the lantern and disappeared into the dull whiteness of the night. Next to her, Isben's head drooped.

She touched his elbow. "You can rest in my lap until he gets back. I don't mind."

"Aren't you tired?" he asked as he made himself more comfortable.

"No, too many things to think about." She combed her fingers through his hair, anything to ease the awful ache there.

"Feels nice."

After several minutes, his shoulders relaxed and he drifted off to sleep. Katira was grateful for the fire Darius had left, although with Isben on her lap, she had no way to continue feeding it. If she didn't, it would eventually burn down to embers and leave her in a blank empty world, a thought that she wasn't ready to stomach.

The moon's dark crescent rose into view through the circle of trees and she was grateful for it. It would help her keep the time, help her from growing too restless waiting for Darius to return. The longer Isben could sleep undisturbed, the better he'd feel when he awoke. She relaxed into the comfort of the rhythmic pull and soft sigh of Isben's breathing paired with the gentle warmth of his body next to her.

The first hint of Darius's return came in the form of sound. While he was gone, the silence was only broken by Isben's breathing and Katira's heartbeat which thumped too loudly in her head. It was a relief when she caught the first faint strains of someone talking in the distance.

Soon, the dark puddle of Darius's lantern bobbed and rocked closer. He carried a pair of bedrolls tucked under his arm. A basket dangled from his fingertips. To Katira's surprise, a sturdy woman followed close behind carrying a large basket that overflowed with books and papers along with a number of wrapped parcels and fruit.

Like Darius, the woman's clothes were too fine for spending time in the woods. Her richly embroidered yellow mantle hung in pristine folds over an equally fine black kirtle. A white belt lined with all sorts of pouches lined her waist, and she wore her hair in two practical braids that were neatly coiled and pinned to the back of her head. Unlike Darius, she smiled easily and radiated a rare type of kindness that made Katira want to trust her.

The conversation died off as they came closer to the glade. Katira wondered if it was because they were discussing something she wasn't meant to hear, or if Darius had told the woman that Isben was unwell and would be sleeping.

"I apologize for the wait. It took a bit to find what I wanted." Darius spoke quietly as set the lantern down by the fire and brought the two bed rolls over next to where she sat. "Any change?"

"It's hard to tell." Katira answered. "He's been asleep this entire time."

"Next he wakes, we best find out. If he's worse than before, then we'll need to discuss our options." Darius turned to the woman he'd brought with him. "Introductions are in order. Hannah, this lovely young woman is Katira. She activated the sequence I set into the barrier. The young man is Isben. Katira, this is Hannah, my personal secretary and good friend."

Hannah's eyebrows drew together as she studied Katira up and down. "I thought you needed a fully trained Stonebearer. She's far too young." Her whisper was loud enough that Katira was sure the woman meant her to hear it. *And she seemed so nice.*

"She's the one. I'm sure of it. We can make our plan work." Darius shot back a withering look. "You must excuse her, Katira.

She hasn't talked to anyone new in centuries and has clearly forgotten her manners."

A fierce blush spread across Hannah's cheeks. "You must forgive me. I didn't mean to offend." She gave a tidy nod. "It's a pleasure to meet you. I hope you aren't as stubborn as he is."

Katira's doubts about the woman dissolved as quickly as they'd come. Something about how she spoke her mind was vastly appealing. She gave a polite nod in return, ensuring no hard feelings.

"That depends on how you define stubborn." Isben stirred and sat up carefully as if trying not to move his head too much. "She can be awfully determined when she wants to be."

"Traitor. I thought you were sleeping."

He watched Hannah as she started sorting through the basket she'd brought. "And I thought we were alone. What's going on?"

"Darius is back. He's brought some supplies as well as his friend, Hannah." She studied him the way Mamar showed her, observing how he moved and learning what she could without bothering him.

At the introduction, Isben's eyes flew open and he made as if to rise to his feet before deciding against it. "Lady Hannah." He gave a stiff formal bow of his head. "It's an honor to meet you." All that movement was too much too soon. Isben clamped a hand over his mouth as if he was going to be sick.

The woman returned his greeting with another kind smile, clearly flattered. "Please, just call me Hannah. I insist." She dug around in the basket she'd brought and fetched out one of the bottles and a pair of cups before offering them to Katira. "Here, some tea for the both of you. It's my own special blend and I find it very soothing. Might help."

Katira took the bottle and the cups with a nod of thanks and Hannah turned her attention back to Darius, who had busied himself studying the collected papers. As much as she wanted to listen in to their conversation, Isben needed her attention. She poured a cup of the tea for both of them and pressed one into his hand.

Isben sniffed it carefully. "Do you think it's drugged?"

"Doesn't smell like it." She took a small sip and was surprised to find it perfectly sweetened with notes of lemon and other herbs. "Drink. There's chamomile and other nice things in there. It won't hurt you."

He watched her for a moment, as if waiting for her to fall victim to whatever might be in the unknown mixture. When she didn't, he took a sip. "Shame it's not hot, because then it would be perfect."

"Did sleeping help at all?"

"A little. Not nearly as much as I'd hoped."

She pulled her pack closer so that it rested against her leg once more and rummaged through it for something that might be helpful. If the bizarre colors and light of the mirror realm caused his headache, then perhaps it would be best to shut them out. Her hand closed around a roll of bandages.

"Choose, would you rather be blindfolded, or risk the headache getting worse?" She held up the roll.

He snatched the roll from her hands and proceeded to wrap it around his eyes. "I'd hate to consider what worse feels like."

When he'd finished, Katira took his hand in hers and let the cold rush of power fill her. A quick delving would be enough to give her a better sense of what was going on. The ache filled his head and radiated down his neck, not so much a throb but a clanging sharp pinch as if his head were being squeezed. While he appeared calm, beneath the surface a gnawing worry rivaled his frustration about not being able to leave.

When she pulled her hand away, he shuddered and drew up his shoulders to his ears. "That's disturbingly cold you know, like having frozen slugs crawl through your veins."

"Sorry." She placed a kiss on his knuckles. "Didn't think about that. Finish your tea. I'm leaving the bottle here next to you, as well as my pack."

"Good thinking." He felt around where he was sitting as if looking for something. "What about mine? We should keep them together."

With a jolt, Katira scanned for his pack amidst the washed-out details of the ground only to find it missing. It had been right next to hers when she sat with him, but it wasn't touching her. She mentally kicked herself for not being more careful.

"It's gone, and it's all my fault. It must have faded away while we were waiting."

He shrugged. "Don't worry about it. Unlike yours, I didn't have anything helpful in mine. A few foodstuffs, some clothes, my writing stuff, that's all." He took another sip of tea, carefully guiding it to his lips so he wouldn't spill. "Go figure out what's going on, and I'll behave myself and drink the tea. It tastes far better than your medicine."

Katira fought the urge to nudge his shoulder as she normally would when he got too cheeky. With him blindfolded as he was, it would spill the tea. If it was helping, then she wanted him to drink as much as he could stomach.

In the center of the glade, Hannah knelt next to the lantern with several of the papers arranged in front of her and ran her finger along lines of text. As she did, Darius leafed through the remaining papers in the basket. Katira had caught fragments of their conversation here and there, something about finding a way for two wielders to work together.

Hannah tapped one of the papers. "Take a look at this."

Darius read where she was pointing. "That's good. Keep track of that one."

She folded the paper and tucked it into one of the pouches at her belt. "You find anything in the Healer's papers yet? I was pretty sure they'd have something to say about this."

"A few things. I've snatched the passages that might serve us. I could have sworn there were more." He handed over half the remaining stack. "See what you can find in these."

When Katira looked back to the papers laid out by the lantern, several had already disappeared. "What are you trying to figure out?" She scooped up one of the papers left behind and found the letters and symbols on it foreign.

The page had been torn from a book. She glanced at the other pages and found with horror that they'd all been. Back at Amul

Dun, the tower archivists cared for books as if they were children. Ripping out pages was unthinkable.

Hannah took notice of her dismay. "Remember, they reappear back in their books as soon as we stop paying attention to them. Same with anything we touch. Same with ourselves in a way. Speaking of ..." She bent over the basket and selected one of the remaining apples and took a bite. "You'd better grab whatever else you'd like from the basket. Whatever you hold onto will stick around long enough for you or your friend to enjoy, but the rest won't." She glanced at Darius. "I don't know when I'll have a chance to collect more."

Only half of the items remained of what was in the basket when Hannah had brought it. Katira selected two rolls, the last apple, and a small wedge of cheese neatly packaged in cloth.

"You didn't answer me. What are the two of you trying to figure out?"

"Oh, that. Sorry. It's two things, actually. The first is one we've talked about endlessly over the years — how two wielders can link glyphs without being companions. Lucky for me, there are a handful of helpful texts on that. Made it easy to grab the pages." She patted the pouch on her belt.

Darius, who had been reading nearby, stepped back into the conversation. "The other has to do with how power originating from the mirror realm will work with that from the real world. Not much written about that, I'm afraid. We have to lean on the little we've learned from Rose and trust that my intuition combined with yours will guide the rest."

There it was again, the belief that Katira would be part of a plan that sounded so big that the chances of them both obliterating themselves while trying was far more likely than she was comfortable with.

"You've made a critical mistake." She set the paper down. "You assume that I'm willing to help you, eager even, all while I don't know if what you're asking is even possible. What you propose sounds insane."

Darius's mouth fell open as if what she was saying made no

sense to him. "But, by doing this you will heal a broken world. Don't you want that?"

"You said you explained it to her, that she understood what you were asking her to do." Hannah rolled up the stack of papers in her hands and thwacked him on the shoulder. "This plan of yours, it's monumentally big. Not to mention more dangerous than any one of us can predict. If you want her to help you, you have to ask her. Nicely."

Darius had the decency to look shamefaced. "My dear Katira, you don't know me, and you didn't ask to be a part of this crazy plan of mine. I suppose haven't made a good argument about why fixing what is broken in the world is so important, or how long I've worked to put this plan into action. I promise to explain everything in as much detail as you need before we do anything. Are you willing to trust me for the time being?"

Katira glanced back at Isben, who sat blindfolded as he nursed his tea, then at the mottled purples and browns of the broken world Darius had been living in for so long. What he was asking her felt right, just like how taking the rod felt right, or how delving the barrier and being drawn in felt right. Whether it be the intelligence within the power, or her own sense of humanity, she needed to be a part of his plan. She was a healer at heart, and this world was sick.

"Yes, but only under one condition." She pressed the apple between her palms and prayed Isben would forgive her. "First, Isben needs to be returned to the real world."

CHAPTER 15

When Jarand arrived at the cottage, he hesitated to open the door. He repeated over and over to himself that this wasn't his home anymore. He shouldn't seek out the pieces of his life that he'd left behind. He shouldn't breathe in the subtle hints of Mirelle's herbs. He shouldn't hope to see her standing at her worktable preparing one of her various medicines. By opening the door, he'd have to face the hundreds of memories he'd pressed into the pages of time.

"Would it be easier if I opened it?" Issa's voice was soft and carried with it a warm understanding.

"No, it's all right. I just needed a minute. That's all." He opened the door the same way he'd yank an arrow from his thigh, quickly and with the expectation of pain.

The first few steps inside were the hardest. Every sight, every smell, every item he touched, brought back fragments of the life they'd lived like shards of glass. The grief struck hard, as if he had never healed from losing her, but had simply found a way of surviving. He couldn't lose himself to it, not when there was work to be done.

Bremin leaned over the table, studying the pages of notes he'd gathered from their most recent encounter with the barrier and jotting down anything helpful that occurred to him. Cassim dozed in a chair, one of the papers still pinched in his fingers. Onyx poked at his free hand, wanting more petting.

Upon their entry, Cassim snorted awake. He set down the page before returning Onyx to the makeshift perch he'd cobbled together in the corner of the room. "I thought one of you needed to stay on duty."

Issa set her sword on Mirelle's worktable, something she would have been scolded for if Mirelle were still there. Jarand didn't have the heart to do it.

"We've figured something out," she said.

"Okay, that's nice." Cassim helped Jarand unbuckle and shrug free of his baldric and belt and set them, along with his sword, alongside Issa's. "I still think one of you should be out there."

"You don't understand. If this works, it will do a better job than any stationed guard." Jarand gathered up the swords and set them in the rack on the wall.

Cassim sagged back into his chair, ignoring Onyx's chirps to be picked back up. "I suppose that's worth considering then. What is it?"

Issa slid a blank sheet closer and stole the pen and ink Cassim had been using to start sketching the patterns they'd discussed. "It's a modified sensing net, similar to what we did at the Tower after the last attacks. I remember most of the sequences. With Jarand's help, we can have it up within the hour." When she finished, she slapped the table with a smile. "There."

Bremin's head snapped up from his work. He'd been too deep in his thoughts to be listening. "Do you mind? Some of us are working here." He glanced at the page pinned under her palm. "What is that?"

"I want to pair Jarand's sensing net with one of Lady Alystra's new Tower wardings, make it so we know the moment a hound slips in regardless of what we're doing." Issa pushed the paper toward him. "All we need is an expert set of eyes on this to make sure it won't blow up in our faces."

"The flattery is nice, but unnecessary." Bremin pulled the paper closer and a hint of irritation crossed his face. He'd never liked shifting his focus when he could help it. But, he wasn't stupid either. He understood exactly what advantages this type of protection would grant. His eyes darted over the diagram with practiced ease.

"This is nice work." He snatched up his pen and altered a few patterns here and there before handing it back. "How soon can you have it in place?"

From his seat, Cassim craned his neck to peer out the small window over Mirelle's worktable. "What about the town?"

Jarand settled himself into his old chair, his tired bones appreciating the familiar curves in the wood.

"We fought off two already, that might be it for the night. But if you're worried, you can stand watch. You could even set your bird out, if you want. She's good at sensing when a predator is near."

Cassim pressed his lips shut and shot a pleading look toward Issa.

"I agree." She joined the three at the table. "Even if they do come, they'll come straight here first. We're not that far from the center of the town. Our time is better spent getting the net in place."

Bremin nodded his agreement. "Who will hold the signaling line first?"

"I will," Issa answered before Jarand could speak.

"No, you won't. I know this town and every building in it." He straightened in his seat, the need to protect Namragan and the people in it surging against his conscience. "When the warning comes, I'll know precisely where they are and what that means in terms of fighting them."

Cassim gave an ungentlemanly scoff that he tried to hide. "By that logic, you'd be the only one who holds it. Bad idea. What if something happens to you, then what? Besides, the town's not that big. Issa will do just fine."

The man had an annoying habit of keeping tabs on everyone, which was one of the reasons he was so good to have on a campaign. He didn't continue his lecture, but Jarand knew where he'd go with it if he did. Issa needed to take the first turn because Jarand had pushed himself too hard ever since Katira had disappeared.

All the same, Jarand didn't appreciate being told he was wrong. "Fine. We do it fair. Four-hour watches. Agreed?"

"Look, I don't care who holds it, I just needed to know before you make the thing. Issa, you form the outer framework, including the additions. Jarand, you'll build your part inside. Wait to spark anything so I can check the sequences."

Issa gave a quick, well-practiced salute and stood to the side of the cold hearth to allow space for the glyphs to assemble. Jarand placed himself in front of her and fought to regain the calm this level of glyph weaving required. He'd rarely interwoven glyphs with anyone other than Mirelle and found he had to summon a far greater degree of focus to keep track of how Issa worked. Glyph weaving with a companion was easier, because the flows themselves were already partially matched.

As the last of Jarand's glyphs fell into place, Bremin came closer. "Hold it a moment."

That was easier said than done. A completed pattern was an anxious pattern. The moment Jarand finished, the pattern itself tugged and pulled at its confines awaiting release.

"Well done." Bremin stepped back a safe distance. "Cue the sparking sequence as outlined."

Jarand locked his gaze with Issa, watching for her readiness just as she watched for his. On her mark, they activated the first patterns, creating a bright ring that surrounded where they stood. With the second, the ring settled on the ground before sending out the net that would encompass the entire town. Jarand grimaced at how his power pulled away from him as if he were a spool of thread. Setting the net was the most demanding part, if they could manage it, then the rest would be easy.

As the last of the net flowed outward, Jarand sensed it catch against something briefly before moving on, as if the fabric of the net itself had gotten snagged on something sharp. The net itself was engineered to only catch on the unique properties of the hounds and nothing else, so any change could mean something.

The last of the pull lessened, then stopped as the net settled into position. As Issa created the tether that would allow them to monitor the net without being drained, Jarand sparked the inverting pattern and watched as the net vanished except for where it wrapped around Issa's forearm. After another moment, that disappeared as well.

"That should do it. How does it feel?" Bremin asked.

Issa held up the arm with the invisible anchor. "Much like those we use in the Tower. I'd call it a success."

"Excellent." Without missing a beat, Bremin turned back to the table and sorted through his notes, passing pages to both Jarand and Issa. "I'd like you to take a look at these, see if you can figure out what any of these glyphs might mean. Cassim and I have pinned down a few, but not nearly enough to make sense of it."

Jarand took the paper. The question about the strange snag perched on the tip of his tongue, but he thought better of asking, especially if Issa hadn't taken notice of it. Figuring out the broken set of glyphs found in the barrier was their best chance to get Katira and Isben back; time spent anywhere else was time wasted.

At Katira's mention of sending him back, Isben lurched to his feet, hands outstretched to keep himself from falling. He knocked the bandaging around his eyes askew, so that it sat crooked.

"I won't go. Not until whatever work you're meant to do here is done." The second he finished speaking, he grabbed his head with a cry and his knees buckled beneath him.

Hannah, who was standing closest, managed to grip his shoulder and slow his fall. She glared at Darius, "I thought you said it wasn't serious. This looks pretty serious to me."

Isben curled in on himself, the same way he'd done when Surasio had used the death oath on him. Only this time, there was no hope that the pain would lift. Katira hurried close and set a hand on his back, anything to ease his discomfort.

"If you still have ...that other vial, can I have it?" he said between shaking breaths. "It might give me enough time to help you."

It wouldn't give him enough time, and even if it did, it didn't matter. It was the only thing that could grant him some comfort. Katira fished out the vial and helped him drink it.

"What was that?" Hannah asked.

"Willow bark tincture. It helps with pain."

Hannah lowered her voice so Isben wouldn't hear. "If the problem is finding more, I can help."

The part of Katira that hated the idea of sending him away leapt at the chance. However, she knew that using the tincture was like using sand to stop up a river. Unless they could stop it at the source, the pain would keep coming.

"The longer he stays, even with medicine, the more likely he'll suffer permanent damage. I can't take that chance. He must return to the real world as soon as possible."

Hannah gave a solemn nod. As all this was happening, Darius kept his distance, his brow furrowed with concern. When Hannah took him aside to speak to him, she seemed upset.

On the purple grass of the forest floor, Isben worked his way to sitting with slow deliberate movements. "See, I'll be fine. Eventually. Is there any more of that tea? That tincture tastes awful."

Katira knelt in the grass facing him. "I know you don't want to go, that you'll do anything, even suffer like this, to stay here with me, but it isn't right. I'm worried about you."

"Don't be. We don't know what the future holds. Who knows, I might get used to this place and be fine." Even as he said it, Katira watched as he swallowed back a wave of nausea. His face had a greenish cast to it.

"The way things are going, I'll consider myself lucky if you are still conscious in a few hours. You have to go back. The mirror realm has taken too much away from me. It can't have you too."

He gripped her arm and forced her to look him in the eye.

"Even without the bond, we're still meant to be companions. That means we're stronger together. I need to stay with you."

Katira forced herself to be brave. Sending him home was the right choice. "You're right, I do need you. But not here. I need you on the other side. You might be the only one who can save me if anything goes wrong."

"Do you think things are going to go wrong? "

"Maybe. I'm scared." She shivered.

Isben reached out to her. When his fingertips brushed against her, he pulled her so close that his breath warmed her ear. "I don't like it. I don't like any of this."

"I don't either, but I need to see this through." She let him hold her and breathed in the vanilla of old books.

When he finally let go, Katira left his side and pushed her way into the animated discussion occurring between Darius and Hannah. She poked her finger against his chest.

"I'll see this plan of yours through to the end, you have my word. But only if you send Isben back. You brought us in, so I trust you know how."

Darius stood dumbfounded at her sudden change, mouth hanging open until he remembered to shut it.

"I need you to be sure. Once we commit to healing the barrier, there's no going back."

She glanced back at Isben before answering. "I'm sure."

"That settles it then. Yes, I believe I can send him back." Darius's scholarly air fell away, revealing a man of action. "First, we need a place here that still exists in roughly the same state in your world. Somewhere he'll be safe when he appears on the other side. I'd hate to send him through only for him to end up halfway inside a wall."

Katira considered all the places in Namragan that might work. The square, while open, was too exposed. The fields outside the gate were a good option, but she wasn't sure exactly where the sheep wall crossed the space. Inside the cottage posed the same problem, there was no telling exactly where it was. Behind the cottage, however, was still wild. She'd roamed those woods as a child and knew each tree and rock.

"Behind my father's forge. It's still wild there in the real world."

"Good. Take us there." Darius tucked a handful of the papers inside the safety of his doublet.

Hannah collected the few remaining parcels of food and tucked them in several pockets secreted around her person. Katira slipped on her pack, unwilling to part with the small amount of comfort it provided, and took Isben by the hand.

When she returned back to the valley that would one day grow into her childhood home, she scanned the edge of the forest, seeking any detail, any feature that looked familiar, and only found differences. The trees crowding the edges of the valley were generations, if not centuries, younger than the ones she'd come to know.

With so much changed, she turned to the contours of the valley itself. She traced the lines of the two imposing mountains on either side and how they shaped the valley floor. In her time, the Kanth river wandered along the eastern edge of the city before twisting to flow under the bridge near the main gate.

She followed the river and found where it turned, tracing her steps as if she were there. The main road would have cut through the center of the meadow with shops and homes on either side. She walked into the forest, letting her memory guide her. Ahead, she would see the fountain and the edge of town square. She counted the invisible houses on her left until it felt right.

"I believe the cottage sits here." She released Isben's hand and imagined herself opening the small gate into Mamar's garden and then through the front door. She walked past the heavy worktable, past the hearth, then the kitchen, then out the back door and into the forge. The sheep wall that separated the forge from the forest lay twenty steps beyond. She scanned the forest floor, seeking out where the land began its climb up the mountain. Several steps to her left, a large granite boulder cut upward out of the long grasses.

She rushed to it, running her fingers along the familiar grooves and ridges. "Here. This same boulder sits outside the wall near my father's forge."

Darius turned in a slow circle as he studied the area. "Perfect."

"No, it's not perfect." Isben protested from where Katira had left him next to Hannah. "What would be perfect is for you to find a way for me to stay. We're meant to be together. Meant to solve this together. You need me." He pulled off the blindfold and squinted into the sudden brightness beneath the trees.

"I will always need you." Katira tugged his head down and pressed a chaste kiss to his lips as she led him to the side of the boulder. "And right now, I need you to share what you've learned with my father. With Bremin. They need to know."

He scowled at her. "You can't just kiss me and expect me to feel better about any of this."

"Fine." Katira raised an eyebrow. "Next time I won't."

It took the space of a breath for her meaning to sink in. "No, wait, I didn't mean it like that." Isben scrambled to change his answer.

Darius crossed his arms, impatience making him look more like a father than a king. "Okay, you two. We best get started. The moment Rose senses me touching the barrier, she'll come to investigate. I'd like to be long gone before she gets here. Hannah, keep watch, just in case."

He turned his attention to Katira, his face far stonier and more serious than she'd seen before. "As for you, I know how much Isben means to you, but I have to ask you to trust me. Stay back unless I tell you otherwise."

"But what if—"

"No buts. I've been a student of the power longer than anyone alive. If I can't do this, no one can."

CHAPTER 16

Katira stepped back to the edge of the small clearing, away from Darius, Isben, and the chunk of granite. Despite Darius's assurances, she refused to stand by and do nothing. She bound her stone to her palm and let the frigid chill of her power fill her. Should something happen, should some need arise, she'd be ready.

Darius summoned his first glyphs in a smooth line before binding them into circles. Again, Katira had to swallow back the horror at how the lines on his arms glowed dark and the ribbons of his power shone in an unworldly black.

Just like Wrothe's.

She gripped her stone until her hand ached. This fear was a reflex, nothing more. The darkness had nothing to do with the intent or madness of the one wielding it. Just as the colors of the world had inverted, the colors of their Khandashii had changed as well. If her theory was correct, Hannah's lines would also glow dark.

If Isben was uncomfortable with allowing those dark ribbons to touch him, he showed no sign of it. Instead, he watched with wide curious eyes as Darius's power danced around him. After all his years of studying the legendary man, seeing him work like this must be a dream come true.

The initial series of glyphs wrapped cocoon-like around Isben until he resembled a spider's egg sac. With the wrapping complete, Darius shifted his focus to the barrier itself, bringing it into view with a new series of glyphs.

No sooner than it became visible, Darius's flows changed once more. Threads of the barrier looped up and around Isben in a dance that rang true to Katira's memory of being pulled through. For the first time since Darius began, she allowed herself to believe all was well.

Then, something shifted.

A change in Darius's flows caused the threads of the barrier to twitch violently as if agitated at the intrusion. A muffled cry pushed its way through the thrum of power and the crackling hiss of the barrier.

"Stop. You're hurting him." Katira's own power surged against its confines.

"I've almost got it. Don't interfere." Darius's face had gone red with the strain. His glyphs no longer flowed in smooth ribbons, but in erratic bursts.

She scanned the forest for Hannah. If there was anyone he was more inclined to listen to, it was her. The woman was nowhere in sight. Isben cried out again and twisted in the bindings. Whatever Darius was doing was hurting him, possibly killing him.

Interfering directly was too risky; one wrong glyph and Katira might tear Isben in half instead of saving him. A single desperate option remained, to join with Darius and force him to see what he was doing through her eyes.

She set a hand on his back and let her power flow, let the connection form, let the sense of him fill her. The hard thump of his heart echoed in her head as it fought to sustain that level of effort. He sucked in breath through his teeth. A wrongness churned around the point where his glyphs interacted with Isben and the barrier.

She pressed in on him, using the full force of her need like a battering ram. "You know something is not right. Withdraw before you kill him."

Through their connection, she felt the jolt of awareness strike him. His focus had been so locked on the process, he'd not realized anything was wrong. His flows slowed, then stopped, and the barrier faded from view. The cocoon around Isben loosened and he fell to his hands and knees.

Katira was by his side in an instant. "Talk to me. Are you okay?"

Darius staggered back and slumped against a tree as he tried to catch his breath.

Isben wheezed as he rolled onto his back. He flung an arm over his face to block out the light. "What in the Stonemother's own name was that?"

"I'm not sure." She pressed a hand to the side of his neck, the delving glyph already flying from her fingers. If Darius had hurt him, king, or no king, she would rip into him like a harrow turning soil. "Don't worry. We'll try again, something different."

"I'd rather not." He shivered and gingerly touched a spot under his ribs. "Right at the end I thought I was going to be sliced into ribbons."

Katira lifted his shirt. A series of welts painted stripes across his chest and belly. Isben wasn't wrong. Had she not stopped Darius when she had, they would have cut him apart.

She stormed over to Darius needing answers. "You nearly killed him. What went wrong?"

Darius released his stone and massaged the mark it left in his palm. "You have every right to be upset. I truly believed my plan would work without Rose's glyphs. They're dangerous even when applied with caution, but now I see they're necessary."

"Why, what do they do?"

"They manipulate whoever she's caught to draw upon their own power, form the glyphs needed to break through." He winced as if remembering something awful. Katira suspected she'd done the same to him more than a few times. "She's so good at it you probably didn't realize what you were doing until after it was done, and worse, it probably felt oddly pleasant. Does any of this sound familiar?"

Up until that moment, Katira had believed that the comfort and peace she'd felt while being drawn through the barrier somehow came from the barrier itself. His description was so exact that it made her stomach twist.

"You see now why I'm loath to try it the same way. Why my attempt failed."

She worked the moisture back into her mouth. "You're saying that for it to work, he needs to create part of the flows that allow him to pass through, but without Rose's glyphs to draw the right patterns from him, he won't have any way of knowing when or how?" She glanced back to Isben who sat with his head between his knees. At any other time, he might have been up to the task. "There has to be another way."

Jarand hunched over the table as he tried to decipher the glyphs on the paper Bremin had assigned to him. As the night grew deeper, he found it harder and harder to focus his eyes. He touched the invisible tether wrapped around his wrist, grateful for the peace of mind it brought. As long as it stayed quiet, the town was safe. Issa had passed it off less than an hour before, and under Bremin's orders, both she and Cassim had retreated into the bedroom to sleep for a few hours.

In some ways, his bond to Katira did the same thing. Worlds apart as they were, the sliver of awareness wasn't much, but it was enough. She was safe.

A soft snore came from where Bremin had fallen asleep with his chin in his cupped hand. Jarand debated whether he should wake the man and send him off to a real bed, or simply let him sleep as he was. In the end, he decided to leave him be. Any sleep was better than none, and if he woke him, the man would return to work.

The stone walls of the cottage held onto the last remaining warmth from the day, keeping the kitchen comfortable enough that

Jarand hadn't bothered to keep the small cooking fire going. Thin moonlight passed through the shutters and created lines on the floor. In the center of the table, a single lantern cast its flickering glow over Bremin's notes. Alone, and in the quiet, Jarand let the memories he'd kept locked away since he'd walked through that door trickle back. He'd cut and placed each beam of the ceiling, hung each shelf on the walls. He'd built this place, every piece of it, with Mirelle by his side and baby Katira perched on her hip.

As he allowed each recollection to come and go, an unfamiliar ripple of power brushed over his senses. It started so softly Jarand wasn't sure if it was real. He homed in on where it was coming from as it grew stronger, calculating distance and direction.

Bremin stirred, blinking himself awake and rubbing his eyes as if surprised he'd fallen asleep. He glanced toward the back of the cottage. "That's disturbingly close. I'll get the others."

Moments later, Issa emerged from the bedroom and collected her sword and its belt from the rack. Cassim followed close behind, his hair sticking up in all directions and his long tunic twisted around him as if he'd been fighting with it.

"Is it just me, or is it coming from just beyond the forge?" Jarand fetched his own sword and left the cane against the wall.

Issa gave a curt nod and buckled her sword belt over her loose linen tunic. "It can't be a coincidence. If Katira has anything to do with it, she might have chosen this place because it is familiar to her." She followed him as he led the way out the back door of the cottage and through the forge. "Or, she can tell where you are, and wanted to be close when she passed through. I'm not complaining either way. Had it been back at the campsite, chances are we wouldn't have made it in time."

Ten paces beyond the low sheep wall, a patch of air shimmered and twitched. Threads of the barrier strained and stretched as if an invisible hand tugged at them. Bremin, who'd managed to get there first, was already examining the opening with his keen eye.

"Did it do that before?" Jarand heaved himself over the wall to get a closer look.

"You might want to give it space." Cassim warned when he

reached the wall. "Those things can slice skin if they snap and you're too close."

Bremin took a single step back. "Do you sense either of them? Are they doing this?"

Jarand held his power at the ready, hungry for every last scrap of information he could wring from the encounter. He'd missed their earlier attempt. He wouldn't miss any part of this one. He fed in a cautious flow and extended his senses into the mass of threads, this time staying wary for any traps. To his disappointment, he sensed neither Katira nor Isben's unique signatures.

Issa stood opposite him, feeding her own sensing flows into the mass. A second set of eyes was always better than one. He pushed further, if their presence was somewhere in there, he didn't want to miss it.

Buried in the writhing mass, a dark flow brushed against his. He yanked back, unwilling to give Wrothe anything to grab hold of. The last time she'd touched him with her dark power, she'd quite literally killed him. If it wasn't for Katira, his heart would have never started beating again. He had no intentions of falling victim to her again.

"There's a dark ribbon of power in there. It's unmistakable."

Bremin hurried closer. "Yes, but is it *her*? Can you tell? Issa, what about you?"

Issa's ribbons remained in the weave of the barrier, cautiously exploring the space Jarand had just left. She closed her eyes as she searched for any trace of what he'd described.

"There. I touched it for a second and now it's gone. But you're right, it is a dark flow." She withdrew from the barrier. "I know it sounds crazy, but I don't think it's her. I sense none of that maniacal anger like we saw at Amul Dun."

Before Bremin could ask anything else, the barrier's hum grew to a roar. The sharp crack of snapping threads filled the air.

"Get back, you three!" Cassim shouted from the safety of the wall.

Jarand didn't need further convincing. A lifetime of facing all manner of danger taught him there was no sense in taking a hit when he could avoid it. He bolted to the shelter of the trees as several threads cracked through the space where he'd been standing.

As soon as it had started, the barrier calmed and faded back into nothingness. Without its glow, the moon's narrow crescent gave little light to see by. Bremin stared, locked in thought, at the place where the threads had appeared. Judging by the deep furrow in his forehead and how his mouth twisted, he was already piecing together what he'd witnessed against the vast stores of information in his head.

Cassim and Issa made themselves comfortable against the sheep wall where they talked quietly. Jarand itched to join them, wanting to know what else Issa noticed while she explored the barrier. Had Bremin wanted to speak with all of them together, he would have returned to the comfort of the cottage. Something was puzzling the man, and Jarand wanted to find out what.

After several long minutes, Bremin let out a pent-up breath and scratched his neck under his scarf. "I can only assume that was a failed attempt to cross the barrier. Nothing else makes sense. If we learned anything from Master Ternan's involvement with Wrothe, it was that she required power from the real world to do so. Whoever was trying to open the barrier this time was trying to make do without." He walked a short distance down the wall, putting more space between them and the other two. "I've been meaning to ask you, did Katira's power take control of her again when she was pulled through?"

Jarand had kept Katira's rare lapses of control secret, sharing it only with those who absolutely had to know. Cassim and Issa were numbered among those few, as they worked closely with her in her training. But he'd not shared Lady Alystra's suspicions that she might be an Innate with a single soul, including Katira herself. Bremin only knew because of his relationship with the High Lady. For him to be asking meant he suspected something, and not something Jarand was eager to hear.

"What of it? She still loses control when something scares her. I'd be scared too." Jarand knew he was in denial. Knew what had happened was something different, something more. He just wasn't ready to admit it to himself.

"You know that's not what I'm talking about." Bremin leaned against the wall and stared into the darkness of the forest. "If this is it, if this leads her to the thing she's fated to do, then who are we to impede that process?" When he returned his attention back to Jarand, sympathy furrowed his brow. "Is this it for her?"

"I don't want it to be." Jarand found himself wringing his hands together. "I'm not ready. She's not ready. I thought we'd have more time before fate showed its ugly head."

"You believe it is, then. There must be something bigger going on here that we can't see just yet." Bremin shifted his gaze to the crescent moon as it crept higher in the sky. "We must assume that things are going to get far worse before they get better. The others need to know, but I'll leave it to you to decide how you will tell them."

CHAPTER 17

Katira hauled Isben to his feet despite his many colorful protests and made quick work of replacing the bandage around his eyes. The sooner they could put space between where they made their attempt and themselves the better.

Darius scanned the surrounding area, his jerky movements revealing the panic that his face refused to show. "No doubt she felt that surge, even down in Khanrosh. We best not linger here too long. Quickly now. Back to the cabin. We'll collect Hannah on the way." He motioned for them to follow as he made his way back through the watercolor violets, greys, and whites of the forest floor.

As soon as Darius was far enough away, Isben leaned in and caught a better hold of her elbow. "Did he tell you what went wrong?"

"He did." Katira did her best to guide him through the tangled woods and found the process too slow.

"And?" Isben pulled back, slowing her even more. "What is it?"

She pulled his blindfold off without warning. "If we don't move faster, Wrothe is going to catch us. You'll have to do without this until we get back."

He winced at the sudden change and pressed his eyes shut. "If you put it that way, fine, but warn me next time."

Katira took hold of his hand once more and dragged him through the woods. "For it to work, he'd have to use Bending glyphs on your mind."

"I don't like the sound of that." The run, even as short as it was, was already taking its toll. The color had drained from his face. "Does he think he can do it?"

"That's what I'm worried about. He doesn't have Wrothe's talent. Any mistake is going to end up hurting you."

He stubbed his foot on a raised root and cursed under his breath. "Why use Bending glyphs at all?"

Darius waited anxiously for them at the edge of the woods. "She's onto us. Get to the cabin, fast as you can. Hannah's set up the warding there."

Isben gripped her elbow tighter, still needing her for balance as they hurried across the purple meadow with its dark mounds of sleeping sheep and through the cabin door. As soon as Darius burst in behind them, Hannah made short work of throwing up the last pieces of her shielding glyph.

The woman fell against the door and dabbed her neck with a handkerchief. "How long until she gets here?"

"Minutes. Enough for me to catch my breath." Darius braced himself against the single chair.

Isben made his way to the narrow bed and snatched the blindfold from where it dangled from Katira's pocket. He made quick work of tying it back on with a sigh of relief.

Hannah tucked the handkerchief back into its pocket. "You better get out there then, be the first thing she sees. Throw her off the scent of these two." She glanced out the tiny window. "Do you need me to come with you? Because I'd rather not."

"No, I'll be fine." He released his hold on the chair. "If you're out there, she'll start asking questions, and we can't have that. Stay out of sight." He stared at Katira, as if waiting for some response.

It took Katira far too long to realize he wanted her promise that she'd stay put. The moment she agreed with a nod, he slipped out the door.

With Darius gone, Katira turned her attention back to Isben. "Are you all right after all that?"

"Okay enough. Now I know for sure that the blindfold is helping, the medicine is helping a little too." His color had partially returned after sitting a few minutes. "I know I said I wanted to stay here with you, but would you be upset if I changed my mind?"

"You really are feeling horrible, aren't you? I hate that I can't do more to help."

"Getting me back to the real world is the best help I can ask for." He reached for her hand and she took it. "Until then, tell me everything. Figuring out things like this is something I'm good at. It'll distract me for a while."

With Darius gone, Hannah settled down in the chair and began removing all the packaged goods from her different pouches and pockets.

She unwrapped one of the cheeses. "What do you want to know?"

"Mostly why sending him back failed." Katira gave his hand a reassuring squeeze. "But anything else you can tell us would be most welcome."

Isben pursed his lips. He hated when she spoke for him, and here she'd done it again. "Katira said something about him needing to use bending glyphs on me to make it work. Do you know why?"

"Ah, yes. Getting to the meat of it. I like that." She sliced the cheese and proceeded to polish an apple on the fabric of her cloak. "The barrier is composed of both real-world power and that of the mirror realm. To breach it, if you can call it that, you need both powers. Darius thought he had it figured out using just one, but you're still here, so I'm guessing it didn't work."

"You can say that again." Isben touched at the sore spot on his ribs and grimaced. From what Katira saw of the welt there, a deep bruise was probably forming beneath it.

Hannah sliced tidy sections of apple and set them on the plate. "The bending glyphs would force you to provide the real-world power against your will. Rose did something similar to that poor soul she'd ensnared in your world."

Katira tried to spot Darius from the small window, but he'd moved to a place in the meadow where he couldn't be seen. Knowing him, it was probably on purpose.

"Are you worried about him facing her alone?"

Hannah glanced toward the window and sighed. "Of course I am. Rose can be downright terrifying when she wants to be." She arranged the cheese on the plate, taking care to lay out the slices in an even line. "The saddest part of all of this is how used to it we both are. Dealing with her is exhausting." She gestured to the modest offering of food. "All that's left to us is to keep trying. I know this isn't much, but I find a snack helps me from getting too worked up. Have you ever tried cheese and apples together? It's quite nice."

The thought of eating while Darius willingly faced Wrothe alone twisted Katira's stomach into a knot. She declined. Isben's stomach, having only subsided on tea and a few bites of mush all evening, gave a needy growl.

"I won't think less of you if you have some." She selected a slice of the cheese, paired it with some apple, and pressed it into his hand. "Here."

Together, they sat in an awkward silence as Hannah arranged the other small food stuffs on the table. Katira wanted more than anything to pull on her power and let it fill her so if anything happened, she'd be ready. But with Wrothe so close, doing so would serve as a beacon. Instead, she was left with the selection of foods on the table and her own tormented thoughts. Maybe Hannah was right; maybe eating would be enough to calm nerves that were stretched to breaking. She took one of the two remaining soft rolls and ate it one tiny piece at a time.

Darius didn't return until the roll was gone and Katira had picked at some of the cheese. He burst back into the cabin, all nervous energy and trembling hands.

"That was too close. She was seconds from checking her trap when I drew her attention away. For all of our sakes, I hope she entirely forgets that she wanted to."

"What did you tell her you were doing?" Hannah held up a slice of the cheese that Darius refused.

"The usual, testing new patterns that might restore a portion of the world. It's not entirely inaccurate."

"So she still doesn't know we're here?" Katira asked.

"Thankfully, no." Darius had begun to calm, his hands no longer shaking. "The longer we can keep it that way, the better."

Hannah stood and offered him the chair. "What are the odds of convincing her to create another trap? It would be far easier to simply use her expertise again rather than trying to recreate it."

"Drawing her attention to the idea of traps is too dangerous. I'd rather not talk to her at all if I can avoid it. It never ends well. But that gives me an idea." Darius tapped on the table as if the idea might desert him if he didn't act. "Paper, pen. I need to write."

Hannah retrieved a small writing case from one of the many pouches on her belt as he snatched up the pen.

She laid out a piece of paper that had seen better days. "This won't last you five minutes. I can go fetch more."

"It's enough. Stay." He removed the cork from the tiny inkwell and dipped the short quill.

"You keep mentioning going places and coming back as if it were nothing, but neither of you are Travelers. Am I missing something here?" Isben asked from behind the blindfold.

With nowhere else to sit, Hannah resigned herself to leaning against the mantle. "You're right. We're not. But here, we don't need to be. In some aspects, this bizarre world is more dream than real. Traveling any sort of distance is more a matter of letting your mind shift to the idea that you're already there and then walking until your body catches up."

Katira must have made a face as she tried to wrap her mind around the idea. The night was growing far too deep for thinking about time and space and how to bend it. She stifled a yawn with the back of her hand.

"Don't think too hard about it, it'll make you crazy." She gestured to the remaining food in front of her. "What matters is that it lets me collect all sorts of tasty delights from anywhere in the world that I'm familiar enough to remember clearly. It's one of my few joys in this place."

Isben sat up from where he'd leaned against the wall. "Are you saying I could visit the home I grew up in if I thought about it and started walking? That I could see the famed library of Khanrosh?"

Hannah smiled at his sudden excitement. "I would take you anywhere you wanted to go if circumstances were different. As it is, we best be careful.

Darius continued to jot down lines and draw diagrams at the table, reminding them why they were there, why the circumstances were what they were.

Isben drew in a quick breath and his excitement fell away. "It works the same for Wrothe, doesn't it?"

Her smile faded as quickly as it had come. "Sadly, yes."

He reached for Katira. "That decides it. We both need to go back. Now. Before she appears on the doorstep."

"Would the three of you stop talking? I've almost got it." Darius dipped his pen and jotted down another few words. "Besides, I'm bonded to her, remember? I'll know if she gets close enough to worry."

Katira pried Isben's fingers loose from where they clung vise-tight to her hand. His determination to keep her safe was admirable, but she'd made a promise and she didn't break promises easily. He released his grip with a quiet apology.

After several more minutes of writing, Darius set down the pen in triumph. "There. That might just do it." He leaned back in the chair and rested his hands over his chest, the very picture of success. "First, I owe you an apology, Isben. My pride nearly got you killed."

Isben released a jaw cracking yawn and made no effort to conceal it. "You did what you thought was necessary. But thank you, I accept your apology. What's your solution?"

"In concept, it's fairly straight forward. I need power from the real world to push you through. Both you and Katira possess it. We'll have to work together."

Watching Isben made Katira yawn again. She wiped at her eyes. "Is this saying you need me? What about that whole of *because you've worked with the power longer than anyone else, that if you can't do it, no one can?"* The words left a bitter tang in her mouth.

Hannah scoffed. "You didn't honestly use that line on her, did you? You shouldn't be surprised that she balked at it, since you know how much I don't care for it."

"I was wrong. There, I said it. Happy? You try being king for a while, it's harder than you think." His grip tightened on the pen and ink splattered on the paper. "Listen. I know what I said. I know how it turned out. I'd like to make it right. Katira, if you're willing to forgive an old foolish man, I'm more than willing to do what it takes to get Isben back so he's not suffering anymore."

"That makes two of us." If it meant getting Isben back to the real world, she was willing to try anything. Still, a string of doubts tugged itself through her tired mind. What if she lost control? What if she failed and it hurt Isben, or worse, killed him? What if she killed Darius?

"There's no guarantee that our powers will combine nicely with each other. There are risks. Isben needs to agree," Darius warned.

Isben lifted his head from his hands briefly. "I agree. I trust her. I'm willing to take the risk."

Hannah shook her head. "No, I can't approve of this. She's too young, and she's untrained. Trust isn't enough. This is foolishness."

"With all due respect, you don't know her like I do." All traces of exhaustion vanished from Isben's voice, replaced with a cast-iron conviction. "You haven't seen what she's capable of. There isn't anyone alive I trust more."

Darius cleaned the tip of the pen and set it back into the small case. "That's all the assurance I need. You two get some sleep. We'll try again at first light."

CHAPTER 18

Sunrise in the mirror realm brought with it the violent punch of color and detail that the night had stolen away. The hope Katira clung to, that the ash streaked white of nighttime was somehow harder on Isben than the crisp dark of day, evaporated as she watched him crumple in on himself and fumble at the makeshift blindfold which kept slipping as they walked. He wouldn't have to suffer for much longer, her intense need paired with Darius's skill would succeed where Darius alone had failed before. It simply had to work.

She tried to distract Isben as they walked, talking about anything and everything, but Isben had few words to share. He allowed himself to be led back to the granite boulder without a single protest.

Nearby, the dark glow of Darius's lines peeked out from the collar of his shirt and from under the hems on his sleeves as he readied himself to start the process. Hannah hovered close this time, muttering something about danger and foolishness as she tried to talk him out of it. When Darius wouldn't respond, she found a fallen tree within sight of the boulder and perched on it with her arms folded, looking every bit like a grumpy pigeon.

Katira led Isben back to the place he'd stood only hours before. "Are you ready for this?"

He pulled the blindfold away and tucked it into a pocket. "I'm not sure anyone could be, but I meant what I said. I trust you. I've seen what you can do."

She leaned in, resting her head against his chest and breathing in the lingering scent of old books and ink. "You're needed out there. When I come back, if I come back, I want your face to be the first thing I see."

He wrapped his arms around her and pressed his lips into her hair. "You will come back. I will do everything in my power to make sure of it."

Darius held out his hands and the first ribbons of power began to flow into their patterns. "It's time."

Katira took one more moment to soak in the comfort and quiet strength of Isben's arms before letting go. She couldn't afford to be weak now, not when Isben needed her.

She opened herself to the power and filled herself with the overwhelming need to send Isben back. In the past, the deep intelligence hiding within the power often waited until her desperation hit its peak. She'd never been successful in forcing it to act before, but if there was ever a time she wanted it, it was now. As her flows rushed over Isben, the connection between them opened. His trust in her was overwhelming and all the more tender knowing he sensed her every last insecurity. She hoped she could live up to it.

If she'd learned anything from their earlier encounters with the barrier, it was that Isben needed a bubble of protection to stop any thrashing threads from touching him. She'd never tried to create glyph-forged armor for anyone but herself. Wrapping each piece around his distinctly different body was both awkward and difficult. As the minutes stretched on, the chill of the power sank deeper. Her fingers lost feeling and her teeth rattled against each other. With the armor complete, there wasn't a moment to lose.

"He's ready," she said.

Darius stepped closer, enough that they were nearly touching shoulders. He brought the flows he'd been forming in front of Isben and awoke them with a spark. Katira felt an immediate pull, as if his power were a magnet and hers was iron. His next flows emerged in hues of orange, guardian force glyphs meant to move and hold. Next, came an array of sickly red that wove into the edges of his pattern and reminded her of a bruise. The presence of bending glyphs sent a shiver of worry scurrying down her back. While Darius had earned her trust, her experience with Surasio had left plenty of hard feelings she hadn't been able to work through.

Darius's flows slowed as he laid his final sequence in place, a series of unexpected purple traveler's glyphs. On his signal, the dancing pattern tightened in on itself and reached for the barrier which buzzed at his intrusion, sounding every bit like a kicked beehive. The comparison was apt; one wrong move and they'd all get stung. The pattern combined with the barrier, forming a rough, glowing surface the size and shape of a door.

"Allow your raw energy to touch the surface and mingle with what's already there," Darius instructed Katira. "The pattern I've built will take hold of it and fill in the gaps."

Katira isolated the flows wrapping Isben's protective armor in place and formed a new ribbon. She had to remind herself that touching this dark power was different, this was for something good, this was for Isben.

When her light flows drew close to Darius's dark, the attraction between the two pulled at each other. She took a steadying breath and allowed them to touch. The instant she did, her inner intelligence burst to life. A sweet sense of calm filled her and pulled her mind into a safe place. The intelligence knew exactly what it was doing, and the raw ribbon of energy flowing from her fingers formed into elaborate flows of glyphs that interacted with the framework Darius created, improving it, correcting it, and filling in the missing pieces.

"What are you doing?" Darius demanded. His maintaining flows shrank back at her unexpected contribution. Wrapped up in the calm as she was, she couldn't answer.

When she stayed silent, he moved as if to stop her. She willed him to wait, to watch, to see that what she was doing made his pattern better. With their power working together, he'd sense her much like she could sense Isben. Before he could do anything, the understanding dawned on him, and his expression shifted from that of an angered schoolmaster to one of a curious child.

He returned his flow of power into the pattern, this time full of eager anticipation. Their two flows melded together, weaving back and forth into the barrier until the surface floating in front of Isben smoothed into a perfect mirror through which reflected the warm greens and browns of the real world. The harsh buzzing faded into a pleasant hum, as if the barrier welcomed their weaves.

Through all this, Isben stood stiffly with his fingers splayed against his thighs to keep from moving. The shimmer of the blue glyph-formed armor radiated around him in a halo. The echo of his confidence, along with the worry and pain he'd tried to hide from her, had grown into something much bigger, pride. He'd trusted against the odds that her gift would manifest, and it did. She met his gaze, hoping that he understood how much she wanted for him to stay if it were possible.

"Isben, are you ready?" Darius asked through the noise.

He gave a clear nod of his head. Katira sensed his grim acceptance.

Darius drew in a handful of his flows and redirected them toward Isben, forming a net around him. "Touch the mirror."

Isben stepped closer and raised his hand, allowing a single finger to brush against the shining surface. Ripples formed as if he'd touched the surface of a calm pond. These ripples bounced off the edges of the frame and grew larger and faster as they returned to him. When they touched him, they didn't stop, and instead climbed up his arm. He jerked back in surprise, but the mirror held him fast. More dark flows extended from the frame and pulled him forward.

He craned his head back, trying to keep his face from touching the rippling mirror until the last moment. Terror rolled off him and through their connection in waves. He looked to Katira one last time before taking a gulping breath and plunging beneath the surface. The mirror rippled again as if his passing were no more than a stone dropped in a pond.

The moment he disappeared, Katira's connection to him stretched until it was spider silk thin. She held onto it tightly, using it as a lifeline to maintain his armor. The barrier fought Isben's presence, wrapping tightly around him and pushing against each crack and weak point as if trying to take and change him. She couldn't let that happen. She strengthened her flows around him, pulling power away from the parts of the mirror that were no longer needed. The frame around the mirror crumpled.

The thread grew thinner, and her sense of him smaller, with each passing minute.

"Is he through? Is it safe to close the portal?" Darius's voice came in a strained gasp as he fought to maintain his hold.

She shook her head. Surely, she'd sense his relief when he reached the real world, and it hadn't come yet.

Something yanked against her flows, nearly tearing them from her grip. She fought to hold on to him as their connection stretched impossibly thin. For a brief second she sensed his fear dissolve and the barrier's assault on him stop.

Then, the connection snapped apart. Katira's flows flailed for something to hold onto as Isben disappeared. She didn't want to let him go. Once she did, she would be alone in this strange space, and she wasn't ready for that.

When she reached for him, she caught a glimpse of the real world reflected in the now still mirror. Papan rushed forward, his power slamming into the barrier and clinging to its edges as if trying to force it to stay open. She gripped her stone tighter, seizing this chance to make him understand that she was okay, that she needed to stay, that she'd return as soon as it was finished. His desperation changed into something more complicated, something she couldn't begin to understand. He didn't withdraw.

Darius fell to his knees, the stream of energy flowing from his outstretched hand growing thinner by the second. Hannah drew closer, stone held at the ready.

Katira untangled her power from the mirror as it started to break apart. "It's done. He's safe." He's gone.

As soon as Darius heard, his arms fell to his sides, and he let go.

The mirror broke apart and fell to the ground in glittering pieces before disappearing like frost in sunshine. They'd done it.

She sunk to her hands and knees. The power's chill had seeped into every part of her. With each pump of her heart, every part of her burned as her body fought to warm itself. She knew the dangers of cold, the signs of when a body's limits had been pushed too far. When muscle tremors struck hard enough to send her to the ground, it was a relief. Cold was a deceptive killer, often comforting its victims before stopping their heart. If she was hurting, she'd live.

No one in Jarand's proud company wanted to return to sleep after the barrier had opened itself behind the forge. Bremin perched back in his seat, inking glyphs and patterns that if worked into the glyph rod might be enough to make the barrier believe both powers were present. Issa took up her seat next to him, attention fixed on one of the papers that he'd just finished. She traced patterns in the air as she considered each combination.

Cassim, on the other hand, busied himself in the kitchen assembling something for them to eat as they worked. Cooking, he reasoned, was not much different than preparing medicines. The biggest challenge was knowing what went together, and what didn't. Soon, sandwiches layered with thick slices of cold chicken and pickled vegetables were stacked neatly on a plate.

Jarand paced the length of the cottage, too agitated to sit, but wanting to hear and weigh each possibility that anyone shared. Bremin's belief about how their situation might be linked to Katira's destiny as an Innate was too big to set aside, as was his order to share his suspicions with Issa and Cassim.

They passed several hours this way, until the first light of day warmed the sky to the east. Cassim left his place at the table and approached Jarand.

"You're doing it again." He snatched up a mug, filled it with warm broth, and pressed it into Jarand's hand.

"Doing what?" Jarand took a sip and found he was hungry.

"You're pushing past your limits. I know you didn't sleep last night, and possibly not the night before either." He scrubbed a hand through his hair, making it stick up more than it already was. "Don't make me mother you. Should something happen and you're too tired to think clearly, you'll never forgive yourself."

Jarand didn't meet the man's eye, choosing to study the surface of the broth instead. "I appreciate your concern. I'm making it harder for you to perform your duty and I'm sure that's frustrating you to no end."

"It's infuriating, really. Things should be quiet for a few hours. I insist you get some sleep." Cassim gestured toward the door of the small bedroom to make his point. "No one would think less of you."

A fresh surge of energy vibrated through the air. Despite Cassim's best intentions, fate had other plans. Jarand immediately recognized Katira's familiar signature within the surge and set the mug down, sloshing its contents dangerously close to Bremin's papers.

Issa straightened. Her full attention tuned in to the subtle change. "Is that ...?"

"It's her. She's trying to get through." Jarand rushed toward the door leading to the work yard. "Come, quickly, maybe we can help from this side."

The disturbance in the barrier hung in the same place as it had before, but instead of an angry flailing mess of power fighting against the barrier, the threads writhed and snaked outward in a coordinated dance.

"Your orders?" Issa asked, poised and ready with her stone in hand.

"Not sure." Jarand opened himself to the power and sent a careful ribbon toward the shimmering mass, testing it to see if he could make any more sense of it than he did before. The barrier's weave near the edges of the mass endlessly folded back on itself as it maintained the shape. Tucked within that weave, Katira's power laced itself tightly within the dark power they'd sensed before.

"Issa, have a shield ready." Bremin hopped over the low wall.

"Whatever comes through needs to be restrained until we know they aren't corrupted."

"Even Katira?" Jarand asked, hating the very idea of his daughter being restrained like some criminal.

"You know how strong she is. If Wrothe has turned her against us, we can't give her a chance to strike."

"Yes, sir." Issa assumed a fighting stance, feet wide and hands ready. A series of shield glyphs spun over her palm.

Cassim and Bremin took up flanking positions, far enough back that they'd have time to react should anything unexpected happen.

The shimmering mass calmed and smoothed until Jarand could see his reflection in broken colors in its surface. He reached out to touch it but stopped when a hand emerged, followed by an arm. These were not Katira's familiar pale slender fingers. Instead, this hand bore traces of ink smudged up the side. Katira must be sending Isben first. Lines of her power chased over Isben's skin alongside those of the unfamiliar dark.

"Keep your distance, Jarand." Bremin warned. "We have no idea what we're dealing with here."

Jarand drew back as the rest of Isben's body emerged. The boy's eyes were clenched shut, as if he were avoiding looking into a bright light.

"Do you still want me to shield him?" Issa asked.

"We can't take chances. If Wrothe's drained Katira and taken Isben as a host, it might as well be her walking back into this world."

She gave a sharp nod and flung her shield the moment Isben stepped clear of the mirror. The force of it knocked him to the ground and pinned him there. With one clean sweep, the shield severed the flows of power laced around him.

With the connections gone, the mirror returned to a glassy calm, but this time it reflected Katira standing with power streaming from her hands. She made no move to leave. A man stood next to her who looked strangely familiar. As quickly as it had formed, the mirror began to crumple in on itself.

Jarand threw his power into the collapsing weaves, hoping he could force it to stay open a moment longer to allow Katira to pass through as well. When she didn't move, he pushed even harder. Whatever hold that stranger had on her, he had a stronger one. He would pull her through by force if he needed to.

Bremin set a hand on his shoulder. "She's trying to tell you something. She doesn't want to leave yet."

"We're so close. If I just grab hold then maybe…" Even then, he sensed her confirming Bremin's words through the thin stretched line of their bond.

"Do you trust her?"

What remained of the mirror had shrunk down to the size of a plate. The collapsing weaves crushed his flows like paper. He pulled them back as the last of the mirror disappeared, taking that short glimpse of Katira with it.

"Of course, I do. But that doesn't mean she has to face this alone." As soon as Jarand released the power, exhaustion struck and his heart stuttered from the strain.

Bremin eyed him briefly. "She won't be. We'll be there every step of the way."

CHAPTER 19

*K*atira shivered on her hands and knees as she waited for the pinpricking angry burn of her body warming itself to fade and her thoughts to quicken. Darius and Hannah knelt close, talking to her, talking to each other. The staccato burst of each pressed question, each urgent phrase, came faster than she was willing to make sense of it.

Through the fog of her thoughts, one thought rang triumphant — they'd succeeded. She and Darius had worked together with their power and pushed Isben back into the real world. He was safe. Cassim would take care of him.

Darius patted her face, as if trying to rouse her, and drew back in surprise. "Your skin. It's like ice."

She lifted her head and cracked open one eye. The unnatural riot of color stabbed at her senses, and she pressed it shut again. "Leave me be for a few minutes. I'll be okay."

"I can't. Rose is coming." He gripped her beneath her shoulder. "We must get away from here."

The name jolted her cold-addled brain back to alertness. She grabbed at Darius's wrist with weak, numbed fingers. "Get me up."

Together, Darius and Hannah hefted her to her feet against the wishes of her legs, which refused to cooperate. She nearly toppled over again. Her frozen joints protested with each step. With their combined efforts, she made it across the field and back to the cabin. As soon as she set foot in the door, Darius broke away.

"I'll go talk to her, see if I can convince her to leave. You two stay out of sight." He straightened his doublet and ran a hand through his hair. Despite everything, he put on a masterful show of duty under pressure.

Hannah guided Katira to the edge of the bed. The soft features of her face twitched with the effort of pretending to be calm. She ran her hands over the fabric of her mantle over and over.

She managed a weak smile between uneasy glances out the small window. "Not sure if it makes any difference, but you're the first to manage using power from the real world here. Congratulations."

"I'm the only one, I imagine." Katira couldn't stop her teeth from chattering. "Why didn't Darius freeze?"

Hannah pulled up the tattered shepherd's quilt and set it around her shoulders. "The real question is, why did you? If I recall correctly, the power is supposed to burn."

"It was cold like this for Isben as well, something to do with us being here." Katira wrapped the quilt around herself and held it as tight as her frozen hands would allow.

"Must be. As for Darius and myself, and Rose as well, feeling that searing heat when we opened ourselves to the power stopped when we broke the world. With the absence of temperature here, I guess it makes sense." She touched the handle of the clay mug. "I can't tell you how much I miss holding a comforting mug of hot tea. It would be the perfect thing to thaw you out." She glanced out the window again and her knuckles went white around the handle.

"What is it?" Katira pressed her teeth closed to keep them from chattering. It did nothing to calm the shivers that threatened to shake the quilt off.

"Nothing that hasn't happened hundreds, no thousands, of times before. Doesn't mean I've grown used to it." A bitter sadness crossed the woman's face. "He'd prefer me not to tell, but it's important that you understand the imbalance that exists between Darius and Rose."

"It's okay. If you're trying to tell me how she's much stronger than him, I already know."

"It's more than that, I'm afraid. Both members of a companionship must be roughly matched in their strength in the power. That way, one companion can't unfairly oppress the other simply because they're stronger. Darius and Rose used to be equally matched."

"What happened?"

Hannah pressed the mug between her hands. "When the world broke, it harmed both of them. For Rose, it tore her mind, leaving her stuck in a state of constant fear and paranoia. Her anger stems from trying to protect herself."

"And Darius?" Katira glanced out the window to where he confronted Wrothe. From the look of it, things weren't going well.

"It broke his power. Weakened him enough so she can take advantage." Hannah set down the mug and massaged the blood back into her fingers. "And she does. As his companion, it's all too easy for her to drain away his power and make herself stronger. He can't fight against it."

Mention of a companion sharpened the ache left by Isben's absence. "But why? Is it just to be mean to him?"

"Yes, and no. She'll do anything to avoid reliving the moment the world broke. By stealing from him, she can remain awake as long as she wants."

The mention of sleep reminded Katira of how little she'd had since she'd arrived. The weight of it pressed down on her, making her feel heavy and slow. "You mean she hasn't slept the whole time she's been trapped here?"

"Not exactly, but lately it seems that way. It makes her more unpredictable than usual. People aren't meant to go without sleep for a reason." She peered out the small window again, this time giving a relieved sigh. "He's on his way back. Promise me you won't say anything."

Katira agreed with a nod that grew into a tremor big enough

that it shook the quilt from her shoulders. Hannah scooped up a portion of shepherd's mush into the bowl and offered it to her.

"I know it's not hot, or even that good, but having some food in you will help you warm up faster."

Darius let himself in and closed the door carefully behind him, as if trying not to make any noise. His shoulders slumped and his feet dragged as he crossed the floor toward the table. Hannah left her chair without a word and joined Katira on the edge of the bed.

"How is everything?" His gaze flicked toward Katira as he asked.

"We're both lamenting the lack of hot food in this place," Hannah answered in a tone that was supposed to sound cheerful, but instead sounded strained. She watched him carefully as he lowered himself into the seat. "What's happening with Rose?"

"She's livid. Beyond livid at this point. With all we've done, we've pushed her right up against her breaking point, and we haven't even started the real work yet." He rubbed at his eyes. "And here I thought healing the barrier would be the hard part."

Katira slid the bowl onto the table, her hands still unwilling to grip anything heavier than a spoon. "I promised I'd help you if you sent Isben back. You kept your end of the bargain. I intend to keep mine. I need to know exactly how you plan to heal the barrier. Tell me everything."

"And I will, but like all complicated things, I'd prefer you to be at your best when I do. Rest a while, get warm, we're safe for the time being."

Jarand extended his hand through the place where the strange mirror portal had appeared, hoping there'd still be some trace of Katira lingering in the air. She'd been right there. He'd seen her, had felt her power woven into every part of the exposed barrier, had felt her commitment to stay. As much as he would have it any other way, she was now in fate's hands.

A strained groan rose from where Issa had Isben pinned so tightly to the dirt that he couldn't blink, let alone speak.

"Shall I continue to hold him?" she asked.

"Cassim needs to check him." Bremin stepped away from Jarand's side to take charge. "Keep him pinned until he's declared clean."

Cassim's brow twisted with questions as he drew closer. "Why would Katira do that?"

"Later," Issa said. The strain of maintaining the shield pinched at her voice. "See to Isben first. This isn't comfortable for either of us."

Cassim blinked, noticing the boy on the ground for the first time. "Yes, of course." He brushed off his impeccably clean hands and adjusted his grip on his stone. "If he has been ... corrupted ..." He swallowed hard. "Delving him will give whatever has him a chance to take me as well."

"None of us will let that happen." Jarand promised, although Cassim had every right to worry. This was precisely how Wrothe had possessed poor Catrim, and they all knew it. "Just think, you will be the first to delve anyone who has entered the mirror realm and returned. You could write a paper about it."

The healer's face suddenly lifted, like a sunflower towards the first rays of morning sunlight. "Well, when you put it that way, let me take a look."

A delving usually only took a few moments. Having needed all manner of fixing over the course of his life, Jarand was more familiar with the process than most. When those moments stretched into minutes, his worry spiked.

What if something had gotten hold of the boy, something worse than Wrothe? Was Katira's unusual calm the truth, or a trick meant to put him at ease? What if something had already taken Cassim, and it was too subtle for them to notice?

Jarand caught Issa's attention and a silent exchange passed between them. He needed answers. She was growing impatient. She furrowed her brow and nudged Cassim, a touch rougher than necessary. "Would you stop already? Jarand's about to chew through his cheek with worry."

"Fine. He's clean. Release him." Cassim rose-colored flows retreated away from the pale blues of Issa's shield. "I found no evidence of Wrothe or corruption or anything else. What he does have is Katira's signature all over him and a massive headache."

Issa cut her flows in a single swipe, leaving Isben shaking and coughing on the ground.

He moaned and clutched his head. "What in the Stonemother's name was that for?"

"A precaution," Issa answered simply as she tucked her stone beneath her shirt.

"Against what? A hoard of shadow hounds? Wrothe herself?" He wiped his face and spat out the dirt from his mouth. "I'd hate to see what you'd have done if you'd found something."

Bremin, who'd been watching the delving intently, held out a hand and helped Isben to his feet. "Do you blame us?"

Isben had been at both Khanrosh and Amul Dun when Wrothe played her hand. He was all too familiar of what she could do. He shook his head. "I suppose not."

Jarand returned his stone back around his neck. "I imagine you have plenty to tell us. Let's get you inside."

Isben stopped at the low wall and set a hand on it as if relieved to see it. "You have no idea how right you are."

CHAPTER 20

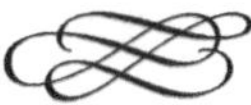

*I*t took a minor eternity for everyone to get settled inside the cottage. Jarand held back the need to grab Isben by the shoulders and demand to know what Katira was doing. The ache to go after her, save her, bring her back, had grown so large he feared he might burst. Judging by the bruise-like dark circles under Isben's eyes and the falter in his step, they wouldn't have long to ask their questions before Cassim put a stop to it.

Bremin ushered Isben into one of the two comfortable upholstered chairs near the fireplace and arranged the remaining chairs from the cottage into a circle around him. At Issa's insistence, Jarand took the other comfortable chair. She had an uncanny knack for knowing when the ache in his back had grown too insistent to ignore.

Cassim was the last to find his seat, having taken a detour to gather a pile of seeds to appease Onyx while they talked. The second he quieted, Jarand let fly the only question he could manage to hold onto. "Is she ...?"

Isben didn't need to hear the rest. "She's okay. Nothing has happened to her."

"Did she intend to return with you?" Bremin asked.

"No, she needs to stay. You won't believe who's behind all this." Isben gave a half smile and shook his head as if he still couldn't believe what he was about to share. "King Darius himself. He's been trapped there this whole time."

Cassim lost his balance and fell off his chair with a loud thud. The room erupted into chaos as they all demanded more information. When he tried to answer one question, another filled the gap.

Bremin held up his hand. "Enough. I trust Isben to tell us what we need to know. Let him talk."

"Thank you." Isben cleared his throat and ran his hands over the faded red of the chair's armrests as if needing time to organize his thoughts.

Jarand opened his mouth to ask another question. The sooner he learned about the dangers Katira faced, the faster he'd be able to form a strategy to counteract them. It was the kind of information Isben wasn't likely to share without prompting.

Issa set a calming hand on his knee. "We've all had a long night, Isben included from the looks of it. Let him talk."

Cassim handed Isben a mug of hot tea with the steam curling up from its surface. "You don't have to do this now if you don't feel up to it."

"No, this is important." Isben wrapped his hands around the mug and breathed in the warm steam. "I'll be okay."

Once Cassim had settled back into his chair, Isben began his tale.

"Our own history tells us that King Darius and his companion died in a tragic accident. His story has been used as a lesson against recklessness when it comes to using the power for as long as anyone can remember. But there's more to it, a part that remained secret for all these years." Isben truly was a storyteller at heart, pausing at crucial moments to build tension before releasing it.

"The accident that we believed killed him was the same accident that created the mirror realm and trapped him in it. When Katira touched the barrier here in Namragan, she triggered a sequence of glyphs he'd placed there in hopes of finding a Stonebearer with the right talent to help him fix his mistake and heal where the world was split apart."

"Why her? Why not any of us?" Jarand blurted out the question before he could stop himself. "Both Issa and I touched the barrier here before she did, why weren't we pulled in?"

"That's where it gets complicated." A trace of hesitation crept into Isben's voice. "King Darius has been waiting for someone with a rare gift, someone through which the power can act as it sees fit. When Katira fought against Wrothe and survived, he had good reason to believe it might be her." He looked toward Jarand. "I'm not sure I'm making any sense. Katira has always been different, but this seems so much bigger than that."

Jarand swallowed down the knot forming in his throat. Across the circle, Bremin gave a small nod. If there was any time to share the truth, it would be now.

"You're right. She is different. We've all seen her do things that she shouldn't have been able to do, things that no Stonebearer has ever done. Lady Alystra believes Katira is fated to fulfill a greater purpose, that her talents indicate she might be something more — an Innate."

A silence hung in the air as the word settled over them. Cassim sucked in a breath and exchanged a glance with Issa.

"But that means ..."

"I know what it means," Jarand said in a quiet voice. "This task set before her will most likely lead to her death."

"That might not be true," Isben offered. "It didn't kill Darius like we once believed."

"No, but it apparently trapped him in a prison with a monster for the better part of a millennium. That's worse than death if you ask me." Jarand rubbed the tension from his forehead. Talking about if his daughter was going to die or suffer something worse wasn't helping. It was time to change the subject. "You said something about repairing the split. What does that mean?"

"It means reversing what happened at the time of the accident and," Isben clasped his hands together which had started to tremble, "healing the mirror realm. If they succeed, the barrier and the mirror realm will no longer exist."

For months, ever since Lady Alystra had first mentioned the possibility of Katira being an Innate, he'd wanted to know what she was fated to do. This was his answer. Each hurdle they'd conquered before was merely clearing the way for her to reach this, the final test. He went cold at the immensity of it. How could one person heal the rift between two entire worlds?

"How?" It was the only question left, and Jarand feared what the answer might be.

"I didn't stay long enough to hear the specifics, but I do know that it requires power from both the mirror realm and the real world working in tandem. I wish I could tell you more."

"You've already told us more than we could ever expect to learn on our own." Bremin touched the papers on the table. "For that, you have my gratitude. Is there anything else you can tell us?"

"What about Wrothe. Did you see her? How much of a threat is she?" Issa asked.

Isben cast his gaze toward the ceiling and gave a wry laugh. "Oh, she's a threat all right, but it's even worse than you think, if that's possible. She's Darius's companion."

Bremin grabbed one of the papers on the table, flipped it over, and snatched up the pen from where he'd left it when they'd dashed out earlier. He scratched off the ink that had dried on the nib. "Are you certain?"

Isben stammered before answering. "Yes. But Wrothe isn't her name, it's what she started calling herself after the split when madness got the best of her. Her name is—"

"Rose," Bremin finished the thought. "A cunning Bender, the histories of that are clear, and what we've seen of her recently confirms it. I can't believe I didn't put the two together before. It's so obvious." He continued to write words and phrases over the paper as they came to him. "That's the key I needed. It's all coming together now. If it was the combination of his and her power that broke the world, he needs that again if he has any hope of fixing it.

Stonemother knows Wrothe won't cooperate in her present state of mind. He needs Katira as a substitute."

"That's why she wouldn't leave." Jarand whispered, sounding too calm for how he felt. He wanted her home. He wanted her safe. He wanted her to have nothing to do with ancient legend, much less anything that imprisoned the ones who attempted it in the first place. There was too much at risk, too much that could go wrong. He flexed his hand, wanting to grip something solid. "This isn't her fight. She shouldn't have to do this."

"While she wasn't given a choice, it doesn't mean that any of this is wrong." Cassim started. "If they can do what they set out to do, we'll never have to worry about shadow hounds or anything else creeping in from the mirror realm ever again. Can you imagine what life would be like without those monsters?"

Jarand glared at him, unamused. Cassim flinched but continued on.

"Hear me out. She's got natural talent. She's young, but she's been able to do some remarkable things. Stonemother knows she's strong enough. If destiny has this in store for her, I can't think of a better cause than to fix what we never knew to be broken."

The room pressed in on Jarand. In the space of a single conversation, his fragile hope that perhaps Katira wasn't an Innate, wasn't destined for something great, fell and shattered. "I need some air."

~

Darius and Hannah had moved in and out of the cabin through the course of the morning, talking in hushed tones, and trying not to bother Katira as she laid curled up under the quilt. She drifted off to sleep listening to their quiet discussions. When she awoke, Hannah was gone, leaving her and Darius alone.

From her spot on the bed, she watched as he poked at the fire's unchanging flames with a stick. He'd been deep in thought for some time, his gaze distant. She hoped he was carefully planning through their next steps, but he might have been lost in a memory. It was impossible to tell.

Stonemother knew she'd been doing a fair amount of thinking over the course of the past day. They'd succeeded in melding their two powers together, but it came at the unexpected price of nearly freezing her to death. Healing the barrier would be much harder. How could she help him if she froze solid in the process?

Darius picked up one of the smaller burning logs with his bare hand and dashed it against the back of the open fireplace. The motion was so unexpected that Katira yelped in surprise as the log exploded in sparks and sent embers tumbling out onto the cabin's packed dirt floor.

"Oh, sorry." Darius brushed off his hands, although they held no trace of ash. "I thought you were still sleeping. I didn't mean to startle you."

In a world where anything he did vanished the moment he let his mind wander, Katira reasoned that being able to destroy something over and over again might be one of the few things that kept him sane. She sat up in the bed and pulled the quilt around her to hold onto the warmth she'd collected inside of it.

Darius sat back in the chair. "After so many years of only having Hannah and Rose for company, it's been strange having someone new to talk to. I know so little about you." He nudged one of the glowing embers back into the fire with a toe. "How do you feel? You had me worried."

She flexed her fingers, testing their strength. "Better now. Although, I'd kill for that cup of hot tea Hannah talked about earlier."

Instead of smiling, like Katira expected him to do, Darius pressed his lips together until they turned white. "I hope it doesn't come to killing. But, knowing Rose, things will get ugly before we finish."

"I can't imagine how hard this must be for you." She watched as he touched the stone hanging over his shirt, something Papan did when he was thinking about Mamar. She couldn't imagine what it might be like to constantly be at odds with someone he had to hold so close. It would be better for both of them to steer the conversation back to safer territory. "You promised to tell me how you intend to heal the barrier. Is now a good time?"

A sound at the door made them both turn. Hannah walked in backward, using her hip to hold open the door as she struggled to carry a large basket brimming with different foods. A long baguette stuck out of one side along with a pair of bottles. Inside the basket, several baking dishes nestled in the folds of mismatched towels.

"To celebrate our success, I've rounded up a few of my favorites. I hope you're hungry."

Darius reached for the bread and Hannah slapped his hand away. "We'll have a proper lunch for once, so no sneaking. You can help by setting the table. With the three of us together, I'm pretty sure we can keep this feast here long enough to enjoy it." She handed Katira a stack of fine black porcelain plates. "Set these out, if you would."

Hannah produced dish after steaming dish from her basket, more than enough to feed a crowd. Beautifully poached fish rested on a bed of blue lettuce. Perfect tiny potatoes swam in a dark buttery sauce. Roasted vegetables of all shapes and sizes dripped with a savory dressing. The crowning dish was a perfectly tender roast that fell apart when Hannah served it.

Katira couldn't help but marvel. Hannah had outdone herself. She served herself a chunk of the bread and delighted in the texture and the sound of it breaking. Unlike the coarse brown bread she'd grown up eating, this was light and airy with a crisp crust.

"Where did all this come from?" she asked.

"The bread, meat, and fish are from the palace kitchens in Fordzala," Hannah answered with pride. "The cheeses are from the green seaside valleys found on the eastern seaboard. The wine is from the coastal region east of here." She set a few glistening apples and a large bunch of grapes on the table. "And the fruit is from the marketplace carts in the valley of flowers."

"When I asked you to find us a nice lunch, I wasn't expecting a feast." Darius served himself several messy scoops of the various dishes. "I guess I shouldn't be surprised, knowing how skilled you are at finding good food."

"I'm also terribly good at finding the information you need from time to time. I'll have you remember that." Hannah placed a final scoop onto Katira's plate and topped it with a swirl of one of the sauces before serving herself and pouring a glass of pale blue wine.

Even with a plate full of good food in front of her, Katira itched to get back to the question she'd asked before Hannah arrived. Talking about it over the meal was as good of time as any. She picked up a small bunch of grapes. "Speaking of information, Darius was about to share his plan about how he intends to heal the barrier."

Hannah took another sip of her wine and set it down with a nod. "Oh good. I wanted to be here when he did. Fill in the gaps if necessary."

Darius arched an eyebrow at Hannah. "It all comes down to our current understanding of the barrier and then reversing what we believed happened at the time of the split." Darius fetched the thick shepherd's plate and set it in the center of the table. He then poured a small puddle of wine on one side and another of oil on the other. "You see, the barrier isn't really a barrier. It isn't like a wall or a door. It's more like what happens when two liquids with different properties, like oil and wine, meet. The barrier is that space between the two where neither one wants to cross the other. It's composed of strands that come from both of these worlds. I believe healing it is a matter of getting the two to mix together once more." He swirled his finger around the plate until they appeared to have mixed. The moment he stopped, the wine immediately separated itself into tiny bubbles that merged into larger and larger ones.

"But this is the entire world we're talking about. There's no way we could possibly heal it all," Katira interjected.

"Technically, it's not." Darius broke off a piece of bread and dunked it into the oil and wine. "Khanrosh was the center of the break, but it only extended outward from there about a hundred leagues, give or take. This valley sits along the outer edge which explains why the hounds can slip through here. For that same reason, it should be easier to begin the healing process here as opposed to at Khanrosh, which is the most affected point."

"So, you're saying that all we have to do to bring the two worlds back together is encourage the strands of the real world and the mirror realm to mix?" Katira studied the oil and wine of his example as another bubble merged together. "Something tells me there will be far more to it than that."

Hannah sighed. "He's done a right proper job of not explaining it at all. Shush, you silly fool. Let a historian have a crack at it." She selected a piece of bread and flattened it against the table with her palm. "Let's suppose this is the world before it was split apart." She gestured to the bread before reaching for the butter. "Almost forgot. Bread always needs butter." She proceeded to coat the flattened piece of bread with the butter and took a large bite.

"Hannah, you were explaining. Don't eat your example." Darius gave an amused smile and waved her on.

"Oh, sorry. Pretend I didn't do that." She tore the bread into two pieces. "When the world was split, a portion of reality tore free. This piece isn't connected to the whole, so time doesn't function here. It's a reflection of that which existed when the accident happened." She then layered the buttered sides of the two pieces together. "The barrier is where the two pieces of bread are touching, which makes the butter the strands of the barrier that I believe are the frayed edges of both worlds. To heal the barrier, we need to press these strands together until they become one again." She proceeded to firmly press the bread together until butter oozed from the edges. "I'm not sure if that helps, but that's what I've got." She proceeded to grab a jar of preserves and spread a layer on top of the squashed bread, which she ate with relish.

"So, which is it?" Katira tore off a piece of bread and dipped it into the oil and wine. "Squishing bread, or mixing water and oil? It seems both will cause a great deal of destruction."

"What we are trying to say is, we aren't entirely sure." Darius took a sip of wine. "But we are willing to try, and that's what's important. With your help, we'll find a way to bring the two parts back together."

The dishes that had once filled the table had started to disappear one at a time. As they finished, Hannah handed Katira one of the fine napkins remaining on the table. "Go ahead and tuck away a few things for later, just in case."

Katira bundled up a wedge of hard cheese, a piece of bread, and a bunch of grapes. "When do we start?"

Darius set down his glass. "Now that your friend is safe, as soon as possible."

CHAPTER 21

A pounding on the door jarred Jarand awake from where he'd dozed off in his chair by the fireplace. He cursed, realizing he must have fallen asleep during his watch.

Bremin, who had been talking quietly with Issa at the table, set down the page they'd been studying. "It would be best if you answered that. Whoever it is seems awfully eager, and not in a good way."

The knocking came again. Bremin collected the papers into a tidy stack and left out the back door with Issa following close behind. Jarand rubbed his eyes in a futile effort to clear the sleep from them before opening the door where Lucan stood with his hand raised to knock again. Behind him, Elan shifted back and forth on the balls of his feet.

Lucan pushed past Jarand and entered the cottage without waiting for an invitation. "The whole town is in an uproar. What happened last night?"

He plopped himself into one of the chairs at the kitchen table the same way he used to do when consulting Jarand about town council matters. Except, this wasn't a town council matter; this had everything to do with him being spotted the evening before, Jarand was sure of it.

Isben, who lay sprawled on the small cot in the corner like a discarded ragdoll, stirred briefly in his sleep. Cassim's gentle snoring remained unchanged as it worked its way through the open door of the bedroom. If Lucan kept talking as loud as he was, he'd wake them both.

Jarand stepped back and gestured for Elan to enter. "Good morning to you too. Please, come in." He did nothing to conceal the irritation in his voice.

Elan gave a curt bow and joined his father at the table.

Jarand's sarcasm wasn't lost on Lucan. "Don't pretend to be pleasant. You know why I'm here. You wouldn't believe the rumors I've heard flying around town this morning. There was a mob at my door at sunrise." As expected, the noise woke Cassim. His snoring had abruptly stopped with a loud snort. "What were you up to?"

"I did exactly what I promised." Jarand collected the mugs scattered around the cottage and carried them to the sink to give them a quick wash. "Gonal talked, didn't he?"

"Of course he did. That boy loves sharing a good story. Although with him, there's no way of separating fact from fiction. Hopefully, most of the town will take all his talk about seeing dueling magical knights with glowing swords as yet another one of his creations. Had I not known better, I would have struggled to believe him as well."

"Dueling magical knights, eh? That's not terribly far from the truth." Jarand rested his forearms on the table. "Had I known he was watching, I would have been more discreet."

"Seeing as no one fell afoul of the beasts last night, you have my thanks all the same. Whatever you did worked well enough." He traced his finger along a dark streak in the woodgrain of the table. "I was surprised when you didn't come to this morning's meeting. Your being there would have dispelled the more colorful rumors."

Jarand glanced over to where Isben stirred in his sleep and lowered his voice. "We had a few challenges that forced us to work through the night. They're not all resolved yet."

Elan scanned the room. His grip on the edge of the table tightened when he realized Katira wasn't there. "Where is she? Is she okay?"

From the moment Jarand saw Elan waiting at the door, he'd been expecting this question. Even with time to consider his answer, he hadn't come up with anything that sounded less than horrible.

Isben stirred on his cot and pressed his hands to his eyes. From what Cassim said, the more sleep he could get, the faster he'd recover. When Elan spotted him, he relaxed his grip and breathed a sigh of relief, which made what Jarand had to say that much worse.

"No, she's not. There's something important she needs to do." As much as he tried to sound neutral, he couldn't help how his voice wavered.

Lucan tilted his head and his eyes narrowed. "You said nothing about this last night. What's going on? Is she in trouble?"

Jarand expected anger from Elan. In the past, the boy had been quick to assume the worst and act accordingly. His hands didn't tighten back into fists, but instead balled together into a tight, worried knot, a feeling Jarand understood all too well.

"If it was important, why would you send her alone?" Elan gestured toward Isben. His voice grew louder with each question. "You promised to keep her safe. Shouldn't you be with her? Shouldn't *he* be with her?"

Isben groaned and sat up in the bed. "We're not with her because we can't be." He looked marginally better than when they'd insisted he sleep for a while. "It's not his fault."

Elan's mouth worked soundlessly, his worry turning into agitation. "But why? There's something more going on, something that's got you troubled. What aren't you telling us?"

"Stop," Lucan said in a low voice heavy with warning. "I trust Jarand to share what we need to know." He turned his attention back to Jarand. "Tell me, old friend, what can we do to help you? Can you tell us where she is?"

"That's where I run out of answers. Explaining where she is, is the easy part. She's in the same place where the hounds come from, the mirror realm." This time Jarand managed to say it without his throat tightening. He found himself wishing Mirelle were there. She had a way of explaining things that put others at ease, even when the situation didn't warrant it.

Isben came to his rescue. He held tight to the frame of the bed and brought himself to his feet slowly as if he didn't trust them.

"If it makes you feel any better, Master Jarand has nothing to do with what's happening to Katira. What's more, he's done everything in his power to help her." He gingerly lowered himself into the last remaining chair at the table. "The best thing you can do for us is to calm the townspeople. Tell them the truth. Some might be angry, but I believe most will appreciate knowing what's going on."

Elan quieted, and he released his viselike grip of the table. "It was you who saved her at the ruins, wasn't it?"

Isben gave a somber nod. "You're not the only one who cares for her. There's something she needs to do. Something only she can do. If it works, the threat of those cursed hounds will be gone for good."

"And if it doesn't?" Elan asked, eyes widening.

"It's a risk we have to take," Jarand said in a near whisper.

"What do you mean? What's the risk?" Elan asked.

"She might not survive." The words rasped like thorns in Jarand's throat. He studied the surface of the table, unwilling to see the anguish erupt across Elan's face. "We'll do everything we can to help her, but we have no assurance that it will be enough."

"But, your powers? Your strength? Do you mean to tell me that with all that, there's still a risk?" Elan stood so abruptly his chair fell backward to the floor.

"It's part of who we are," Jarand said. "As Stonebearers, we carry the burden of knowing one day we'll take on something bigger than ourselves. Katira understands this, as do I. All we can do is hope our sacrifice might make the world that much better for future generations. That said, I'll do everything I can to bring her out of this whole. I hope you'll do the same."

Elan swallowed hard. "Of course, I will." He exchanged a look with Lucan who gave a solemn nod. "We all will."

Lucan braced his knuckles against the table and stood. "I'm sure by now there's an angry crowd gathered at the Mad Rabbit trying to make sense of what they've heard. It would be best if you came and addressed them yourself, told them the truth like Isben said. Can I let them know you're coming?"

The truth. The very thing he'd kept carefully hidden the entire time he'd lived there. The thought of it sucked the moisture from Jarand's mouth. But if he knew anything about rumors, it was that they had a tendency to turn sour if left to themselves. It would be better to put the wilder ones to rest, even if it meant risking turning the anger of the town against him.

He stood to walk Elan and Lucan to the door. "Yes, I'll come."

As soon as possible. Katira had expected nothing less from the man, but still, the prospect of what they were about to do felt far too large to even be spoken about casually, and here he was mentioning it in the same tone he'd use to ask for a cup of tea.

Hannah was already on her feet, gathering up the papers she and Darius had spent the morning debating over and tucking them away in the larger pouch at the back of her belt. "We best head out. The first challenge will be to find the right place. Stonemother knows that might take ages."

"Why?" Katira followed Hannah's example and slipped her pack over her shoulders, making sure she took mental note of all that was in it. Even with her best efforts, some of the smaller items had disappeared, like her comb and a spare shirt.

"It's got to be close to a natural outcropping of motherstone for starters. And it can't be where Rose will think to look for us either." She opened the door.

"Also, it shouldn't be anywhere close to where people might be in the real world," Darius added as he stepped outside into the whites and purples of the pasture. "The wrong kind of interference could jeopardize everything."

"What about where we sent Isben back? Would that work?" Part of Katira craved the familiarity of the place. Ever since Isben had left, she'd felt strangely untethered.

"You said that was close to the rear of your father's forge? How close are we talking about?"

"Perhaps thirty paces give or take, but it's on the edge of the town. The only thing beyond it is the forest."

Darius cast a questioning glance toward Hannah, who shrugged.

"I'd prefer it be more isolated if possible, but the motherstone in that area should be sufficient," she said. "We might as well go take a look."

As they made their way back across the meadow, Katira noted the familiar dips and rises of the ground and placed where the village square fountain would stand, as well as the Mad Rabbit Inn and finally the place where her home stood.

Hannah and Darius walked on ahead, retracing their steps from that morning back to the large boulder sticking out of the ground. When they reached it, they continued on and worked their way deeper into the woods. Katira stopped to rest her hand on the top of the boulder. Somewhere close by, Isben was hopefully sleeping off the last of his headache under Cassim's gentle care at the cottage. Somewhere close by, Papan was coming to terms with what she had to do. No matter what happened, they would be safe.

Katira kissed the tips of her fingers and set them on the tip of the boulder before hurrying to catch up to Darius and Hannah. She found them examining a rocky grotto formed where one of the mountain's many small springs had cut away the softer rock, leaving a narrow pocket with a tiny pool at its heart. Darius ran a finger along the different layers of rock, no doubt looking for sufficient traces of motherstone as Hannah sat fanning herself with a handkerchief.

Katira momentarily forgot the absence of smell in the mirror realm as she tried to breathe in the beauty of the place. She imagined the richness of the dirt at her feet, the unique perfume of wet stone, and how the sharp resiny pine would punctuate the end of each inhale.

"Yes, this should do nicely." Darius brushed the dirt off his hands. "As far as we can tell, this grotto sits right on the edge of the break. If my theory is correct, the barrier should be easiest to work with here."

"Not to mention it will be easier to conceal." Hannah tucked her handkerchief away. "With the right combination of glyphs, it shouldn't be too hard to keep Rose out of our business for a bit longer than usual. As long as there isn't anything here in the real world, I say this is our best option."

"Here, Katira. I want to show you something." Darius pointed to the thin webbing that laced through the stone. "That's what motherstone looks like in the mirror realm. I find my intuition is sharper in places like this. All the more reason to make our first attempt here."

Hannah fidgeted with her stone where it hung around her neck. "The only thing I don't like about this place is how we'll be hemmed in like rats in a trap. It will be that much harder to get away when she comes."

"All the better that she doesn't know where we are. Even if she comes after us, it will take her a while to find us. Enough time for you to escort Katira somewhere else."

Hannah twisted the chain around one finger, as if deciding between arguing or agreeing with him, and then let it go. "Fine, but this better work. If I have to spend another century in this hell, I'll lose my mind." She placed herself in the entryway of the grotto. "Please be careful. I won't be able to watch you as closely as I would like."

Darius waited for Hannah to get settled before returning his attention to Katira. "Might as well get started. Are you comfortable enough? This might take some time."

Katira loosened her stone from around her neck and bound it to her palm. "I don't understand. Is she angry with you? Or protective? Or both?"

Darius held his own stone loosely between his fingers. He lowered his voice so Hannah couldn't hear. "Both, I imagine. I've made her too many promises that I haven't been able to keep. If I were her, I'd be skeptical as well. Healing the barrier would allow her to finally be at peace."

The sentiment struck Katira. She'd always assumed the two were simply close friends, but this hinted at something more. "We best get started then."

Darius tugged his doublet straight. "You've proven yourself more than capable. Trust yourself, trust your instincts and intuition, and I'll do the same. Hannah is far wiser than she lets on, and she'll do everything she can to give us the time we need." He said this last part loud enough that Hannah was sure to hear.

In return, she gave a curt nod that appeared more like a salute.

He wove the series of glyphs into place that made the threads of the barrier visible again. "Take a moment to simply observe the threads for what they are. Take in how they differ from each other and how they are the same."

Katira stepped closer, reassured at the barrier's steady hum. She'd seen it a dozen times, but this felt different. Within the chaos, she found an abstract beauty woven into the colors and pulsating patterns that flowed through the space. If it were possible, she'd watch it for hours the same way she'd watch the sunset transform the world into night.

"My mother used to talk about seeking out beauty amid the chaos of the world, talked about how it helped her cope with all the ugliness she faced. I never thought of the barrier as something beautiful before, but then again, I've never had the chance to really look at it."

"Even the most beautiful things can be deadly, as you well know. Like we discussed, the barrier is where the two worlds touch. As such, half the threads are those of the mirror realm, and the other half are of the real world." He selected one of the threads and isolated it from the rest with a flow of his power. "This thread is from the mirror realm. As you see, it doesn't fight against my touch.

Had it been from the real world, it would have lashed out like a wild thing."

Katira studied the thread in his grasp, trying to tease out what made it different from the others. As she did, she couldn't help but wonder how many times Darius had tried to fix the barrier on his own. "You've tried this before, haven't you? That's why you knew you needed me. You can't touch the other threads to bring them together on your own."

"Exactly." He regarded her carefully, as if he was unsure about something. Whatever it was, it passed quickly. "When you're ready, extend a ribbon into the barrier. In theory, there should be a thread from your world that matches this one. Seek it out."

Katira pressed her stone into her palm, drawing comfort that amidst all this change, it had stayed the same. She'd delved the barrier before; it was what sucked her into this world in the first place. The irony of having to do the same thing to heal the barrier didn't escape her. Opening herself to the power came with a rush of cold as if she'd jumped into an icy river. She expected it, but the shock was just as unpleasant as the flash of searing heat that came when she worked with the power in the real world. Just as with the heat, once the initial surge of cold passed, the intensity faded into a tolerable chill.

Forming a delving ribbon came as naturally as breathing. She guided her flow around his and the thread he held, sensing, learning, and picking out its unique qualities. Darius's dark flow pulsed with a golden glow, like a spring sunrise, which drew light inward instead of radiating out. The thread he held drew in a shade of blue that reminded Katira of the narrow throats of bluebells. This drawing in of light instead of radiating it out must be what marked them both part of the mirror realm.

Then, there was the unique vibration of the energy. Where Darius's felt clean and clear, like the ringing of a bell after it was struck, the thread he held resonated like the deep thrum of a large drum. Maybe that was enough. Maybe all she needed to find was a blue thread with drum-like energy from the real world to make the match.

She turned her attention to the writhing mass of the barrier, repeating the words *Blue drum, blue drum, blue drum* in her head like a mantra, as if she'd forget. Dark, color-eating threads shifted away from her flows in much the same way that soap cleared grease from the top of water, making her search marginally easier.

It still left hundreds, if not thousands, of threads to sift through. *Blue drum, blue drum, blue drum.* Several blue strands winked at her from within the mass. She selected one and studied it. Instead of a drum, this one's energy buzzed like a fat bumblebee. Not a match. She selected another, and another, still not finding anything close to what she thought she was looking for.

When she'd picked up the fat bumblebee thread for the third time, she realized she had no way to track the ones she had checked and the ones that she had not. She pushed the fat bumblebee to the side, deliberately this time, hoping that it would stay put. But as soon as she let go, it burrowed itself back into the mass.

She called back her delving flows and flexed her fingers. The cold was certainly there in her joints, but no worse than working to fetch water on a cold spring morning. Delving held the power but didn't use it. Perhaps the cold would only become dangerous when she triggered glyphs to act. If most of the work was seeking out matching strands, maybe she'd be able to do it after all.

"Don't fret, we have all the time in the world here. Let your intuition guide you." Darius coached.

Her intuition, that's what she was missing. When she'd worked with Darius before, that intelligence had sprung to life the second her power touched his. Why wasn't it waking now when she was doing something so similar? If this was what she was meant to do, the intelligence within the power should have already taken control and showed her the way. She needed to try something different, with the hope that it would spark the intelligence to act.

"The second I let go of a strand, it mixes back in with the others. There's no way of telling what I've studied and what I haven't. Perhaps if we switch, you'll have more luck."

"If you wish." Darius released his strand and it retreated back into the mass of threads. "Select one from the real world and I'll see what I can do."

Behind them was the distinct pop of a cork being pulled from a bottle of wine. When they both turned to look, Hannah grinned back shamelessly over a basket full of books and wrapped parcels that wasn't there before.

"From the looks of it, you won't be doing anything worth catching Rose's attention for hours yet. I figured I had time."

"Your confidence is overwhelming." Darius replied, his tone flat. "Go ahead, Katira, choose your strand."

Katira chose her strand carefully, believing that the right one might make it easier to hold it for as long as Darius needed to find its match. When she spotted a docile strand the green of new spring wheat and radiating the energy of the sweep of a butterfly's wing, she reached for it with a ribbon of raw power as she'd seen Darius do. As soon as she tightened her grip around it, it slipped away like soap in a washbasin. She grabbed for it again only for it to slip away once more.

Clearly, forcing it to be held wouldn't work. Darius's gentle reminder about using her intuition only served to frustrate her. She wanted this; wasn't that enough? *The power is a partnership, it can't be forced.* Papan had repeated the phrase each time she'd tried to force a solution with her will alone.

She calmed her breath, drawing it in and out the way Papan had taught her, and voiced her intentions to the power itself. A spark of that intelligence stirred, not enough to take control, but enough that her mind quieted and the ribbon wrapped itself around the strand.

"Good." Darius's own ribbon hovered close, ready to study her strand as she'd done with his. "It should stay as long as you maintain your focus."

With such a wealth of talent and time perfecting his craft, Katira wanted to learn from every practiced motion and every precise glyph. Whenever her attention followed him, the thread from the real world squirmed in her grasp. Darius pulled back until she regained control and then tried again.

After his fifth attempt to study the thread only to have her lose focus, he drew back with a huff. "I'd like to identify one matched pair and attempt joining them before we call it quits for the day."

"I'm sorry. It's hard not to watch what you're doing."

"You'll have to trust me. Be one with the thread you're holding and pretend I'm not here. I'll do my best not to come close to your flows, which should help."

When Darius tried again, he showed a mastery of control that rivaled that of Lady Alystra herself. Katira did as he asked and kept her attention fixed solidly on the thread in her grasp. After several long moments of study, he sent dozens of seeking ribbons into the threads of the barrier. Each wandered carefully, choosing, studying, separating. It wasn't long before he'd selected one and brought it forward.

"This is where we both need to rely on intuition and trust. I will bring this thread alongside yours and see if they truly are a match. It's my hope that if they are, they will lock together."

Katira nearly lost her grip on the thread again as she listened to his instructions. She calmed herself and sought out that focus and intention once more. "What happens if it isn't a match?"

"I believe we'll both sense it. You will continue to hold your thread, while I seek out another."

That wasn't the answer she was looking for. Unease tightened the back of Katira's throat. The barrier had lashed out when they'd guessed wrong before. If it happened again, they were standing so close that they'd be sliced to ribbons. She tried not to think about it.

"Ok, try it. I'm ready."

With that masterful deft touch, Darius lined up his selected thread next to hers. She sensed its color, its energy. She'd assumed it needed to be green, but Darius had selected a deep pink thread with the energy of a bright horn. The two threads seemed opposite in every way. There was clearly a reason he'd chosen that one, even if she couldn't see it.

Katira willed the two threads to join, willed the intelligence to restore them. As they touched, she braced herself for anything.

Nothing happened.

The threads slid against each other like two slippery fish in a bucket. Darius shifted his thread and tried again, and again. There had to be something she could learn here, something she was meant to see.

She extended the tiniest of delving ribbons toward the threads. The intelligence within the power hovered near, as if it too was watching and listening. It was only when she pressed her ribbon to take a deeper look at the first thread that its vibration expanded from one impression of sound to a distinct song full of harmony and life.

She sent a separate delving ribbon to the other thread, this time seeking if it too had a song. Sure enough, it sang with its own unique voice. When she layered its song with that of the first, the notes clashed against each other.

"They don't match. Can you hear it?"

Darius was busy readying his thread for another attempt to join them together. "Hear what?"

"Their energy. It's like a song, and the songs of these two threads don't match."

He stilled the motion of the thread. "What do you mean?"

"When I delved the two ribbons here, the vibrations reminded me of music or of a sound you'd hear in the forest. My thread made me think of a butterfly in flight, while yours was more like a horn. The more I studied them, the more complex each of their songs became. They didn't match."

Darius let the thread he was holding slip from his grasp. "To think I've been fighting this problem for hundreds of years and I never considered that."

Hannah set down the book she'd been reading and took a dainty sip of wine. "It's because you're no poet, that's why. I might have thought of it eventually."

"Eventually could be a very long time." Darius shook his head and gave Katira a smile. "Let's take a break and regroup before trying again."

Katira couldn't have agreed more. Even without using a single glyph sequence that would have frozen her solid, the persistent cold of holding the power took a toll. She shivered and wished for the real warmth of her real-world sunshine.

As she plucked a slice of seasoned cold sausage from its wrapping and reveled in the taste of peppercorn and fat on her tongue, Hannah pulled Darius to the side where they spoke in low voices. Judging from the serious expression on her face, something had her worried.

They must be talking about her. Maybe her idea was so unfounded, so wild, that Hannah was once again trying to convince Darius to reconsider if Katira was the right choice.

All around them, unearthly white-trunked trees and their purpled leaves stood deathly still like sentries. The silence, strangely enough, brought Katira's thoughts back to all the songs of life in the real world that she used to take for granted. Both Darius and Hannah had been isolated from those sounds for so long that perhaps they'd forgotten.

Katira leaned closer, hoping to catch hints of what they were discussing without being obvious. If she could figure out what she was doing wrong, then she could fix it or try something else.

Hannah lowered her head as if she were ashamed. "I thought it would work better, that it wouldn't take as much."

The statement caught Katira off-guard. It had nothing to her ability or being too young. If anything, it sounded like a different worry entirely. Somehow, that didn't make Katira feel better.

Darius's back was facing Katira so she couldn't hear his answer. He lifted Hannah's chin and leaned in so close that their foreheads touched.

Whatever he told her made her stand straighter. "I suppose you're right. I'll do what I can."

Hannah turned her attention back to the basket and Katira and acted as if nothing had happened. "Oh good, you found the sausage. I thought you might like that. I know Darius does."

Instead of joining them, Darius walked deeper into the trees and set his hand on one of the trunks, his head tilted as if trying to hear something.

"What's he doing?"

Hannah poured a cup of the tea she'd brought earlier and handed it to Katira. "You gave him a lot to think about. He'll return when he's ready."

CHAPTER 22

*J*arand had already taken the time to clean his face and comb his beard and hair and now rummaged through one of the old chests he'd left in the cottage for a clean shirt. It was no use talking to the town unless he looked completely respectable. If he tried as he'd looked earlier, after sleeping in his clothes and with traces of blood still on his face, things wouldn't go well. This time, however, he'd wear his sword openly and roll up the cuffs on his sleeves so that the lines on his forearms showed. There was no use trying to hide what they already suspected.

Issa busied herself with buckling on her armor. Cassim stood in front of her, serving as a makeshift armor stand. He held a pair of bracers in one arm and a strip of leather in his teeth. Onyx took advantage of his predicament by standing on the top of his head and preening his hair like a dutiful mother.

"Have I mentioned that this goes against everything we've ever done?" Issa tightened the last buckle at her waist and reached for her sword.

"A few times." Jarand set his hand on the door and debated whether he needed the cane that rested next to it. "Trust me, facing these rumors head on is far better than the alternative. Northerners might be stubborn, but they respect the truth."

Cassim chased Onyx off his head and set her on the table. She squawked and nipped his finger. "Right. Does anyone else see the irony in all of this?" He turned to Issa, this time clearly concerned. "Are you sure you don't want me to come along? I'd hate it if the mob turned on you. Pitchforks are more dangerous than they look."

She grimaced. "If they turn on us, they'll turn on you as well." She leaned in and kissed him on the cheek. "It makes more sense for you to stay here."

Bremin took a quick glance of who remained in the cottage. "I'll stay at the edge of the crowd. Be a second set of eyes and ears on the ground, just in case."

"Wait, why do you get to go, and I have to stay?" Cassim protested.

"You forget who you're talking to," Bremin said. "I've spent a lifetime being invisible."

Jarand checked the secret knife tucked into the top of his boot. "That's enough. Issa stands as my second. Gonal spotted her last night, and no doubt she's part of these rumors. Bremin, you watch for any situations developing, listen to the whispers in the crowd. Cassim and Isben, stay here. If something, anything, should happen, I want you far from the crowd and ready to respond."

Isben gave an assertive nod, while Cassim gave a wave that could only be described as dismissive. The tether to the warning system they'd put in place glinted on his wrist. "Go already. Your public awaits."

So late in the morning, the square was nearly as empty as it had been the night before. Most would have done their shopping earlier in the day, in hopes of picking out the best fruits and vegetables from the different carts. A crowd clustered around the front of the Inn, waiting for him.

Issa walked next to Jarand with a smooth controlled grace that could transform into a strike at a moment's notice. She kept her silence, preferring to keep careful watch as the marketplace took notice. Somewhere in all of this, Bremin worked his way unnoticed into the crowd.

The whispers started immediately. Ahead of him, a pair of women carrying baskets of laundry halted midstride and leaned in close to talk behind their raised hands. In the crowd, more than a few started to point. The attention made Jarand itch to unroll his sleeves and check his collar, anything to ensure that his markings remained hidden.

"Easy. You're getting tense," Issa said, even as she checked her blade in its scabbard. "Don't give them a reason to second-guess your intentions."

"It's too late to back out, isn't it?"

He'd drawn close enough to the crowd that they'd parted to either side to allow him and Issa to pass through. As expected, first one, then several people gasped as they saw his marks. It might have been his imagination, but it seemed as if the crowd drew back away from him even further.

"You wouldn't, even if you wanted to. You made a promise." He heard the hint of a smile in her words.

Lucan stood on the steps leading up into the inn, waiting. The crowd launched into shouted questions before Jarand and Issa managed to climb the three steps onto the Inn's landing, a noisy mix of demands to know who they were, why he'd lied to them, and what their intentions were.

It took several moments of Lucan staring them down before they quieted enough for him to speak.

"As many of you heard, Master Jarand returned not long ago in the company of several friends," Lucan started, but was immediately interrupted by Stefan, the town weaver, a gangly fellow with more teeth missing than present.

"Wielders, you mean. He's brought evil among us." He pointed to Issa. "She's one of them too."

The crowd erupted into noise again, some arguing against the accusation, and some yelling their agreement. Lucan was right; there had been a lot of talk, enough to divide the town.

"They're the ones responsible for those monsters lurking in our streets!" a woman, possibly the weaver's wife, shouted the moment the noise died down, whipping them all into a frenzy again. It seemed they all agreed on this point. Pity.

Jarand drew in a breath, ready to make himself heard over the crowd, when Gonal joined them on the landing.

"All of you, just stop it," the young man demanded before he realized what he'd done. His face turned an impressive shade of plum when the entire crowd went quiet to listen to him.

He stammered before regaining his bearings. "For weeks we've tried everything to get rid of those things. We can't even touch them, let alone kill them. Last night, I watched as these two brought down not one, but two of the beasts as if it were nothing. If I hadn't seen it, I wouldn't have believed it myself. Those swords they wear, they know how to use them. Maybe we should listen to what they have to say."

Stefan yelled something and was shushed by those standing near him. For the moment, Gonal had captured their attention and quieted their building anger.

"He's right," Jarand said, grateful for the opportunity Gonal created. Mirelle had told him it was always best to give people what they thought they wanted. It was as good a place to start as any. "My friends and I can kill those things. Our goal is for them to never return to the valley again. They aren't welcome here."

The crowd cheered, or at least most of them did. Stefan continued to scowl. Martin, the town brewer, a barrel-chested man with an elegant mustache, had joined him.

"How can we trust you? You lied to us!" Martin's voice boomed over the crowd, causing it to hush once more.

Jarand let his palm rest on the hilt of his sword, drawing strength from the familiar steel. He knew he'd have to come clean. "I admit it. When I lived here, I kept a secret from you. You knew me as nothing more than a blacksmith and a council member. You knew Mirelle as a capable healer. Our intent was never to deceive, but to watch over you and keep you safe."

He drew his sword and set its tip at his feet. Slowly, he drew upon his power and let its heat fill him, let the marks on his arms and neck glow to life, and sent streaks of brilliant blue down the sword's blade. Next to him, Issa did the same. The sight of it sent a ripple of astonishment through the crowd and even Stefan watched on with troubled curiosity. Bremin's red scarf caught Jarand's eye. He gave a signal telling Jarand to wrap things up.

"Many of you don't understand what we are. You fear what those who can wield the power are capable of. But you know me. You knew Mirelle. You know that I would never do anything that would bring harm to anyone. My friends, including Issa here, are good people. You have my word on it."

Just as he was about to release the power, a wave of energy washed past. The shock of it made him forget what he was about to say, and time slowed to a crawl. Bremin was already in motion, slipping out of the crowd and toward the wave's source.

Issa replaced her sword and turned toward him. "Your orders?"

"Follow Bremin, make sure neither of you are followed." He kept his voice low, trying to read what he could of the eddies and vibrations surging through the air. "I'll be right behind you."

There had been a few more shouts from the crowd during this exchange, none of which Jarand paid any attention to. If the barrier was active again, then it could only mean one thing. Katira and Darius were making their first attempt to heal it. He needed to be there.

Lucan drew closer, his brows drawn together. "Something's happening, isn't it?"

Jarand gave a slight nod as he watched those in the crowd move out of Issa's way. "The barrier has reopened somewhere outside of town. I need to be there, just in case." He slid his sword back into its scabbard. "Was that enough truth for now?"

Lucan leaned his weight against the wooden railing and looked down at the crowd, who were growing more restless by the minute. "I suppose so. They'll need some time to consider what you shared. Make their minds up about what it might mean." When he looked toward Jarand, there was earnestness there. "I know there's not much I can do to help, but I'm asking anyway."

"If you can keep the people of the town from turning against me, that will be enough. More than enough."

Lucan patted him on the shoulder. "You underestimate the goodness of people. I think they'll be more understanding than you think."

Before Jarand had a chance to reply, Lucan turned his attention back to the crowd to address the buzz of questions that still hung in the air. Yes, most people were good honest folk, but Jarand had made the mistake of misplacing his trust before and had the scars to prove it.

As soon as Jarand was clear of the crowd, he broke into a lopsided sprint back toward the cottage. The damage Wrothe did to his heart made him weaker, reduced his stamina to a fraction of what it used to be. Cassim would have several choice words for him, but Jarand couldn't bring himself to care.

Isben was convinced that Katira's next move would be to attempt to heal the barrier. Trying anything new with the power was a dangerous pursuit. Doing so while also working to mesh glyphs together with someone else, even more so. Attempting both while engaging with a power-laced entity like the barrier was suicidal at best. He didn't want to consider how Katira's lack of experience made the odds of success that much worse.

When he reached the cottage, he wasn't surprised to find it empty. He grabbed hold of the solid kitchen table and sucked in several breaths as he waited for his heart to stop stuttering. Lady Alystra would have chastised him for chasing down the worst possible scenario before he had any real information. But it was what made him a good General. He was always prepared, no matter how bad a situation became.

He homed in on the ripples and eddies of power washing through the air, letting them guide him back into the forest and along deer trails and hunter's paths. He couldn't shake the feeling that the barrier would close at any second. Even if he could run the entire distance, he'd most likely miss it. He ran anyway, keeping hold of the power to better sense what was happening, to feel Katira more clearly in the mix, but moreover to give him a much-needed boost of stamina. When the vibrations finally dulled, then disappeared, he clung to those last tiny traces of Katira as a small assurance that she was safe.

He dropped back to walking, knowing he was close. When he finally found the grotto, he found Cassim sitting outside its narrow entrance.

"Did any of you make it in time?" Jarand asked between panting breaths.

"Thankfully, yes. Isben got here first. The kid is like a mountain goat, I swear. He's making a full report to Bremin as we speak, best let him get it all out before he forgets anything important." Cassim straightened his tunic and tugged at his sleeves. "Tell me you didn't run the whole way here."

"Okay, I won't." Jarand adjusted his stone from where it slipped from its bindings in his palm. "I need to hear this report."

Cassim grabbed hold of his sleeve as he tried to walk past. "Bremin will tell you what you need to know. We need to talk. Here. In private."

"I don't need your lecturing." Jarand tried to tug himself away, but Cassim held firm.

"I know you don't, but I wouldn't be a good friend if I didn't try." He released Jarand's sleeve once it was clear he was going to stay. "I'll keep this brief. You can't help Katira if you're dead."

Jarand was hoping for one of Cassim's usual "kind-but-stern" warnings, the type that could be easily shrugged off. This was anything but that. The shock of it caught him off guard.

"What do you mean?" He knew exactly what Cassim meant, but he needed the man to somehow soften the blow.

"Exactly what I said. The damage to your heart was beyond severe. Sure, Katira put the pieces back together and managed to get it working again, but you know as well as I do that there are limits. All I'm asking is for you not to push up against yours quite so often."

Jarand's shoulders sagged. He hated looking weak, especially at a time when being strong made all the difference. "I can't promise you anything. Not with this. There's no knowing when the worst has happened until all is said and done. I'm sorry."

"I had to try." Cassim rubbed a hand over his face. "Go on then. Duty awaits."

Inside the grotto, Bremin leaned against one of the walls as he asked Isben and Issa questions. From the sound of it, no one had the answers he was hoping for.

Issa looked up from the knife she was toying with. "There you are. I was wondering how long it might take you to get here."

Jarand ignored her playful jab and dove straight into the first question on the list of many. "Any idea why they chose here and not back behind the forge?"

Bremin patted the rough stone wall of the grotto. "Plenty of motherstone in these layers, good distance from the populated area of the valley, fairly well concealed ... I could go on, but most of it's pretty obvious. What you're really asking is if you believe they'll use this spot again. Am I right?"

Jarand settled against where the rough stone wall jutted forward like a shelf. "And?"

"I don't see why they wouldn't." Bremin joined him and let the toes of his boots dip in the narrow stream. "They weren't successful, but you probably guessed that already. From what Isben told me, they're trying to match up the threads and get them to join. But with so many, it'll be a real challenge to find which matches with which." He picked up a pebble and tossed it into the water with a splash. "It seems the townspeople were being fairly reasonable. It's a good thing you already have a reputation here or things might have turned out differently."

"For now. That could change in a heartbeat if anything happens. For their sake and ours, I hope this barrier business stays in isolated places. Felix was doing something much more subtle when they caught him, and they nearly strung him up. I can only imagine how they'd react if they caught sight of the barrier when it's open."

"Agreed. For now, it's best we stay here for a while, see what happens." Bremin drew in a deep breath. The air in the grotto was wonderfully cool compared to the rising heat of the day. "I can think of worse places to work."

CHAPTER 23

Katira sat with Hannah and picked at the grapes and cheese still in the basket. As she waited for Darius to return, she mulled over the pieces of the conversation she wasn't supposed to be listening to and tried to piece together what Hannah had been worried about. It didn't seem right to ask the woman directly, and Hannah hadn't seemed eager to talk either.

It wasn't until she spotted Darius wandering back that she had formed a theory of what might be going on. Hannah wasn't just watching over them, she was testing what it would take to shield their actions from Wrothe. They'd hadn't needed it, as they hadn't managed to join a thread, but sometime while they worked she must have realized that she wouldn't be able to hold a shield for nearly as long as the work would require.

Without something blocking Wrothe from sensing them work, they wouldn't have enough time to do much of anything.

When Darius reached them, he set a hand on Hannah's shoulder and they exchanged an unspoken greeting. He poured himself a cup of the tea and took a deep drink.

"Right. We best see if that idea of yours works. Would you like to hold or to seek this time?"

Katira got to her feet and popped one last grape into her mouth. "Seek. I think I know what I'm looking for now."

"Good. Let your intuition guide you, and we'll see what happens." He ushered her into the sheltered space of the grotto.

Inside, Katira turned to him. "Should I be worried about Hannah? She seemed upset." She kept her voice low. If her theory was correct, she needed to know.

He raised an eyebrow. "Last I checked, eavesdropping was considered rude."

"I don't like secrets."

He returned his stone back into his palm. "Her concerns are between me and her. Trust that she'll do everything she can to give us the time we need."

Katira bound her own stone to her palm, letting the familiar motions ready her for the task ahead. His answer didn't satisfy her, but it was enough.

Darius watched on with interest. "Why do you do that?"

"Do what?"

"Wrap your stone and tie it?"

"It's what I was taught to do. No matter what happens, it stays touching skin."

Darius grunted in amusement. "Interesting. Never really thought about doing that. I've always held it. The flows never seemed to mind." As he spoke, the series of glyphs for bringing the barrier into view danced over his hand, and he sparked it to life. He selected a thread from the mirror realm and brought it forward. "Whenever you're ready."

Katira invited the power's icy rush to fill her and extended her awareness along his newly captured thread. Fresh determination straightened her spine and put a fire in her bones. She drew in the thread's personality like drawing in breath, a warm purple like the deepest part of a flame, and its energy, like wind through a chimney. Her delving flow settled deeper, revealing the thread's true song, a rich symphony of energy and vibration.

She let this deeper, more complicated song fill her until it resonated alongside the thrum of her own power. With it, she extended herself into the mass of threads, letting the song course along her seeking ribbons. Threads shimmered and danced as her ribbons came close, some darting away, some leaning in, as if they too were listening.

Darius had taken notice but thankfully held his tongue. Any other sound would make holding the song that much more difficult. She blocked out everything except the dance, the music, and the way the threads called out in response.

And then, she heard it.

A melody beckoned to her, its song weaving itself around hers and harmonizing in a way that could only be described as perfect. She sank her delving ribbons into the mass of threads, seeking out the source of the melody until only a handful of threads stood out from the rest. She tested each one, seeking that match, that perfect harmony, until she was sure.

She willed a ribbon of raw power to wrap around the matching thread and drew it out until it rested alongside Darius's. As she carried it, she had the impression that what she held wasn't just a thread, but was something more, something vibrant and alive. The songs of the two threads sang brilliantly against each other and a joyful anticipation radiated within the sound. She sought out a point on Darius's thread where the harmonies locked together. When she found it, she allowed the two threads to touch.

The song continued, but the threads did not join.

It should have worked. She had done precisely what Darius did when he found what he believed to be a match. *Trust your intuition,* he'd said. She'd assumed that meant for her to allow the intelligence within her power to act, but again it had stayed distant. She'd have to figure it out herself.

When performing other work with the power, the sequences needed to be activated with a spark, and maybe this was no different. Katira touched a bright spark to the point where the harmonies intertwined. Darius, who had been watching closely, did the same.

The moment the two sparks touched, they formed a brilliant point of light that then shot down the threads. Slowly at first, but then faster and faster, the threads drew on Katira's power as they began to fuse together. She braced herself against the strain. Her vision narrowed down to the that singular point where the threads continued to fuse.

Near her, Darius uttered a strangled cry. Hannah leapt to her feet and activated the shielding around the grotto before hurrying closer. If healing each of the threads pulled at that rate, it wouldn't be long before they'd both be drained to husks.

Tight bands wrapped around Katira's chest and her head prickled as swirls of ice laced up her arms. Hannah reached out to Darius just as the two threads finished. In their place hung two glowing orbs, one shining with a bright white light, the other glowing darkly.

Katira stumbled on her cold deadened feet. "What are those?"

"Not sure. I believe it's a gift." Darius touched the dark shining sphere. It melted over his hand and sank through his skin. He breathed out a sigh of relief and stood straighter. Color returned to his face. "Quickly, take yours before it fades away."

With Hannah's support, Katira reached out and touched the brilliant ball of light, and it shivered under her fingers like a living thing before melting over her hand and racing up the lines of her power. It was wonderfully warm and eased the pain from where the cold had frozen her solid. When it reached her heart, it curled into her and resonated a sense of peace and gratitude.

Hannah didn't release Katira right away. Her brow was still knotted with worry. "That was far more intense than I was expecting. What happened?"

Darius cast his gaze to the burnt tar of the sky. Tears sparkled in his eyes. "It worked. By the Stonemother above and the power itself, it actually worked."

Katira gingerly shifted her weight on her feet, remembering before how the cold had locked her joints solid, and was amazed to find herself completely restored. She took a few steps to both reassure herself and to show Hannah that she was fine. While they'd only joined one strand, the barrier seemed smaller, less daunting. They could do this. They could heal the barrier safely.

Darius ran a hand through his hair and chuckled to himself. "That was brilliant. What inspired you to work that way?"

"You said to trust my instincts. It felt right to let the songs find each other. The rest of it seemed right too."

Hannah laughed as if she couldn't believe it. "It's so obvious now. We assumed the threads had to be identical in some way, but this is much more beautiful."

When Katira found the match, she had a sense that the threads were something more. It seemed the right time to ask about them. "Just what are the threads, exactly?"

The smile faded from Darius's face, replaced by something that could only be described as regret. "I suppose it's better that you learn sooner than later." He took a slow breath and his gaze shifted off into the distance. "They're people."

"What?" Katira didn't expect that. "But, how?"

"When I tried to stop Rose, back on that fateful day, she'd woven her power into thousands of souls before I realized what she was doing. I tried to cut them away, but it was too late. The world was tearing, and the souls she'd captured tore with it."

"Healing the threads is restoring those souls, so they can finally find peace," Hannah added quietly. "You haven't seen them, locked in the same day forever, aimlessly repeating the same motions. It's one of the many reasons we've kept you isolated."

Darius continued to stare into the distance, as if lost in the memory.

Katira fell back a step. She set her hand on the wall of the grotto as the reality of what they were saying swirled in her head. Thousands of people trapped all those years.

Another question pressed against her. "What about you? Do you and Darius have a thread?"

Hannah looked to Darius for a moment, as if hoping he might have something to add. When he didn't, she continued, "Being so close to the tear affected us differently. We aren't like the others trapped here. That said, I believe we do have our own threads in there somewhere."

She clapped a hand on Darius's shoulder, her smile returning.

"What matters is that we managed to heal one of the threads and that's a reason to celebrate. It looks like you won the bet, dear friend. I owe you yet another fine dinner."

Darius still didn't turn away from what held his attention down in the meadow.

"I'm thinking of those beautiful shrimps we found down in Camberton paired with ..." Hannah trailed off when she realized she wasn't being listened to.

Katira scowled. "You bet against me?"

"A friendly wager, nothing more. All it means is another lovely meal for us to enjoy tonight." Hannah looked over Darius with a kind smile that shifted to worry when she still couldn't draw his attention. "Making bets keeps things interesting. Like I said before. There's not a lot going on here."

"What did you ask for?"

"Darius agreed to help me read a book."

Katira was unsure she'd heard correctly. "What kind of bet is that?"

"Think about it. Things here disappear if they don't have someone paying attention to them. To read a book you have to always keep your hands on it, or tuck it somewhere on your person. If you set it down, say, to talk to someone or get a drink, it disappears and returns to its home, wherever that might be." She sighed wistfully. "I've been wanting to reread the Ballad of the Quaking Shore for ages, but the effort to go find it each time and then remember what page I'm on is too tiring to make the reading enjoyable.

"If I'd won the bet, Darius would agree to hold onto the book while I wasn't reading and make sure it didn't disappear. If it did, he'd fetch it for me." Hannah squinted in the direction Darius had turned, her attention sliding away from the conversation.

"She's coming, and fast." Darius went pale. "I thought the shield held."

All Hannah's good humor fell away. "It was a near thing, but it did. Whatever she felt, it wasn't from you. It must have been from the barrier itself."

Darius held Hannah by the shoulders. "I need you to hide Katira somewhere far enough away where Rose can't find either of you."

"I should stay with you," Hannah protested. "Together we might be able to convince her that we were experimenting again, nothing more."

Darius pressed his stone to his chest, as if praying for any other answer. "She's already enraged beyond reason, so there will be no convincing her of anything. If I'm lucky, I'll get her to take all that anger out on me in one massive outburst. If I fail, you're the last person to stand in her way before she discovers Katira. Go, now!" Darius pushed her, urging her to move faster.

Hannah gave a curt nod before catching Katira's sleeve and pulling her up and to the side of the grotto, her face a mix of bitter anger and determination.

"We must hurry. Shadows like Darius and me are safe enough, but she'll kill you without a second thought. We need you alive at all costs."

~

Jarand fidgeted with the invisible tether binding him to the sensing net he and Issa had put in place. At the grotto, the increased distance made wearing it far more uncomfortable than when he was at the cottage. Enough so that he found it hard to concentrate on the theory Issa was trying to explain. It didn't help that Katira's first attempt to heal the barrier had failed. If he knew why, he'd at least have some idea how to help her when she tried again.

Issa held up a paper covered in her tight tidy script. "The moment we sense a hound passing through, we can release this pattern of glyphs down through the net which will mark out exactly where. If we can pinpoint the specific weaknesses that exist in the town, we can seal them up and problem solved."

He took the paper and studied what she'd written before handing it back. If her plan worked, they'd both be able to dedicate more energy to helping with Katira's efforts at the barrier.

"We'll need the glyph rod for this. What are the odds that Bremin will part with it for an hour or two?"

"Based on what I've overheard, not great."

Nearby, Bremin was locked in his own discussion with Isben and Cassim. Jarand had only caught bits and pieces of it as he worked with Issa, enough to know that Bremin wanted to use the glyph rod to see if they could manipulate the threads from this side of the barrier.

Both plans were completely practical and necessary — exactly what their strategy should be — but everything inside Jarand screamed that it wasn't enough. Yes, he wanted to prevent the hounds from passing through. Yes, he wanted to help Katira sort the threads, if that's what she needed. But it didn't feel like enough.

If healing the rift between the worlds was what she was fated to do as an Innate, then something about the process would lead her to her death. Nothing they'd discussed considered that as a possibility, and none of their plans included steps to prevent it.

"Jarand?" Issa asked. "Is everything all right?"

"Sorry." He held up his wrist where the tether was. "I don't know why it's bothering me so much."

She set the paper down. "We both know that's not it. You've commanded entire armies with an arrow lodged in your thigh. Discomfort has never been a problem for you."

He gave a hollow laugh at the memory. "It made Cassim so mad. I remember." He absently rubbed the spot on his leg. "I've never been good with situations where I don't have enough information. That's all."

Issa tapped at the other papers that Bremin had left pinned under a rock. "I know it's not the kind of information you want, but there might be something in there that helps."

"You know what I mean. I need intel on the movements of my enemy, not pages of theoretical glyph work."

Before Issa could respond, the air in the center of the grotto thrummed to life and the barrier came back into view. Behind the forge, there had been plenty of room to move away from the threads. Here in that sheltered space, they were all forced to stand far closer than Jarand was comfortable with. Should the threads whip, it would be that much harder to shield themselves.

Bremin studied each shift and motion of the barrier intently. "Isben. You saw more of what happened last time. Stay alert. If anything appears different, tell us at once. Jarand, watch for Katira's flows. We need to know if she's leaning into her gift as she works. No one interferes with the barrier unless I say so, because we don't want to disrupt the process."

Jarand held his power in check, ready to leap into action at the first sign of trouble, regardless of Bremin's orders. At first, there wasn't much to see. Of the multitude of threads displayed before them, none appeared to shift or react. No flows or glyphs came into view.

"There." Isben pointed to the lower corner. "That one shifted. Look at how it appears to pull in light instead of glow."

Bremin leaned in closer to Isben. "Yes. You mentioned something about that before. I agree. It must be a thread from the mirror realm. Which means ..." He trailed off as a brilliant shimmer of flows burst through the threads like a shoal of tiny fish.

"That's ... that's her." Jarand hadn't known how much tension he'd been holding until it released. He sank back to the low shelf of rock behind him. "She's seeking a match."

Isben watched on with an intensity that Jarand had only seen among Benders as they worked. "It's more than that. There's direction there, purpose. They must be trying something different. It's working much better. Look." He pointed at how a few of the threads seemed to shift away from her seeking ribbons. "They didn't do that before."

"What's different, can you tell?" Bremin asked.

"I'm not sure, because nothing I can see has changed — wait." He held up a hand and closed his eyes. A gentle glow danced down his arm.

"Don't touch it. We mustn't disturb them," Bremin warned.

Issa took a step closer to Isben, waiting for the order to either protect him or stop him. The lines at her neck flared as she readied herself for either. The threads of the barrier moved, manipulated by

Katira's invisible touch. One thread shifted apart from the others and moved toward the first thread.

"It must have something to do with feel, with the energy." His outstretched hand flexed as if trying to reach something just inches out of his grasp. "Just one delving ribbon? Please. I've almost got it."

"No," Jarand said with a tone that brokered no argument. As much as he knew the information was important, Katira's safety came first. "Not yet."

Bremin exchanged a look with Jarand, clearly conflicted with the turn of events. Information was his strength; the more of it he could get, the better decisions he could make. If Isben could learn something new, something vital, it could make a difference.

Cassim, who had been watching from the safety of the grotto entrance, stepped closer, keeping Issa as a shield between the barrier and himself. "Why did it stop? She selected a strand and was moving it, but now it's stopped."

"They've pulled the two selected strands together, like before," Isben said. "Come on, Katira. You can do it."

The droning buzz of the barrier filled the air of the grotto and pressed in on Jarand until he felt as if it might flatten him against the surrounding rock. It was all he could do to remain still and vigilant.

"That. There." Bremin pointed to where a bright spark formed between the strands. "I think they've got it. Look, the strands are fusing." He cheered and clapped his hands together. "In all my years, I never thought I'd see such a thing."

Jarand watched on with a mix of wonder and horror. With the barrier open, he could feel Katira as if she were back in the real world. He felt the moment her exuberance shifted to worry, then to fear. He felt how the reaction pulled power from her far faster and far more than was safe. If it didn't stop soon, she'd be overdrawn.

The glee on Bremin's face faded when he glanced over at Jarand. "Oh, that's not good." He returned his attention to the threads as if weighing what he saw. "How much longer can she hold out?"

"Not much."

When Isben realized what was happening, it struck him like a blow to the stomach and forced the air from his lungs. He crumpled in on himself. For a long moment, he stood there blinking before he remembered that he was supposed to be keeping track of what was happening with the barrier. "I think they're nearly there. A few seconds more, that's all." His statement sounded more like a plea.

With another bright flash, the two threads disappeared, and with them, the barrier also. Its insistent hum lifted from the grotto and left a jarring silence in its place. Jarand strained to sense Katira through their rapidly thinning connection.

Everyone in the grotto looked to him, waiting for the answer to the question no one dared to ask. Isben had gone so pale his face was practically bloodless. Bremin and Issa stood as if they didn't dare move. Cassim gripped the end of his tunic and wrung it between his hands.

With the barrier closed, she felt impossibly far away, but she was still there. "She made it." Jarand sighed and slumped forward, cupping his face in his hands. "She'll be okay."

"It's too much," Cassim gave voice to what they were all thinking. "There's no way they can do that for every strand. As it is, it might take days for them to recover enough to try joining another. At that rate, finishing what they started will take years. If they are able to finish at all." Cassim made a helpless gesture with his hands.

"There are forces beyond our understanding at work here." Bremin sat next to Jarand. "Katira's fate wouldn't be tied to a fruitless quest. The Stonemother is not known to be cruel."

CHAPTER 24

Katira scrambled after Hannah as she climbed further up the steep rocks. Below, Darius had crossed half of the meadow. At the edge of the meadow Wrothe stepped into view, her blood-red dress flowing behind her despite the stillness of the air.

Hannah threw herself into the shelter behind a large boulder and yanked Katira down beside her. "This should do it. Darius will keep her distracted enough that she won't seek us out."

Katira couldn't keep her hands from shaking. "But what if she does?"

"You have every reason to be scared. I am too. But I'm pretty good at staying out of her way when she's angry like this. As long as neither of us draw her attention, we'll be fine."

"That's not reassuring." Katira peered down into the valley and was relieved to see where Darius and Wrothe stood face to face.

"I miss the centuries she was locked up. It made our research so much easier." She closed her eyes and leaned her head against the rock. "She couldn't use him like she does now."

A dark flash appeared in Wrothe's outstretched hands, and a

ripple of energy flowed across the field. Darius stepped back, hands outstretched and placating.

Hannah gripped Katira's shirt and pulled her back out of sight. "There's nothing worth seeing. Trust me. It's not worth the risk of her spotting you."

The last thing Katira wanted to do was wait, not while someone was in danger, certainly not when she was the cause. She crouched on the balls of her feet and fought the urge to sprint down the mountainside. She understood why she had to stay, but her heart pounded, urging her to do something. If she couldn't run, she could distract herself by getting answers to the endless questions she still had.

"When I first encountered Rose, I didn't even think she was human." Katira started, hoping to encourage Hannah to open up and share more. "Does Darius, you know, still care for her?"

"It's complicated. If you asked him, he'd say that he did. But, after fighting her like this for so long, the heart can only take so much. There's a part of him that will always love the person she used to be. I can't fault him for that. Then there's the other part of himself that has to live through every day. That part of him has moved on."

Hannah rested her hand on her stone. "It's the same for me, I still love my companion, but he was too far away at the time of the split. All that remains of him here is a shell, endlessly repeating the same day over and over again."

The sudden revelation startled Katira. She'd never considered Hannah being anything other than a friendly Seeker who enjoyed a good meal. Learning that she too had lost someone dear to her made her kindness and smiles that much more bittersweet.

"What is his name?"

"Gaitan of the Ones who Walk with Fire. He came from a place far to the east of here. The names are all like that there." A slight smile crept up the side of her face as she thought of him. "The man loved language, loved words the same way a gardener loves the new buds of spring roses. When we first joined, first felt that connection, that completion between us, it was simply right. Perfection."

"You miss him." It wasn't a question.

"In some ways I have it easy. He's still technically here, with me. I can talk to him if I want to. Touch him. Connect with him, in a way. The trouble is, he's stuck in the same day while I move on. To make a rotten comparison, he's not that much different than the food in the baskets. The moment no one is paying attention to him, even if I leave his sight for a few minutes, he returns to the pattern of his day as if I had never been there."

She let her head fall back so that she was looking at the dark sky. "The worst part of it all? He'll never understand the pains and frustrations I've gathered from the hundreds of years of being stuck here. When we're together, he can sense all of them and wants to fix them, wants to make them better, and he simply can't. This ..." She vaguely gestured toward the meadow. "... is something that he can't fix. It's upsetting for both of us, so I stopped visiting him. He continues to live that shadow of his life day in, day out and doesn't know he's trapped. Doesn't know I'm gone."

"You said it was easier, but that doesn't sound easier at all. I'm so sorry. I didn't know." Katira edged her way back up the rock. The bursts and waves of energy in the air had subdued a fraction. Perhaps Darius had managed to calm Wrothe after all.

Hannah tugged her back down. "I swear she has the senses of a hawk. She'll feel you watching. If she comes after you, there's only so much I can do before she kills me." She winced and rubbed her chest. "I'd rather not go through that again if I can avoid it."

Katira dropped back down, momentarily stunned by how casually the woman spoke of her own death. She tried to not think of her mother, of not being there when she passed. She understood why she had been kept away, but the place where that memory should have been ached like a bruise.

"What's it like?"

"What's what like?" Hannah rummaged around in her pockets and pulled out a parcel wrapped in fabric and tied with string.

"Dying."

Her fingers slipped as she tugged at the knot. "I don't recommend it. Rose only caught me once. Rammed an iron poker straight into my chest. I've made a point to avoid her when her temper was up after that." She pinched at the knot, and it finally came loose. "It took hours before it was over. The power forced my heart to keep beating. Darius stayed with me, kept my mind on other things. I refused to let him end me, even when I knew I wouldn't survive. It was horrible."

She sighed and unwrapped the parcel, revealing a small moist cake. "But, near the end, everything changed. As the last of my power drained away and I started to slip, there came an indescribable peace. Everything I'd ever worried about, the whole lot of it, fell away. In those last moments I found complete clarity, like my whole existence suddenly made sense. And then it was over. I woke up back on the floor in Khanrosh, not remembering any of it until much later." She gestured with the cake toward Katira. "Would you like some? I have some of the other treats in here as well if you'd like something else."

"Where did that come from?"

"I had it in my pocket when the world split. It reappears when I've forgotten I've eaten it. Even after all these years it still tastes good. You'd think I'd tire of it."

Katira broke off a piece of the dense cake. It was studded with dried fruit and felt heavy and decadent in her fingers. "This feels wrong. We shouldn't be enjoying something while he's down there trying to hold her off."

"He'd want it like this. He hates the thought of anyone, even me, sitting and worrying about him. The cake is a distraction, and right now we both need distracting."

As Katira had neither heard nor sensed anything worrying coming from the meadow for several minutes, she sat back and took a bite of the cake and let its richness melt into her mouth. Hannah did the same and closed her eyes as if retreating into a memory of a better time.

With Hannah distracted, Katira rose to her knees and peeked out over the edge of the boulder. Even at this distance, Katira could see the anger in Wrothe's movements as Darius tried to calm her.

Whatever he was saying, it wasn't helping. Dark ribbons of power crackled around Wrothe like a halo.

"That's not a good sign."

Katira was surprised to find Hannah peeking over the edge of the rock next to her.

"She rarely backs down at this point. It doesn't matter what he says or does, she's going to allow her anger to win." She lowered herself back down and dug her nails into her palm. A tear gathered in the corner of her eye.

"What does that mean?" Katira didn't want to hear the answer.

"It means that unless some miracle happens, Darius is going to suffer." She leaned her head into her folded arms. "I hate this." Her voice was muffled through the fabric of her sleeves. "Don't watch. Please. You'll never be rid of it. It will haunt you forever."

Katira couldn't turn away. In the short time she had known Darius, she had come to like him. The thought of anything happening to him tightened her throat. Wrothe raised her hands over her head, and a dark sphere collected between them. When she released it, it swarmed around Darius so thickly that Katira couldn't see him. Then came his screams.

She reacted before she could think, lunging back toward the meadow with every intention to put an end to the horror that was unfolding. She'd stopped Wrothe in the past, and she could do it again. No one would be hurt like this because of her. Before she could take a single step, Hannah seized her arm and held it with surprising strength.

"I know it's hard. When it's all over, he'll come back. He always has. But if she gets you, you will not. Stay here."

"She's torturing him. We have to do something." Darius's screams had changed into something primal and raw. It would be easy to break Hannah's hold and bolt down the trail, but the pleading desperation in her eyes stopped Katira cold.

"You must remember what we are trying to accomplish. Darius can't heal the rift between worlds without you. You are the first in hundreds of years with his gift. If you get yourself killed, it might be another thousand years before we find someone else. *If* we can find someone else. By then, we might be as insane as Rose. That's hundreds of years that the real world will suffer as shadow creatures find their way in. Hundreds of years for Wrothe to continue to work her mischief. She won't stop, she can't die. Who's to say what she'll destroy when she breaks through again?"

Darius's terrible screams faded into silence.

Hannah released her grip. "It's done."

Jarand wedged his hands between his knees to keep anyone from seeing how they trembled. Katira had done it. She'd healed one of the strands of the barrier. For months, he'd worried and wondered about what being an Innate would mean for her. At one point he'd even believed he'd feel better if he knew, because then he'd would have been able to train her for it. Maybe that's why his hands shook. No one could have been prepared for such a task, and here his brave girl had to face it on her own.

Across the grotto, Bremin and Isben had set to work analyzing what they'd seen. Jarand listened in as Isben spoke of how they could help organize the strands from this side and make it that much easier for Katira to find the one she was looking for. He left them to it. There was something far more pressing on his mind, and Cassim had the right knowledge to help him.

The Healer had remained near the grotto entrance, keeping a safe distance from where the barrier might appear in case anything unexpected happened. Onyx dozed in the sun and blinked lazily when Jarand came close. Nearby, Issa stood as sentry.

"Cassim, a word? You too, Issa. Any insights here are welcome." Jarand plucked up his cane. Between the previous night's events and all that had happened that morning, the ache in his back was making itself known the longer he remained standing.

Issa didn't move from her vantage point. "If this is about the power drain, we're already working on a few ideas."

"It is. I'd feel better if we had some kind of plan should we sense it happening again. You two come up with anything so far?"

Cassim's gaze darted to where Jarand's stone hung around his neck. "How do you feel about using the apprentice bond to reach Katira through the barrier?"

Jarand couldn't help reaching for the stone at the mention of the bond. It was the only thing that gave him any reassurance that Katira was still okay. "Any ideas how? I don't imagine the barrier being friendly toward that type of intrusion."

"I was hoping Bremin might have a few theories on how it could work. Of all of us, Stonemother knows he'll have an opinion on it." Issa leaned back against the rock behind her and dropped her voice lower. "Listen, we all want Katira to walk away from this. Don't think for a moment that you're carrying this worry and fear alone."

"Thank you." And he meant it. Issa had fought in enough campaigns alongside him that she knew his tendency to wall people off when things got hard. "I want to be there when you talk to Bremin. Hear what he has to say."

She gave a curt nod and peered in to where Isben pointed to something with the pen tucked in his hand. A dark smudge of ink wandered up his cheek. From the look of it, he and Bremin were coming to the end of their discussion.

Jarand gathered up all the reasons why using the apprentice bond could or couldn't work and found his list shorter than he'd hoped. Maybe he should have spent more time studying Bremin's notes. As he searched what he knew for anything useful, the tether pulsed against his skin. Something down in the valley had activated their warning network.

He held it up. "We've got a problem."

She narrowed her eyes and peered down toward the valley below. "Nonsense. It's the middle of the day. Hounds avoid daylight."

"All the more reason to see what's going on. What are the odds of something happening here anytime soon?" The idea of leaving filled him with a bitter unease that tightened the muscles of his neck.

"Hard to say. Katira won't be able to heal another strand until she's regained some of what she lost. It might be a while," Cassim said.

"Good." The tightness eased a fraction. "Issa and I will go investigate. You discuss your idea with Bremin and Isben. We'll return as soon as we can."

CHAPTER 25

$\mathcal{B}$ack at the cottage, Jarand leaned against the outer wall and caught his breath while he refocused his attention on what the tether was trying to tell him. He hoped now that he was closer, it would make more sense than the muddy signal he received back at the grotto.

"If there's a threat, we best head it off, and quickly." Issa rested one hand on the hilt of her sword and fixed him in her gaze. "You ready?"

"That's not the issue." He sucked a breath past the flare of pain in his chest. "I can't tell where it's coming from."

"What?" Issa furrowed her brow. "Nonsense. It's designed to show us." She held out a hand. "Give it here."

He passed the tether over and rubbed his wrist. Issa grit her teeth as she slipped it on.

"That's ... strange." She walked along the side of the cottage a few steps. "If I were to make a guess, it feels more like an echo than an alert, like it's picking up activity from the mirror realm." Her eyes widened. "Should we get the others, bring them down?"

He checked the thin sending from his bond. "I don't think it's the barrier, because it doesn't involve Katira."

Issa's face tightened. "It's getting stronger. Whatever is happening, it's significant." Her attention shifted toward the center of town. "I've got a location."

She hurried back along the side of the cottage, taking long ground-eating strides that Jarand did his best to match. When they reached the town square, a dark mass hovered to the side of the fountain. Not threads, or the barrier, but something utterly different. A small crowd had gathered at the edge of the square and watched it with fear-filled eyes.

Jarand bound his stone to his palm and placed himself between the people and the dark mass. "Have you seen anything like this before?"

"Can't say I have. You?" Issa's lines around her neck flared.

He shook his head. "Anything new from the tether?"

"Afraid not. It's tuned into things breaking into our world, not —" she gestured to the thing, "—whatever this is."

As they spoke, the mass grew darker. Tendrils whistled and whipped around its edges. Jarand gave it more space. If his past had taught him anything, it was that anything with tendrils like that was certainly not something he wanted to be close to.

He cursed through his teeth. "I'll give you three guesses where we've seen something like this before."

Issa whirled her sword through the air, changing her stance from a relaxed neutral to one ready to take down anything that dared get too close. "I'm getting really tired of that woman. If she's trying to break into our world, she's in for a terrible surprise. I'd love to stick my sword down her—"

"Issa." Jarand said, the warning clear in his voice as he tilted his head toward the crowd. "We're trying to keep them on our side. Best keep your more creative ideas to yourself."

The mass bulged again before collapsing down on itself into a sphere so dark it seemed to pull the light from the air around it. Someone in the crowd screamed.

"Quickly, a shield." Jarand flared his power to life.

Issa followed the order, her shield joining his in a brilliant display of light. "What do you hope to accomplish? Whatever this is, I don't think it's real."

"They don't know that. They need to see that we're taking care of the situation." He drew together the familiar shielding sequences and sparked them to life to form a larger than necessary sphere which spun into existence around the mass. "And ... if it turns out we do need it, we'll already have something in place."

Jarand had never been one to show off, he knew that, but if this tipped the scale in their favor, it was worth a bit of showmanship. No sooner than they'd formed the sphere, the mass contracted one final time and then swirled down to nothing.

"That was ... odd." Issa withdrew from the shield, causing it to fizzle and then collapse.

From behind them, shouts of praise emerged from the crowd, starting with a few and growing until they were all cheering.

"Odd, but worth it."

Lucan approached them, staying well away from where the mass had been. He'd been impressed when Jarand had showed him the sword, but this was the first time he'd seen Jarand wield glyphs. The man's eyes practically bulged from his head.

"Do I want to know what that was?"

"Probably not," Jarand answered. Stonemother knew he wasn't sure either, but he wasn't about to tell Lucan that.

The answer didn't satisfy Lucan, so he kept pressing. "Well? Was it dangerous? Is it going to come back?"

Issa shot Jarand an amused sidelong glance as if eager to hear what Jarand came up with.

"It might." He tried to sound like he knew what he was talking about to reassure Lucan that they had the situation under control, that the town was safe. Well, safe enough. "Rest assured, we'll know if it does and we'll deal with it, just like we did today." It wasn't technically a lie. The sensing net was still in place.

Lucan stepped closer. "Stop being intentionally vague. Of everyone here, I deserve to know the truth." He lowered his voice. "This has to do with the mirror realm, doesn't it? You said the hounds had a way of getting into the town. Are we still safe?"

"You're safer than you were. We're heading off each threat as soon as it shows itself." Jarand adjusted the sword hanging off his belt as a reminder. "The town still needs to take precautions, especially at night."

The next question was even quieter, but it struck twice as hard. "What about Katira? Any news?"

"She's still there, still working. We believe she made a breakthrough this morning." Jarand glanced toward the crowd where they remained gathered in a tight knot. What Katira was doing would keep them safe from shadow hounds forever. If she succeeded, they would no longer require a Stonebearer hidden among their ranks to protect them. This was for Namragan and a hundred other small towns like it. Healing the barrier was something worth dying for.

Lucan let a small, relieved sigh escape. "That's good to hear."

Issa shifted her weight, a subtle sign that she was eager to leave. Lucan picked up on it.

He stepped back and raised his voice back to where the crowd could hear it. "Thank you again. We appreciate all you've done for us. Best let you get back to work." He lowered his voice one final time, "Take care. I mean it. I expect to see you, Katira, and your friends all in one piece when this is over."

"Agreed." Issa gave a sharp nod that felt more like a salute and turned to leave.

Katira's need to run down to the meadow, to see what had happened to Darius, coursed through her entire frame with such force that she practically shook.

"When can we go to him? Must he die alone?"

"Rose needs to be long gone," Hannah explained again. "I promised him to keep you safe. I will not fail."

Katira worked her fingers deep into the ground-hugging tiny wildflowers growing next to her and made a tight fist, finding some satisfaction as the roots pulled free. "How can you be so calm while this is happening?"

"I'm not calm, far from it." Hannah tucked the remaining part of the cake away. "Every time something like this happens, a part of me curls up and goes blank. I lose myself a little more. One day, there will be nothing left."

The way she spoke. There was something deeper hiding beneath the surface. No, not something. Someone. "Do you worry that you might become like Gaitan?"

Hannah said nothing for several minutes. Instead, she tilted up her head to the rusted sky and blackened sun. "It wouldn't be so bad to give in to the nothingness of this world. All my fears, my hopes, my dreams would lose their sharp edge. Sometimes I wonder if I should let myself slip into it. It would be so easy." She sniffed. "I wanted to when I realized that the Gaitan that remained here was only a shadow of himself. Darius woke me up, forced me to keep my mind alert and active, kept me working toward a solution to this mess. He's always been driven. You'd think losing so much would change that, but if anything, it's made him all the more determined."

"If we manage to heal the barrier, what will happen to Gaitan?"

"We're not sure. I'm assuming the part of him that remained in the real world is long dead by now, so his shadow most likely will disappear as well." She sighed and picked at a crumb that had fallen in her lap. "I've been mourning him for ages already."

When Katira returned her attention to her open palms, the broken stems and tiny blossoms had disappeared. Wrothe had to be gone by now. She resisted the urge to peer over the lip of their hiding place. Should she be wrong, should that demon still be lingering around, it would be foolish to expose herself after she'd made it so long without being caught.

"It must be safe now." Katira rose to her feet but stayed hidden.

"Let me take a look." Hannah took her time getting up and dusting off the hem and back of her mantle before looking down into the meadow. The moment she spotted Darius, she gave a tiny involuntary gasp.

"You never do get used to it, that sudden shock of seeing him lying there. We've argued about whether it's worth it to even look countless times." She began climbing back down the trail. "For me, it's a reminder of what we are fighting for, what we are trying to put a stop to."

Katira finally gathered the courage to peer over the edge of the rock. Hannah was right; seeing him like that sent a piercing ache right through her. She thought of Mamar. "I agree. Whether we like it or not, pain is part of the experience of being alive. Shielding ourselves from it doesn't serve anyone."

At the edge of the meadow, far from where the sheep peacefully grazed unaware of any change, Darius lay as if he were sleeping. No blood stained his skin, no unnatural angles marred the lines of his body, no evidence of the torture Wrothe inflicted upon him remained. His face had fallen slack in death, the lines of his smile had disappeared and his brow, usually bunched in thought, was smooth.

Hannah knelt close to the body, her motions indicating that this was something she had done many times. She rested her hand on Darius's chest and bowed her head. Katira followed the woman's example and knelt on the other side.

"I was devastated the first time Rose killed him. I thought I'd lost him forever," Hannah said. "I buried his body and stacked a cairn on top of it. It took almost a year before all the stones of the cairn eventually disappeared. It was the longest I'd kept anything in this world on my own. My sorrow held him in place. You can imagine my surprise when he came waltzing up to me a few days after the last stone disappeared, the cheeky bastard. Scared me out of my skin."

Katira held back a short laugh, the image of how startled Hannah must have been struck her as tragically funny.

"It's good to see you smile, even at a time like this. Soon, this will all be a memory. The barrier will be healed, the mirror realm gone, and no one will ever suffer from Rose's anger again."

Katira's thoughts turned back to Wrothe. No one could hold that much anger inside themselves without being destroyed by it. "What does she want, Hannah?"

"To go back. It's as simple as that."

"Yes, but why? What does the real world have that she's so desperate for?" Katira finally convinced herself to let her hand rest on Darius's arm, not enough to feel how his heart no longer beat, how his chest no longer rose and fell, but enough to sense that this body no longer had him in it.

"I used to believe her rage centered around being ripped away from everything that gave her life meaning. Most of it is, but there's something else as well." Hannah's gaze wandered back to the sheep grazing in the field. "I believe she's holding on to a terrible guilt over what happened. The world would have stayed whole if she'd listened to him."

"Then why is she so mad at Darius for trying to fix it? Shouldn't she be pleased?"

"Because it's happening all over again. Just when she's found a way of making this world work for her, he's doing something that will take it away." Hannah withdrew her hand and tucked it in her lap. "She's always been stubborn and as temperamental as any ocean. A wise sailor knows when it's safe to cross the waters. Stonemother knows I'm not brave enough to try." She gave him a respectful bow. "Thankfully, he was."

"It's not fair." Katira sniffed back a tear. "Here we are working to fix all this, save her from this nightmare she's been stuck in. The least she could do is let us work in peace. Maybe he should tell her about me. If she knew we'd figured it out, it would give her a reason to hope. Hope can be a powerful thing."

Hannah's gaze regained its focus as she let it settle back on Katira. "It's not worth the risk. Every time she's gotten her hands on someone from the real world, she's caused death and destruction. If she gets her hands on you, she will find a way to seize your power and create a portal, or change herself, or something else horrible so that she can return to the real world. Neither of us are willing to let that happen." She patted Darius's chest one final time, gently, tenderly. "For the good of everything, we best leave now and let him return. The sooner you two can resume your work, the sooner we might put all this behind us."

CHAPTER 26

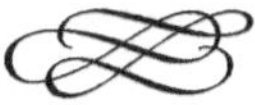

*B*ack inside the small cabin, Katira buried her head in her arms and tried to force from her mind the sight of Darius sprawled lifeless on the ground. All the while, Hannah paced the length of the small room and asked her question after question in hopes that it would draw her thoughts to something, anything else. After an hour, Katira was ready to pull her hair out in frustration.

She gripped the quilt's worn fabric in her fists. "This place reminds me too much of him. We need to try something else. Go somewhere else."

Hannah stopped pacing and leaned against the back of the chair. "Where would we go? Most places familiar to you don't exist yet, and the places I know would be no comfort. We don't know if you can travel the way I can. If we were to go anywhere, we'd have to walk. We don't have time for that."

"If I can't stop thinking about him, then we're stuck waiting until I can. We have nothing but time. A walk would do me some good." Katira went to the door and didn't wait for Hannah to follow. When she opened it, Darius's body drew her eye like a magnet. She took a steadying breath and stepped out into the deep blacks and browns of the afternoon.

Despite being several centuries younger than how she remembered the narrow road leading south away from Namragan, it still held a familiar comfort. Katira found herself longing to hear the sound of the Kanth River bubbling off the side of the road and to smell pine and rain on the breeze. Anything would be better than this soundless, lifeless world.

Hannah followed along, staying mercifully quiet as they walked. If she was ever going to make peace with what happened to Darius, then she needed to allow herself to wade through the mess of emotions that came with sudden loss. Then, and only then, would her mind be able to let Darius go. They'd been walking for some time before Hannah finally broke the silence.

"I shouldn't have pushed you to forget so soon. It wasn't fair. Would you like to talk about what happened?" The question seemed strange after her earlier efforts to distract Katira.

Katira swallowed down the knot forming in her throat. "You were doing what you thought was right."

"That doesn't make it any better." Hannah quickened her pace until she was walking along beside her. "If anything, it probably made it worse. Go ahead, ask me anything."

Katira studied the purple trees with their grey and white trunks as she considered what was bothering her most. "What happens to him after he disappears from here?"

"He goes back to the beginning, where it all started. He'll wake up crumpled on the floor of the testing chamber in Khanrosh having no memory of what happened. His first panicked thoughts will be of Rose and trying to figure out what happened. I do everything I can to be there when he wakes so I can help him remember." Hannah gave the explanation as if she was doing everything possible to stick to the facts. Then, her voice broke. "He does the same for me."

"What happens if you're not there?"

Hannah swallowed and continued, returning to the safety of the facts once more. "It takes longer. He might stay and relive the past for hours before he remembers that it isn't the first time."

Katira stopped walking. "That sounds horrible."

Hannah gave a dry laugh and looked to the dark sky. "We try to avoid it."

Walking through the canyon that separated Namragan from the rest of the world, Katira had no way of knowing if she'd managed to push thoughts of Darius away long enough for their plan to work. Being away from the cabin certainly helped, but had it helped enough?

She glanced back up the narrow winding road, knowing they'd gone too far to see anything more than trees and hillside behind them. "At what point do we check to see if he's gone?"

"That's entirely up to you. At any point during our conversation did you forget he was dead?"

Hearing Hannah speak so plainly about it, even after she'd done it several times, still jarred Katira. After Mamar died she'd made every effort to be careful when she spoke about death around Papan with the hope that it would make his burden less difficult to bear.

"It's hard to say, I believe so. That's why I want to check. If he's already gone, then the sooner we can go help him remember, the better."

Hannah furrowed her brow. "There's no 'we.' You're not going anywhere close to Khanrosh, and that's final. If he's gone, I'll go get him and that's that."

The woman's sudden resolve startled Katira enough to shake the idea from her mind. Going to Khanrosh, to where Wrothe would most likely be, would be like offering herself up on a platter for that monster. It would be best to keep her distance.

"I didn't think. I'm sorry. Staying here is a better idea." If Hannah was going to Khanrosh, that meant she'd be traveling in the strange way she'd mentioned before. It gave Katira an idea. "Before you go, could you show me how you travel? I'd like to know."

The furrow in Hannah's brow tilted to amusement. "You are just like him, you know that? I suppose it won't hurt to try. I'm curious to see if you can." She stopped in the center of the road. "Okay, first things first. You must be familiar with the place you want to go. Much like Traveling with the power, the easiest places to travel to are ones where you've been many times."

"That's going to be a problem," Katira said. "I'm guessing that only places that existed at the time of the split will work. I don't know many of those."

"That's true." She tapped on her lip. "The Namragan from your memory didn't construct itself because you came, so it holds that other places in the world you're familiar with won't either." She reached out a hand. "We'll start small, then I'll try to take you back to the cabin with me as if you were a basket of fruit. As long as you can keep your mind clear, it should work."

"I didn't have much luck with keeping my mind clear earlier." Katira took the offered hand.

"This is different. It certainly won't hurt to try."

With their hands linked, Katira focused on her breathing like Papan had taught during all those lessons on meditation at Amul Dun. Even then, in the familiar surroundings of the Tower, she'd never succeeded in clearing her mind for more than a few minutes at a time. There was always something to do, always some problem to think about. She hoped those few minutes she could manage would be enough.

They walked together in silence for what felt like far longer than necessary. During that time, Katira's thoughts flitted from subject to subject faster than she could stop them. The moment she released one, another rushed in to take its place. Was Isben okay? Could she learn to move through the mirror realm? Could they actually heal the barrier?

"Keep your focus on the sound of your breathing, nothing more," Hannah urged as she continued to take slow steps.

Katira pulled back on her hand, stopping them both. "I'm afraid that's harder than it sounds."

"What if I let you direct us instead? It might be easier to think of the cabin than to try to keep your mind clear. It's a small enough distance and we just walked it. All you'd need to do is imagine yourself walking back and arriving."

A flutter of worry swept through Katira. Moving through space like this was all too new. At the Tower, she hadn't started learning Traveling with glyphs yet. It was considered an advanced skill that required absolute mastery of both the foundational and secondary glyphs before being allowed to start. Stories of horrible things happening to even experienced travelers kept her from even thinking of trying.

"The worst that can happen is it not working, right?" she asked.

"I believe so. It's a small test and we've limited the variables. When you're ready, walk with the intention of returning to the cabin. Let the desire to go there fill your mind." Hannah held out her hand. "I'll be with you every step of the way.

Katira considered the long narrow road once more and the many times she'd walked it returning home from selling Papan's wares in the other villages. She knew each bend and rise without thinking.

"I can do that."

She fixed the image of the cabin in her mind with its gentle pasture and grazing sheep, and started walking. The way Hannah explained this kind of traveling seemed too easy. Katira would have preferred there to be a prescribed sequence of actions and a more confident guarantee that it would work. With each step, with each breath, she willed herself to relax into the idea that all she was doing was walking back. Hannah walked behind her and held on lightly to her wrist.

Perhaps it was *too* easy. While her goal was to return to the shepherd's cabin, she couldn't stop thinking of the why of it. Her mind kept slipping, returning to thoughts of Darius like a magnet. Khanrosh was his home; he might be there waking up dazed and confused at that very moment.

She'd been there. She'd suffered there. She'd fought for her life and for her father's life there. Her mind locked on that memory so powerfully that it shut out all other thoughts. She continued to walk, but no longer saw the trail or the familiar aspens and granite of her home.

"Katira? What are you doing?" Hannah gripped her wrist hard and pulled. "This is wrong. Bring your thoughts back to our goal.

Imagine the cabin, quick, while the world is still shifting around us."

~

As hard as Katira tried to alter course, the lonely cell in the dungeons beneath Khanrosh continued to materialize around them. It was in this cell where she had found Papan bleeding and barely conscious. She'd never dared to revisit those memories for fear of being overwhelmed. Instead, she'd bottled them up and hoped she'd never have to think about those dark days ever again.

"What have you done?" Hannah seized her by the arm, not to drag her anywhere, but out of alarm.

Katira circled the room, stunned, not quite believing what she was seeing. "I'm sorry. I'm so sorry."

"Why here? What could possibly be here that would pull you that strongly?"

Katira touched the door's smooth iron and found no trace of rust, no rough places where the metal had been damaged from use.

"I was here, not long ago. This was where it all happened."

"It, what? What happened here?"

Katira closed her eyes and rested her forehead against the metal, wishing it were cold. "After Rose had escaped from her prison, she wanted revenge more than anything. She locked me and my father in these cells. She tortured him, trying to get him to serve her as a twisted form of payback. Every time he refused her, she hurt him more. I nearly lost him."

Hannah covered her mouth as it fell open in shock. "With that kind of story, those are bound to be powerful memories. I'm sorry you had to live through that. It sounds truly terrible."

More visions from the past broke over Katira like a drowning wave. Wrothe drinking away her reserve of power. Isben plunging his dagger into Surasio's chest over and over. The triggering of the death oath. The overwhelm of it made it hard for Katira to breathe.

"Easy. You're okay now. You're safe." Hannah gripped Katira's shoulder, the strength of her hand welcome and grounding. "Best we find a way out of here."

Katira let Hannah's calm presence bring her back down to where she could think once more. She'd created this problem; she'd do whatever she could to help solve it. "Is there any reason we can't Travel out of here? Like, with the power?"

"Several, unfortunately. Khanrosh is glyph-shielded, especially the cells. In my day, we kept a fair number of dangerous wielders down here. It wouldn't do for them to disappear on us."

"We can't walk travel either, I'm guessing?"

Hannah looked up from where she studied the lock. "It's a pretty small cell. I'm not sure how well it would work."

"If we closed our eyes and walked in place. You know, pretended we're somewhere else?" Katira cringed. "No, that's stupid."

"Maybe not. You might be onto something." She closed her eyes and walked in place as if testing the idea. "It's all a mind puzzle anyway. If we believe we are heading somewhere else, in theory, this world will do the rest." Hannah held out her hand once more. "We know you can travel now, so it won't hurt to try."

The longer Katira stayed in that cell, the more memories each sight and sound stirred up, none of them welcome. She closed her eyes against it, willing them to be anywhere else.

They walked in place for what seemed like forever. Each tiny sound, even the grit of hewn stone under her feet, drew Katira's attention right back to the horrors of the place. She wanted to return to the cabin, but she couldn't convince her mind to let go.

"Try humming a song, something that you've known forever. Fill your head with it," Hannah suggested.

Mamar used to sing a lullaby to her as a child when she couldn't sleep. She let the soft melancholy notes fill her head, drowning out the noise of the dungeon, covering up the worries and fears that plagued her memories.

After another long effort, Hannah released her hand. "It's not working. I don't know what to do. Darius won't think to look for us here, and if either of us use the power, Rose will be on us in seconds."

A shift of light in the corridor marked where one of the shadow guards was making his rounds.

Without warning, Hannah pushed her back into a corner and spread her dark mantle around them both. Fear radiated from her.

"Best they not see us."

Katira hated the unfairness of it all. The woman was a friendly historian, not a fighter. She should never have been pulled into this.

"Listen," Katira whispered. "It's me that's keeping us from getting out of here. Force me to sleep, knock me out, whatever, but make it so I can't think."

"No, that's a horrible idea." She pressed the mantle closer as the footsteps in the hallway came and went. "I can't risk hurting you."

A tight knot of uncertainty formed in Katira's throat. "I'd rather you try that than having Rose find either of us here. Anything she does is bound to be worse. Knock me out, then hold my hand as you travel back. If that doesn't work, forget that I'm here long enough that the world returns me back to Namragan. As soon as I'm gone, you can follow."

"This is madness. Absolute madness." Hannah pressed her stone between her fingers. "If you don't see me before Darius finds you, tell him what happened. He'll know what to do. He always does." Something in Hannah's eyes betrayed a worry that she wasn't sharing.

She reached her hand around Katira's neck and pressed her fingers along the sides of her spine. A hot rush of power filled her head and she felt herself falling, felt Hannah guiding her to the floor, felt the woman's fingers trembling as she pulled them away and darkness rolled in.

When Jarand reached the cottage, he rested his hands on the low garden wall and let the heat of the midday sun beat down on his back and shoulders to ease where the muscles had locked up.

Issa squinted upward as if gauging the time before sitting on the wall next to him. He'd caught her monitoring him since they'd left the grotto and wondered if it was under Cassim's orders, or simply her natural protectiveness for a fellow soldier. Either way, he resented that they felt they needed to. He could manage himself well enough.

She drew one of the smaller knives from her belt and absently picked at something lodged under her nail. "Judging by the time, we best stay here. The others should be returning for a bite to eat sooner than later. Cassim's not one to skip meals lightly."

He bit back a groan as he pushed himself up from the wall. The cramped muscles refused to release, leaving him standing hunched. "The barrier could open again at any minute. I want to be there."

She slid the knife back into its sheath. "What good will you be to Katira if you can barely stand?"

"More than I'll be staying here."

"Not necessarily." She stood and opened the gate leading inside the low wall. "I have those new glyph patterns I'd like to weave into the sensing net. After what we saw in the town square today, I'd prefer to have all possible protections in place to prevent trouble in the future. Your help would be most welcome."

He weighed his options. If he returned to the grotto and nothing happened, he'd only tire himself. Helping Issa, on the other hand, would ensure the town's safety. It was the better strategic choice.

He followed her through the gate. "Fine. But if the barrier opens while we're working down here, I'm going back."

"And I'll be right behind you. I promise."

Inside the cool of the cottage, Issa made short work of laying out the design she had in mind. This level of glyph weaving required focus and attention to detail. As soon as they started, Jarand lost himself in it. He wasn't sure how much time had passed when the door leading to the forge swung open.

Bremin slipped through and took note of what they were doing. "Get to a place where you can stop, then we'll talk."

Isben closed the door behind them and leaned against it to watch. Cassim wasn't with them.

Jarand nodded that he'd heard, unable to do much more as he

worked to hold several sets of glyphs in the air while Issa compared them to her notes. When she was satisfied, she sparked them to life and watched them weave themselves into the net. It was only after the net had disappeared that she let her attention shift.

"You know Cassim hates it when you leave him behind, right?" Issa gathered up her papers as she rounded on Bremin.

Bremin stepped into the space where they'd been working, set his bag on the table, and fished out several sheets. "Yes, but he also glares at me when I slow down to match his pace. At least this time I had a good reason to hurry ahead. We discussed using the apprentice bond as a tether and gathered up a few ideas on how it might work. He insisted I share them with you two as soon as possible."

He placed down several papers, each filled with lines of script and diagrams that twisted and wandered. Jarand found that with Bremin, the more confusing the writing, the more inventive the man had been. If any problem needed an inventive solution, it was this one. Thankfully, the man had the uncanny ability of organizing and storing all the important information in his head. The writing served more as an exercise to help him pull his thoughts together.

He pushed one of these papers toward Jarand. "You said you felt Katira more strongly through your bond when the barrier was open, correct?"

"That's right." Jarand briefly scanned over the roaming lines.

"Good. I think I've got a way for you to instill energy in her using that connection. It's complicated, but I believe it will work."

Cassim shuffled his way through the door and carefully set Onyx on the makeshift perch in the corner before making his way straight to the water bucket. He took several long drinks before falling into the nearest chair. "I assume you've started explaining what we discussed?"

"Yes, I was about to show him the specific sequences." Bremin indicated the paper.

As much as Jarand itched to see what Bremin had come up with, his sense of duty required him to finish what he'd started with Issa. It didn't help that she was watching him intently from across the table.

"I'll look at them the moment we finish this improvement to the sensing net. It's no good to the town the way we left it."

Cassim slapped his hand on the table, startling Jarand into silence. "Don't be ridiculous. I'll help Issa finish with the net, as it's the least I can do. As for you, you're the only one who can make those work, the only one who can help Katira if the need arises." His hand trembled on the table ever so slightly, betraying just how worried he was. "I pray it doesn't, but we best be ready, just in case."

CHAPTER 27

The thought of opening her eyes made Katira's stomach twist uncomfortably. Her head pounded as if it had been stepped on. The last time she felt like this it was because she'd overdrawn from her reserves of power. She strained to remember what she'd been doing only to come up with nothing. Strange. Stranger still was the gritty sand pressing into her cheek. She listened for Papan, he never went far when she'd hurt herself, he was sure to be close by.

Instead of hearing him, she found herself surrounded by an eerie emptiness. It wasn't just quiet, it was dead silent. The sand triggered a thin memory that teased her from the edge of her brain. They'd been camping near a river; she must be there.

She risked cracking open one eye. The sight that greeted her made her wish she'd kept it shut. The world seemed broken, its colors wrong and jarring. She pressed her eyes shut, hoping what she saw was nothing more than the last clinging bits of a dream. As she did, more of her senses awoke. She smelled the strange nothingness of the air and the absence of the sun's heat which should have been beating down on her back at this time of day. More memories returned fitfully. She'd been at camp above Namragan, and they'd attempted to view the barrier using the glyph rod. Something happened then, but the idea of it was still vague and hazy.

She opened her eyes again, which triggered a different memory, this one enough like a nightmare that she wasn't sure it was real. She'd been inside Khanrosh with someone who'd never appeared in her dreams before.

Hannah.

The name jolted her back to awareness. She was in the mirror realm. She was working with Darius to heal the barrier. She rushed to her feet only for her knees to soften beneath her, sending her back to her hands and knees in the sand. Her tongue felt thick and dry in her mouth and the world spun around her.

Memory couldn't be forced; it needed space to flow into. Katira allowed her mind to clear, waited for the memory to come. They hadn't meant to go to Khanrosh. It was a mistake. Hannah was trying to keep her mind off something, that's why she'd talked of traveling — as a way to forget, if only for a moment.

With time, the remaining pieces of the story snapped back into place, each one hitting like a punch to the gut. Wrothe had killed Darius. They'd succeeded in healing a strand of the barrier. Hannah had knocked her out so she could escape Khanrosh.

Katira eased back to her feet, slower this time. The campsite on the river's elbow against the sheer wall of the canyon was familiar, even with its bizarre colors. She'd been there with Isben when they first arrived. If all had gone according to plan, then Darius and Hannah would be waiting at the cabin to reunite with her.

At the meadow, Darius's body was thankfully nowhere to be seen. That much of their plan had worked. As for the other part, the cabin stood empty. Katira cursed. They should have been back already.

Hannah made it clear that Wrothe was strong enough to over-power Darius's best defenses, break down his walls, and steal into his mind. If she found him before Hannah helped him leave Khanrosh, it would only be a matter of time before she discovered that he'd altered her trap for his own uses, and that Katira was in the mirror realm. If that had happened, the woman would drop everything to hunt her down.

And Katira could do nothing but wait. She briefly considered hiding again to buy herself more time if Wrothe did come, but doing so would make it harder for Darius to find her and continue the work. Instead, she sat on the front step of the cabin and watched the dark orb of the sun drop towards the horizon. The muddy daytime sky shifted from shades of rust, to amber, and then to milk as the sun finally dipped out of sight. With each passing hour, her unease grew and other, more horrible, scenarios built themselves in her mind.

Katira flared her power, letting it race along the pathways of her skin, and shuddered at the sudden chill. She couldn't use it, shouldn't use it, not without Darius's protection in place. If she did, it would be as if she'd personally invited Wrothe to come find her. Utter foolishness. But holding it would do no harm. With it, she could sense the slight eddies and vibrations of power being used somewhere to the south.

In this soundless, empty, shadow-haunted world, at least holding the power, no matter how cold and uncomfortable, felt real. With the coming dark, her doubts assailed her. What if Wrothe had destroyed Darius? What if it was up to her to piece the barrier back together on her own? At what point did she stop waiting and take action? She allowed a single ribbon to stretch forth and formed a small series of glyphs inspired by those she'd seen Darius use when he'd opened the barrier.

"Stop!" came a shout from nearby. Darius rushed toward her, eyes wide, hand outstretched, and lines blazing dark against his skin. "What do you think you're doing?"

The shock of seeing him broke her focus. Her power retreated. "When you didn't come back, I got scared."

He gripped her outstretched arm, unwound the cord binding her stone into her palm, and replaced it around her neck. "I admire your curiosity, but you know the risks."

A thousand protests sprung to Katira's lips, each one losing its sting before she managed to speak. All of her fears of the past few hours needed a target. "I had no intention of sparking it to life. I'm not stupid."

"All the same, had you managed to complete that sequence and activate it, it would have been the same as offering yourself up as a sacrifice."

Katira wanted to argue her position, explain how if she could find a way to work without him, then no matter what happened, she could heal the barrier and they would accomplish their goal.

Her argument's intensity dried up as soon as she saw the quiet desperation in his eyes. He'd been waiting centuries in this hell for a chance to heal his broken world, and she was being reckless.

"Forgive me. I didn't mean to scare you," Katira said, and she meant it.

Darius accepted her apology with a nod before turning to look around. "Where's Hannah?"

"I thought she was with you." Katira had assumed the two of them would return together, that perhaps Hannah had already left to fetch some interesting morsels for the evening meal. If she hadn't, if Darius hadn't even seen her, it could only mean one thing. "She was supposed to find you after—"

Darius's face turned from serious to stony. "What happened?"

She walked a few steps away, unable to meet his eye. "It was an accident. I didn't mean for it to happen. I asked her to show me how to travel the way the two of you do, that it might help me get away from Rose if I needed to."

He clenched the muscles of his jaw, pulling his face into tight lines. "The fool. I warned her against even trying. There are too many uncertainties. The world you know is far different than this one."

Katira found herself suddenly defensive. "She did it to help me. I'd just watched you *die*. I couldn't get the horror of it out of my mind. By teaching me, I was able to forget for a few minutes. You're here, so it worked well enough."

Darius's face softened until he looked almost apologetic. Almost. "Being here has been hard for you. I keep forgetting how different this world is, how everything that happens for you is so new and painfully fresh. Don't fret. I'm here now, and we'll figure this out." He faced the fading light of the last of the sunset. "Ugh. That also means she won our bet. I owe her now," he muttered, almost too quiet to be heard.

"Wait, you bet against me to be able to travel?"

"It's not important." He turned to meet her gaze. "Where is she?"

Katira hung her head. "Somewhere in Khanrosh." She took a shaky breath. "I was supposed to travel back to the cabin. It was supposed to be so easy. But knowing you might be waking up in Khanrosh, that you might be in danger from Rose, summoned up my own bad memories of being there. I couldn't get it out of my head."

Darius winced. "But you escaped, how?"

"Had Hannah been alone, she could have gotten away, but she refused to leave without me. I couldn't clear my mind enough to allow her to guide both of us out. So, I convinced her to knock me out, hoping that I'd return to the campsite as soon as she stopped thinking of me. As soon as I was gone, she'd be able to make her way back soon after."

Darius completed the thought. "She got stuck there."

Katira pressed her eyes shut, hating that her idea had failed. "It was our best chance. Hannah knew if I was caught it would be worse."

"She risked getting caught for you."

"I truly believed that she'd be able to leave before Rose found her." Katira pressed her toe against a purple tuft of grass. "The worst thing that could happen is that she gets killed and has to start over, right?"

"She didn't tell you the worst possible outcome." Darius's fists clenched. Distress laced over the wrinkles of his face. "If she did, you wouldn't have agreed. Rose learned early that killing wasn't the worst thing she could do to someone. As long as she doesn't let her attention shift, she can torture someone for weeks."

Katira wrung her hands. "If Hannah's tortured, will she tell Rose about me?"

"Most likely. Even the strongest mind won't last long when Rose is determined, and she's already suspicious."

"Then we have to go save her. Get her out of there." Katira started back down the path leading south.

Darius didn't move. "She wouldn't want that. She would want us to continue the work and heal the barrier. Anything to end this horror once and for all."

"I can't let her suffer." Katira grasped her shirt sleeve and twisted it. "There has to be something else we can do. Something to distract Rose long enough so Hannah can get away."

Darius tugged his doublet straight. "Wait, come back. That's it. That's the solution. By working on the barrier, it's as good as calling to her. She will feel it and come after me like she did before."

"And what if she doesn't?" Katira smoothed out her tortured sleeve. "What if she keeps hurting Hannah until she tells her everything? We're practically gifting Rose what she needs to know to sabotage our efforts."

Darius's shoulders fell, and he pinched the bridge of his nose. "What would you have me do, Katira?" He drew a deep breath and held it for several long moments before letting it out. "Hannah has been my only friend for several hundred years. I want her safe as much as you do. No matter what we do, Rose will learn of you and of what we're doing eventually. The best we can do is work as hard as we can, get as many of the barrier's strands healed before she comes after us again."

"But—" Katira started before he cut her off.

"When Rose broke into your world, it cost you your mother. Whose life will you risk the next time she manages it?"

"That's not fair—"

"I'm surprised she didn't guess at your unique talents when the two of you crossed paths before. The second she sees us working together, she'll know. You are a threat. She won't stop until you have been eliminated or brought to her side. I'll kill you myself before I let that happen."

Katira flinched hard at his last statement. He'd never threatened violence against her before, but she knew he meant it.

Should Wrothe get hold of her, the woman would become unstoppable.

~

Katira charged into the dense trees as she followed Darius. She assumed they were going back to the sheltered grotto, but he stopped when they reached the large stone where they'd sent Isben back.

The lines on his arms glowed to life. "Time is of the essence, and this is as good a spot as any." He immediately brought the barrier into view and isolated the first few strands. The patient teacher she'd seen in him before was gone, replaced by an intensity that confirmed how desperate he was to see Hannah safe.

The change of place caught Katira off guard. She'd been successful at the grotto, and only at the grotto. Trying to heal the barrier somewhere new, somewhere already charged with the memory of nearly losing Isben, all while not letting her worries about Hannah overwhelm her, seemed like a bad idea.

"No, not here. Please. We should go back to the grotto. It's safer there."

"It'll take too long to get there. We already know this area is safe in both worlds. There's no time to waste." He pulled his selected threads further from the weave of the barrier. "Find a matching strand."

She glanced around and tried to dislodge the creeping sensation that Wrothe might sneak up on them at any moment and seize her. It would only take a moment of Darius being distracted for it to happen. Wrothe was strong enough to overpower Katira and weave those awful glyphs into her brain that would make her the woman's slave. She shuddered. It did no good to think like that. Besides, Darius would know the moment Wrothe came near, it was in his best interest to keep Katira safe. She had to trust him.

She brought a delving glyph to life and with a touch filled herself with the song of the first strand. Somehow, knowing that this was a person made it all the more compelling to heal the two halves of the thread. The barrier hummed in a rich contented buzz, with no trace of the anger they'd seen before. So far, so good. With the song filling her head, Katira plunged her seeking strands into the threads.

Just as before, threads from the mirror realm shrank back, while those from the real world surged forward as she let the melody resonate through the mass. At the song's touch, more threads fell back until a proud handful stood out, hopeful and shining. She touched each of these, comparing their song to the one she held until she found the one that formed a perfect harmony. While the process seemed far easier this time, it still took more time than she wanted. There had to be a way to work faster.

She lined up the matching thread to Darius's and sparked the joining. Just as before, it violently yanked her power away. As the first thread they'd restored hadn't taken everything, she had to trust that this one wouldn't either, but nothing was certain.

Katira's head spun as the last of the thread finished fusing together. She held firmly to her power, leaning into it to keep upright. Aching cold pierced her through. She needed the thread's gift, the restoring orb, or it would be impossible to continue. When the orb finally took shape, she reached for it without hesitation. Like before, it granted a fraction more than what she'd lost.

Darius added a new thread to those he held. "Again, quickly, before that extra fades away."

Katira wasted no time learning the next song. As she did, an idea took hold. If they started fusing the next thread before the previous finished, they could create a continual loop using the orb's gift at the same time they spent it. Then they could maintain the work as long as they could keep focused.

It all came down to how fast she could find the match. With the new song ringing in her mind, she dove back into the mass, hoping to find a faster way. Without warning, the barrier heaved, and its contented buzz rose into an angry hiss.

Darius grabbed her collar and pulled her back with a mighty heave just as dozens of threads whipped through the air. One caught a nearby branch, severing it as if it had been cut by a freshly sharpened axe. Just then, raking hot lines of pain echoed through the bond and for the tiniest moment, she could have sworn she'd felt Papan's flows inside the surge. He must have been close to the barrier when it erupted and been hit. The disturbance faded as soon as it started.

Darius found his voice first. "You okay?"

Katira rubbed at where her shirt had rasped her neck, her attention fixed on her bond with Papan until she sensed the prickling of Cassim's healing flows. It was enough to know he was safe.

She nodded. "What was that?"

"My best guess is that one of your friends tried something new. Let's hope they learned their lesson."

She winced at the remembered pain. "I have a feeling that they did."

Darius hadn't dropped his threads like she had, and it took several long minutes before she found the match from before. She was impatient now, needing to see if it was possible to loop the energy and spare both of them the violent losses and gains of power as they worked. When she sparked this thread to its match, she didn't wait for it to finish before choosing another.

As soon as the song filled her, she rushed to find its match, eager to test if it was even possible to join more than one at a time. When the bundle of potential threads came into view, she leaned into her intuition, hoping that perhaps if her need was great enough, it would guide her to a match that much faster. By the time she found the next match, the joining in progress was close to finishing. The extra energy of the first thread's gift still pulsed under her skin. If there was any time to try, it would be now. She brought the second pair together and set the spark.

"Easy Katira, slow down." Darius's hands were shaking. "We're not all as strong as you."

As expected, the new orb appeared. Katira took hold of it and guided its energy through her and back into that bright point where the next set of threads were beginning to join. If they continued like this, each new match would fuel itself.

"I have to keep going. It wants to keep going." She selected a new thread and again found herself struggling to find its match fast enough to start its joining as the next orb appeared. As she searched, she could have sworn she sensed Isben there among the waiting threads.

"You must slow down. This is getting out of hand." Darius's threads waiting to be matched scattered. "We have to be able to stop."

"Don't you see? We could finish it now. The barrier wants to be healed. It wants this to happen." Katira pleaded. The extra energy from the orbs pulsed under her skin, and she no longer felt the cold.

"You don't understand. We have to stop." Darius showed his empty hands.

The thought of letting go of the music made her throat tighten and her focus slip. The momentum gained from each healing pushed her to keep going. Without Darius supplying the next thread, she had no choice but to gather up the extra energy instead of using it.

"Good. We need to be sure it's safe to do it this way." He continued to coach, but there was a tremor in his voice that couldn't be from the work. He should be revitalized just as she was.

"What's wrong?"

"Focus on finishing this last thread." A tiny thread of desperation wove through his words.

Him not telling her made the apprehension worse, made her focus slip more. As she worked to line up the last thread, it kept slipping in her grasp. She nearly lost it before being able to spark it to its match. Without another of Darius's threads to study, Katira found herself growing more anxious about why he needed to stop.

"The orb, Katira. Take it before it fades."

She did, allowing its warmth to fill her. Without another thread to heal, the extra energy coursed through her and made her skin prickle uncomfortably.

Darius let the barrier snap closed and gripped her by the shoulders. "What you did was amazing. Now, get away as quickly as possible. I'll hold her off." He pushed her toward the grotto.

Suddenly, the reason he wanted to stop made sense. Wrothe was coming. Katira pivoted on the balls of her feet to sprint into the trees, only to be cut off by two snarling shadow hounds. She backed up and drew the knife from her belt.

"So, this is your big secret. Interesting." Wrothe's voice filled Katira's head with its oily black film. The woman stood at the edge of the small clearing in all her terrible majesty. The crimson fabric that trailed behind her billowed as power streamed off her in waves. At least a dozen hounds formed a circle around the clearing, trapping the two of them inside.

Wrothe shot a bolt at Darius. "Don't you dare move."

Darius deflected the shot as if it were nothing. "What did you do with Hannah? She's innocent."

His tone surprised Katira, as it was full of venom and utter hate. She'd assumed he would grovel and plead, like all those times before, anything to appease the crazy woman so she would go away. Seeing him stand up to her like this was both thrilling and terrifying.

Wrothe crossed her arms over her chest and scoffed. "You always assume the worst of me. I hate it. I'll have you know, I didn't hurt her — much."

Katira's heart caught on that last word. It was true then, Hannah had suffered because of her. Katira couldn't undo the past, but she could remove herself from the situation and make it so Wrothe couldn't use her as leverage. She studied the forest, taking note of the three hounds that now blocked her escape. If she was going to run for it, she'd need to get past them.

Darius kept himself squarely between Katira and Wrothe, and kept the woman's attention trained on him. "Where is she?"

"You shouldn't have lied to me," Wrothe said, her voice now strangely sweet. "Had you simply told me what you were doing, I wouldn't have had to pull it from her mind like I did." A ring of Bending glyphs formed in a circle over her outstretched hand. If she got inside Darius's mind, she could convince the man to do anything she wanted. "Give me the girl and I won't have to use this on you."

"Never." A shield sprung to his fingertips. "After all these years, I finally found a way to be free from this hell forever. Isn't that what you want?"

"That's not freedom. That's the end." Wrothe lunged forward, forcing Darius back. "With her, I could enter the real world whenever I desire and take what I want, live like I want. All without risk."

"Your slaves never last long. What will you do when she's all used up?"

"That's not your concern." Another bolt shot from her fingers and burst against his shield. "You can't fight me forever. I always win."

"I don't want to fight you forever." He gave Katira a small push, reminding her that she needed to leave. "If I'm allowed to finish, I'll never have to fight you again."

It was happening once more, Darius was sacrificing himself for her, for the greater goal, for the hope that they could put an end to this madness once and for all. If Katira couldn't stop it, then the best she could do was make it count and get as far away as possible. Only one place existed in this world where she could take shelter from that monster—

Amul Dun.

CHAPTER 28

*E*ven after several hours of practice, Jarand still didn't feel confident in the patterns that Bremin believed would enable him to strengthen Katira through their bond. At any other time, he would have preferred to learn something like this over the course of weeks, until the use of them came as naturally as breathing. But they didn't have weeks. They barely had hours.

To his credit, Bremin had the patience of a stone when necessary. He watched as Jarand brought each sequence to life, only correcting when necessary, only giving advice when asked. Hundreds of years of teaching other Stonebearers might have had something to do with it.

It wasn't until the sun hung low and lazy in the sky that Issa and Cassim finished fixing the new pattern into the sensing grid, and not a moment too soon. It would be dark before long, and Jarand was sure they'd see more action with the hounds. Issa caught his eye and touched where the tether wound around her wrist.

"It's your turn to wear this."

Seeing as she'd worn it the better part of the day, it was only fair. He held out his arm. "Pass it over."

The tether's glowing strands uncoiled from Issa's wrist, not unlike a snake. "It's a touch more cumbersome than before. I'd refine the pattern if there were more time, but seeing as there's precious little of that, I figured it'd be best if you got used to it before trouble finds us."

She fixed it to his wrist with a swift wrapping motion, and with it came the unnerving sense that he was everywhere in Namragan, all at once. If he thought wearing the tether was uncomfortable before, it was just shy of irritating now. But, if her new sequences did as she promised, neither of them would have to wear the thing much longer.

Isben's head snapped up from his work, and his pen clattered to the floor, splattering ink as it rolled beneath the bed. "Something's happening. It's close this time."

The tether had distracted Jarand enough that he'd missed the first ebbs and surges of power. Isben threw open the door leading to the forge with a thump and charged outside with Bremin close on his heels. Jarand checked the stone, which was still tucked secure in his palm, as he hurried to follow. In the fading light, the bright threads of the barrier shone like a beacon over the same large boulder where Isben had returned back to the real world.

"Why here? Why not at the grotto where it was more secure?" Jarand asked as soon as he reached Bremin.

"Speculating will only waste time." Bremin walked a quick circle around the disturbance as if inspecting it. "I'd much rather you test that new sequence, see if it works before we find we need it."

Earlier when dealing with the barrier, Bremin's counsel had been to stay back, to not interfere, anything to avoid causing problems for Katira. While Jarand wanted nothing more than to have the security of knowing that he could help Katira should she be overdrawn, being the one to potentially cause a problem made him pause.

"Well? What are you waiting for?" Bremin asked when Jarand didn't immediately move into action.

The question that dug into Jarand's skull wasn't worth asking. Bremin wouldn't make him try anything that he hadn't already weighed out all the odds for. If it was a better choice to test the sequence than to risk causing a problem with the barrier, then it was worth trying.

Cassim and Issa had already taken up their positions with Issa ready to shield and Cassim safely behind her. Isben stood near Bremin, lines already alight and brow furrowed.

Jarand formed the first sequence, designed to lock around the invisible connection between himself and Katira like a bead on a thread. As it completed forming, it rested on the bond like a weight. Not uncomfortable, but definitely there. This would serve as the vehicle that would carry a ribbon of pure power from him to Katira, a risky move, but the only solution they could come up with that would allow him to keep her alive without being able to touch her. It shone like bright gold as he wove it securely into the bead.

"There, that's it." Bremin's eyes shone with an eager excitement. "Now, wrap it in the modified shielding. We must see if it will pass through."

Jarand tried his best not to be distracted by Bremin's encouragement and continued on. At least shielding was something he was skilled at. He wove the adapted shield around the bundle, being careful not to let it touch the ribbon of raw energy.

"She's found the first match," Isben reported from behind Bremin.

"Any faster than the last time?" Bremin asked.

"Not much, no."

Bremin shifted his attention away from Jarand. "Are you getting a better sense of what she's looking for, what the match needs to be?"

"I believe so. I think I could help her. It wouldn't be perfect, but it would be a start." A delving glyph formed over Isben's palm.

Bremin held up a hand. "Wait. Jarand must complete the test first. Then we'll see what you can do."

His glyph lingered a moment, then winked out. As the night deepened, the show of light became that much more dramatic. Anyone from the town wandering remotely close would be drawn to it more surely than a moth to a flame.

Jarand didn't wait for Bremin's attention to return. Managing a raw ribbon of power alongside so many other flows required more focus than he was accustomed to. As with all glyph weaving, time worked against him, making it more likely for him to lose his grasp of the sequences. He slid the shielded bead along the bond and toward the surging threads of the barrier.

He didn't realize his mistake until the barrier's hum snapped into an ugly hiss. He'd forgotten a single sequence, something meant to mimic the dark energy that radiated from the mirror realm and keep the barrier from reacting. Hundreds of angry threads whipped outward, dozens of which struck Jarand, cutting wherever they touched. The flows he fed into the barrier stuck fast, preventing him from pulling away.

"Issa, cut him free!" Bremin ordered from behind Isben's ragged shield. "Now!"

She'd been standing ready, the glyph already perched on her fingertips. The cut was clean, efficient, and far too close to Jarand's face for comfort. He staggered back a few steps before Issa forced him to the ground and covered both of them with a shield as the angry whipping threads slowed and stopped. Jarand fought to catch his breath. His heart raced in an erratic lurch. The glyph work had been challenging, but not enough to do that.

The glow of Issa's shield winked out as she called over her shoulder. "Cassim, help him. Those things cut deep."

Jarand pulled at Issa's hand where she had him pinned, needing to get up, needing to try again. He already knew what went wrong, and her fussing over him wasted precious time.

She slapped his hand away. "Not until Cassim's done with you. Calm down before you bleed out."

Bleed out? Those threads couldn't have cut him more than scratches. "It's not that bad," he mumbled through lips that had turned weirdly numb. Maybe it was that bad. His head fell back against the ground as Cassim bustled around him.

A voice from the past swirled up from the dust of his memory. Master Iosephe, the long-dead Captain of the Guard and Jarand's first teacher, had taught him how to calm his mind in times of conflict. More than a hundred years later, Jarand could hear his stern lecture as it echoed through the silence of Amul Dun's practice yard. *Observe everything, take note of each sound, each smell, the firmness of the ground beneath your feet, the brush of the breeze on your skin. Take note of that which stays the same, that which changes, and act accordingly.*

It was good advice and had served Jarand well in the past. It would serve him now. At first, the shifting pitches within the hum of the barrier filled his ears, blocking out any other noise. With a sigh of submission, he allowed his focus to open so that the world outside of his awareness of the barrier could enter. Overhead, a falcon rode the warm currents of air. Its cries echoed off the granite of the mountain. Onyx clicked her beak at it from the safety of the nearby trees. The breeze coming down the canyon from the north hinted at rain and rustled the leaves as it cooled the beads of sweat that had formed on the bridge of his nose.

When he finally relaxed, Issa released her hold. "That's better. Lie still until Cassim finishes, then you can get up."

"I'd prefer it if you didn't, not for a good while at least." Cassim protested from somewhere to his left. "I can't guarantee all these will hold, rush job and all."

Jarand winced as the healing flows hit a tender spot. "I can't see. What's happening?"

"You're ridiculous, you know that? Here you're bleeding to death, and you still can't step back for even a second." Cassim moved to the next spot. "They've got everything under control."

"Don't exaggerate, it wasn't that bad." Jarand tried to push the healer to the side to see for himself.

Cassim obstinately held his ground. "It was bad enough. Bremin's letting the kid see if he can identify matching pairs. From the sound of it, he's close, but hasn't quite figured it out." He wiped his brow and sat back on his heels. "What of Katira? Did the threads get her?"

Jarand hadn't considered that the threads might have burst out on both sides; he'd assumed it had only been toward him. With the barrier open, the bond that pulsed between himself and Katira was much easier to read. If anything had happened, it hadn't touched her. She was, however, concerned about him. She would have sensed the threads cutting him in the moment it happened. With Cassim nearly done, that worry was fading.

"Jarand?" Cassim gave his shoulder a small shake.

He shook his head which was unpleasantly fuzzy. "She's fine, as far as I can tell."

"And the energy drain?

Bremin, who'd always been one to listen in, even when it was unwelcome, answered instead. "The joining of each thread still takes a massive amount of power, but it seems as if the barrier itself is releasing some back to her with each strand restored."

Cassim returned his stone around his neck. "That does it. At least try to stay still for a bit, would you?"

Jarand would do nothing of the sort. He carefully pressed himself up to sitting and ignored the distressed sounds coming from the healer. Several of the newly healed cuts stretched uncomfortably, but held. Cassim wasn't considered one of the best healers at Amul Dun for nothing.

"Should I try to reach through again?"

Bremin thought for a moment before answering. "No. Another incident could cost someone their life. We were lucky this time."

Isben raked a hand through his hair, making it fluff larger than usual. "No, no, no, no, no. She's started fusing a second pair before the first is finished. It's taking too much. She needs to go back to one, because there are too many ways this can go wrong."

Through the bond, Katira practically radiated with energy as a second thread fused with its match and formed a bright star. Should she keep chaining them together like this, the risk of being killed by giving too much was reduced to an afterthought.

Bremin held up a hand to quiet Isben as he continued to plead with Katira to stop. "Talk to me, Jarand. What's happening?"

"Whatever she's doing, it's better this way. It's not pulling as much."

"Do you trust in her ability to finish?"

The question struck Jarand hard. As much as he wanted to accept the relief this turn of events had brought, he was painfully aware of all the risks.

"She's still so young. If anything happens, she doesn't have nearly enough experience or training to guide her."

"That doesn't answer my question. Can she finish this?"

"Yes. She can." A knot formed in Jarand's throat, this time not from fear, or pain, or grief, but from hope. "The Stonemother has blessed her with an uncanny ability to make things work. She'll see this through."

Bremin lowered his voice. "You're still scared for her."

"Of course I am." Jarand ran a hand over his face. "Every time she's faced a challenge like this, it's left its mark. If she's an Innate, then..." He trailed off, unable to finish the thought.

The barrier's pitch shifted briefly, drawing Bremin's attention long enough to check on Isben's progress. When he turned back to Jarand, the look on his face spoke of grim resolution.

"Death has come for both of us enough times that we stopped counting. Each time, we have to choose whether to take its hand or fight it off. It's the same for her. I know that doesn't make it any easier for you to bear, but all the same, you must."

Isben's stance shifted and his head tilted to the side, as if trying to figure something out. "Something is happening. They're slowing down."

"Why?" Issa drew closer, so she was looking over Isben's shoulder. "It seemed like things were going well."

Jarand forced himself to his feet and gripped his cane as the world swerved to one side. A sense of uneasy worry washed through the bond.

"She's in danger."

Bremin held up a hand. "Don't let your imagination get the best of you. For all we know, it's King Darius erring on the side of caution. Maybe he wants to stop."

"It's not that." Isben's grip tightened around his stone. "It's like her focus has slipped. She's struggling to find the match." Determination tightened his fists, as if he believed he could make her stick with it by his willpower alone. "There, you've got it."

When the thread finished healing and disappeared, the barrier snapped shut, leaving them in sudden darkness. Jarand was about to release his power when the tether pulsed at his wrist. As if they didn't have enough to deal with, shadow hounds had crossed into the town, and worse, there were far more than before.

His heart tripped and he grit his teeth as he held up the tether to Issa. "We have a problem."

CHAPTER 29

Katira ran.

Behind her, a pair of shadow hounds writhed in the dry undergrowth, downed by two bolts that thankfully had hit their marks. She hated every step that took her away from Darius, through the trees, and up the rocky slope. She ran to fill herself with the desperate need to breathe and the pounding of her heart, anything to keep her mind from the events unfolding behind her. If she were to think of Darius, even once, this world would take her right back to him and directly into Wrothe's hands.

The Pathara Mountains ringing Namragan were made from the same grey granite as the mountain where Amul Dun perched. It should have been easy to imagine herself already there, to fall into the measured strides of the long sentry path that circled the keep's expanse.

The landscape blurred at the edges of her vision. It was working; the world was shifting. It wouldn't be long before she found herself back in the comforts of Amul Dun. The harder she ran, the more compelling that want became. Back at Amul Dun, she could pretend, at least for a little while, that all this was over, that everyone was safe, that the world was back to normal.

A single thought stabbed its way into her mind. *Wrothe is hurting Darius because of you.*

She couldn't go back, not when so much depended on her staying out of Wrothe's grasp. But no matter how hard she fixed Amul Dun into her mind, the world had already set this new path in motion. It snapped around her like a giant spring and pulled her back into the clearing.

Darius stood hunched. He pressed a hand under his ribs where a spreading stain marred his doublet. The air around the two of them crackled with ribbons of their dark energy as they each fought for the upper hand. Katira turned to run again, anything to get away like she promised.

When Darius spotted her, his grim determination changed to anguish. Before Katira could take a single step, a dozen of Wrothe's dark ribbons darted around her like hissing deadly vipers and pinned her in place.

"This world works in mysterious ways, doesn't it? It's almost as if it wants us to be together." As Wrothe spoke, a motherly charm and false sense of comfort flooded over Katira, much like when Wrothe had tried to bend her will back in Khanrosh.

It wasn't going to work this time. Katira was no longer that innocent girl. She wouldn't freeze, not knowing what to do. Her time spent training with Issa had changed all that. Any hesitation would mean death, or worse, being turned into the madwoman's slave. Katira's power leapt to life, and glyphs meant to cut herself free sprung to her fingertips.

Before she could use it, Darius slammed his own complex flows around Wrothe. A dark blossom of power burst around her, then contracted and disappeared, taking her with it. The ribbons pinning Katira vanished like smoke.

Katira blinked at where Wrothe had stood, unsure at what she'd just seen. "What in the Stonemother's name was that?"

"Are you determined to get yourself killed?" Darius yelled at her, face reddening, eyes pleading.

His anger caught her off guard. "I tried to get away. I almost made it. The same thing happened as before."

Darius grimaced and lowered himself next to the boulder in the center of the clearing. "She'll be back in a few minutes, will try to get to you, to snare your mind. Get away from here. I don't care how."

"What if I can't leave? What if it brings me back again?" She reached for him, needing to see how serious the wound was. After all her time studying with Cassim, it was the least she could do.

"You have to. It's your only option." He coughed, and blood spotted his lips.

When Issa taught Katira how to defend herself, she often spoke of the importance of moving beyond the obvious choice. A Guardian who stayed one step ahead was that much harder to beat. There had to be something better than to simply run away forever.

An idea struck Katira, one that was almost too crazy to consider. "Let me heal you. Please. I have an idea."

"No." His voice took on a harder, colder edge, and he pushed her away. "Get out of here."

"Listen to me. If we can heal Rose's strand, she'll disappear from this world. All we have to do is find it."

Darius gripped Katira's sleeve with his bloodied hand. "She'll return long before we come close." He coughed, and his face contorted with pain. "Put me out of my misery. If you know she can't hurt me, it will make it all the easier to leave this place. It's exactly what you did in Khanrosh with Hannah, except you'll be the one running."

"It didn't work. It let Wrothe trap Hannah." Katira willfully ignored that he'd just asked her to kill him.

"It has to. Let your intuition take control. It will help you." His grip on her arm faltered and his hand fell away, but his steely gaze did not.

Katira was familiar with death, but she'd never killed. She choked on the pain. "I can't. Don't make me."

"I trust you. Don't think of it as death. You are ending my suffering. It's a form of healing, really." A weak smile tugged at the corner of his mouth.

He was right, damn him. Her worry was locked around him

suffering needlessly. If Wrothe couldn't hurt him, it would free her to run. The power's cold wash flooded through her, strengthening her resolve.

"Forgive me."

If she hesitated, even for a moment, she'd falter. She pressed the glyphs into him, one to render him unconscious, one to keep him from feeling pain, one to stop his heart.

There was no time to mourn, to think about what she'd done, to dwell on how that last spark of his life flickered and faded. Dark energy gathered on the edge of the circle, and Katira ran. She filled her mind once more with the tower of Amul Dun, of being safe, of falling into her father's arms and letting him hold her until the pain subsided. As much as she told herself that she'd saved Darius from something far worse, her heart fought her.

So she ran, away from Wrothe, away from death, away from everything.

She didn't stop until the rugged slope beneath her boots changed to smooth tile and the narrow slash of sky transformed into the familiar vaulted ceiling of the great hall.

Katira stopped herself just short of running headlong into the wall near the audience chamber door. She pressed her hands into the solidness of it, holding tight to her need to be there and willing herself to stay. When the world didn't tilt away and drag her back to Darius, she slid to the floor with relief.

In the real world, she'd stand in the colored puddle of light shining in from the stained-glass window and let the warmth soak through her apprentice robes. Quiet conversations, soft footfalls, and the rustle of paper always filled the place with a sense of purpose. For just a moment, she allowed her imagination to take her to a time when her biggest worry was performing her apprentice duties up to the standard Papan expected.

She knew this Amul Dun would be different, but still the riot of unusual color assaulted her from all sides. The dark stones that formed the tall walls of the great hall shone an icy blue, as did the floors where they weren't already whitened with the coming night. This place was not her home. This Amul Dun was new. Many of the long winding hallways and wandering corridors hadn't been built yet.

Katira stepped out of the way of the eerie blue-white specter of a woman soundlessly hurrying past with a stack of papers under her arm. Had Hannah not warned her about the people trapped in the mirror realm, she would have thought the woman was a ghost. Amul Dun would be full of these shadows, all of them broken pieces of Stonebearers who lived at the time of the split.

It had been less than a year since Wrothe targeted Amul Dun and Papan, less than a year since she tried to assassinate Lady Alystra, and less than a year since they'd cut her binding cords to Master Ternan. It wouldn't take long for Wrothe to figure out this was where she'd gone to hide. Katira had no intention of being an easy target. If Wrothe came for her, she would be ready.

A younger man with a smooth-shaved head entered the great hall and passed through the large doors leading to the audience chamber. Katira followed him, taking care not to come in contact with any part of him. To him and the rest of the shadows, she didn't exist outside of the familiar pattern they'd been following for centuries.

The audience chamber contained none of the familiar sights. A simple split-log table with benches, much like the ones seen in roadside inns, stood in the place of the finely carved council table. Heavy wooden shutters served as window coverings instead of the magical stained-glass panels that would change as she walked past. Everything about the room spoke of an austere plainness brought about by being new.

On the other side of the room, the man exchanged a few quiet words with an older woman who leaned on the casing of the window furthest from the door. At first glance, she might have been someone's sturdy grandmother taking a break from kneading bread or sweeping the floor. She stood with her head bowed, her snow-white braid coiled neatly on the top of her head like a crown. With a curt nod, the man turned and left the room as quickly as he'd come, leaving Katira alone with her.

She recognized the stole draped over the woman's shoulders, which was much like the one Lady Alystra wore during official occasions. This was Amul Dun's High Lady. If Katira was to find any help from the shadows, she might as well start at the top.

She gave the woman's shoulder a gentle tap, hoping it was enough to wake the woman from her usual pattern. Several moments passed before the woman showed any sign of noticing.

She didn't turn from the window when she spoke. "I asked to not be disturbed."

For the High Lady, the awful news of King Darius's unexpected death would have reached her a few hours earlier that day. She would still be reeling from the shock of it.

Katira chose her words carefully, thinking of what she might say to Lady Alystra, *her* High Lady, to gain her attention even at the worst possible time.

"An enemy is coming. I need your help to stop her."

"Her?" The High Lady's shoulders straightened a fraction, but she still didn't turn. "Why would we fear a woman coming by herself? Surely you've been misinformed of this threat."

"I can assure you, she's dangerous. She's broken her oaths. She must be stopped." Katira balled her fists in the sleeves of her shirt, willing the woman to look at her.

"You are unfamiliar to me. I don't recognize your accent." The woman finally shifted her gaze and a tiny gasp escaped her mouth. "What are you?"

"An apprentice, my lady. I've been sent to request your aide."

She reached out a hand and set her fingers against Katira's cheek, startled when they made contact. "You aren't real, can't be real. The news of King Darius's death was too much, it's making me see things." She buried her face in her hands. "Be gone from me, specter, I pray you."

As much as Katira wanted to convince the poor woman that she was, in fact, real, the time it might take to explain was more than it was worth risking. Staying there in the audience chamber was too public, because it would be too easy for Wrothe to find her. She murmured a soft apology and left the High Lady to her grief.

Back in the great hall, two corridors branched off into the east wing leading to the High Lady's offices, the library, and stairs to the upper level. Katira took the stairs, dodging another set of shadowy figures on the landing. During long summer days, when her work was done, she and Isben often climbed up to the roof above the library to watch the sun set. It was as good of hiding place as any.

As she turned onto the second story corridor, a sight stopped her cold. A young Master Ternan bumbled out from one of the doorways carrying a tea set.

He must have been no more than twenty and still an apprentice, judging by the grey robe hanging from his shoulders. Instead of the white fringes of hair rimming the sides of his head, dark curls framed his all-too-serious face. Instead of a fragile, bent frame, he stood tall and lean. He had yet to write the famous histories of King Darius's reign and tragic demise. While she'd known he was alive at this time, seeing him surprised her. Of anyone in this world, he was the one most likely to understand what had happened. Maybe if she had a chance to speak with him, he would be able to rally the protection she needed.

She discarded thoughts of going to the roof and followed him into a room she knew as his office. Instead of piles of papers and books teetering on every available surface, the few items in the room clearly had a place and a function. A dignified woman sat at the wide desk, bent over a stack of neatly arranged pages as young Master Ternan arranged the tea on a small table in the corner of the room. Her hair was pulled up away from her face, leaving the rest to hang loose down over her shoulders.

Katira recoiled when she saw the simple green trim on her collar. If the woman was a Bender, she would know Wrothe as Rose. The two of them would have certainly worked together over the years when Rose was sane. Convincing Ternan or this woman that Rose was coming to destroy them would be impossible.

As Katira backed herself out of the office, the truth of the situation smacked her upside the head. Just as the grass appeared purple, the purples that marked Seekers would appear green. This woman was Amul Dun's Head Historian. If anything, her being in Master Ternan's same office should have made that clear. If Stonebearers were anything, they were creatures of habit. Knowing this made enlisting either of them for help a much better bet.

The woman wrote careful notes with a steady hand, stopping here and there to dip her quill. Katira slid away one of the finished pages which had been set to one side, being careful not to break the woman from her pattern by accidentally touching her.

It was full of unfamiliar words and characters, reminding Katira of the ancient books in her timeline that required special care to even touch. A knot formed high in Katira's throat when she saw that the woman was recording the details regarding King Darius's death. The same as with the High Lady, the news would have come to her only hours before.

Young Ternan organized the items on his tray and poured two cups of tea, adding a spoonful of honey to each. "After so much bad news today, a spot of tea sounded like the perfect distraction. Would you like to join me?"

The woman didn't look up until she'd finished writing. She then cleaned the tip of the quill and set it down, reminding Katira of Master Firen and his overly meticulous nature.

"Ternan, I've told you countless times. Allow me to finish before you ambush me with your words. I know you are there, it's impossible to miss you."

His gaze fell to the floor. "My apologies. I can't help it."

"Yes, you can. You simply choose to let your impulses win. As you are my apprentice, I will eventually break you of it. It's a valuable lesson for anyone who wields the power. It forces you to think first, act second." She straightened from the desk, stretched, and the sternness in her eyes softened. "As for the tea, you're right. It's perfect for a day like this."

Katira hurried out of the Head Historian's way as she left the desk and joined Ternan at the small table. Normally, the idea of eavesdropping on someone else's conversation would make her uncomfortable. She had to remind herself that this was no longer real, but a moment caught in an endless loop of repeated time.

Young Ternan held his cup between his palms but didn't lift it from the table. "The whole world seems different. I know that death comes to us all, but his? It's like part of me has been ripped away. I can't help feeling that something more has happened than what the reports say."

The woman gave a somber nod. "You have lost something dear to you. We all have. It's bound to leave you hurting."

"I've suffered loss before. I know what it feels like. This feels different. I feel hollow, like something is missing."

She held her cup close to her face and breathed in the steam. "We believed nothing could ever hurt him, that he was too strong. It's a hard reminder that what we do is dangerous, even for the best of us. Give yourself time."

Katira wanted to shout at her. Whether he knew it or not, Young Ternan had clearly felt the aftermath of the world splitting apart, and she was dismissing it as standard grief. Had she listened to him, they might have figured out the truth of what had happened to Darius and taken steps to correct it sooner. It wasn't fair.

A hand on her shoulder made Katira jump. She threw her elbow at her would-be attacker, who grunted in surprise and doubled over.

"Sorry," Hannah said between coughs. "I should have said something. You probably thought I was someone else."

Jarand followed Issa back to the cottage to collect his sword and the leather armor he'd discarded earlier. He hoped the latter would help Cassim feel better about him going after the hounds. As it was, the man was practically in hysterics. He scrambled after Jarand with a different protest bursting from him at every turn. Onyx clacked her beak and fluffed her feathers, annoyed at being awakened by the noise. When Jarand reached for his sword belt, Cassim snatched it from off the long table near the front door and held it hostage.

He yanked the belt back when Jarand went to grab it. "Even if you did feel up to it, if they spot you drenched in your own blood, there will be all manner of uncomfortable questions to answer."

Issa plucked the belt from Cassim's hand and returned it to Jarand. "Unless you're offering to come with me, which you aren't, then it's got to be him. I'd rather not do this alone."

Jarand nodded his thanks and tugged the belt around his waist and fastened it, taking care not to pull too tight against the newly healed cut on his hip. The room still spun whenever he moved too quickly, but not as violently as before. Issa studied him the same way she'd watch one of her students. She was about to say something when he cut her off.

"We best hurry before they scatter too far." Jarand opened the door to leave.

Cassim threw his hands in the air. "Bremin, can you talk some sense into him? He nearly fainted on us less than ten minutes ago. The last thing he should be doing is fighting monsters."

Bremin, who had already taken up residence at the kitchen table with his pen and paper, gave a noncommittal shrug. "He knows the risks, probably better than you do. If you're worried, you should go with them." He methodically dipped his pen and started writing. "Once that new sequence in the sensing net is spent sealing up whatever weakness it finds, someone will have to take care of whatever's left. As our healer, I imagine you'd be rather good at it."

"No, thank you." Cassim blanched and tugged his vest tight around himself. "My talents are needed here." He turned his attention to Issa and took hold of her shoulder. "Please be careful out there. Keep an eye on Jarand. Two, if you can spare them."

Issa pressed her hand over his and held it there. "I will. I promise."

She slipped out the door behind Jarand, and he pulled it shut faster than necessary, unwilling to be caught by any other objection Cassim might raise. As soon as it latched, Issa turned on him.

"Tell me the truth. Are you okay to do this?"

Jarand shifted his sword so the weight of it didn't pull at the older injury in his back. Dealing with the new discomfort of the barrier's cuts wasn't bad enough. "Were you defending my honor in there? For a moment, I thought you needed me."

"I know exactly how stubborn you are. Now that we're alone, tell me the truth, warrior to warrior." She hooked her thumbs into her belt. "It's safer for me to face them on my own than to believe you've got my back when you can't."

A howl split the summer evening's quiet and was answered by several more. Jarand was grateful that Lucan had taken his request to keep people inside after dark seriously, not a soul walked the lamplit streets. He didn't want to admit to Issa how tired he was, how all those cuts from the barrier seemed to drain away his will to keep going, and how his heart staggered from the recent strain. She needed him, they all needed him, and he worried there would come a point where he simply could no longer rally enough strength to act. At moments like this, he missed Mirelle more than ever. She was his strength when his had failed and his hope when the road was darkest.

"Jarand?"

He tapped the tether, letting it relay its information in a series of mental impressions. "The closest crossing point isn't far. We best get a move on."

"You didn't answer me." She blocked his path. The worry in her voice stabbed deep. "Can you fight?"

He loosened his sword in its scabbard. This was for Katira, so he would do everything he could. "It won't be any sort of impressive display, I can tell you that. But I can keep them from flanking you."

Her worry didn't fade as she gave a curt nod. "Good enough. Lead the way."

CHAPTER 30

While Katira knew that Darius or Hannah would find her as soon as they could, she'd half expected Wrothe to find her first. As far as she knew, Hannah was still tied up somewhere in Khanrosh suffering the aftermath of Wrothe's torture. It took her several moments to recover from the shock.

"How? I thought you were…" She trailed off, unable to put those thoughts into words.

Hannah straightened, still clutching her stomach. "You forget, I'm extremely good at finding things, including people."

Katira couldn't help looking over Hannah for any clue as to what might have happened to her, for why she didn't return with Darius after they'd parted ways in Khanrosh. She found none. But then, would she? The mirror realm could have easily erased any mark as soon as she stopped thinking about it long enough.

"I worried about you, about what might have happened. Are you okay?"

The slightest crease marked Hannah's forehead. "I understood the risks when I agreed. What's important is that it's over and I found you before she did."

"What about Darius?"

Hannah narrowed her eyes as if just realizing which room they were in. "For a man who just woke up in Khanrosh, again, he's good enough. The moment he regained his bearings, he insisted I hurry and find you. I didn't stick around to ask questions." She looked Katira up and down. "What about you?"

"Good enough. She didn't get me, if that's what you're asking."

Hannah took the paper that Katira was still holding and set it back on the desk. "You might not know if she got you or not. She can alter memories, remember?"

The thought turned Katira's stomach, she steadied herself on the edge of the desk. "Why would you say something like that?"

"To see your response. Sometimes I can spot when Wrothe's compulsion takes hold, when she's put some kind of block in place."

"And?"

Hannah took longer to answer than Katira was comfortable with. "As far as I can tell, you're still you. We best get moving. If I could find you here, Rose will be able to as well."

"Wait." The sensation of Darius dying under her hands still clung to every thought. Maybe if she talked about it, it would lessen the sting. "Did he tell you what happened?"

"Whatever happened wasn't your fault. It was Rose's. She was already on her guard before you two started. Something Darius said earlier had caught her attention. As for him ending up in Khanrosh, I can only imagine that she got to him again. Don't beat yourself up about it."

"It's not just that." Katira pressed hard against her stone bound to her palm. "I had to end him. It was the only way to stop her from hurting him, at least for a little while."

Hannah tugged on the hem of her coat. A tear shimmered in the corner of her eye. "No one should be made to do that. Least of all you. I should have been there."

The study faded whiter as the sun dipped below the horizon. A puddle of color formed a halo around the candle on the table where the two shadows sat deep in their own thoughts. Ternan stared into his cup as if hoping to find answers there, seeing as his master wasn't willing to talk more regarding Darius's death.

Katira glanced toward Ternan. "You knew him, didn't you?"

Hannah set her hand on the doorframe and leaned into it. "Not as well as I would have liked. He only spent a few months at Khanrosh before being assigned to his master here. It was this discussion that helped Darius and me figure out what happened." She took a shaking breath. "I can't help but think this was the clue that led Rose to binding herself to him and using him. We all have our weaknesses, and Ternan's was being too intuitive. I can only imagine how much he suffered at her hand before the end."

Katira studied Ternan one more time, remembering how they found him pinned to this same study floor, heels scraping against the wood. "If it makes you feel better, even when he knew he couldn't win, he fought against her. He died a hero's death."

"He shouldn't have had to. Both Darius and I could have done more, tried harder to keep Rose from binding herself to him. We were too absorbed in our own problems, didn't realize what she'd done until it was too late. We didn't know, couldn't know, how far Rose had fallen into insanity until she started targeting us as the enemy." Hannah pressed her eyes shut. "If this doesn't work, if after all we've done we can't heal the barrier, I fear my sanity might slip just like hers. After so many years of fighting and failing, I worry that I'll stop caring, or worse, grow cruel."

The dark orb of the sun sank out of sight; another night was approaching. Hannah slipped out of the office and back into the hall. "Come along, we'd better get back."

Katira released a bitter laugh. "And then what? She'll just keep finding us. There has to be a better way. We can't keep running like this, not if we want to succeed."

Hannah heaved a frustrated sigh. "Running is all we have. Each healed thread brings us that much closer to the end. We do what we can, and we run, and we keep trying."

Running couldn't be the only option, it just couldn't. If Hannah worried about slipping, about losing herself, then Darius had to feel the same. For his sake, they couldn't let Rose keep hurting him. As strong as he tried to be, the mind could only take so much abuse.

The thought sobered Katira. "If we keep going on like this, keep running, Darius will fail. His mind will break, and when it does, no amount of resetting or reawakening will bring it back. If that happens, she wins. You're smart, you have a world of resources at your fingertips. There has to be a way to keep her from hurting him."

"You say that like it's easy," Hannah snapped back, her voice heated with anger. "Like there's an answer hiding in one of the books of the Tower. You forget, I've been fighting her for centuries. Believe me, I've tried everything to protect him so the barrier could be healed. I don't appreciate your criticism. Not at a time like this." Her anger softened to a plea. "If you want to protect him, finish what you started."

Arguing would do nothing, not when it came to Hannah. She wasn't the type to budge in the face of a challenge, especially when that challenge came from someone her junior. Darius hadn't objected outright when Katira mentioned attempting to heal Wrothe's thread and remove her from the world. The only reason they didn't try was because there wasn't enough time to find it. If the split originated in Khanrosh, it stood to reason that Wrothe and Darius's threads would be easier to find there. It was worth trying.

"Fine. Then take me to him."

Hannah's eyes widened. "In Khanrosh? Have you lost your mind?"

"If she's just going to keep killing him, we might as well be somewhere close. Make restarting the cycle that much faster," Katira blurted out the lie. Concealing her plan of healing Wrothe's thread made no sense. Hannah would want Wrothe removed from the picture just as much as anyone, but some instinct kept Katira from telling her the truth.

Hannah balled her hands into fists and paced the width of the hall. "And risk her killing you? Why are we even debating this?"

"We both understand that the longer this takes, the greater the risk. Take me to him."

Hannah stopped pacing. "No. Darius gave me one job and made me swear to it. I'm to keep you safe at all costs. I won't deliver you to her." She seized Katira by the shoulders. "You must return to

Namragan. Travel there as soon as we part ways. I know you can. You brought yourself here, you can do it again."

"Wait, where are you going?" Katira went cold with the thought of returning to the valley alone. Everything bad that had happened to them had happened there. "I thought you were supposed to stay with me."

"The sooner I can help Darius remember, the faster you two can get back to work, and I refuse to take you to Khanrosh. I'll only be a few minutes behind you, I promise." With that, she turned, made her way down the long hall, and disappeared into the stairwell.

For a moment, Katira could do nothing but stare as she watched her go. What if she couldn't travel again like before? What if Wrothe found her alone here? What if Hannah fell into a trap at Khanrosh? She wrung the life out of her sleeve as each imagined disaster scenario grew increasingly worse. This was ridiculous, and she had every intention of telling Hannah just that. She darted to the stairwell only to find the woman already gone.

Return to Namragan.

Katira closed her eyes and walked down the echoing corridor outside Master Ternan's office. She fixed her mind on the small valley, the sheep grazing in the field, the way the ground felt as familiar as childhood beneath her feet. Each step summoned a new way their plan could fail, or how Wrothe would seize this opportunity to confront her when she was the most vulnerable.

Once again, the world grew soft at the edges. Amul Dun dissolved around her, and the whisper of her soft boots against the intricate tile patterns shifted to the gritty drag of packed dirt. The second she sensed the change, the memory of Darius dying beneath her hands surged back. She'd killed him. It didn't matter if it was for all the right reasons. He'd ended up in Khanrosh again. Wrothe could have both him and Hannah trapped again. It might be hours, if not days before they returned to find her, if Wrothe didn't find her first.

That worry was enough to alter her course. The grit beneath her feet smoothed to glassy polished marble. Katira fixed the idea of the cabin, the purple grass, the familiar earth back into her mind. She'd promised she'd be there. She had to be there. No matter how hard she tried, the marble stayed firm beneath her feet. The mirror realm delivered her directly into Khanrosh's great hall.

She shouldn't be there. *Couldn't* be there. Not now, not when they'd finally figured it out. She urged her heart to calm and her mind to stop spinning towards the disasters that awaited each wrong choice. Like at Amul Dun, the space was far from empty. Grey-robed apprentices hurried along the colonnade that stretched along either side of the hall, delivering messages and trays to the different offices. Several stately Stonebearers stood off to the side of the empty throne, locked in serious discussion.

Somewhere nearby, Hannah would be gathering up Darius and helping him remember. She heard the woman's voice through the oppressive silence and followed it to one of the doors off to the side of the hall. Inside, Hannah knelt beside where Darius lay curled in on himself.

"This is where it happened, isn't it?" Katira asked quietly, as to not startle either of them.

Hannah sighed, her shoulders falling forward. "I had a feeling you might end up here. Why is it so hard for you to do as you're told?"

"I didn't mean to—"

"I know. I know. Don't bother trying to explain," she said, not unkindly. She touched the ring of symbols in the floor. "This room, these symbols, were supposed to protect us, but in the end I believe they amplified Darius's intentions."

Darius gave a soft groan and reached out his hand.

"I hate seeing him like this." Hannah took it in hers and pulled it close. "Hello, old friend."

Darius stirred slowly. His eyes regained their intense focus, first on Hannah, and then to the rest of the room. Katira watched on as realization seized him like a noose around his neck. "Where is Rose?

Is she okay?" He gripped Hannah's hand tighter. "What happened?"

Hannah helped Darius up and into one of the few chairs in the room that hadn't been knocked over. "It's okay. Give yourself a chance to remember."

Katira stepped closer. "I thought that he already remembered. That you already talked to him."

"I did. There's a moment right as we wake up where the event that sent us here hovers near, much like remembering a dream. His first thought was to find and protect you. After I left, he slid back into the memory of the day it happened."

Darius's gaze darted around the room. "She's not in here. Where is she?" Panic crept into his voice. "I've hurt her, haven't I? You must have cared for her first and taken her to the infirmary. I must go to her. I can walk." He peeled Hannah's hand away from his. "Let me go to her!"

"Look at me," Hannah pleaded. "You've done this before, so many times. Let yourself remember." Anguish rolled off her in waves.

Katira came closer, hoping Darius would remember faster if he saw her. "Is it like this every time?" she asked in a whisper.

Hannah nodded grimly, keeping her attention fixed on him as his terror-filled gaze swept the room.

"It's the same for you as well, isn't it? If you fall asleep without someone watching over you, you wake reliving this moment." They'd told Katira about this, but seeing it drove home the horror of what it meant.

Hannah swallowed as if trying to press down the memory. "As hard as we try to avoid it, it still happens far more than either of us would prefer."

"What about Rose? Does this happen to her?"

Darius's hands flexed in his lap and Hannah took them into hers once more. "Not like it does to us. When the split tore away a portion of his power, she took it up. Made it part of herself. It gives her enough strength to go months without sleeping, longer if she steals power from him." Her breath caught. "He doesn't stop her, can't stop her."

The confusion knotting Darius's brow fell away. He rubbed at his face.

"There you are." Hannah breathed a sigh of relief. "Do you know how you got here this time?"

"It's still in bits and pieces. Did Rose get me again?" His gaze shifted to Katira and a world's worth of questions crossed his face. "Oh. Oh, my. Is she...?"

Katira opened her mouth to speak, but Hannah silenced her with an upheld finger. "It's better to let him work it through."

Darius leaned forward to rest his head in his hands. "It's coming back, all of it."

"Then you know what we must do. As soon as you're ready, we need to go," Hannah said.

Katira ran her fingers along one of the columns running up the wall, unable to shake the idea that if they were able to heal Wrothe's thread, all their struggles would be over. As her companion, Darius was sure to be able to find it given the chance. If being there at Khanrosh made the process any easier, then the sooner they could try, the better.

"Will she come in here willingly?" she asked.

"What are you getting at?" Hannah tugged her kirtle straight, preparing to leave.

"Hear me out. We could attempt to work on the barrier here. Either she'll leave us alone, not wanting to enter this room, or she'll strike one of you down, and you'll reappear here anyway. We'd save a lot of time."

"That's insane. She's literally two rooms away. When she feels us working and tugging on the barrier, she'll be on top of us in a heartbeat," Hannah protested.

Darius straightened, all traces of confusion falling away as he returned to himself. "Katira has a point. This room represents everything painful in Rose's life. It might keep her away longer. It's worth a try."

Hannah wrung her hands, more agitated than Katira had ever

seen her. "There are so many things wrong with this plan." She went to the door and pulled it shut before sealing it against intrusion with several glyphs that wove themselves into the symbols inlaid into the floor. "Even Rose will struggle to break through that, at least for a while. The minute she gets close, we're leaving. Can we at least agree on that?"

Darius gave Hannah a somber nod as his lines came to life. "I remember what you said earlier, about finding her thread and seeing if we can remove her from the pattern. I'll do my best to select any threads that might be her, but I can't make promises. Should the Stonemother be merciful, we might end this today."

"For all of our sakes, I hope so." Katira flared her power and embraced the rivers of ice that swept through her. Just like with the heat, it calmed her and brought back that focus she needed.

With a bright burst, he opened up the view of the barrier revealing a far denser mass of threads compared to what they worked with in Namragan. As he gathered his selection of dark threads, Katira noted him taking more care in which ones he chose before stretching them toward her like the strings of a lute.

Katira didn't hesitate. Each healed thread brought her that much closer to finding Wrothe's. The dark threads sang their songs. To her disappointment, none struck her as belonging to a half-crazed woman. There was no help for it; she'd just have to keep working until it revealed itself.

When she sparked the first match, she had every intention of finding the next in time to feed its joining using the gifted energy like before. She'd just filled herself with the next thread's song when the joining of that first thread caught on something and stopped. She took hold of the thread and pulled, hoping it was only a matter of freeing it so it could continue. It didn't budge. She tried again, but it was as if the entire barrier there was one massive knot.

Darius pushed another thread toward her. "Leave it. It might free itself if we fuse a few others first."

It made sense. When the threads of a loom became tangled, it was best to free the looser strands of the knotted yarn before attempting to untangle the larger mass. She studied Darius's outstretched thread, hoping that perhaps once she'd freed it and a few of the others, that the knotted thread might come loose. To her horror, this thread was stuck as well. She tried another, and another, but not a single one was willing to budge. Something here tangled up these threads, binding them around something she couldn't see.

Hannah stood by the door, shifting from foot to foot as she kept watch.

"It's not working. There's something wrong here." Katira sought out yet another strand and sparked it, hoping that this one might take. The fusing pulled at it, but it did not come free.

Darius released the remaining threads in his grip. "I was afraid this might happen. There's too much power infused in these walls, too many people affected here. Even if we did find her strand, it would be tangled into the same knot as the others."

Hannah pressed another glyph into the web she'd laced over the door. A hollow boom sounded from the other side. "She's onto us. The sooner we travel out, the better."

"My apologies." Darius seized Katira by the neck. "Can't risk any mishaps."

A blindingly bright glyph exploded inside her head and the world fell dark.

Katira's awareness returned in fragments starting with the sound of Darius and Hannah arguing over her in hushed tones. At least her head didn't throb like last time; whatever Darius had done was far gentler than what Hannah had done earlier.

"I didn't have a choice," Darius said in a quiet voice.

"Then explain yourself."

"She's young. I can only imagine how frightening all this must be. If even one of those fears surfaced during our escape, it would have dragged her back just like it did before. I wasn't willing to let that happen, not again. This was our best option. Our only option."

The lap beneath Katira's head shifted. Someone stroked her

hair in a slow, absent-minded way. Her awareness of the world returned in fragments.

"You could have hurt her, made it so she couldn't help you. Then what would you have done?"

"And Rose wouldn't have hurt her if we stayed? Come now. There's something else bothering you. Out with it."

"She was worried about you when I fetched her from Amul Dun." The hand stroking Katira's hair fell still. "It's just ... are you slipping?"

"Slipping? No. Well ... maybe. These last few returns to Khan-rosh have been harder. My desperation to see this done stronger. I fear my judgment isn't as sound as it's been in the past."

"Will you be able to see this through?"

"I have no choice. I won't fail. I can't."

Katira stirred and the remainder of her senses flooded back as she managed to crack open an eye and take in the changing colors of the sky above.

"See, I told you I was careful."

Hannah helped Katira to sit up, all while watching her every move with a healthy dose of concern. "Are you okay?"

Katira shook away the last of the disorientation. They were sitting in the middle of the meadow as if they'd simply stopped at the spot where they'd returned. The last of the color had faded from the sky, returning it to an ashy milk. The moon hadn't crested the ridge of the mountain yet.

"Okay enough. What happened?"

"We needed to leave." It wasn't the explanation, or apology, that Katira was hoping for. From the looks of it, she wasn't going to get one either. Darius extended a hand to her. "Our time grows shorter by the minute. Can you return to the work?"

Katira took it and leveraged herself to her feet, half expecting the world to spin the moment she did. She was relieved when it stayed put. "I suppose so. How long do you think we have?"

"It's best not to think about it." He opened the view to the barrier right where they stood.

Hannah shifted her weight and looked to the sky, as if it held an answer to a question she didn't dare voice. "How long do you need to finish?"

"What are you talking about?" Darius collected several threads and held them ready.

"If you were to finish it all, right now, without interruption, how long would that take?"

Katira's attention shifted to the now familiar work of learning the song of the first thread. With her flows this close to his, she felt, rather than saw, the stab of emotion pierce Darius as he realized where Hannah's questions were leading.

"Hours, most likely the rest of the night. But—"

"But, nothing. I can slow her down, keep her away from here. Maybe even convince her that what you're doing is something that must be done. She's believed me in the past." There was a glint of a tear in Hannah's eye. "It's time for me to do my part."

The stab of emotion twisted deeper. "I can't ask you to do that. You know the risks. What if she refuses to listen? What if her anger gets the best of her? If she tries her mind tricks on you?" He grasped the stone around his neck even tighter. "Will you be able to resist her?"

"I'm tired, Darius. So tired. I want all this," she gestured to the world around them, "to end. This world is tired too. The ghosts who have lived this same day over and over for hundreds of years, they deserve their rest. Gaitan deserves his rest. I'm willing to try anything if it grants you what you need to finish."

"Are you thinking this might be goodbye?" Darius stepped closer. His voice had grown husky and uneven.

Katira lost her hold on the song. It was too soon for endings. They were supposed to work for days and days more, not mere hours. If Hannah succeeded, they'd get what they'd been wanting since the beginning, to work on the barrier without Wrothe bringing destruction down on their heads, but this was not how Katira wanted it.

"Don't leave. Please. We need you here. I want you here," Katira pleaded.

Hannah let out a small laugh. Her lips hinted at that soft smile that helped Katira trust her when they'd first met. She set a hand on Katira's shoulder before thinking better of it and instead pulled her into a fierce hug.

"I know you can do this," she whispered intently into Katira's ear. "Don't worry about me. I'm at peace with my decision. If this is the last time I see you, then promise me you'll go on to have an amazing life." She gave one last squeeze before letting go.

Darius bowed his head and pressed a hand over his heart. "May we awake in the presence of the Stonemother at last."

"Oh, stop it." She grabbed him and pulled him into her arms. "You better make this count."

All pretext at formality fell away. Darius softened against Hannah and pressed his face into her hair. If anything was said between them, it was too soft, too precious for Katira to hear.

When Hannah finally walked away, Katira felt her loss with every step. Duty pressed them all forward like boats in a current. The Stonemother, indeed the power itself, had a plan for Katira, and the boat was picking up speed. If Hannah could willingly push past her fear and sacrifice herself to give them a chance, she could press on as well.

"We best not waste this time." Darius broke his gaze from where Hannah disappeared into the featureless white of night. "Are you ready?"

Unshed tears dragged Katira's vision into a narrow slit. It didn't matter if she was ready or not, they had to heal as much as they could, while they could.

She gripped her stone into her palm. "For Hannah."

CHAPTER 31

*E*ven in Hannah's wildest dreams, she'd never seen herself as a hero. The entire idea of confronting Rose, alone no less, made her feel sick. Each step returning her to Khanrosh brought her closer to what was certain to be an awful experience, she was sure of it. Less than a day had passed since Wrothe had trapped her and forced her to reveal everything. Her hands shook thinking about how the woman had pinned her against the wall and pulled away the information she wanted as easily as plucking the petals from a flower. Hannah was no match for her. Even with surprise on her side, what chance did she have to stop the woman now?

It's worth it. She repeated the words over and over, a mantra to keep her feet moving in the right direction. If she could keep Rose occupied, even for an hour, it was worth trying. All too soon, the path's rough dirt beneath her feet smoothed to fine marble. The cursed familiar walls of the testing chamber took shape around her. Rose's efforts to break through the power-sealed door continued unchanged.

Hannah faced the door and racked her brain for a plan. If Rose took even a moment to catch her breath, she'd feel the shifts in the barrier. That was it. Hannah would have to find a way to keep dragging Rose's attention back to the task at hand. Even before the split, Rose worked with such a ferocious singlemindedness that it was hard to pull her attention away.

If Hannah could keep Rose fixated on breaking down that door, she could hold the woman there for as long as it took to come up with a better plan. Should Rose exhaust herself in trying to get through, all the better. Hannah threw a series of glyphs at the door to strengthen it, each chosen because it couldn't be easily ignored. As those glyphs leapt to life, she checked the seals, reinforcing where they'd started to crack.

Compared to the glyphs originally embedded in the door, her work seemed weak, childish even. Had she been a Guardian, she could have done better, created a stronger unyielding wall. Maybe it was better this way. Her weakness would make Rose that much more eager to break through.

As Darius's friend, Hannah owed it to him to throw everything she had at the woman to keep her occupied. *Think.* At the rate Rose was breaking apart the inner workings of the door's seal, she'd breach it in a matter of minutes.

In the distance, the work on the barrier continued. With each thread healed, Hannah swore she could sense the world lightening, that her heart felt less burdened. All the more reason to come up with something, anything, to compel Rose to stay at Khanrosh. She scanned the room, and her attention was drawn to the protective glyphs embedded into the floor.

A series of crystalline cracks pinged across what remained of the door's seal as Rose threw another wave of power. It wouldn't be long before it gave, so Hannah needed to hurry. She'd never created a projection before, never had to. That odd skill was something only Darius used when he needed to work behind Rose's back. She'd watched him make one of himself a handful of times, enough to understand the general idea.

Her glyphs came together fitfully. It took several tries before she succeeded in getting a mirror of herself to form and that was the easy part. The hard part was the reflective weave that would make it appear as if she was still working to strengthen the door. The only reason Rose kept fighting was because someone was on the other side trying to keep her out. Why protect a room if there was nothing there to protect?

Seeing a copy of herself sent a scurry of shivers up her back. It was a decoy, and a poor one at that. It was a good thing Hannah didn't need Rose to believe it for long. Her plan, if she could call it that, only needed a few seconds to work. With her decoy in place, she set her focus to return to the great hall and began walking.

This will work. This has to work. The testing chamber blurred into a fog before reassembling itself into the vaulted space of the great hall. Spotless white marble slipped under her feet. Inside the testing chamber, the sound of Rose's attack was blunted to dull thuds. Out in the hall, it made Hannah's ears throb with the intensity of it.

She fed more power to the decoy as she placed herself into position behind the pillar nearest Rose. This was the moment where either her plan would work, or everything would come crashing down on her head. Her plan would be so much easier if she could convince her heart to stop trying to beat its way out of her chest.

There was nothing for it. Either she'd succeed or she'd fail, and if she waited too long, she'd certainly fail. She formed the glyph sequence, choosing carefully which patterns to include. With one smooth step, she seized the back of Rose's neck.

"Sleep."

～

The warm summer night didn't call for a fire in the hearth, but Isben busied himself with preparing kindling. The longer he stayed busy with apprentice work, the longer he'd have to think through a way to help Katira find the matching threads uninterrupted. When the barrier opened again, he wanted to be ready.

Bremin sat hunched over pages of diagrams and glyph sequences scattered across the table, also lost in thought. Once Isben finished with the fire, he lit the lantern with a twist of paper for him and earned an appreciative nod. While Master Jarand's accident had been a setback, it had truly been an accident. Bremin, however, didn't see it that way. Someone got hurt following his orders. He'd spend as long as it took to figure out exactly what went wrong and how to prevent it from happening again.

Over in the kitchen, Cassim dug through their meager pile of foodstuffs to pull together some kind of meal. While he'd stopped grumbling about stubborn Guardians and not being listened to, he wasn't happy. If he'd had his way, he'd have Master Jarand bundled up safe in one of the beds and not wandering the town looking for a fight.

Hearing Cassim in the kitchen made Isben's stomach rumble, betraying a hunger he'd been ignoring. It was loud enough to catch Cassim's attention.

"If you're that hungry, perhaps you can give me a hand?" the healer asked, using a carrot to point to the pot on the hearth. "That needs filling."

Isben reached for the pot. Fetching water was another of those mindless tasks that allowed him to think. Just as he lifted it from its hook, a fresh wave of barrier energy pressed through the air. He set the pot back down.

Cassim stopped his rummaging. "Well, that's just perfect. I suppose dinner can wait."

"You've suffered worse. Come on, we best go." Bremin wiped the pen nib with a cloth and headed for the door at the front of the cottage. "From the feel of it, it's in the worst possible place."

"Shouldn't we wait for Jarand and Issa?" Cassim still held the carrot as if unsure what to do with it. "You can't possibly face the barrier with only me as protection."

"I'm willing to take the risk. It's somewhere in the middle of the town so we need to be there. The people have to see us taking control of the situation." He ducked into the lamp lit street without another word.

Isben hurried after Bremin and rushed out into the darkness. Behind him, Cassim muttered something unpleasant under his breath about Bremin's complete disregard for their safety as he followed along. The mutterings stopped when he spotted the barrier hanging in the middle of the street like an angry specter, both menacing and completely out of place. Off to the side, a curtain twitched shut. Someone had already taken notice. According to Katira, the people here were stubborn, not stupid. If they saw something they believed to be a threat, it wouldn't be long before they'd get brave enough to poke a stick at it.

Isben stopped next to Bremin and waited for him to relay orders. He didn't have to wait long.

"Are you ready to try finding a match again?"

Isben bound his stone to his palm, hoping the action would help him feel more confident. The horror of seeing Master Jarand being sliced apart still lived behind every blink. "What if I anger it?"

"Do you think you will?" Bremin asked in that dry tone he often used when teaching.

On the far side of the town square, streaks of light flashed from the edges of the two Guardian's blades as they worked. There was no telling how long it would be before they returned.

"Well, no," Isben said. "I'm not trying to pierce through the world like he was, but that doesn't mean what I'm doing is safe."

Bremin gave a soft laugh. "Fear is funny sometimes. It likes to wrap itself around where it doesn't belong. Is your fear greater than your desire to help her?"

Curse the man for always knowing what to say. Or bless him. Isben wasn't sure which. "Of course not. You know I'll do anything."

"Then you best try. We don't know how long we have." Bremin returned his attention to the barrier. "I'll give whatever guidance I can."

Isben drew on his courage and pressed away the distractions of the square. Cassim had just arrived and entered into a whispered conversation with Bremin. The two Guardians fought against shadows he couldn't see. The square itself felt as if held its breath. If he could help Katira match the threads faster, the whole matter would be finished that much sooner.

He opened himself to the burning heat of the power and let the world fall away as he extended his awareness into the barrier. Within that space, direction had no meaning. There was no up or down, no side to side. It was a world filled with endless patterns of energy and a constant sense of being watched. Finding where Darius kept hold of the next strands for Katira was fairly easy. He radiated his own unique dark energy that stayed in one place. It was finding Katira among the threads that gave him trouble.

If he was going to spot her, he couldn't be distracted. He squashed back the squirming thought that something might go wrong, that one wrong turn might result in him bleeding out on the ground. Cassim was right there to knit him back together should something happen, but somehow it didn't make him feel better.

A familiar presence brushed against one of his delving flows, drawing all of his attention to that single point. It was her. He rushed to follow her, afraid he might lose her among the threads. This time, she slowed at his touch, as if unsure. *Yes, it's me. It's okay.* He drew his flow around hers and was rewarded with a burst of relief mingled with joy. *I'm here with you.* He would have given anything to speak to her, to explain what he was trying to do, to let her know that everything was going to be all right. *Keep going. Show me.*

"Talk to me, Isben," Bremin urged. "Tell me what you're doing."

Isben had nearly forgotten about the two masters watching him. "I've got her. If I stay close, I'm hoping I'll spot how she goes about finding the correct match. It's the only part of this that I'm still struggling to figure out."

When Katira's flow moved, Isben followed, watching on carefully as she sifted through thousands of threads and let those from the mirror realm fall away while collecting up likely candidates. But that wasn't quite it. Several of the threads appeared to drift closer to her while others shied away. He was missing something, and he couldn't put a finger on it.

After several minutes, she selected one and brought it to where he'd sensed Darius. Isben had witnessed fragments of the joining before, but never this close. He studied the two threads, taking this rare chance to see what made them fit together. At first it all felt like a random jumble of color, tone, vibration, and energy. Nothing about the two threads seemed like they should match. It wasn't until the moment when Katira shifted her strand into its proper alignment that he sensed how the distinct vibrations locked together to become one.

That was it.

He wasn't an Innate, but if there was one thing he had a knack for, it was sensing unique patterns. That's all Bending really was, identifying the unique properties of a material and shifting them into a slightly different position to make something else. In theory, if he could identify threads with patterns that could lock together like that, then he should be able to find a match as well.

Katira moved on to study the next thread, and he again followed, watching how her unique signature took on the idea of the thread's vibration and carried it. He reasoned that it must be this vibration, this bait, that the matching threads were attracted to. He watched on as she selected the correct thread and then sparked it to its match, each step of the process confirming his theory about how it worked.

When she left to find the next thread, he didn't follow. If he was going to help her, he'd have to try finding a match on his own.

Hannah paced a tidy square around Rose's sleeping form with only the echoes of her footsteps for company. She watched on as the colors of the Great Hall shifted from brilliant to dull. Puddles of white shadow formed in the corners.

As long as she kept watch, and stayed awake herself, she could keep Rose like this for days. That was the plan and she intended to stick to it. It would have been easier if the place wasn't crawling with the shadows of people caught up in the tear. Even at this hour of night, runners and messengers moved through the space. More than once, Hannah had to slide Rose's body out of the way to keep her from being stepped on. If a shadow's unending cycle was disturbed, they made all sorts of trouble. Hannah couldn't imagine what kind of a ruckus they'd make if they thought she'd hurt Rose, the woman had strong allies at every turn.

A series of windows lining the top of the hall ushered the moon from one frame to the next as the hours of the night slid by. Those hours piled heavy on Hannah's shoulders. She continued to pace to keep herself alert, but the strain of her constant vigil along with her aching feet made her thoughts wander.

You don't get to complain. You have the easy task, she kept telling herself. If only she could dart across the great hall and fetch the book of folktales stashed in her small desk inside Darius's private office, then she'd have something to keep herself occupied. She could immerse herself in a story and let the hours slide by. As long as she kept Rose in sight, or even sat so they were touching somehow, the woman would stay put under the weight of the sleeping glyph. Would it be wrong to rest her feet on her?

She dodged out of the way of one of the kitchen staff carrying a steaming tray and cursed under her breath at coming so close to being touched. Pacing wasn't working. It would be better to stay put somewhere out of their way entirely. Better yet, it would get her off her aching feet. It had been days since she'd slept properly. Gritty exhaustion ground at the corners of her eyes.

A familiar lump pressed against her hip. It certainly wasn't a book, but it was better than nothing. She removed the cake from her pocket and unwrapped it. The last time she'd given in to eating it, Darius was dying at Rose's hand. It served as a distraction for both her and Katira.

With that thought, enjoying it while keeping watch didn't sound as appetizing. It wasn't enough to put it away, but enough to make her pause. This might be the last time she indulged in her pocket cake, and she wasn't sure how she felt about it. If Darius succeeded, if the tear between the worlds was repaired, then she'd either find herself back in the real world, or she'd finally find the rest she'd been craving for centuries. Whatever happened, the decadent cake would stop appearing in her pocket, and the thought made her sad.

She sank down on the smooth floor next to Rose and set her feet against the woman's shoulder as a precaution should her mind start to wander. Off in the distance, the steady lull of the work at the barrier ebbed through the air in a gentle rhythm. Paired with the sweetness on her tongue, she found it strangely soothing.

CHAPTER 32

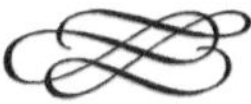

nside the barrier, the world was reduced to the quivering hum of hundreds of threads all vying for attention. Katira continued to press through the mass, one precious song at a time. All she could do was keep going. Each healed thread meant fewer threads she'd need to sort through. With fewer threads, finding each match would be easier.

Darius had been patient as he carefully selected new threads, checking to see if they were caught up in the giant knot they'd found before presenting them to her. The fact that this was gifted time, that every minute was one they'd been given as a result of Hannah's efforts, made each struggle and delay in finding a match that much more grating on Katira's nerves.

"Growing agitated won't help you. It is what it is. Simply keep moving," Darius reminded her, although his own calm was a thin weak thing.

"I know. It's just—"

"All you can do is your best. If there was a better way, we'd have stumbled on it already." He selected another strand and tested it before laying it out with the others. "Fall into the rhythm and let your instincts guide you."

"Was Hannah successful?" He could sense Wrothe, so he would know.

His flows stilled momentarily. "Best keep your focus on the work. Let me worry about her."

It was the kind of answer that made Katira worry more. She skipped over the matching thread she was seeking twice before properly listening to it. "You'd tell me if anything went wrong, wouldn't you?"

He waited to answer until after she'd lined up her thread and sparked it. "Only if it affects the work. Otherwise, it can wait. Don't let your imagination get the best of you. Hannah knows the risks."

Maybe he was right; maybe it was better to not know what horrible things Wrothe might be doing. All the same, being blind to it, but suspecting something might be happening, let her imagination take far too many liberties. She didn't know which was worse. It was at times like this when she was grateful to have the kind of work she could dive into when her feelings got too big to handle. She buried her worry, her fears, and her suspicions under the demands of matching the threads and tried not to think.

Her next thread shone in muted yellows and carried an energy that reminded her of the sky right before sunrise. Its song was slow and cautious, as if worried it might wake a sleeping child. As she moved through the mass of threads, a presence brushed against her flow that was so familiar it made her heart hurt. Her mind must be playing tricks on her, Isben couldn't be here, could he? It had to be some cruel coincidence, nothing more, a reflection of something she wanted but couldn't have. With so many threads, and so many songs surrounding her, it would have been easy for one to remind her of him.

When the presence pressed its way toward her flow again, it was clear that it wasn't a thread at all. She stilled, waiting and wanting, all while trying hard not to let herself hope too much. When it drew close, she wanted to cry out with joy.

It *was* him.

It shouldn't have been possible, but there he was. She soaked up his presence and anchored herself onto his steadiness and how with him she felt whole. Pulsing beneath his joy of finding her was the sense of him urging her to keep going. She could do that. He stayed close as she found the match for the muted yellow thread and followed her as she aligned it with its partner and joined it with a spark.

The moment she did, his excitement exploded across their connection. At first, she'd only assumed that he wanted to find her and make sure she was okay. But his reaction proved there was something else he wanted. He'd never been one to stand idly by if there was work to be done. If he could help her, then they could heal the barrier twice as fast. It was too much to hope for.

When she went to select her next thread, she could have sworn he was studying the thread beside hers. He watched the process once more before disappearing into the threads.

Armed with a new song, she set out once more. Not far away, she briefly sensed Isben as he searched but then lost track of him as her focus turned to the threads that rose to meet her. *He'll find a way, he always does.* When she found her match, she hurried back to Darius's threads and hoped he'd be there.

He wasn't.

She sparked her match and snatched up a new song, and then another, and another. It had been long enough since she sensed him among the threads that she started to worry. Had he left? Had something happened in the real world that forced him to stop? She could do the work without him, but the possibility of having him working by her side had lit a hope that she was reluctant to lose.

The matching had to continue if he was there or not. She left the thread he'd taken an interest in alone. If he was still searching, it would be unfair for her to find it first. She let herself fall back into the rhythm of listening, finding, sparking, listening, finding, sparking until she lost herself in it. It was the only way to keep going. If he was still there, still trying, they'd cross paths again.

Dozens of threads later, she brushed against Isben's familiar flow as she set about lining up and sparking her next match. She sensed a confidence there, something that bordered on smug. Wrapped in his flow was a thread from the real world. She studied it against the one held in Darius's array, and it sounded good. The two threads together felt right. When she gathered and lined them up, they matched.

He'd done it.

Darius's hold on the waiting threads slipped a fraction. "Wait, how did you do that so fast?"

She studied her next thread and couldn't help but smile as Isben studied one of his own. "Isben's working from the other side. He figured out how to match the threads."

"He did?" Darius laughed in that wild unrestrained way that only came with a welcome surprise. "He's quite the clever one, isn't he?"

"He certainly is." A knot of emotion tightened around her throat, betraying how much she missed him. These teasing glimpses of his presence weren't enough. She wanted, no *needed*, to finish, if only to be back with him once more.

The familiar slick smoothness of polished marble pressed against Hannah's cheek. Her entire left side ached as if she'd been flung against a wall. When she blinked her eyes open, she found herself in the testing chamber, which meant she probably *was* thrown against the wall. It wouldn't be the first time. Even with the most stringent controls, testing new ideas was a dangerous pursuit.

She moved slowly, checking for any injuries other than her bruised pride. By her presence alone, whatever happened was at least partially her fault. A vague memory crawled back of Rose trying something big, something she wasn't supposed to be doing.

If there had been some kind of power-fueled explosion, help should already be on the way. If it was, she was half-tempted to lay back down and wait for it. Her head pounded from behind her temples. She strained to hear any hint of that help coming and was met with silence. Not just a lack of footsteps, but an utter abject quiet. *Odd.* She tapped her ears, making sure whatever had thrown her hadn't blown out her eardrums in the process. It wouldn't have been the first time for that either.

A panicked breath came from a corner concealed by curtains. Hannah couldn't shake how she'd heard that sound precisely in the same way before. She crawled to the corner, not ready to trust her feet yet, and found Rose trembling with her head in her hands.

"They're gone. They're gone." She kept muttering over and over, her eyes still closed.

Hannah touched her hand, trying not to startle her. "Whatever happened, it didn't kill either of us. You're okay."

Rose jerked back her hand and balled it into the fabric of her dress. "No, something's wrong, can you feel it?" She opened her eyes and glanced around the room. "By the Stonemother's throne, are you seeing this?"

Hannah followed her gaze. The wrongness of what she saw struck her as hard and as unexpected as a ledger to the face. The colors of the testing chamber and everything in it had changed into a bizarre mimicry of themselves. The smoky grey marble of the testing chamber floor had plunged to darker tones of charcoal. The deep red of the curtains were now a lush purple. Once again, Hannah had the strange sense that somehow she'd seen all of this before.

"Where is he?" Rose grew increasingly frantic as she searched the room. She pointed to the ring of glyphs embedded in the floor. "We were standing right there. He should be here."

That small detail snapped Hannah's memory back into place, along with the maddening realization that they had done this hundreds, no, thousands, of times before. Darius wasn't there because, after hundreds of years, he'd found a way to put an end to this cycle.

"He's not here, but he's safe." Hannah tried to calm Rose and ease her fears. She'd promised to keep the woman here at Khanrosh to give Darius and Katira as much time as possible. The thrum of their work still coursed through the air.

Rose must have felt it. Her fear and panic fell away, replaced with that calculating glare she'd adopted after the split. It put Hannah's nerves on edge.

"We've done this before. Haven't we?"

"I'm afraid so." Hannah quietly opened herself to the power. If she could put the woman to sleep once more, then none of this would matter.

Rose's knuckles turned white where she still gripped her dress. "He tried to stop me. Tried to cut me away from all those people." The lines of her power flared to life, and her beautiful face twisted into that of the monster Hannah feared most. "He doesn't want me to have that kind of influence. He's jealous of my success, can't stand that I'm better than him."

"That's not true." Hannah hurried to her feet, grateful that the room no longer spun. "What you were doing was forbidden, and you know it." In all the years they'd been trapped together, she'd never raised her power against Rose with the intent of striking her down, even in her own defense. But if it gave Darius more time, if by some insane stretch she managed to come out on top, then it was worth trying.

"Since when did you grow a backbone?" Rose stood. A wicked smile crossed her face.

"What Darius is doing will free us all." Hannah squared her shoulders. "There will be no more pain. No more endless existence. This hell we've endured for so long will finally be over. You will never wake in this room again."

"That's where you're wrong." A hint of a deeper insanity twisted the corner of Rose's lips. "What he's doing will destroy everything I've worked for these past centuries. I found a way back into the waking world. There, I can actually live. There, my efforts don't turn to dust."

"This must end." Hannah formed a memory glyph, a clever bit of Seeking that would force Rose to remember all the times she trusted Darius and sought his advice, with the hope it would counteract the looming violence growing in Rose's eyes.

Before she could use it, Rose released a wild burst of energy with a defiant shout. Hannah managed to dodge, and it slammed into the wall behind her, shattering the stone with the impact. With the noise and chaos as a distraction, she sparked her glyph to life and dodged another of Rose's bolts as it wrapped itself around its target.

As memory glyphs went, Hannah had limited control of what kind of memory she summoned and to some degree, its intensity. She'd thrown everything she had into this one, anything to make it strong enough to counteract Rose's fury. As it took hold, Rose gasped against the intrusion and gripped the back of one of the narrow wooden chairs. She sagged into it as her expression softened and her gaze turned glassy and distant.

There was no telling how long it would last. Hannah reached for the woman's neck to send her back to sleep. As she did, her fingers grazed the side of Rose's cheek. The intense focus, that burning anger, leapt back into the woman's eyes.

"You'll pay for that," Rose whispered, then pressed her palm against Hannah's chest and released a killing glyph.

CHAPTER 33

*L*ess than a hundred threads remained when Katira first noticed hints of blue stretching into the mirror realm's milky night sky. The barest edges of the buildings surrounding the town square traced a circle around her and Darius in the empty meadow. When she breathed in, she caught traces of woodsmoke and water and summer warmth. Beneath the smoke lingered the tiniest hint of old books and ink, Isben.

He was near. Not just his flows seeking threads within the barrier, but *him*. If they healed a few dozen more threads, maybe she'd be able to see him. At the rate they were working, it wouldn't be long. He'd gotten fast enough at finding matches that they were often joining two and three threads at a time.

But was it enough? Katira kept telling herself that as long as Darius stayed quiet, they were safe to keep going and she didn't need to worry about Wrothe showing up when they least expected it and slaughtering them all. Even with Darius's reassurance, the looming threat that she might wore Katira thin. The orbs kept the process of joining threads going, but a new, much deeper exhaustion dragged at her.

She sparked another thread, and Isben's faint outline materialized next to her, his roughly chopped hair making him instantly recognizable. Her breath caught in her throat, and she wanted more than anything to reach out to him. Close by, a taller, lankier man came into view, the red scarf at his throat identifying him as Bremin. If the two of them were there, then Papan should be there also, but he was nowhere to be found.

"Are you seeing this?" she asked.

Darius set forward another handful of threads. "The division between worlds is growing thinner with each one we heal. Stay focused. It won't be long now."

He was about to say something else when a wave of dread crossed his face. He didn't have to tell Katira what was happening, she already knew. Rose had bested Hannah.

The thread's song Katira had just learned disappeared from her mind. "How long do we have?"

"It doesn't matter. There's no use hiding from her anymore. No more running. No more playing games. This ends today."

A thousand protests sprung to Katira's lips. They'd worked so hard to get this far, why take the risk? After all of their efforts to avoid facing the woman head on, something had to have changed for him to act like this.

She was about to ask why but stopped when she saw the square of his shoulders and how he clenched his jaw. He needed this to be over. If they weren't going to flee, then they'd have to fight. The length of that fight would be determined by how long it took to finish healing the remaining threads, Wrothe's thread included. Finding hers would put an end to his suffering.

Katira picked up the song she'd been holding, yet another that didn't belong to that monster. "Let's finish this."

A series of howls erupted at the edge of the field signaling Wrothe's arrival. Hounds flooded across the moonlit field, skirting the edges and shadows of Namragan that continued to take shape.

Darius tightened his grip on his threads and turned to face the approaching wave. "I'll keep them back. Keep going."

Again, Katira wanted to protest. There were far too many hounds for one man to handle alone, and she couldn't continue to heal the barrier without him. There had to be something else she could do. She felt for the dagger she kept on her belt, needing something, anything, to put between herself and those things should they come too close.

Something brushed her cheek. The touch was so feather-light she barely felt it. She turned to find Isben holding out his hand. His lips formed three simple words, *I see you.* She reached for him, needing his touch now more than ever. Her hand passed through him as if he were fog, there, but not quite.

"I see you too." She choked on the words.

Hounds from all directions returned the call of those coming with Wrothe. They were being hemmed in. The lines on Isben's neck glowed brighter as he strained to see something in the distance. He must have heard them too.

Keep going. I'll come back. I promise.

"Stay, please," she begged. With him, they could work so much faster, put an end to this insanity that much sooner. More than that, she needed him. They were stronger together.

She grabbed for his arm, catching only air as he hurried away.

The narrow alleyway running alongside the Mad Rabbit Inn smelled of blood, both Jarand's own and that of the hound he'd cornered and killed. At least eight hounds had crossed into the town. Between his and Issa's efforts, they'd downed seven. He pressed a hand against his side to slow the bleeding where one of the newly healed cuts had split open. As if things couldn't get any worse, the barrier must have opened in the square while they were fighting. The air vibrated with its thrumming energy.

Issa met him at the entrance to the alleyway. Sweat plastered her short hair to her forehead, but she still stood tall and held her sword with a firm grip that said she could take on another dozen hounds if need be.

"Any idea where that last one slunk off to?"

Jarand shook his head. "Lost sight of it when I entered the

alley." He returned his sword to its scabbard, needing a lighter weapon to compensate for the loss of strength in his hands. "How do we know if your improved sequence in the tether worked?"

"Easy. No more of these damned hounds show up in the town." She tapped his wrist where he still clutched his side. "Sense anything new?"

He grimaced. "Nothing since the last wave. We better track down that last hound. Whatever is happening in the square is bound to draw its attention. Stonemother knows it has mine."

Issa agreed with a curt nod just as a fresh chorus of howling filled the air. She lowered her sword with a resigned sigh. "That's more than we can handle."

He freed the long-bladed knife from his belt and watched the blue of his power chase down its edge. Its weight would be easier to manage than that of the sword. "Hurry back to the square, protect the others. I'll be right behind you."

She hesitated, her brow creasing as she looked him over. "Perhaps it would be better if I let you lean on me. Get you back to Cassim faster."

He'd only slow her down when speed was essential. It wasn't worth the risk. "Go. That's an order."

With a stiff salute, she hurried toward the square. As soon as she turned away, Jarand let himself slump against the nearby wall.

A small gasp came from someone near the door of the Mad Rabbit. Lucan snatched the lantern from its hook and came closer.

"By the gods themselves, Jarand, are you all right?"

Jarand let his power fade and along with it the glow of the knife in his hand. He wasn't ready to deal with this. "It looks worse than it is. Go back inside, please. It's safer."

"Looks worse? Not sure how that's possible." Lucan hurried down the steps and offered Jarand his arm, which he refused. "You're not alone in this, friend. Tell me what's happening."

Jarand didn't have the energy to concoct a lie even if he wanted to, nor did he have the time to stand still and explain. He motioned for Lucan to follow him. "The situation is coming to a head. More hounds keep pouring in."

Lucan hurried along as he marched toward the barrier where Issa already stood at attention waiting for the first hound to dare come close.

"I'm not talking about the hounds." He held out his hand to the column of light. "What is that?"

"The barrier between worlds," Jarand answered simply. "Katira found a way to bring the two halves together."

Lucan stammered before answering. "Well, that's good then. That's what you were hoping for, wasn't it?"

As Jarand drew closer to the barrier, he swore he saw an all too familiar silhouette there in the flickering light. Katira's shadowy form was beginning to take shape. The shock of seeing her made him forget what he was going to say.

When he didn't answer, Lucan grabbed hold of his shoulder and stopped him just shy of reaching the fountain. "Knowing who you are, what you are, there's far more going on here, isn't there?"

Jarand drew a calming breath. Seeing Katira and being stopped from going to her strained his cast-iron control. He pulled the man's hand free and continued walking.

"Yes, there is. Please, go back inside. There's nothing you can do here."

Again, Lucan hurried to follow. Curse the man for his loyalty. "I don't believe that for a minute."

As he drew closer, another shadowy figure came into view. If Isben was right, this would be Darius himself. After spending a lifetime regarding him as a legend, Jarand's mouth went dry at the prospect of meeting the man.

He joined Bremin and Cassim where they stood at a safe distance to keep an eye on Katira and Isben as they worked. Issa stood at attention nearby, monitoring the perimeter of the square for any signs of trouble. The moment he arrived, Isben and Issa both broke away from their work to join them.

"The hounds?" Jarand asked, ignoring how Lucan stood too close. At this point, it didn't make sense to hide anything from him.

Issa handed a waterskin to Jarand. "I dispatched the last one inside the town. The rest are lurking just outside the warding wall.

If they're determined, it won't be long before they manage to get through."

"And the barrier?" Jarand took a long drink, not realizing how thirsty he'd been.

"They've made good progress," Bremin said. "Isben figured out how to find matching threads, so it's going faster." He jerked his head toward Lucan. "Why's he here?"

"He deserves to know what's happening. It's his town."

"Fair enough."

Another round of howls broke through the night, a sobering reminder of what lay ahead.

Cassim approached Jarand and shook his finger at him. "I warned you this might happen. Would it kill you to be more careful?"

"It might." Jarand winced as the first healing flows pulled harder than necessary. "Fix it as best you can. The night is only getting started."

Concern wrinkled Cassim's brow. "There are dozens of them, from the sound of it. The two of you won't be nearly enough to keep them back."

"Three," Issa started. "You can wield steel, Cassim. But you're right, even with you it's still not enough."

"Four." Bremin stepped forward. "You've got me."

Cassim shot him a scowl. "Not an option unless we're truly desperate."

"Five." Isben loosened the knife at his hip.

Jarand was about to protest. The last thing he was willing to do was put Katira's future companion in any sort of danger.

Lucan pushed himself back into the conversation. "Twenty stubborn northerners. We'll do what it takes to keep this town safe."

Jarand admired the man's heart. Lucan knew the enemy well enough that he was aware of the danger and was willing anyway.

"No. Your weapons are useless against the hounds. Gather everyone and hide up the river away from all this. Don't return until it's over." He pushed the man away. "Go now. Save as many as you can. Save your family."

Lucan stood firm. "For once in your life, Jarand, take help when you need it. There has to be a way."

Isben, who had been watching on as Cassim finished his work, spoke up. "We can fuse a simple glyph into their weapons, something that will allow the cutting edge to make contact with the hounds." He removed his knife and a glyph chased down the blade before gathering at the thickest part of the metal and forming a seal. "Something like this."

Jarand took up the knife and weighed it in his palm. "It would give them a way to fight back. We should do it just for that."

"For that matter, I wouldn't mind having one either." Bremin loosened one of his own blades from his belt and handed it to Isben. "How long do you think a fusing like this will last?"

Issa took Isben's first glyph-fused blade from Jarand and flipped it over in her hand, catching it neatly by its hilt. "Depending on how it's done, at least a few days. Long enough to make a difference."

Lucan patted Jarand on the shoulder. "There, that wasn't so hard, was it? I'll gather up as many blades and capable hands to hold them as I can. Those hounds won't stand a chance."

With each thread healed, Katira's view of the town square sharpened from vague shadows to distinct shapes to the beloved sights that she called home. Not far from where she stood, Papan and Isben, along with Bremin, Issa, and Cassim, stood locked in what looked to be a serious discussion with Master Lucan.

All she knew was that she wanted Isben back by her side. Eighty-three matches remained. Without his help, finishing would take far longer, increasing the chances that more people would get hurt or killed, either by the hounds or by Wrothe herself. That worry was enough to shatter away the last of Katira's calm, and she couldn't hear the next thread's song.

Darius set his hand on her shoulder. "We knew it would come to this. Take a breath. Center yourself."

Katira tried to follow his advice and failed. "What will you do when the hounds come? When *she* comes? I can't do the work without you."

"I have a few tricks up my sleeve that will keep her and the hounds away if need be. They should buy us a bit more time." He gave her shoulder a gentle squeeze before releasing it. "I promise you this, I'll keep holding the threads and sparking the matches even if it's the last thing I do." His voice took on an intensity that reflected the strength of his commitment. "Are you with me?"

"Even if it's the last thing I do." Katira dug deep and sought out that intelligence within her power. If anything would help her see this through, it would be that detached calm that its influence brought. In the face of overwhelming odds, it stirred, then woke.

Hounds burst into the town square. Several bounded straight for the barrier. Darius formed a shield glyph causing his hold on the threads to waver, but as he promised, he didn't let go. Katira braced herself for the noise and the sudden snap of light as she gathered up the next song. Before he had a chance to use his shield, Issa leapt into the hounds' path. Her bright-edged sword cut arcs of light through the night air.

Other glowing blades appeared in a wide ring of protection around Katira and Darius. As they did, a warm and welcome presence returned next to her. Isben pressed a ghost-like kiss into her hair, the sensation of him far more solid than when they'd touched earlier.

This time when his lips moved, she could hear the barest trace of his voice. "I'm here. I won't leave you until this is done."

With the reassurance of Isben working by her side, the world around her, with all its noise and bursts of light, shrank down until she lost herself in the work once more. Together, they set back into the rhythm of finding and matching threads as chaos erupted all around them.

When Wrothe finally came, time itself seemed to slow. On the far side of the square, Papan barked orders as he organized townsmen bearing glowing blades into position. Nearby, but just out of sight, Issa gave her own orders to maintain the ring of protection she'd created around where they worked.

In that ring, Elan stood near Lucan with his own glowing blade. A spike of fear sliced through Katira, threatening to disrupt her calm. Elan had an entire life in front of him. She couldn't stand the thought of him losing it fighting against odds he didn't understand.

She grabbed hold of the next thread's song, needing more than ever for the healing to be finished if only to protect those in the square.

Wrothe stalked forward. Dark ribbons of power whipped through the air around her in a frenzy and murder shone in her eyes. Papan stepped forward to meet her, his face that mask of firm resolution he wore when he needed to take control. The barrier's light revealed dark stains in more places than Katira dared to count and he no longer held his sword.

"You will go no further," he ordered.

She snarled. "This doesn't concern you. Get out of my way."

Her hounds regrouped behind her, along with Wrothe's favorite pet, a large, yellow-eyed wolf that Katira hadn't seen since their fateful day back in Khanrosh. With a flick of her hand, Wrothe sent them charging into Papan and his men.

Less than seventy threads remained. Katira pushed herself to work faster, anything to finish. Papan's knife flashed as he fought and felled hounds right and left. More flashing blades revealed the men waiting behind him.

Papan rushed toward Wrothe, using the chaos and distraction of the hounds to close in on her. The moment she spotted him, a new set of glyphs formed between her palms, something larger and more dangerous.

"Issa, shield!" Bremin shouted from where he controlled his unit of armed townsmen in their fight against the hounds.

Issa sprinted from the protective circle, forming and sparking glyphs as she went. A wall of power leapt up around Wrothe just as the woman released her weapon. It collided against the shield with a deafening screech and shattered it.

Before Wrothe could form another pattern, Darius shouted at her over the noise. "Stop this, Rose. It's time for all of this to be over. I'm tired. I know you are too."

Sixty-two more strands. Katira nudged Darius to spark the next match. They had to keep going.

"Why?" The writhing dark ribbons surrounding her quieted a fraction. She gestured to town surrounding them. "Why do you want this? If you let me have my way, we could take control of all these people, keep them from fighting, keep them from dying. We'd rule as benevolent gods. No one would ever suffer again." Her voice caught. "I already know how. With your help we'd be unstoppable."

Papan stood at Wrothe's back, knife held at the ready, power flaring along his skin. "Give the word and I'll end her."

Darius held out a hand in a rush. "No, you can't. Whether she understands or not, we need her before all this is over."

A wave of mad rage crossed Wrothe's face, and insanity shone from her eyes. Ribbons of power whipped and spun around her, forcing Papan back. Faster than Issa could summon a new shield, Wrothe formed a cutting glyph that shot like lightning toward Darius's chest. He flung up his own small shield at the last moment, deflecting the blow enough that it didn't kill him. The glyph sliced through the meat of his shoulder instead. Several dark strands broke free from his grip from the shock of it, but he didn't let go.

Hounds surged through the square again, another wave of chaos breaking against everyone gathered there. Papan retreated to the group of townsmen he commanded. His shouted orders rang over the noise of Wrothe's power and the persistent hum of the barrier.

As Katira went to select her next strand, Wrothe's cloying voice broke through her concentration and wrapped around her mind like a drugged smoke. *Healing the barrier will kill Darius and Hannah. If you care for them, you will stop, let them live.*

They were just words, a trick. Katira wouldn't be swayed that easily. But the words kept coming. They crawled into her ears and nibbled at her brain. They stung and bit and buzzed so loudly that she lost the song.

"Katira?" Isben's voice barely surfaced through the onslaught. "What's happening?"

She reached out, needing something to cling to as Wrothe's

words pushed her under. Her hand brushed the front of Isben's shirt, and she grabbed hold of it.

"She's in my head. Make it stop."

His eyes went wide and he pulled back his flows from the barrier. "Hang on. I've got you."

With a precise glyph, he severed the ribbon of Wrothe's power tangled around her head. The flood of poisonous honeyed words silenced, leaving her gasping for breath.

He studied her face carefully, clearly worried.

She released her hold on his shirt. "I'm okay. We need to keep going."

Before she could take up the next song, a new commotion erupted at the edge of the town. Hannah ran as if her life depended on it, with her skirts gathered up over her arm and her head thrown back.

"She's coming!" she yelled. "She got away from me. Prepare yourself!"

Bremin's men moved to block her path, weapons raised and ready to eliminate what they saw as a new threat.

"Let her in! She's with us," Darius shouted, a note of panic clear in his voice. The effort of it combined with his fresh wound and the exhaustion from healing the barrier sent him to his knees.

With a barked order from Bremin, the ring of townsmen held back their weapons and allowed her to sprint past. When she reached Darius, she could barely breathe.

"I held her back as long as I could." She finally took a moment to study the scene and her shoulders dropped. "Damn it. She's already here."

CHAPTER 34

As with any battle, the difference between winning and losing often came down to how well Jarand understood the enemy. He understood Wrothe well enough to know this wasn't going to be a fair fight. She'd play dirty and use every last trick tucked up her sleeves to win. Even with a dozen of Namragan's strongest men behind him, he wasn't sure it was enough.

The deepest part of night approached where even the best of those men would begin to tire and their attention wander. He had to remind himself that they were no soldiers.

The most recent clash with the hounds left more than a few bleeding. Cassim hurried from man to man, burning away the venom as fast as he could before it managed to kill.

Andril, Lucan's oldest son and Elan's brother, drew close. "Your orders?" There was an uncertainty in his voice. Good. He had every reason to be afraid. It would keep him, and hopefully the rest of the men, cautious.

Jarand took a moment to regroup. While Wrothe was the biggest threat, the hounds presented the greater danger to every soul there. "Maintain the perimeter around our side of the square. No hounds leave."

Andril tipped his head toward Wrothe as she shot another bolt at those gathered at the barrier. "What about her? Why haven't you stopped her already?"

For now, Issa kept Wrothe's attention firmly engaged by firing a variety of bolts and glyphs at her, forcing the woman to dodge and shield. Judging by the look on Issa's face, she appeared to be enjoying herself.

"It's complicated." Jarand adjusted his grip on his knife as a rogue bolt soared overhead and smashed into the front of a building. "If you and your men can handle the hounds, Issa and I will deal with her. Bremin will issue orders as needed."

Andril pressed his fist to his chest in a salute. "Please be careful."

Jarand returned the salute and hurried back to the barrier. With only forty or so threads to go, the situation had moved far past the point where being careful would do them any good. This was a time to be bold, to strike hard, to not second guess. Anything to give Katira the time she needed to finish.

Wrothe spotted him the second he drew near. She shot one last bolt at Issa, which was easily deflected, before turning her whole attention to Jarand.

"We could have been great together." Wrothe's voice rang through the square, amplified by a clever glyph anchored to her neck. A new sequence formed between her hands. "Your strength here in the real world paired with my genius could have done amazing things. It's not too late. Will you join me?"

"Never," Jarand shouted back.

"What is she doing?" Issa yelled over the noise.

"Not sure, but it can't be good. Keep a shield ready."

"They're anchors." The woman who had barged into the square earlier called out from where she tended to Darius's shoulder. "To turn your men against you."

This had to be the Hannah from Isben's story. Which meant she had just as much history with Wrothe as Darius himself. She stood next to Issa, her face pale and hands trembling. It was clear she was no Guardian and facing Wrothe tested the limits of her bravery.

"Then we break them before she can finish." Jarand formed a cutting glyph.

"No!" Hannah's voice went tight and scared. "You can't. That's what split the world in the first place." Her grip around her stone tightened as she stepped toward Wrothe. "We must force her to see reason."

Jarand grabbed Hannah and pulled her back. "This fight has moved well beyond reason. Save your breath."

Wrothe laughed. "Yes, go back to your books, Hannah. You're not wanted here."

If they couldn't break the sequences, they could certainly contain them. Jarand exchanged a glance with Issa, who'd already begun forming patterns for a much more sophisticated shield, something that even Wrothe would struggle to break. He still had nightmares from when she'd tried to break his mind. He wasn't about to let her do it to anyone else.

He wove in his own flows to make the shield stronger. To his surprise, Hannah added her own unique flows to the mix as well.

Wrothe's eyes shone with triumph. "I'll make this simple. Get Darius to stop and I won't use this." Her sequence grew larger and the noise of it grew to a roar.

"Any moment they'll find your thread," Hannah shouted. "Give up. It's over."

Wrothe's shoulders sagged forward a fraction. Jarand wasn't sure if it was an act, or if she knew she was defeated.

"Then I have nothing to lose." With a dismissive wave, she sparked the mass of glyphs dancing around her to life.

On Jarand's cue, he and Issa slammed the massive shield down around her, the raw energy of it sparking and leaving the air smelling of acrid smoke. Issa and Hannah immediately set to work lacing stronger bonds around it, much like the cages they used during trials.

Jarand wove his own strength into the weaves, reinforcing each layer. The effort made his heart skip on itself, and his hands shook. Cassim's warning about pushing too hard rang through his head. If he kept going, this could kill him, but it was a gamble he was willing to take. With only twenty or so threads left, he would do anything to ensure that Katira finished healing the barrier. Seeing her work, seeing how Darius trusted her, and seeing Isben's quiet strength by her side, let him know that regardless of what happened to him, she'd be okay.

Inside her prison, Wrothe threw bolt after bolt at the walls to bring them down. Sweat poured down Jarand's back and soaked his shirt. He staggered under the strain.

"It's too much. Jarand, you must withdraw." The fear in Issa's voice stabbed him through. She still stood strong. Her flows didn't falter as his did. "Hannah and I can hold it."

Fourteen threads.

Jarand doubled down, pulling power from what was left of the raw shielding and feeding it into the stronger webbing. "I will not let go. This is my town. These are my people. She will not take them while there is breath in my body."

Eleven threads.

The first cracks in the shield echoed through the night like ice breaking.

"Don't be stubborn. Not now. Please." Issa's barked order turned into a plea. Bremin shouted for the townsmen to stay back and find cover.

"Not stubborn. They only need a few more minutes," he said between labored breaths. "I can give them that."

Seven threads.

Wrothe's assault on the shield changed from wild bolts fueled by anger to systematic cutting. Even with the three of them frantically working, they couldn't repair the lines of the cage as fast as she severed them.

Five threads.

Wrothe's onslaught slowed, then stopped. A strange silence fell over the square.

Three threads.

The prison exploded outward. Jarand drew on what little power he had left and flung up a shield as the blast caught him. The effort paired with the blast strained his heart in the worst possible way. A crimson shock of pain lanced through his chest as he was thrown across the square.

If Isben hadn't yanked Katira to the ground when he did, the explosion would have thrown her across the square like it had the others. As it was, the sudden percussive force of it pierced through her head. The world around her quieted to a muffled murmur. Isben curled around her like a heavy blanket and didn't move when she shifted against him.

Bremin ran toward the two of them from across the square, his face covered in dust and his glowing blade still held at the ready. He yelled something, but he might as well have whispered for all Katira could hear of it. She pulled herself free from Isben, afraid to see him wounded beyond what she could fix. To her relief, he stirred and opened his eyes. The blast had only momentarily stunned him.

As she straightened to face Bremin, a crushing pain ripped through her chest and sent her back to the ground. She clutched at what had to be a mortal wound. Isben rolled her onto her back, his hands shaking as pulled her hands free. When he did, she expected to see blood, but there was none.

This wasn't her pain. It was an echo of Papan's. She scanned the square for him, seeking him among the handful of bodies on the ground and found him fallen to his knees, face ashen, and blood spotting his lips. Cassim was already with him, his motions rushed, and all traces of his usual humor gone. If she felt his pain, then he was still alive. For now, that would have to be enough. She pushed Isben back and tried to tell him she was okay, but he refused to let go.

When Bremin reached them, he hurried them both to their feet. Katira couldn't make out the orders he shouted, but she could read his actions clearly enough. They were to continue the work, and he and his men would stay close to make sure they could do so without distraction.

Katira rushed over to where Hannah knelt next to Darius, and her mouth went dry when she saw the blood staining his doublet. Nearby, the last remaining shreds of the barrier hung in the air. Despite being flung across the square, he'd managed to keep his promise not to let it close. Still, he lurched unsteadily when Hannah helped him back to his feet.

In the center of the square, Wrothe stood bent, her hands braced on her knees and shoulders heaving. The effort required to break the prison walls had cost her dearly. The only person who didn't seem affected by the blast was Issa. She stood with the tip of the sword resting in the dirt as she waited for the woman to make her next move.

Before the blast, Katira heard the songs of these last three threads as they harmonized with the melodies of other threads, creating a unifying force that sustained the entire barrier. The entire world pivoted around those three remaining threads. Everything they had done, all that they had suffered, came down to this moment.

She tapped at the side of her head, then shook it, but the sounds around her remained muffled. Without being able to hear the melodies, she had no idea how she was going to find the right thread, and line it up with its match.

With a solemn nod, Darius took hold of the remaining three dark threads and lifted one toward her. His command was unmistakable.

Finish her.

They'd healed every other thread, removing them one at a time from that giant knot that prevented them from reaching Wrothe's thread before. Katira leaned on her instinct, hoping the intelligence within the power would guide her, and selected a thread, only for Isben to shake his head.

His flow spun around hers and led it back to one of the other two threads. As he did, something he'd said to her earlier came back in full force. *I can help you the same way you know you can help me when I struggle. Promise you won't shut me out?*

She was such a fool thinking it all came down to her. Through everything that had happened, even in her darkest moments, she'd never been alone, and she wasn't alone now. With Isben's help, they'd bring this madness to an end.

Katira took hold of Wrothe's thread and with Isben's guidance aligned it with its dark twin. While she couldn't hear the moment when the two melodies became one, she felt their vibrations lock into place.

Darius held a spark ready. After waiting centuries for this moment, healing Wrothe's thread deserved some kind of reconciliation or final words. Katira waited, giving him space to ready himself and to say something if he felt so moved. An expression of grief tightened his brow as he looked at Wrothe, his Rose, one final time. With a grim nod he set his spark against the threads.

As he did, Wrothe shot a mass of dark ribbons at the exposed barrier, a futile attempt to stop the joining. Issa stood poised and ready, releasing a brilliant sequence of glyphs that blossomed outward, catching the ribbons and repelling them.

"If it's a fight you want, then come and get it," Issa taunted.

A blazing sword formed in Wrothe's hand, and she yelled in frustration as she charged forward. Whether she meant to or not, Issa had become the perfect distraction to keep Wrothe away during these last critical moments.

Katira tore her attention away from the fight and added her spark, waiting with uneasy anticipation for the two threads to fuse. When the moment came and went, she looked to Darius, hoping for an explanation. His face reflected the same confusion she felt. With Isben's help, she realigned the threads together again to be sparked. Once again, they refused to join.

A blast of energy swept through the square, throwing Issa back several feet. The pressure of it made Katira's ears pop painfully. The sense that her head was full of wool disappeared and was replaced with a persistent ringing. She could hear well enough to catch Issa cursing as she threw herself back into the duel.

"Do something," Hannah urged Darius. "That Guardian woman is starting to tire."

Darius stammered and gestured to the stubborn strand, as if that explained everything. "I don't know what else to try."

Hannah flinched back as a hound bounded straight at one of the townsmen closest to her before being cut down. "This is not the time to act as if you're defeated. What if I try?"

"Say that again?" The spark of an idea lit Darius's eyes.

"You're exhausted and hurt," Hannah explained. "Maybe I should try. All I need to do is hold the thread and add the spark, right?"

Darius snapped his fingers. "That's it. The world broke the three of us differently than the other shadows. We're still thinking, breathing people. We have to spark our own threads." He shifted his gaze back to Hannah. "It has to be you."

"Oh, no." Hannah recoiled. "You still need me. You're still fighting. Don't make me be first."

At the edge of the circle surrounding them, Cassim hurried to Bremin's side and spoke urgently to the man while gesturing to where Jarand stood with his knot of townsmen. While Katira was encouraged to see her father standing, she knew through their bond how little strength he had left. No doubt Cassim was appealing to Bremin to order him to stand down.

He didn't need to fight anymore. The hounds, far fewer than before, weren't challenging each weak point around the square as they were earlier. When Bremin answered with a shake of his head, Cassim threw up his hands. Whatever response he had hoped for, he didn't get.

A cry of pain came from the center of the square. Issa gripped her arm where Wrothe had scored a hit. Bremin caught Cassim by the sleeve before he could run to her. Katira overheard him say something about the healer needing to stay.

The strain in Darius's voice drew Katira's attention back to the matter at hand. He presented Hannah with her thread. "This isn't goodbye. I promise."

"I love you too, you old goat." Hannah's lips pressed hard against each other as she took in the world around her one last time. "I'm ready."

Katira wrapped her flow around Hannah's thread from the real world and aligned it with its twin. She formed the spark reluctantly, knowing that with it she'd have to say goodbye.

"Thank you for your kindness, Hannah. I won't forget you."

Hannah touched her spark to the bright point. "You're a remarkable woman. I'm glad I got the chance to know you."

The two energies swirled together before sinking into the threads. For several anxious seconds, nothing happened. Katira gripped her stone, willing the threads to join. Just as her heart started to sink, a brilliant streak of light leapt up and coursed along the threads, sealing them together.

Even from the start this healing felt different, demanding far more power than that of the other threads. Thanks to the extra power gifted to her from the orbs, Katira would have enough, but just barely. Just as the real world had come into view as the threads were healed, Hannah faded from view, becoming more ghostlike as the length of her thread shrank.

"Goodbye, my friend," Darius whispered as the last portion merged together and disappeared.

Katira laced her hand into Isben's and they stood in silence waiting for the next orb to appear.

It never came.

The dark reality of what it would cost Katira to finish healing the barrier struck her like a blow to the stomach. Without a word, Isben drew her into his arms and joined with her. She didn't dare tell him that it wouldn't be enough.

CHAPTER 35

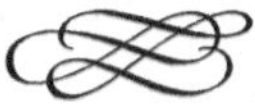

nother angry shout came from the center of the square where Issa and Wrothe remained locked in combat. Hannah had been right; Issa wouldn't last much longer. Her short hair was slicked to the sides of her head with sweat, her arm bled freely into the dirt at her feet, and she favored one leg. Wrothe hadn't fared much better. Her raven black hair looked singed in places, as did her dress. She held one arm tightly against her chest.

Katira watched on in horror as Darius charged through the ring of townsmen and headed directly toward Wrothe. The last time he'd done anything like this, Wrothe had killed him outright. Katira could still hear his screams. Darius didn't stand a chance against the woman, and yet he approached her with the conviction of a man who believed he had every chance of success.

Bremin seized him by the arm.

Darius pried, unsuccessfully, at Bremin's grip. "Let me close to her. I'll make her understand."

"What makes you think she'll listen?"

"Because she has to."

"That's not a good enough reason to let you risk yourself."

With that, Bremin hauled him back to the safety of the circle, where the two of them immediately began arguing over a plan of attack. Cassim hurried over to join them.

Isben loosened his hold from around Katira, and the flow of power from him slowed and stopped. Katira's head felt that much clearer for it, and for that she was grateful.

"We're so close," he murmured in her ear. "Nearly finished. Darius needs us now more than ever."

Katira's feet refused to move. "I know. It's just..." She swallowed down the memory of seeing Darius's body in the field. "Wrothe's hurt him so badly in the past. I can't stand it."

"If this works, she'll never hurt anyone ever again." He held out his hand and this time her feet obeyed.

When they approached, the argument had transformed into a rapid-fire discussion of strategy.

"How long do you think Issa hold her?" Darius asked

Cassim gripped his stone. "She's pushing her limits as it is. It might only be for a few minutes. Is that enough?"

"It has to be." Darius straightened his doublet.

Bremin's brow furrowed. "Are you sure she won't break your mind? Take control?"

"It's a risk we have to take. Stay ready. If I manage it, we won't have much time before she changes her mind again."

Bremin gave a curt nod and signaled Issa with a whistle. She blasted Wrothe to the ground with a wide bolt before hurrying over.

"Do you know how hard it is not to accidentally kill her?"

"I can imagine." Bremin gave an unamused smile. "New plan. Bind and block her as long as you can on Darius's signal."

"Are you insane?"

"Probably," Darius answered with no trace of humor. Wrothe was already on her feet.

"Fine then. Your plan better be better than the one I'm imagining." She turned back to face Wrothe, new glyphs forming between her hands. "On your order."

Darius hesitated for the space of a single breath. "Now!"

The first half of Issa's binding glyph snatched Wrothe's hands and yanked them behind her back. The second, more difficult half, forcefully blocked her from reaching for her power.

"It's now or never. Go!" Issa ordered, her face already going red with the strain.

Darius closed the distance between himself and Wrothe. His hands trembled as he reached for her. "This is for the best."

"No!" Wrothe struggled against her bonds. "Don't touch me."

The closer the two came to each other, the more Katira itched to push them further apart.

"It's over. All of it." His fingers grazed the tip of her shoulder. "Let me help you understand."

"Get away." She yanked herself back from his touch.

Undeterred, he set his hand gently on the side of her neck and the other over her heart even as she arched away. The lines of his power glowed softly, quietly, against the chaos surrounding her.

She took a shuddering breath, her body tense as a spring. "I don't want this. Why can't you leave me alone?"

His motions remained gentle, careful, calm. He'd found his confidence. He knew what he wanted. "Let me in. Let me help you."

When Darius connected with Wrothe, she released a keening low cry so laden with anguish that for a moment Katira forgot how dangerous she was.

The woman softened a fraction. "It's too much. I don't want to feel this."

He wrapped his arms around her. "I loved you once. Was utterly devoted to you. In some ways, I still am. This was never the life you wanted for yourself. It's time to let go."

For a fleeting moment, Katira caught a glimpse of something kinder, something calm, in Wrothe's eyes. She stopped fighting against him.

"Release her." Darius glanced toward Issa. "It's okay."

Issa hesitated, this looked like the worse kind of foolishness. Releasing Wrothe was the ultimate show of trust, a trust the woman hadn't earned. But then again, maybe it was enough. Maybe it was the last piece to a puzzle they didn't understand. With a sigh and a shake of her head, Issa let the binding glyph fall away but stayed close. *He* might trust Wrothe, but it would take a miracle for anyone else to take that leap.

Katira eased her flows back into the barrier, ensuring that Wrothe's thread stood ready for the woman's spark should it happen.

Darius drew Wrothe closer to the barrier, speaking in a soft, almost hypnotic voice. One of her dark ribbons teased along the barrier's edge as if testing it. When that ribbon skirted too close to Katira's, her head snapped up and the trance shattered.

"What do we need her for?"

"Don't fret." Darius's voice remained quiet and calm. "We need her to make ourselves whole once more."

"This is a trap. You've all tried to trick me." She turned on Darius. "How dare you manipulate me?" Her markings glowed dark and dangerous.

"Get him out of there!" Katira yelled as she fought to free her flows from the barrier.

Issa sprang into action as Wrothe's power raced over Darius's body and pierced him through. His head whipped backward with the shock of it, his mouth set into a silent scream as the barrier swallowed itself up with a frightful screech. Issa's binding glyph took hold of Wrothe and threw the woman several paces away from Darius as he collapsed. She leapt into the space between them, sword held at the ready.

Katira was at his side in an instant, delving him to see what Wrothe had done. "Stay with us, Darius, just a bit longer."

"Cassim! Quick!" Bremin shouted.

CHAPTER 36

As soon as Katira's delving glyph touched him, a sinking sick feeling filled her gut. Wrothe, in her anger, had torn out the roots of his power save one tenuous connection. It was no wonder the barrier collapsed as it did.

Darius blinked at the dark sky above him, his face strangely at peace. "I didn't think I'd ever see the stars like this again."

Katira seized a handful of his doublet. "Don't you dare die on me, not when we're this close. "

"Not dying. I promise. But the stars are quite lovely, aren't they? I'm glad I got to see them before the end." He reached out a hand for Isben to help him sit up.

"Careful!" Cassim protested. "You should stay still until I take a look."

"It's nothing you can heal, I'm afraid." Darius pushed away Cassim's hand. "We'll overcome it, just like we have everything else."

Cassim leaned in close to Katira and kept his voice at a whisper. "I don't remember him talking like that before. Did he hit his head?"

"This is serious. If he can't help me fuse his thread, then this will never end. Can you do anything for him?"

"You know I can't." He gave a helpless shrug. "What if he sleeps? Doesn't that restore him?"

She was glad he didn't suggest the alternative. Darius had suffered too much death already. "Maybe. But with the entirety of the mirror realm boiled down to those two threads, there's no way of knowing what might happen."

A new desperation coiled inside of Katira. They were so close. Wrothe would be on her guard now. She wouldn't fall for the same trick again.

Darius lurched to his feet using Isben as a crutch. The sight helped Katira feel slightly better about their odds. Slightly. Not far from where they stood, Papan sat on the edge of the fountain next to Lucan. The color had returned to his face, and he breathed easier.

Issa continued to stare Wrothe down. She hadn't held this binding like before, choosing to conserve her strength for whatever would come next. Between the two of them, it was hard to tell which was more exhausted.

Beyond them, the townsmen stationed around the edge of the square watched on in a silent vigil, their glowing blades held at their shoulders. Katira couldn't remember the last time she'd spotted a hound prowling at the corner of her vision. Perhaps they were gone for good. *Good riddance.*

The silence in the square was so complete that it startled her when Darius spoke again. "When the barrier was opened from your side, how did you do it?"

Katira couldn't stand the irony of it. That stupid rod was what triggered his trap and forced her to become part of his plan in the first place.

"A glyph rod. I'm not sure where it is."

"I have it." Issa fished out the slim rod from one of her secure pockets and held it toward them, not taking her eyes off Wrothe for a second. "Here."

Isben took the rod from Issa and presented it to Darius. "It's a nice piece of Bending, if I do say so myself."

He weighed it in his palm. "Can you use it?"

"Yes," Isben answered. "All it needs is a spark."

Katira didn't like where this was going. She much preferred for Isben to remain by her side. If he was the one keeping the barrier open, then she'd be sealing up Wrothe's and Darius's thread alone.

She took the rod and pressed it into the healer's hands. "Cassim should do it."

"No. Lives depend on how fast I can act." Cassim pushed it back. "Isben is a good choice."

"I agree." Darius took the rod and placed it into Isben's hands once more. "Whatever happens, the barrier must stay open until the joining is complete. We can't risk the threads ripping apart if it closes before they finish."

The rod looked out of place in Isben's hands, and Katira saw a thousand apologies in his eyes as he set the spark.

The barrier opened, its light once again too bright in the night's darkness. The two remaining pairs of threads rolled into view. Wrothe snarled at the sight of it.

"I tried to be kind," Darius yelled over the noise. "I tried to be gentle with you. If you won't go willingly. I have no choice but to force you." He took hold of his and Wrothe's dark threads with flows of the power. "Issa, seize her."

This time, Wrothe was ready. She broke Issa's binding apart before it came close and set her own binding that knocked Issa to the ground and pinned her in place. More glyphs formed on Wrothe's fingertips, and an insane glee shone from her eyes.

Katira didn't see the bolt.

Didn't see how its deadly path raced toward her.

Didn't see Darius leap in front of her to take the blow.

And then she did.

He fell at her feet, his eyes wide and his chest ruined. Life faded from him with each breath. Katira expected to hear Wrothe gloat, or laugh, or do something else utterly terrible to celebrate her win. Instead, she heard Isben's strained grunt. In the chaos, he'd seized the woman while keeping hold of the barrier, not with a Guardian's force, but with a Bender's precision. Wrothe stood stiffly, that insane glee replaced with terror.

Katira knelt next to Darius, too shocked to speak.

"It's okay," he whispered, "I would save you again. Go live your life. Make it amazing. I'm done with mine." He held forward his thread and formed a single spark.

She held his thread close, listening to his song one last time. It was radiant, like the sun itself, and held all the power of a nation standing together. Lining up the two halves came easily, effortlessly. She set her spark as he set his, not wanting him to go, but accepting that his trial was finally over.

The pull hit Katira's already strained resources hard and forced a gasp from her lips. Stars crowded around the edges of her vision. Just as she worried she might faint, someone set a hand on her shoulder and their warm flows of power coursed through her.

As the end of his thread disappeared, Darius breathed in one last shaking breath and mouthed the words *Thank you* as he faded from view.

Darius was gone, but the hand remained. She wiped her eyes and found Cassim standing behind her.

"You needed it," he offered before she could how he knew. "You can thank me later when this is done." He gave her shoulder a small push. "Go on, save the world. We're all right behind you."

Isben's face had gone red with the effort of holding Wrothe and he sucked in lungfuls of breath as if he'd just run the gauntlet.

"I've got her. When you're ready, I'll force her to make her spark," he told Katira when she drew closer.

So, he *was* controlling her. Interesting. It seemed fate had a sense of justice. "How long can you hold her?"

Isben adjusted one of his flows with a grimace. "Not much longer. Whatever you want to do, be quick about it."

"That's all I need." Katira placed herself squarely in front of Wrothe and forced their eyes to meet. "You wanted to control people, make them do your bidding to protect the innocent."

Wrothe struggled against Isben's invisible bonds, her nostrils flaring like a frightened horse. "You're no better than me. Look at the evils you've resorted to," she said between clenched teeth.

The barb made Katira flinch. She *was* better. She was righting a thousand-year-old wrong. It had to count for something.

"Be done with it," Isben urged. "Nothing you say or do will bring your mother back."

He was right. It wouldn't. At the end of all this, Mamar would still be gone. Papan would still remain a weakened shell of what he once was. Countless people would still be dead. Nothing Wrothe said would heal the hurts Katira held inside of her. It was time to bring it all to an end.

Katira wrapped her flow around Wrothe's thread. Holding it was like looking down into the depths of a well. "You are a murderer. By the laws of this land, I sentence you to death."

"You'll regret this. You'll carry this weight forever." Wrothe jerked against the bonds again in one last show of defiance as Isben forced her to hold her thread forward and form the spark.

Her defiance never left her eyes. As with Hannah, and with Darius, it took longer for the threads to start fusing together. Each second that ticked past was another second that Isben had to restrain her. When that brilliant flash took hold and the fibers of the threads began to deftly intertwine, Katira could finally breathe again.

She expected the pull, knew it would be just as bad or worse than when she healed Darius's and Hannah's thread, and braced herself. When it came, it sent her to her knees and overwhelmed her senses.

Wrothe writhed again, and something snapped apart like the breaking of a branch. Isben gasped and staggered back as one of her ribbons seized the flow of Katira's power sustaining the healing and snaked up it before burrowing inside, just as she'd done to Papan.

As Wrothe's thread spooled out of existence, it yanked Katira's power along with it. Her world shrank. Time itself came unhooked and flapped like a sail in the breeze. Bremin gave orders. Papan slid the glyph rod from Isben's hands. Cassim's warm presence returned at her shoulder.

Isben knelt next to her. "I've got you. Stay with me." Issa joined him.

The two of them set their flows along where Wrothe had gripped her, burning and cutting away each place where her anchors held tight. As much as they were trying to be careful, they weren't moving fast enough. The last of Wrothe's thread came into view. All that was left of the woman was a ghostly outline. If the thread finished healing while Wrothe was still anchored to Katira's power, it would kill her.

She grabbed Isben's wrist. "There's no time. Pull it free."

Isben glanced at the remaining length of Wrothe's thread and horror crossed his face. "May the Stonemother forgive me." He closed his eyes and heaved on the ribbon with all his strength.

With no threads to hold, with nothing to sustain it, the barrier's edges pulled in slowly at first then faster and faster until all that was left was a single bright point of light. The point burst, sending stars flying out in all directions. The square fell into silence and darkness once more

At each point where Wrothe had dug inside her, something had torn. Katira shivered as her life drained away, grateful she wasn't alone, sad for the pain she saw in Isben's gaze above her.

She had already resigned herself to death when the intelligence within the power rose up within her, filling her with an unexpected warmth and calm. One by one, it sealed up the tears and took away the pain. When it was finished, it drained away like a sigh, and Katira knew this was the last time she'd feel its presence.

The grief in Isben's eyes changed to wonder, and he pulled her close. "You're safe now. Rest."

To the east, the barest hint of sunrise painted the sky behind the mountain peaks. The fight to finish healing the barrier had taken all night, and every hour felt as if it had been burned into Katira's

bones. She breathed in the cool air of the summer morning and welcomed the reminder that she was indeed alive and back in the real world. Isben, with his comforting smell of books and ink, hadn't left her side.

Pieces of conversation drifted to where they sat.

"I warned him. He knew what would happen."

"I know. I warned him too. On rare occasions he even listens to me."

"Best tell her before it's too late."

Katira's ears perked up. Whatever it was, it concerned her. Cassim joined them, his head bowed and his tunic crooked and dirty. Onyx had returned to his shoulder and nuzzled his hair. She'd seen this kind of walk before, when Isben told her about her mother's death. The sight of it here tightened her throat.

"Let me up. Something's happened." She said to Isben who'd fallen quietly asleep. He woke with a jerk as she freed herself to face the healer.

Cassim stammered over his words several times before he succeeded. "You'd better come with me. I don't think he'll be with us much longer."

She nodded dumbly, letting the healer lead her to the side of the fountain where Papan lay propped up against a sack of flour. From the moment she felt that flood of pain in his chest, she'd known this was a possibility, but it didn't mean she was ready for it.

His breath came in shallow bursts, too far apart to be more than a reflex. He gazed up into the morning sky, eyes glassy and unfocused. When he saw her, a smile crossed his lips.

"There you are. I was worried." He held out his hand.

She wrapped it into hers and sat next to him. "I'm okay, Papan. Everything's okay now." There was no need to tell him how her power had changed, how the thing that made her an Innate was no longer a part of her. The barrier was healed, and that was all that mattered.

"I'm not. Cassim's so mad." He gave a weak laugh that turned into a cough. "He ordered me to stay back. Told me that if I tried, it would kill me. And I did it anyway."

"And you're dying because of it." She pressed his hand against her face. The same hand that had held hammers and swords, the same hand that had made beautiful things, the same hand that had comforted her when she needed it most. It was already cooling, his heart not strong enough to warm it.

"It was worth it. Got to be there when you changed the world for the better." He stopped to catch his breath. "I'd do it again."

She leaned in closer, letting her head rest on his shoulder. "You're proud of me then?"

"I never stopped, never will."

When Isben rounded the corner of the fountain, the look on his face said he knew what was about to happen. He sat next to her and set his hand on hers. One by one, the others gathered around them. Bremin, Cassim, Issa, at first, but then at a respectful distance, Lucan and Elan and many of the townsmen.

"Look." She pointed to the gathering crowd in awe. "They're here for you. They've come to honor you."

The hand she held trembled in disbelief. For so long, he'd fought with the belief that if they knew who he truly was, they'd hate him. This proved him wrong in all the best ways.

Bremin finally broke the silence. "This is it, isn't it? After such a remarkable victory, we are still defeated."

Papan's grip tightened around Katira's hand. "Not a defeat. Only a farewell. Watch over my daughter. All of you. I couldn't ask for any better."

"No. I refuse. You're not leaving us, you stubborn thing." Issa held her arms around herself as if they were the only things holding her together. "Do something, Cassim. He can't die like this. Not when we've finally won."

"Issa," Papan pressed and a faint smile touched his lips. "Don't make me order you."

She brought her fist to her chest. "Of course. Like my own daughter."

Cassim spoke quietly to Bremin who gave a solemn nod. "Jarand. It's time. Who do you want to perform your last rites?"

"I'd choose you, old friend, but you need to remember." He paused to breathe. "Issa. Would you?"

Issa lifted her head and there were tears on her face. "Of course."

Issa took her place next to Papan and wiped the corners of her eyes. The ancient words of the rite flowed from her lips and filled Katira's mind with pattern and color before solidifying into memories.

He'd lived so many years and walked so many lives that she had never known. The war had left him haunted and hollow. Her whole life had been in the shadow of the scars left by it. Finally, she understood what it had done to him, what fears it had ingrained in him, the endless nightmares he suffered because of it. Through all of it, Mamar had been with him as close as his own shadow. After Katira's own limited experience with being a companion to Isben, she finally understood the depth of Mamar and Papan's closeness, how in losing her he came so close to losing himself.

Just when Katira began to believe she might not be part of these shared memories, that he'd lived so long that perhaps her part in his life wasn't enough to notice, she felt an undeniable spark of joy breaking through the darkness.

Her.

She watched on in awe as he relived those special moments of his life with her, from her babyhood as he cuddled and cooed at her, from her learning to walk, from when she helped him in the forge, from her standing on tiptoe alongside Mamar and struggling to lift the heavy pestle to grind herbs. Along with that joy came a fresh set of fears and worries she had only started to understand. After everything he'd endured in his life, the thing that scared him more than anything in the end was failing her.

As Papan's life dwindled away, another presence joined them, something larger than life, bigger than love. The intensity of it made Katira forget to breathe. This presence carried her away from the shelter of Papan's memories and to the edge of a circle of stout pines where a cheerful brook babbled to one side.

In the center of the circle, Papan stood tall and strong. The deep lines on his face, the scars, all faded away.

A woman stepped into the circle, her robes flowed out from behind her as if they floated in a stream. Her hawklike features marked her as something not of this world. She walked up to Papan and set a hand on his chest.

"Jarand of Pathara, do you know who I am?" she asked, her voice ringing through the air like bells.

He bowed his head. "Yes, honored one. You are the Stonemother."

Katira grabbed for the nearest tree, needing something solid beneath her fingers. This was the end then. The Stonemother was calling him back to her. It felt too much like a dream and too real all at once.

The Stonemother continued with her ritual questions, "Do you know why you're here?"

He didn't hesitate. "My time has come."

The Stonemother smiled. "The last time we met, you begged for more time, for another chance. What has changed?"

"My daughter is safe now. The danger is passed. My work is done." With each statement, Papan's shoulders relaxed as if he were finally letting go of a great weight.

"You have done well." She extended her arm and a space between the trees came into view. There, sitting at the edge of the stream trailing her fingers in the water, was a figure that was so familiar, it hurt. "Go to her. Find your peace."

"Mirelle?" Her name reverently fell from his lips, as if it was the most beautiful word in the world.

Mamar looked up, her hand stilling in the water, the other darting to her mouth. She jumped to her feet and together they closed the distance, falling into each other's arms. As they did, the Stonemother turned and disappeared into the forest as silently as she'd come.

Mamar touched Papan's face, his shoulders, as if not believing he could be real. "Is it really you? Are you here? What happened?"

He kissed her forehead and pulled her close. "Too many questions. I'm here. Let me hold you."

As they embraced, Mamar saw Katira standing in the circle.

"Katira? Are you...?" She stopped herself short and looked to Papan who shook his head. "Come here, precious one."

Katira's emotions caught in her throat. She had been robbed of her chance to say goodbye when Mamar died, and now getting it back seemed too good to be true. She ran into those arms and let herself be enfolded inside, her tears flowing freely now.

Papan wrapped his arms around the two of them and kissed each of their heads. "She has a long and wonderful life ahead of her. Don't fret. I kept her safe for you."

All Katira's pain of loss, the weariness of doubt, the anger she held, melted away in that embrace. "I've missed you."

Mamar stroked her hair, the gesture familiar and reassuring. "Oh, my dear sweet child. I never left you. I know it's been hard, but you were never alone."

"Then you know about what I did?"

"Of course I do. I'm so proud of you." She nudged Papan with a smile. "We're so proud of you."

The edges of the world began to fade, and Mamar and Papan faded with it. Katira knew she'd never have enough time to say everything she wanted to say, but this was enough. They would see each other again. She fought to hold onto them as they slipped away, clinging to every last moment. The vision faded and the embrace that had wrapped her so warmly faded with it. The real world came back into view. Papan's hand still rested in hers, but his soul had flown. He was gone.

CHAPTER 37

The great hall at Amul Dun, with its grey granite walls and pool of vibrant reds and blues forming on the floor from the stained-glass window above, rested in a solemn silence. Katira stood alone in front of the two massive doors leading into the audience chamber, remembering a lifetime ago when she'd stood there for an entirely different reason with Papan by her side. For the thousandth time that morning, her heart ached at his absence.

She cradled his stone in the palm of her hand, awed over how he'd worn it for centuries, through good times and bad. Bremin had presented it to her the night after he passed, when they committed his body to the sky. In a way, it meant she always had a part of him with her. She touched her own stone hanging at her neck, missing that connection they used to have, missing how she could curl up in the comfort that he was never far away.

Two weeks had passed since Namragan. Two overwhelming weeks of being heralded as a hero all while trying to process Papan's death. Isben moved into Papan's — no, now *her* rooms — on the first day, so she wouldn't be alone. He brought her food and walked with her, being a ready ear when she felt like talking.

She wanted Isben there with her as she stood in front of those massive doors and waited for whatever Lady Alystra had in store. If this had anything to do with healing the barrier, Isben deserved to be honored as well. She wouldn't have been able to do it without him, or without any of them for that matter. Issa, Cassim, and Bremin all deserved praise more than she.

The great door swung open. Issa, clad in her formal blue gambeson and shining breastplate, ushered her in with a warm smile. Lady Alystra stood tall on the dais, her yellow robes resplendent in the morning sunlight. Bremin stood by her side, his crisp, clean shirt trimmed in purple. It was no wonder the great hall was so quiet that morning; everyone in the Tower had gathered inside and now waited in hushed anticipation.

When Katira reached the front of the room, she pressed a fist to her chest and gave a respectful bow.

Lady Alystra addressed the room, her clear, strong voice reaching to the furthest corners. "In recognition of your actions, your bravery, and your personal sacrifice, the Stonebearer Society wishes to commend you, Katira Pathara. You have endured grief, loss, and pain beyond your years. Through your efforts, the injury done to our world that created the mirror realm has finally been healed. For this, we wish to bestow upon you a special honor."

She gestured to her right where Issa stood with her fellow guardians. She and Captain Edmont stepped forward bearing a long ornate box.

"This is your father's sword." Captain Edmont said as he placed it at the foot of the dais. "It rightfully belongs to you now."

He opened the case. The sword had been polished until it gleamed. The delicate words and carvings down the blade caught the light and glittered in a rainbow of colors.

"The Order of Guardians has pledged to continue your training," he continued. "Should your strength mark you as a Guardian, we would be honored to have you." The captain bowed and pressed his fist to his chest before stepping back into the ranks.

Issa knelt in front of Katira. "Regardless of what order you formally join, I offer to continue your training as your father trained me, and to be there for you, not as your master, but as your friend."

Katira bowed the way she was first taught as Issa's student to show her acceptance and was surprised when the woman pulled her into an embrace.

Issa whispered into her ear. "I meant the part about being your friend. That means you can always turn to me if you ever need anything."

Before Katira could answer, Lady Alystra was already moving on. She gestured toward where Cassim stood with Master Firen.

Master Firen stepped forward bearing a parcel wrapped in dark cloth. "The Order of Healers formally pledges to take you under our wing and continue your education. Lady Mirelle was one of our best, and your talent shows that she's taught you well. We would also be honored to have you among our ranks."

He held out the parcel. "This is one of her notebooks from when she was first learning with me all those years ago. I thought you might want it."

Katira gave an involuntary sharp breath in surprise. This was something far more precious than any gift or trinket; this was something her mother had spent hours taking painstaking notes in. The pages were worn and the edges soft with use. "It's wonderful. Thank you."

Cassim adjusted his tunic and stepped forward. "If it's okay with you, I'd like to continue our work together as well."

"Of course. I'd love that." Katira clasped his hand in hers and once again found herself hauled into a giant hug.

The remaining orders each made a similar offering. Master Aro approached on behalf of the Benders, Bremin on behalf of the Seekers, and finally Lady Alystra herself, on behalf of the Travelers. All extended their acceptance. All expressed their desire to continue her training.

When the presentations had finished, Katira wasn't sure what to do. There was no dismissal, and no one made any move to leave. It wasn't until Bremin broke into a smile that she noticed Isben was standing by her side.

"There's one last thing I'd like to formalize, if you're willing," Lady Alystra began. "Seeing as you and Isben have already proven yourselves to be a matched pair, we've ruled in favor of granting you your companion bond today. What say you?"

Katira reached for Isben, needing someone to hold onto more than ever. "Yes, I'd like that very much."

"Then it is agreed. Present yourself at the pedestal." Lady Alystra stepped down from the raised dais.

As soon as the High Lady's attention turned away, Katira pulled Isben close. "Did you have something to do with this?" she whispered in his ear.

A wide grin split Isben's face. "It might have been my idea, but it was Bremin who ran with it. I suppose we should thank him later."

Lady Alystra cleared her throat, although not unkindly. "Your apprentice stones, please."

With a pang of loss, Katira set her stone next to Isben's on the motherstone surface of the pedestal. This small stone represented everything that had changed about her since she left her old life behind, and she was reluctant to part with it.

The High Lady's markings glowed to life. "When you're ready, place one hand on the pedestal alongside your stone and join hands with the other. Then, open yourself to the power."

When Katira met Isben's gaze again, she saw a nervous energy in him that matched her own. She took a slow breath, trying to calm the butterflies taking up space in her chest. When she opened herself to her power, his was already there waiting for her, eager to intertwine.

At Lady Alystra's touch, light laced through the pedestal's surface in delicate patterns that danced around their stones and their outstretched hands. As her flows grew more elaborate, they drew in Katira's senses. The room and everyone watching faded away.

The light held them in perfect unity, pressing away all fear, and filling her until there was no room to doubt and no space for anything else other than the perfect bonding of their two halves of magic.

The stones on the pedestal melded together and formed a new stone much greater than the sum of the two parts. This new stone then twisted apart into two distinct stones that were crafted in such a way that they fit into each other like a puzzle.

Just as when Katira and Papan were bonded, as soon as the stones were fully formed, the heat of Lady Alystra's power began its race around her, Isben, and their two stones. Each pass laid down a thread that strengthened the bond between them, and she continued on and on until the bundle of threads resembled a thick rope.

Unlike when Katira was bonded to Papan, there was no test, no rite of passage to prove they were meant to be. They simply were. The light faded and the dance of power surrounding them slowed and drew to a close. The sense of unity and strength Katira always felt when she and Isben connected remained strong.

Lady Alystra removed her hands from the pedestal and stepped back to where Bremin waited for her. "The joining is complete. Take up your stones."

Katira didn't want to release her hand from Isben's, didn't want the connection to close like it always did. It was only after he gave her a reassuring smile and squeezed her hand again that she finally let go. To Katira's astonishment, the connection didn't disappear.

She picked up her new stone from the top of the pedestal and pressed it into her palm where it felt as warm and hers as ever before. It knew her, belonged to her, and was there to serve her.

The High Lady raised her hands. "May the Stonemother always be with you, 'til the last of your days."

The room cheered back in a thunderous wave. "'Til the last of your days."

Isben stood close to her, smelling of paper, ink, and the uniqueness that was only him. Joy radiated from him across their newly formed bond like a pulse.

"Kiss!" came a shout that sounded suspiciously like Cassim.

Isben turned to Katira, and their hands joined once more. He leaned in, inviting her to do the same. Her lips met his, and an explosion of sensation flooded through her.

If this was what the next several hundred years would be like together, Katira looked forward to every minute.

AFTERWORD

Thank you for reading Stonebearer's Redemption, the final book in the Shadow Barrier Trilogy.

If you enjoyed this book, you can help other people find it by leaving a review!

For news on upcoming books, as well as other goodies and offers, be sure to sign up for My Fantasy Reader Community:

https://www.subscribepage.com/jodilmilner

ACKNOWLEDGMENTS

Here we are, at the end of a project that I never imagined finishing when I started it. The experiences I've had bringing Katira's story to life and onto the page have been both bitter and sweet, and because of them, I've grown as a person. The brunt of the work for this book happened during the peak of the pandemic, a time that proved to be more stressful than I ever thought possible.

I couldn't have done it without the network of wonderful and supportive people in my life. It amazes me how fate has connected each of us at just the right time. First, a huge thank you goes to the talented members of my editing and production team. Not only have they made my books so much better, but they've also served as the best mentors a gal could ask for. I couldn't do it without them. Jana, Melissa, and Fiona, you made my dream of finishing this series come true.

Second, a huge thank you goes to my writing communities, the League of Utah Writers, Wednesday Writer's Whatchamacallit, and of course, Author Snark, all of which have provided a safe space to explore and learn while pushing me to the next level.

Third, and quite possibly the most important, I'd like to thank my family for being awesome and giving me the space to grow my hobby into something that's given me purpose, strength, and a place to express my creativity and talents.

And finally, to you, dear reader, thank you for lending your imagination to make my words take flight.

ABOUT THE AUTHOR

Jodi L. Milner, author of the award-winning Shadow Barrier Trilogy, wanted to be a superhero and a doctor when she grew up. Upon discovering she couldn't fly, she did what any reasonable introvert would do and escaped into the hero-filled world of fiction and the occasional medical journal. She's lived there ever since.

These days, when she's not folding the children or feeding the laundry, she creates her own noble heroes on the page. Her short stories explore the fabric of dreams, while her novels weave magic into what it means to be human.

Jodi is a firm believer that life is what you make it, and she intends to make it a good one. She is an avid student of the interesting and obscure and has an unhealthy fascination with mental health and medical science. This path led to her working professionally in both human and animal medicine.

She still dreams of flying.

Connect with Jodi at JodiLMilner.com

facebook.com/JodilMilnerAuthor

twitter.com/JodiLMilner

instagram.com/jodi.l.milner

9 781734 436754